BURIED PASTS

George Stratford

Copyright © George Stratford 2019

The author asserts the moral right under the Copyright, Designs and Patents Act 1988 to be identified as the author of this work.

All rights reserved. No part of this publication may be reproduced, stored in a retrieval system or transmitted, in any form or by any means without the prior consent of the author, nor be otherwise circulated in any form of binding or cover other than that which it is published and without a similar condition being imposed on the subsequent publisher.

ISBN: 9781794219762

eBook ASIN: B07JHVPQ5C

This novel is dedicated to the Canadian father I got to know only through my mother's memories. It is also for the fifty-five thousand other men from Britain and the Commonwealth who gave their lives whilst serving with RAF Bomber Command during WWII.

**George Henry Stratford (78 Squadron, RAF Bomber Command)
Killed in action 19th July 1944**

ONE

MARCH 1944

Five had already left. It was his turn next. For Flight Sergeant Mike Stafford, touching a lucky mascot was not a requirement. Far too many times he had seen such things bring only fatally bad fortune to their owners.

In the rapidly fading light of a chill Yorkshire evening, he eased the big Lancaster bomber into position at the end of the runway and applied the brakes. The noise from his four Rolls Royce Merlin engines increased to a roar as he ran them all at full revs.

To a pilot of Stafford's experience, these pre-flight checks were second nature. Not that familiarity with the take-off routine ever eased the tension of the moment for him. Nor was it likely to make things any easier for the six members of his crew scattered in their various positions throughout the length of the now violently shuddering fuselage. Each one of them would be going through pretty much the same range of gut-wrenching emotions as himself while preparing for yet another trip to the 'Big City' – Berlin.

Below them all in the darkness of the bomb bay lurked the aircraft's non-human cargo: one 8000lb 'cookie' bomb, plus well over a thousand small incendiary devices.

Stafford shifted slightly in his seat. He prayed that it would be only their bombs, and not the entire bloody plane, that came crashing down on enemy territory. But the odds on another safe return to base were debatable. They had already somehow managed to survive twenty-seven previous ops. Still, he told himself, only three more to go and their tour of duty would be completed. After that there would be a nice spot of leave for them all to enjoy. Even as this pleasant thought formed, he remembered that so many crews did not even get to complete five missions. Was it unreasonable to think that Lancaster K for King may now be flying on borrowed time?

Pre-flight checks completed, and with engines once again running steady, he waited for the green light that would signal his clearance for take-off. There were seventeen Lancasters from 79 Squadron at RAF Wetherditch on operations tonight. They were leaving at one-minute intervals.

The green light came.

Stafford applied full power. The heavy bomber trembled as it began its forward surge. Rapidly gathering pace, it thundered down the runway. Outside, the marker lights set on the ground flashed by. Eighty miles an hour – then ninety – then one hundred.

At this speed, Stafford eased back the stick. Heavily burdened with its bomb load and over two thousand gallons of high-octane fuel, the Lancaster clung stubbornly to the ground before finally yielding to the law of aerodynamics. With the four propellers clawing furiously at the air for more altitude, he raised the undercarriage.

Once again, they were on their way to Berlin.

***

Stafford was well aware of why Berlin had been nicknamed the 'Big City'. Quite apart from the sheer size and importance of the place, the city's ground defences were the most formidable in Germany. Hundreds of heavy flak guns, each capable of destroying a plane with a single shot, had been massed together to protect the German capital. Situated as it was in the heart of the country, a trip there meant that K for King could expect to be in the air and under threat of attack for around eight hours. Maybe much longer if damaged or forced to take a diversion.

Enemy night fighters were an almost constant danger. Those defending the target area would be waiting high above the flak barrage like birds of prey. With their vastly superior speed and armament, these Luftwaffe pilots were sure to find many more easy pickings before the night was over. Tonight's raid numbered nearly a thousand aircraft, making the sky packed with potential targets. Far too many for the German fighters to gobble up entirely before the opportunity had passed. Survival in a Lancaster, and in the even more vulnerable Halifax, often came down to nothing more than the passing whim of an enemy pilot.

'Eeny – meeny – miny – mo,' Stafford murmured to himself in a moment of dark humour.

***

The navigator's voice sounded over the intercom, giving Stafford his course for the first leg of the journey. A few minutes later they crossed the English coast just south of Hull and were heading out across the North Sea. Further snippets of information came from both the flight engineer and navigator. Twice he made slight adjustments to their course to compensate for the strong crosswind they were experiencing.

Twenty-five miles out over the water, he once again flicked the intercom switch on the front of his oxygen mask. His accent was pure Canadian. 'Pilot to gunners. Test your guns now.'

Flight Sergeant 'Geordie' Heatley was the first to respond. Exposed for the duration in his isolated turret at the tail of the aircraft, everyone on board knew that his was the loneliest and most dangerous job of all. With just four lightweight .303 machine guns to defend himself and the Lancaster with, he would make a highly tempting target for the heavy cannons of any night fighters seeking to attack from the rear.

Each of Geordie's guns fired off a short burst into the night sky. Further along the fuselage, their New Zealand born mid-upper gunner, Sergeant Phil Thomas, went through the same routine.

'All guns okay, skipper,' both men reported.

From the very front of the aircraft, the south London tones of Sergeant Jimmy Knight also responded. 'Same here, skipper. All guns okay.'

As the bomb aimer positioned in the nose turret, it was Jimmy's job to double up as their front gunner.

Stafford smiled at his best friend's bright tone. They were both only twenty-four years old, but just six weeks ago Jimmy had astonished everyone by getting married. Stafford could still hardly believe how suddenly it had happened. Not that Jimmy was making the most of his new status at present. With his wife many miles away in London, the couple had seen each other only twice since their big day. There was little doubt in

Stafford's mind how his buddy would be spending his time on leave once they'd got through this tour of duty.

Jimmy's voice came over the intercom again, bringing his mind back to the job in hand. 'Bombs selected on all switches, skipper.'

Stafford acknowledged this, at the same time casting his eyes around the sky. He could see two other Lancasters, but already their squadron was being scattered by the strong crosswinds.

After nearly two hours in the air, Flying Officer Doug Short, the navigator and only commissioned officer on board, came out with the words that the entire crew were apprehensively waiting for.

'Enemy coast ahead.'

Stafford responded to this with a general broadcast. 'Right, you guys. Keep your eyes open and lights out as much as possible.'

They flew over the Danish coast at 18,000 feet and began to climb until Stafford levelled out at 21,000 feet. He glanced yet again at the airspeed indicator. At this higher altitude it was approaching 220 mph.

It wasn't long before Warrant Officer Hughie Smith, the Flight Engineer occupying the seat alongside Stafford, was offering further advice. 'I'd ease back on the revs a bit skipper, we're drinking up the fuel.'

'Thanks, Hughie.'

The engines dropped a tone as Stafford acted on this advice. They sure as hell wanted enough fuel to get them back home. He then checked himself. That was always assuming that K for King would be making the return journey. There was no room for complacency.

***

The Dresden to Berlin train ground noisily to a halt thirty miles short of its destination, bringing a frown to Siggi Hoffman's face.

'Not another delay,' she sighed to herself. They were already running over three hours late. At just twenty years old, Hitler's war had been with her for nearly a quarter of her life. It felt far longer. All she wanted right now was to be home again with her mother and elder sister, Astrid. Although away for only a few days, she was already missing them both a great deal.

Her whispered words must have sounded louder than she imagined. A soldier sitting directly opposite gave her a wry smile. 'Better to arrive late than not arrive at all,' he told her. 'I'm sure there is a very good reason for us stopping again.'

He hesitated before adding: 'Are you from Berlin?'

Siggi studied him briefly before replying. He was only two or three years older than herself. A corporal in one of the infantry divisions she would guess by the look of the insignia on his jacket.

'Yes, I live in Steglitz in the south-west of the city,' she said, deciding that the soldier was being genuinely friendly and not interrogating her. 'I'm just returning from visiting a relative in Dresden.'

'Did you enjoy your visit?'

'It was ...' She shrugged in a vague, non-committal way.

He took the hint and did not press her with further questions.

Maybe the expression on her face had discouraged him as well, she realised. In truth, it was all she could do to suppress a shudder as she recalled the last three days spent with her uncle. She would never understand how her relative had become so indoctrinated into Nazi party ways. When younger, she had always thought of him as being a fair and reasonable man. Now he was a fanatic. Just prior to her departing he'd even had the nerve to suggest she should be proud that her father – his own brother – had sacrificed his life for the Führer on the Russian Front.

She clenched her fists as the memory of this provoked a spurt of anger. Her father had never had the slightest belief in the cause he'd been compelled to fight and die for. She had no belief in it either, nor did her mother and sister. In many ways, all three of them hoped that Germany would lose the war. Better that than a lifetime under the Nazis.

But it was one thing to think these anti-party thoughts: quite another to express them openly. There were people everywhere prepared to report such loose talk to the Gestapo, so on the surface at least, she and her family were forced to go on supporting the Nazis. At the same time, in spite of the increasing demands being made of the civilian population, each of them did as little as they could get away with to aid Hitler's war effort.

Straining her eyes to see in the dimly lit carriage, she looked at her watch. It was 9.30 pm.

'Why have we stopped again?' she asked a passing guard.

The man paused briefly to spit on the floor. Siggi felt disgust at both his manners, and sense of hygiene. 'The British bombers are coming again,' he almost shouted at her. 'Hundreds of them.' He then continued on his way down the carriage, muttering loudly to himself.

Many other passengers sitting nearby could not fail to also hear the guard's words. Almost immediately, a concentrated murmuring developed. An old lady two seats further along began praying in a loud, shrill voice.

Siggi's thoughts immediately went out to her mother and sister. Not Berlin again – surely not? Why couldn't they leave the city alone? She tried to reassure herself. The majority of the bombs were usually directed much more toward the city centre than to suburbs like Steglitz. Their area had escaped reasonably lightly up until now, so why should it be any different tonight? Although it was strictly forbidden under the blackout laws, she tugged nervously at the window blind, raising it a touch to peer outside.

She could see little in the darkness apart from the fact that they were in the middle of the countryside. Then a distant droning reached her ears. It was the all too familiar sound of approaching bombers. A sound that was invariably the prelude to ear-shattering noise, fire and death.

The sound rapidly grew, as did the babble of voices on the train. Disregarding the rules, more people began raising the blinds. Some even opened the windows and leaned out in an effort to spot the planes.

'There's one!' exclaimed a middle-aged man with a moustache clearly modelled on the Führer's very own. 'And another! And another!'

The noise from the bombers was now very loud. In contrast, a hush descended over the carriage, as if the passengers were suddenly realising the vulnerability of their position. Siggi knew they would stand little chance while crammed together like this if a stray bomb were to fall nearby.

The guard returned. 'Everybody off the train,' he ordered.

No one needed telling twice. Siggi was swept up in the mad crush as people began scrambling for the nearest door. For close to a minute it was sheer madness. Then the soldier who she had spoken to briefly was by her side. He placed a protective arm around her shoulder. Grateful for his help, she allowed herself to be guided safely off the train. Together, they walked to the middle of a field. Both of them gazed skyward.

The flak guns had now started, their noise competing for supremacy with the monotonous drone of wave after wave of bombers. Searchlights probed the sky, endlessly searching for targets to trap in their glare.

And then they heard the first of the bombs falling. Even at a distance of thirty miles, the sounds and smells reached them clearly. Looking away, Siggi buried her face in her hands.

Like the old woman on the train earlier, she began to pray.

TWO

The navigator's voice came to Stafford over the intercom. 'Target area dead ahead in about five minutes, skipper.'

'Thanks, Doug. And the rest of you guys, keep a sharp eye out for night fighters.'

With the flak from the heavy defence guns already beginning, the Canadian had more immediate things on his mind. Shells were exploding with increasing regularity in the sky all around them, each one sending shock waves thudding into the aircraft. Such was the extent of the buffeting, it was now taking nearly all of his strength just to keep the heavy Lancaster on anything like a straight course.

'And watch out for any of our own guys as well if they get too close,' he added to his general warning, ever mindful of how tight airspace was going to be in the melee of bombers jostling for position.

The large patches of low-lying cloud weren't helping much either. All crews had been told it would be clear over Berlin by the time they arrived, but once again the weather boys had got it wrong. Flying above these clouds might offer some protection from the searchlights, but accurate bombing was now going to be far more difficult than usual.

Stafford was still considering this problem when he found himself moving into a large area of cloudless sky. Almost immediately the searchlights began stabbing holes in the protective darkness surrounding the Lancaster. He twisted the aircraft to the left – to the right – then left again in an attempt to evade their probing. But the pursuit was relentless. Almost inevitably, one of the lights finally managed to trap him full in its glare. The dazzling intensity of it transformed the cockpit interior from deep gloom to brilliance. The bomb aimer's Perspex dome in front of him became an incandescent fire, throwing a searing blaze of light back into his face. Through squinted and stinging eyes, he tried everything he knew to lose the damning shaft of light, sharply aware that the flak guns would already be zeroing their sights in on him.

Like eager vultures closing in on a dying animal, more searchlights picked up on K for King. Sweat was now pouring from Stafford's brow. Any second now they could expect to be blown from the sky.

There was no choice. As a final desperate manoeuvre, he threw the Lancaster into a steep dive. With the weight of a full bomb load dragging them down, they were soon hurtling earthwards at over 300mph. Still the lights followed them.

From the front nose section Jimmy shouted out a frantic warning. 'We're going to hit one of ours. Left, skipper – go left!'

Even as the bomb aimer spoke, Stafford was banking hard to port. How he missed the other Lancaster he'd never know. But miss they did, and then, miraculously, they were in the relative safety of darkness once again.

'Shit that was close, Mike.' There was a definite shake to Jimmy's voice as he addressed Stafford by his first name.

From the rear gunner's position, Geordie's voice cut in on the intercom. 'Those bloody lights have picked up on the Lanc we just missed.'

There was a pause, then: 'He's hit! The bastards have got him.'

The big aircraft above them literally blew itself apart as the flak guns scored a direct hit on its bomb bay. Brightly glowing fragments began dropping from the sky like some multi-coloured snowstorm.

They had plunged to well below 10,000 feet before Stafford finally managed to pull out of the dive and level K for King. The effort it took left him feeling briefly weak. But there was no time to relax. Pausing only to suck in a few deep breaths, he began to climb once again. Maximum height was vital when anywhere near the defensive guns of Berlin.

By the time they regained altitude he could see parts of the city already burning. But there were no marker flares from the RAF Pathfinder Group. Absolutely nothing to tell him that these earlier bombs had found the correct target. His immediate reaction was to drop his bombs anyway and get the hell out of it as fast as possible. It was suicide to hang around here for very much longer. The flak was now far heavier: the worst he'd ever experienced. A chance shot could bring them down at any time. On top of that, the searchlights were once again becoming too damn close for comfort. And if all that wasn't enough, he had just spotted a pair of night fighters descending for a few easy kills.

Another Lancaster close to them went down in flames. It was becoming like a huge game of aerial dodgems. He was doing all he could to stay out of trouble, but it was impossible to know which direction the next attack might be coming from.

'Wireless has packed up, skipper.' It was radio operator Pete Cowley on the intercom.

Stafford swore softly. That ruled out any possibility of establishing the correct target over the air.

Barely had that thought formed when a large green flare appeared over on the starboard side. 'At last,' he murmured, swinging the Lancaster toward the marker. 'There's your target, Jimmy,' he told his friend.

There was no trace of the earlier shakiness in the bomb aimer's voice, 'I'm on to it, skipper. Try to keep her steady.'

Stafford's teeth clenched tight as the aircraft shuddered violently from the closest flak blast yet. Steady was a damn sight easier said than done under the circumstances.

The bomb bay doors opened. 'Steady --- steady,' Jimmy repeated with methodical slowness while peering down through his sights. 'Go left just a touch --- hold her there --- steady --- right a bit --- steady --- steady.'

Jimmy now had command of the aircraft until after their bombs were released. For Stafford, every second spent holding this vulnerable straight and level course felt like an hour as his friend painstakingly guided him into the correct position.

'Steady --- steady,' Jimmy's voice persisted. Then came the words that everyone on board was longing to hear.

'Bombs gone!'

Suddenly free of its seven-ton cargo, the Lancaster rose sharply and surged forward. There was a new, almost joyous vitality about it.

Stafford came back on the intercom, his relaxed tone belying the nervous tension he was feeling.

'Okay guys, bomb doors closed. Let's get the hell out of here. Give me a course for home, Doug.'

***

Siggi shivered, automatically pulling her coat more tightly around herself. But the involuntary trembling had little to do with the chill of the night air. She knew that it had far more to do with the cold fear she was feeling for her mother and sister.

Thirty miles away, the whole of Berlin now appeared to be ablaze. Even from such a great distance, the intensity of the flames was still making her eyes sting. She looked away. It was impossible to imagine how anyone within the city could ever hope to survive such a conflagration. And yet still the bombers kept on coming. Wave after wave of them.

Along with all the other train passengers, she had been simply standing and waiting in this gloomy field for more than two hours now. Very few people were speaking. It was as if they were all thinking along similar lines to herself. Just like her, most of them would also have close relatives and loved ones living in Berlin.

Siggi's eyes shifted to the sky as more bombers passed nearby. She stood there, trying hard to imagine what kind of men were inside them.

'Leave my family alone,' she muttered softly.

***

Stafford flew due west toward the Dutch coast, all the time battling against the powerful wind that threatened to drag them southwards. Since leaving Berlin behind the flak had been light. Now, having managed to skirt around the heavily defended area of Hanover, an air of confidence was beginning to spread. Even the fighters seemed to be taking a night off in this area, he mused. Not far to go now and they would be back over the North Sea and then home. With four engines all in good working order to get them there, it was beginning to look as if they had once again come through a trip to the Big City unscathed.

The night fighter came swiftly out of the darkness.

In the cold and gloom of his rear turret, Big Geordie Heatley shouted a warning into his intercom. 'JU88 up our arse, skipper! Corkscrew.'

Stafford reacted immediately, putting the Lancaster into a steep dive to starboard. At the same time, Geordie fired off a burst from his guns. The response was a solid stream of cannon fire ripping into his turret.

The heavy bomber rose sharply again, this time to port, before completing the spiral movement that gave the corkscrew defensive manoeuvre its name.

'I can't see the son-of-a-bitch. Where is he, Geordie?' Stafford called.

There was no reply from the rear.

'I can see him, skipper.' It was the nasal tones of New Zealander Phil Thomas in the mid-upper gun turret that now came through. There was a brief pause then: 'Shit, he's slipped below us.'

Stafford did not need reminding of the danger this presented. Once positioned beneath the bomber, the German pilot would know that he was safe from any of the Lancaster's guns. His night fighter, on the other hand, would be equipped with twin, upward firing cannons.

Only seconds later Stafford's worst fears were realised. The first volley of cannon fire tore into the Lancaster's underbelly. The follow-up burst destroyed his inner starboard engine. This immediately burst into flames.

The smell of cordite was strong in Stafford's nostrils as he fought to control his stricken aircraft. Jamming the rudder bar hard over to port in an effort to counterbalance the loss of power, he dived yet again.

The fighter pilot, obviously flushed with success, became a touch careless. Instead of applying the finishing touches, he hesitated a short while to assess the damage he had so far achieved. It was the classic sign of an inexperienced pilot taking risks simply to preserve ammunition for more kills.

Following K for King into its dive, the JU88 strayed briefly into Phil Thomas' gun sights. The New Zealander, unlike the fighter pilot, *was* experienced. There was no hesitation on his part. The mid-upper gun turret shook violently as he put in a long burst.

For once, the lightweight .303's proved to be effective. The nose of the JU88 erupted into a mass of flames. Its graceful dive suddenly became a vertical plunge. Although still rapidly descending itself, the Lancaster appeared to be almost stationary as the doomed fighter shot past them.

'I got the bastard, skipper,' Thomas yelled.

Stafford was too busy to respond. He kept the aircraft in its dive, all of the time praying that the rushing airflow and heat-activated extinguishers would combine to put out the blazing engine. Sweat was pouring from him again when, at a mere three thousand feet, the flames finally flickered away to nothing.

There was an almost reverent silence on board as he levelled the Lancaster. In the seat alongside him, Hughie Smith let out a long sigh of relief before running an expert eye over the instruments. Stafford wound the rudder trim and feathered the offending prop. Satisfied that the aircraft was still flyable, he spoke urgently to the rear gunner.

'Geordie, can you hear me?'

There was still no reply.

'Pete. Get in the back and check on Geordie.'

'On my way, skipper,' the wireless operator told him.

'Is everybody else okay?' Stafford asked.

'I'm all right, but my table's been shot to pieces.' It was a very aggrieved sounding Doug Short.

'Don't worry, Doug. The RAF will buy you a new one.'

'I'm getting cramp.' This time it was Jimmy from the nose turret.

'Well make sure you've loosened up by the time we get back home, buddy. I reckon we all owe our Kiwi mate a few beers.'

'Hey, I'll go along with that right enough, skipper.'

Stafford grinned at the gunner's enthusiastic response.

***

While the banter continued, Pete Cowley made his way along the fuselage to the rear turret. He banged loudly on the sliding doors, but there was no sound coming from the other side. Seizing the dead man's handle, he pulled as hard as he could. It was stuck fast. He banged again, this time even louder. Still no reaction came from inside the gunner's tiny compartment. Not a single sound to suggest that Geordie may still be alive.

Just behind Pete was the regulation fire axe. Seizing this from its mounting, he chopped savagely at the point where the two doors met. The blade bit, allowing him some leverage. But still the twin doors refused to separate.

He continued hacking until there was a hole large enough for him to get a foot into. By wedging his back against the side of the fuselage, he was now able to exert the maximum pressure of his leg muscles. He strained hard for several seconds. The left side door at last gave a little, then, with a protesting screech, abruptly opened all the way. The right-hand door quickly followed.

An icy blast of air immediately cut right through the wireless operator. The turret was a complete mess. Great jagged holes – twisted metal – and shattered Perspex strewn everywhere. Slumped in the middle of all this mess was Geordie, his safety harness the only thing preventing him from toppling forward and out of the turret completely. Cowley stared with mounting horror at his crew mate. The large patches of blood on Geordie's chest and right leg were still spreading, the red standing out with ominous clarity against the bright yellow of his electrically heated suit. He made no movement.

Cowley's hand went to his mouth, struggling to hold down the rising nausea. Rapidly, he disconnected the gunner's intercom and plugged in his own. 'Geordie's been hit, skipper. Looks like he may have bought it. I can't tell while he's stuck in here.'

Stafford reacted immediately. 'Doug, go back and help Pete will you? See if the two of you can get Geordie out of there.'

The navigator joined Cowley within moments. Unusually for a rear gunner, Geordie was a large man – a dead weight that, once his harness had been released, was in constant danger of slipping away from his rescuers' clutches. The confined space made their job even more difficult. They struggled for several minutes before managing to manoeuvre the big gunner completely out of his turret and safe from a long fall to earth. As the pair finally completed their task, Geordie groaned.

'At least he's still alive,' Pete remarked, the anguish he was feeling showing clearly in his expression. At twenty years old, he was the baby of the crew.

'Maybe, but he looks to be in a hell of a state.' Short's face was also full of concern. Everyone on board liked Geordie. Nearly always cheerful, never once had he been heard to complain about his lonely and dangerous role.

As gently as they could, the pair of them carried the big man toward the front of the aircraft. Close to Pete's position was a drop-down stretcher fixed to the side of the fuselage. Carefully, they laid Geordie onto this. Short undid the gunner's suit. In the dim, artificial light his wounds looked ghastly. Even though the big man's heart had obviously not taken a direct hit, it was hard to imagine how he could possibly survive such terrible injuries.

'Christ almighty.' Pete swallowed hard and looked away.

Short, older by ten years, took charge. Not simply because he was an officer. It was just that the situation demanded speedy action.

He moved forward to the pilot's position. 'Geordie's been shot up pretty badly,' he told Stafford. 'Can you spare Jimmy in the back for a while? He's had a lot more first-aid training than me.'

Stafford nodded his agreement. 'Okay, but Pete will have to take over on the front guns while Jimmy's gone.'

Short returned to the back. By the time the bomb aimer and wireless operator had changed places, he'd already opened the first aid kit and was doing his best to tend Geordie's injuries.

Jimmy made a quick examination. 'That needs sorting out double quick or he'll bleed to death,' he stated, pointing to the wound in Geordie's lower thigh. Despite Short's earlier attempts at stemming the flow with tightly applied wadding, the blood was continuing to pump out in rapid little spurts.

Grabbing a lead from the now useless radio set, Jimmy wrapped this around the gunner's upper leg. He then used a stout pencil from Short's collection to twist the lead tight. The blood spurts gradually ceased as the makeshift tourniquet constricted the arteries.

Satisfied, Jimmy administered a shot of morphine. 'If he's conscious enough to be feeling any pain, at least that should help a bit,' he said.

There was little the pair could do for the chest wounds other than finish cleaning them up and apply a dressing. This done, they strapped the injured gunner securely into his stretcher.

'How's it going, Jimmy?' It was Stafford back on the intercom.

'We've done all we can. It's touch and go from now on.'

There was a short silence while the Canadian digested this news. 'Okay, now you're finished with that, go take a look at the rear guns. See if they're still working.'

Short cut in. 'Not a hope. I checked them before we brought Geordie back. Everything's well and truly buggered.'

Stafford's voice hesitated only briefly. 'In that case, come back up front, Jim. I'm gonna take this baby right down. Let's just pray we don't come across any stray flak guns.'

***

Stafford took the big Lancaster lower and lower, until it felt as if they were almost kissing the ground. He knew that at this level the enemy radar would not be able to pick them up. Also, they were far less likely to attract the attention of any other night fighters that might be prowling the area. With their rear guns and one engine out of action, K for King would be a sitting duck if spotted.

All the same, it was a desperately dangerous tactic, and one that was calling on every bit of his flying skills. At approaching two hundred miles an hour, the ground level terrain flashed by. Power lines...high buildings...any kind of sudden rise in the ground: all these were barely visible in the gloom ahead and had to be negotiated with little more than an instant's warning. Pete Cowley was visibly shaking while handing his temporary role in the nose cone back to Jimmy. His expression stated quite clearly that if they were going to fly like this, then he would far rather do it from his usual position where he could see nothing of the outside and ignorance was bliss.

Three pairs of eyes: Stafford's, Jimmy's, and Hughie Smith's all continued to keep a constant watch for any dangers ahead.

'Watch out for --'

Jimmy's shouted warning died in his throat as Stafford found himself literally flying around a church spire that loomed up from nowhere directly in their path. His port wing tip could not have cleared the obstacle by any more than a few feet. It was at this extreme, hair-raising moment that Doug Short came up front to see for himself what was happening.

His gasp of horror at their near miss sounded loud.

'No trouble picking out landmarks tonight, eh Doug?' Stafford remarked, his eyes never leaving the ground ahead for an instant.

Like Pete Cowley before him, a little of life near the driving seat at this altitude was clearly more than enough for the navigator. Rapidly, he returned to what remained of his shattered table.

***

Siggi tried hard to contain her impatience. The last of the bombers had finally departed and everybody was back on board the train. But still they were not moving. An announcement a few minutes earlier had informed passengers that some of the tracks ahead had suffered damage. The few lines still remaining serviceable were in great demand. All trains would have to take their turn.

Even with the air raid over, her concern for the safety of her mother and sister wasn't easing. Constantly, she tried to reassure herself. Although a few other properties close to their home had suffered quite badly, their own little street had so far remained completely untouched by the bombs. It was almost as if an invisible barrier had wrapped itself around this part of Steglitz and was determined to protect it. Besides, she knew that everyone in the house would have spent the entire raid sheltering in the house cellar. It would take an awful lot to harm anyone down there.

Still clinging to this comforting thought, she wondered how much longer they were going to be delayed.

***

Stafford maintained his low-level tactic until they were just a few miles away from the Dutch coast. Aware that there might be strong coastal defences ahead, he then began to climb. They made 15,000 feet and crossed the North Sea without further incident. Now once more back over British soil and close to base, his only real concern was their lack of radio contact.

'Just about enough fuel left,' Hughie Smith informed him as he lined up the aircraft for their final approach.

The Canadian passed a hand over sore and tired eyes. One final effort and it would be all over for another night. He cast a brief thought for Geordie. The gunner's plight troubled him deeply, but he could not – dare not – dwell on it too much. Not until he had first put the Lancaster safely down. He reached for the undercarriage release lever. A buzzer and red flashing light told him that it was dropping. Both would automatically cut out when the wheels were locked into position.

But they did not cut out. Frowning, Stafford raised the wheels and tried once more. Again they failed to lock. He ran through the process a third time, still with no success. It was useless. Something had been badly damaged, almost certainly during the night fighter's attack from below.

The feeling came with a rush. Never before had Stafford experienced anything remotely similar. It wasn't just a vague idea that something might go wrong. There was always a variety of niggling doubts to eat away at you on ops like these. This time, it was far more serious than that. This time, an imminent disaster felt like a full-blown certainty. Just what had planted this crazy thought into his head, he had no idea. There was obviously a fair size risk attached to putting the Lanc down, but it was far from unknown for a crew to walk away from a wheels-up landing. Even with one engine out.

He tried to push the feeling from his mind, but it would not let go. It was overpowering him. Something terrible was about to happen. He just knew it. The premonition gnawed away at his brain, blotting out all else.

All the time they were losing height on their final approach. Then came another blow. The port flap dropped okay, but the one on the starboard wing wouldn't budge. That was the clincher. This landing was becoming more perilous by the second. The lost engine – the undercarriage – and now a useless flap. Much as he wanted to, he could no longer ignore the warning signs.

Stafford threw on the power and began to climb once again.

Hughie Smith in the seat alongside glanced across in amazement. 'What's going on, skipper?' he asked.

'You saw for yourself didn't you? First the undercarriage, then the starboard flap. I can't risk making a landing with all you guys still on board.'

'What are you talking about?'

'Get your chute on, Hughie.'

The flight engineer's face twitched. 'You can't be serious, skip.'

Doug Short came up to join them. Rapidly Stafford told him of the new problems. 'It's too risky, Doug,' he continued. 'Once I've made enough height I want you all to bale out. Make sure Geordie's strapped in good and tight. I'll try and get this baby down, but it's going to be a rough ride. There's no point in the rest of you guys risking your necks as well.'

Short began to say something and then changed his mind. One look at Stafford's determined expression would have told him that any debate was pointless. His senior rank meant nothing. While in the air, the pilot was always the one in command.

'I'll get things organised,' he said, disappearing into the back again.

Hughie Smith at this stage was in the process of removing his parachute from its storage rack. The relatively small pack, which was designed to clip onto his chest using the harness he was already wearing, somehow managed to slip from his fingers. If this was because of nerves, it was understandable, Stafford thought briefly. None of his crew had ever jumped before. The only training any of them had received for this kind of situation was leaping off a high bench in an aircraft hangar and being shown how to land properly. But at least his flight engineer was now appearing to accept his order as being necessary. The Canadian then spoke to his friend in the nose cone.

'Come up here, Jim. Get ready to bale out.'

'What!' There was total disbelief in the bomb aimer's voice.

'You heard what I said. We've got problems, so let's move it, buddy.'

The intercom went dead. Moments later Jimmy appeared on the flight deck, parachute in hand. He made no attempt to clip this on as Stafford repeated what he had told Short. Just as he was finishing, his friend cut in.

'Hold on a minute. You can't really believe I'm going to let you put this crate down on your own. That's not the way it works with you and me. We always stick together, Mike. If you're going down, I'm going with you.'

Then, in what seemed like an attempt to justify his outburst, he let out a short laugh, adding: 'Anyway, you know how I've always been a bit nervous about jumping.'

'I'm sorry, Jim. I want you to go anyway. That's an order.'

It came out all wrong, sounding curt and authoritative. Privately Stafford's heart was going out to his close friend. He wanted to say, *'Okay buddy, you stay and we'll see it through together.'* But he knew he couldn't do that. The feeling that something terrible was about to happen just would not go away.

Jimmy shook his head. 'I don't give a damn what you want, Mike, I'm not going. That's final! What kind of bloke deserts his best mate?' As if to emphasize his point, he threw his parachute hard down onto the floor in disgust. It landed with a thud.

The two men's eyes met briefly in a powerful clash of wills. Hating himself for resorting to such measures, Stafford used the only tactic he felt would break down Jimmy's stubborn sense of loyalty. He spoke slowly and with great purpose.

'Listen hard, Jim. If you don't do as I say, our friendship is finished. That's not bullshit; that's a fact. I'll also have you charged with disobeying a direct order. After the court martial you won't be flying with me, or anyone else, ever again. Is that clear enough for you?'

If he had physically struck his friend, the effect could not have been more dramatic. Jimmy's mouth literally dropped open.

'You don't mean that.'

'Try me.'

Stafford knew full well that he could never carry out such a threat. His expression though conveyed none of this. For an instant Jimmy appeared to be on the brink of real anger. He finally took a deep breath and instead shrugged.

'Okay, Mike. If you want to try and win a VC all on your own, go ahead.'

There was another long and difficult pause. Jimmy then placed a hand on Stafford's shoulder, squeezing hard. His voice was now quiet.

'I'm sorry. I didn't mean that. You'll get her down safely, I know you will. Christ, you're the best bloody pilot I've ever known.'

There was still a lump in Stafford's throat when he levelled the aircraft out. 'We've got five thousand feet,' he announced. 'That's plenty high enough.'

Hughie Smith, who had remained silent and in his seat throughout the confrontation, now headed toward the rear exit point.

'Good luck, skipper,' he said. There was a slight shake in his voice.

'What about you, Jim?' Stafford asked, seeing that his friend had made no move to follow the flight engineer.

'Just give me a minute.' 'If I've got to go, at least let me go out last.'

Stafford nodded. How could he refuse under the circumstances?

A short silence followed. Finally, with a deep sigh, Jimmy turned to leave. 'Mike ...' he began hesitantly.

The Canadian glanced up from the controls and winked. 'Go on, get out of here before I run out of fuel.'

Jimmy gave him one final searching look before moving away.

Alone, Stafford reflected on his choice of action. He was doing the right thing, he assured himself. It wasn't possible to ignore the bad feelings still eating away at him. This landing was going to be a bloody messy business; there was no doubt about that. And even if he did manage to walk away from it, that didn't mean all the rest of his crew would be so lucky. No, they were far better off getting out now. He would never have been able to forgive himself had any of the guys stayed on board unnecessarily and then got badly injured or killed.

Jimmy's voice came over the intercom. 'Everyone's out except me, Mike.' He paused before adding: 'I've got a bottle of scotch in my locker we can crack open later. I reckon we've earned ourselves a drink or two tonight.'

'I'll hold you to that one,' Stafford told him.

There was a short silence. 'I'd still rather hang around here, you know.'

'Go! That's an order, Jim.'

'Okay, have it your way. Just make sure you get yourself and Geordie down in one piece, Brandon Boy.' This was Jimmy's private nickname for him, normally used in moments of good-humoured banter. It was a reference to the small prairie town in Manitoba that Stafford originated from. A complete contrast to Jimmy's own south London upbringing.

'Brandon Boy' was the very last thing he heard Jimmy say. A few seconds later he knew that his friend had jumped.

THREE

Once again, Stafford lined the Lancaster up for his final approach. The fuel gauges were registering just about empty. If he got this one chance wrong – that was it. No possibility of going around for a second try. The only consolation was that, with empty fuel tanks, the danger from fire was greatly reduced.

He thought of Geordie strapped into his stretcher further back. Was he still alive? And if so, was he conscious enough to be aware of what was going on? Stafford hoped that he wasn't. Much better for the guy if he were to wake up in a warm hospital bed. Or not wake up at all if things turned out badly.

His thoughts turned to the rest of his crew. At least they were all safe. It was strange, but now the critical point was almost here, his premonition of doom appeared to be easing off. He felt almost confident. Was it possible that he had over-reacted? All he knew for certain was that he'd done everything he could to ensure the crew's safety. That was the most important thing.

The loss of the starboard flap was a major blow. Without the braking system of the undercarriage, he would have been relying on the wing flaps to help reduce his speed after touching down. But to use just the port flap on its own would result in the aircraft spinning, so that was effectively put out of action too. Even with the engines running at minimum, he could still expect to hit the deck at around 100 mph. It wasn't a great prospect.

Bus drivers – that's how a lot of fighter pilots flippantly referred to those who flew bombers. Well, it was okay for them in their neat little

Spitfires and Hurricanes. Let's see one of those guys put this crippled heavyweight down and walk away from it in one piece.

The first trick was to try and touch down at the very beginning of the runway so as to allow himself as much distance as possible. Feathering the inner port propeller to match the damaged starboard engine, he ran the remaining two at just above stalling speed. The Lancaster came in exactly as he wanted it to: nose up with the solitary tail wheel making contact with the ground first. Not on the hard, unforgiving runway, but on the grass that ran alongside. Stafford immediately shut off the power.

For a brief moment the aircraft appeared almost graceful as it balanced delicately up on its single tail wheel like some giant ballerina. The illusion was quickly shattered. The wheel first of all buckled, and then broke up. What remained of the rear turret disappeared completely in a mass of tangled metal. K for King hovered momentarily before performing a belly flop of earth-shattering proportions.

For Stafford it was like being trapped inside a giant concrete mixer racing around at treble speed. Somehow his harness continued to hold him in his seat, although the strain was enormous as the webbing bit into his chest with crushing force. His head shook violently. His teeth banged together repeatedly with such violence that he grunted out loud with the pain. Pieces of shattered windscreen were flying all around the cabin like a swarm of enraged hornets. The stick bucked wildly and then flew out of his hands as the huge bomber careered on, ploughing an ever-deepening furrow in the grass.

Any kind of control was now out of the question. Everything was down to fate. The back end began to slew to one side, straying onto the hard surface of the runway. Sparks flew from this section, although Stafford, battered and completely disorientated, was unaware of this. A crazy, illogical thought was passing through his mind. He had not paid last month's mess bill yet. He would hate to die in debt.

The last thing he remembered was catching a glimpse of the approaching ambulance. Often he had witnessed charred and mutilated bodies being loaded onto this. The vehicle became a harbinger of doom. Was this it? Were his worst fears about to be justified, after all?

Something caved in behind him. There was a blinding spasm of pain. Then nothing at all.

***

Six more interminable hours dragged by before Siggi's train began moving once again. They eventually pulled into Berlin's Anhalter station just as the first hint of daylight was struggling to show through.

The soldier who had helped Siggi during the earlier panic carried her suitcase onto the platform and placed it beside her. 'So, I must leave you here,' he said. He gave an encouraging smile. 'Try not to worry too much. I am sure that your mother and sister will be safe.'

Although they had exchanged only a few words during the final part of the journey, she had nonetheless managed to draw some small comfort from his presence. She was about to thank him for his kindness when a loud voice from further along the platform barked out an order. A stern looking Sergeant was glaring at them.

The soldier grimaced. 'I must not keep the Oberfeldwebel waiting.'

'No, of course not.'

He hesitated for just a second longer, as if wishing to say something further. Then, just as Siggi was on the point of attempting to thank him once again, he flashed a final brief smile and hurried away.

Sighing, she picked up her suitcase, briefly wondering what to do next. Attempting to call home would be useless. The communal telephone in their large apartment house had been out of action for weeks. But the Universum film studios where she worked as a secretary was only a short distance away. Even at this time of the morning there was a chance that someone capable of giving her a lift home might be around. People there worked all kinds of unusual hours.

Quite why she had not been forced to labour in a munitions factory like so many others she knew of was still a mystery to her. Somebody important at Universum, most probably a leading party member, must value her services more highly than she realised? That, or they were attracted to her? She had been uncomfortably aware for several years now of how sexually appealing most men found her.

She set off under heavily clouded skies in the direction of the film studios.

It was heart-breaking to see the damage done to the city. After all the air raids that Berlin had suffered, Siggi felt that she should be hardened to the terrible sights by now. But she wasn't, and doubted that she ever would be. Everywhere she looked there was suffering, death and destruction. How could anyone ever accept these things as being normal?

The bombs had even mutilated the trees in the Tiergarten, a place where she had spent so many pleasant times before the war. Instead of the happy cosmopolitan crowds that used to congregate in the park, there were now only grim-faced locals – a lot of them homeless – all wondering uneasily when the next air raid might be coming. Everyone spent the dark hours listening for the dreaded sirens that would send them once again scuttling into the nearest shelter. The British planes had been bombing them regularly for months now. More recently, the Americans had joined in too. Often during daylight hours. There was no respite.

Siggi had frequently wondered how the Londoners had coped when it was their city being blitzed. She could feel no great hatred toward the British. Most of them were ordinary folk with the very same day-to-day problems as Germans. If the reports she'd heard were true, huge damage had been done to the English capital. Thousands of lives had been lost.

And now her home city was suffering in retaliation. All because of that madman Hitler and his quest for world domination. How she hated him.

After a few minutes of walking she turned into Prinz-Albrecht Strasse and passed the headquarters of the notorious Gestapo. Amid so much destruction, the building remained virtually untouched.

Siggi frowned. Talk about the devil looking after his own kind.

She turned left, and there ahead of her was Leipziger Strasse where the film studios were situated. She was feeling tired after her long journey. Her suitcase was already becoming heavy. Silently, she prayed that there would be someone around capable of giving her that lift home.

***

After all the problems she had encountered so far on her journey, Siggi felt a wave of relief to have her prayer answered. From the hundreds of people who worked at Universum, she bumped into a young man she knew slightly who was on the point of leaving.

'I can drive you most of the way,' he told her. 'That is, if the roads are still passable after last night's bombs.' His expression grew serious. 'I don't want to worry you, but I heard that Steglitz has been hit quite badly.'

Siggi's heart gave a lurch. 'No,' she whispered. 'Surely not.'

He was instantly contrite. 'I'm sorry – I shouldn't have said anything. The reports are probably wrong anyway.'

'Please. Let's just go,' she implored.

***

The Volkswagen left the city centre behind, allowing Siggi to see the full extent of the new damage. Whole streets had been devastated. Many of them were still burning. Several times they were forced into taking a long diversion in order to get around the fires and fallen rubble.

When they finally did manage to get somewhere close to the south-west suburbs it became horribly clear that the reports were true. Steglitz *had* been badly hit. The flickering glow of flames could already be seen against the still gloomy sky. Siggi felt nausea rising. Her mother and sister had to be safe, she told herself over and over again. Fate had already taken her father. Surely it would not inflict any more punishment on her family?

The nearer they got, the worse the devastation became. Masonry from collapsed buildings lay strewn across roads in great smouldering heaps. Eventually the car pulled up.

'I'm afraid that's as far as I can take you,' the young man said. 'It's impossible to drive any closer.'

He began to add a few words of comfort and encouragement, but soon realised that he was wasting his breath. Siggi had already grabbed her suitcase and was out of the car.

Nothing was going to stop her reaching her family.

***

The air was thick with smoke and dust, making her eyes sting and her breathing laboured. Twice she stumbled on the mounds of debris, grazing her leg on both occasions. It didn't matter. She had to keep going.

The damage to property was now so bad that it was almost impossible to recognise where she was. Whole streets had been totally obliterated, turning the area into a sea of rubble with virtually no distinguishing features. Siggi had an awful feeling that, in her panic, she was now running around in circles. Her eyes searched desperately for some kind of landmark that might have survived the bombs. Anything to reassure her that she was still heading in the right direction.

She moved closer to a collapsed building where a group of firemen were carefully digging. Another fireman was pumping air into a line that had been pushed through a pile of rubble and down into the cellar below. This told Siggi that there must be people trapped but still alive beneath the ruins.

She shuddered. The mere thought of being buried alive absolutely terrified her. Surely it would be better to die instantly from a direct hit? Better that than to spend hours, or possibly even days, imprisoned under tons of rubble slowly choking to death in the dust, not even knowing if others were aware of your plight. Always uneasy in confined spaces, such a fate had been her secret nightmare ever since the air raids had first begun.

She spoke to one of the perspiring firemen, urgently asking him if he knew where her street was. The man paused from his digging to wipe a grimy hand over his sweat streaked forehead. He pointed to his right.

'It's somewhere over there, I think,' he said after a few moments of thought. 'About two hundred metres.'

Without even pausing to thank him, Siggi hurried off in the direction indicated. In her haste she tripped once again, this time cutting the side of her face on a sharp stone. Such was her preoccupation, she barely felt a thing.

And then she knew exactly where she was.

She stared ahead with sickening horror and disbelief at the mangled heap of bricks, roof tiles and plaster. It was all that remained of her home.

The scene surrounding the devastated building was almost a replica of the one she had just left. More firemen, this time aided by a group of interned Italian labourers, were working methodically to remove the rubble. Once again, air was being pumped down.

'Mother! Astrid!'

All Siggi's anguish and pain came pouring out. Dropping her suitcase, she rushed blindly forward, throwing herself bodily onto the pile of debris. She clawed frantically at the rubble, her tortured mind striving to believe that she could somehow make it all magically disappear. Scream after scream flew from her mouth in an uncontrollable torrent.

All at once, she felt a firm hand grasping hold of her shoulder. Words in a language that she did not understand were spoken softly in her ear. Wild eyed, she spun around to see who had dared to interrupt her.

It was one of the Italians: a short, swarthy man with a kind face that was full of compassion. He said something more to her, and although Siggi still had no idea of what he was saying, his words seemed to have a strangely calming effect.

'My mother! My sister!' she sobbed.

He appeared to understand this. Trance like, she allowed him to gently lift her to her feet. Then one of the firemen approached them. Siggi pleaded with him for information.

He looked grave. 'As far as we know, everyone living in this house took shelter inside the cellar. They are still trapped down there. We can only hope that --'

'Siggi!'

A voice shouted out her name, cutting the man off in mid-sentence.

'Astrid!'

It was her sister. Dirty – dishevelled – her eyes full of pain – but it *was* her sister. She was safe.

Sobbing with joy and relief, Siggi rushed to meet her. She clung to Astrid fiercely. Both of them were talking at once, their voices combining to produce an incomprehensible babble. It didn't matter. All that mattered was the huge sense of relief and happiness washing over her.

Then Siggi drew back slightly and saw the look on Astrid's face. Her joy ended abruptly.

'Mother?' she asked, all but knowing the terrible answer before it came.

'She's down there somewhere.'

Even Siggi was surprised that she did not become hysterical once again. Maybe the continuing pressure of shock after shock was now having a numbing effect on her? She desperately wanted to cry, and could feel a huge burden of guilt for not doing so. But the tears simply would not come any longer.

Astrid took hold of her hand, squeezing it hard. 'They'll get her out safely, I know they will,' she promised.

***

There was nothing they could do but wait and pray. Astrid related how she had been visiting some friends in a district a few kilometres away. Once the bombs began falling she had little choice but to remain where she was and take shelter with these friends in the cellar of their house. Despite some damage to the area, the building above them had survived the raid almost intact, with only a few of the windows being blown out by one of the closer blasts. As soon as the all clear had been given, she'd made her way home as best she could. The last few hours had been spent just waiting and praying that their mother was safe.

At this point, she began to cry softly. 'If only I had taken mother with me,' she sobbed.

The roles were now reversed. It was Siggi's turn to be strong. Sitting forlornly amongst the rubble beside her sister, she comforted her as best she could. Her mind flashed back to the previous August. The British had dropped thousands of leaflets on the city warning of the huge bombing raids to come, urging civilians to evacuate their homes. If only they had followed that advice. But at the time it seemed that they would be giving up so much. They were city people, not country dwellers. And at that stage of the war, any bombers getting through to Berlin had been small in number. It was a far cry from the many hundreds at a time that were now coming.

As the pair of them continued to wait they noticed the NSV, a people's welfare organisation, setting up a nearby kitchen. Amid all the destruction they were soon distributing free comforts: soup, sausages, coffee, even cigarettes were being handed out. In the current days of strict rationing, such things were normally very scarce or completely unavailable. In spite of their anxieties, both girls realised that they needed to eat. Hunger, temporarily forgotten, was revived by the sight and smells of such rarities.

While waiting in the queue they recognised several neighbours who had miraculously escaped the carnage. She knew it was wrong, but Siggi could not stop herself from wondering why these people had been allowed to survive when her own dear mother was still buried, perhaps dead. There seemed to be no justice in it. Just how did God select, she asked herself bitterly?

Although only a rare smoker, she accepted a packet of cigarettes with her food. Astrid did the same. The stress of waiting was becoming too much. Right at this moment, both of them needed a crutch of some sort.

They had finished their food and were on their second cigarette apiece when the Italian with the kind face came running over. He beckoned for the pair of them to follow him. No words were necessary. It could only mean that the rescuers had finally cleared a way through to their house cellar.

Siggi could hear her own heart pounding loudly as the first survivors were assisted from their would-be crypt. Each new figure that emerged brought a surge of disappointment. Two elderly spinsters who lived in the apartment next door to them then appeared, clinging protectively to each other for comfort, much as they had probably done throughout the long hours of their ordeal. Both women looked at the end of their tether. This did not prevent Siggi and Astrid from assailing them with questions.

'Our mother – is she safe?'

'When is she coming up?'

'How is she feeling?'

The two old ladies looked nervously to each other for guidance. One of them sadly shook her head.

'I'm so sorry, my dears. She had a heart attack while the bombs were still falling. She passed away several hours ago.'

***

'Nurse, can you spare a minute please?'

The sudden effort of calling out across the ward triggered a sharp stab of pain to Stafford's ribs, causing him to gasp. It was evening visiting time, and every bed apart from his own had at least one visitor beside it.

The nurse, bespectacled and severe looking, stopped dead in her tracks. The brisk clip-clopping of her shoes on the hard floor ended abruptly, much like a machine gun that had run out of ammunition. She spun on her heel to face him.

'Yes,' she demanded.

'Are you sure that I haven't got any visitors? Does the squadron know which ward I'm in?'

As far as angels went, this one was a long way short of getting her wings, Stafford considered.

'Everyone is perfectly well aware of where you are, Mister Stafford,' she told him stiffly, as if daring him to question her efficiency. Without another word, she continued on her determined way. The clip-clopping resumed.

The Canadian sank back on his pillow and sighed. So much for colonial war heroes, he told himself with a wry grin.

But he had been lucky: incredibly so. Apart from a lingering headache, the blow to his head had done no serious damage. The main injuries were a couple of cracked ribs and a dislocated shoulder. Other than that it was just cuts and bruises. He would be laid up for only a week at the most, the doctor had assured him.

To cheer him even further, a short while ago he had been given the good news about Geordie. Although still currently under intensive care, the surgeons had done a fantastic job on him. There was no reason now why the big guy should not pull through okay, and in time, even be fit enough to resume flying duties.

All in all, things could have been a whole lot worse, Stafford reflected. In spite of the overwhelming power of his premonition, it had in the end turned out to be a bit of a dud. Okay, so the guys had to walk a few miles back to base after baling out. But that wasn't the end of the world. And as a consolation, they might all now be able to claim membership of the Caterpillar Club. That should please them.

The only down side at present was his lack of visitors. He would have staked his life on the crew coming in to see him this evening. Especially Jimmy. Perhaps there was some kind of flap on?

Stafford's thoughts continued, now reflecting on life in general. In physical appearance he had often been likened to the famous Hollywood actor, James 'Jimmy' Stewart. It was an irony his best pal frequently made jokes about. In a further coincidence, the movie star was currently also doing his bit in England by flying B-24s on daytime operations with the American Air Force. But while Stewart had already attained the rank of major, promotion for Stafford was proving a whole lot harder to come by.

Although grateful to the RAF for the opportunity to gain his pilot's wings, there were times when he felt more than a little annoyed over this state of affairs. Having volunteered in early 1940 very soon after the outbreak of war – and worked night and day in order to pay for his own fare across the Atlantic to join up – he still remained firmly stuck on the rank of flight sergeant. This, despite the fact that his experience of operational flying was far greater than that of many commissioned officers in the squadron. But it wasn't just himself of, course. Canadians in general throughout the RAF seemed to be regularly overlooked in this way. Hardly fair when you considered that his fellow countrymen made up nearly a quarter of all Bomber Command's aircrew. Were it not for Canada's contribution, plus that made by the boys from down under, they would surely be in a sorry mess for manpower.

Stafford was still musing on this topic when his glance strayed optimistically in the direction of the ward entrance. He immediately spotted Doug Short lingering there. The navigator had an unmistakable air of uncertainty about him.

'I'm over here, Doug,' he called out. This caused yet another stab of pain to the ribs. Not that he cared. Boy, was he pleased to see the guy. With a bit of luck, the rest of the crew would be arriving soon as well.

Short gave him a brief smile, but his uncertainty persisted. He appeared strangely subdued while approaching the bed. It was as if he would much rather be somewhere else.

'How are you, Mike?' His navigator spoke in the kind of voice Stafford usually associated with undertakers.

'Hey, what is this?' he asked. 'Lighten up. I'm not going to die just yet.'

'I know, I've already spoken with the doctor. He said that you'll be out of bed and getting around in no time.'

'And Geordie's going to be fine too.'

'That's what they say.'

'So why the miserable face, Doug? Everything worked out okay in the end, didn't it?'

There was a long, heavy pause before Short spoke again.

'I'm afraid it didn't, Mike.'

Stafford looked sharply at his visitor. 'What do you mean?'

All the bad feelings he had experienced just before landing K for King came rushing back once more.

Short chewed at his bottom lip for a moment, then swallowed hard. 'I don't know how to tell you this.' His face crumpled a little. 'I wish to God it wasn't me who had to do it. I suppose it's all part of being an officer.' He gave a hollow laugh. 'Stiff upper lip and all that rubbish.'

Stafford reached out, seizing hold of Short's arm. The stabbing pain to his ribs caused by the sharp movement now meant nothing.

'Never mind the fancy speech, Doug. Just tell me what's on your mind.'

Short swallowed again. 'I'm so sorry, Mike.'

Still he hesitated. Then the words came out with a rush. 'I'm afraid Jimmy didn't make it. Something went wrong with his chute. It didn't open properly. It was a rotten, lousy, thousand to one chance.'

There was a long silence. Stafford knew that he'd seen the man's lips move. Knew that he'd heard the words coming from his mouth. Even so, he could not accept what Short was telling him. He had misunderstood, that was all. Nothing like that could ever happen to Jimmy. He wouldn't allow it to. They were best buddies.

Short's lips were moving again. 'Don't blame yourself, Mike. Everyone knows that you did your best for the crew under the circumstances. You couldn't possibly have known it would turn out the way it did.'

It was only then that the full reality of the situation finally hit Stafford. Jimmy was dead. That was what he was being told. The realisation arrived with all the destructive force of an earthquake.

'No! Goddamn it to hell – no!'

Stafford's anguished cry reverberated all around the ward. Stunned patients and visitors stopped in mid-conversation to stare at him.

Short put out a restraining hand. 'Steady on, old chap.'

Stafford pushed the hand aside. 'Don't give me that typically British *old chap* garbage. That's bullshit. Don't you understand that Jimmy is ...'

He checked himself, pausing for a long moment. His voice dropped to barely a whisper. 'Of course you do. I'm sorry, Doug. I shouldn't be taking it out on you.'

The navigator gave a half-hearted shrug. 'Go ahead if you want to. The whole crew's been hit hard, but at least we've had a few hours for it to sink in. Honestly, I don't know what else to say. We all loved Jimmy, but everyone knows how close you two were.'

He spread his hands. Further words were unnecessary.

A lengthy, difficult silence followed, during which Short's eyes probed deeply for signs of any reaction. When Stafford did eventually speak, his voice was brusque.

'Push off, Doug.'

'Are you sure there's nothing I can do?'

'Can you raise the dead?'

Short flinched. 'That's not fair.'

'But life's not bloody fair, is it Doug?'

Stafford hesitated before adding: 'Just let me get used to the idea on my own, will you?'

'If that's what you want.'

'That's exactly what I want.'

Short turned to leave. 'I'll come in tomorrow perhaps,' he suggested gently. 'I'll bring the rest of the boys with me if you like.'

Yeah. Bring them all in, Stafford thought, the pain now biting deeper than ever. We can have a bloody party to celebrate the skipper's louse-up.

Out loud he said: 'Sure, Doug. That'll be fine.'

***

Stafford lay still in his bed, oblivious to everything except his own anguished emotions. So his premonition had been right all along, he told himself bitterly. But it had come about in a way that was far from anything he could have anticipated. Maybe – if only he'd chosen to ignore that damned feeling – Jimmy might still be alive.

Or would he? Just because he and Geordie had pulled through the landing okay, that didn't necessarily mean all of the others would have managed to do the same. He knew how badly the Lancaster had been breaking up just before being knocked cold. Everyone on board would have been in danger.

But at least that way Jimmy would have stood a chance, the voice of cold logic persisted. By forcing him to jump, he'd absolutely condemned the guy to death. This was something that he would be forced to live with for the rest of his life. Jimmy's words at the time came flooding back, mercilessly cutting their way into his brain. He could hear them as clearly as if his friend were standing right there by his bedside.

'We always stick together, Mike. If you're going down, I'm going down with you. Anyway, you know how I've always been nervous about jumping.'

No matter which way his thoughts turned, there was no escaping the torment. Jimmy's young wife, Barbara, was also figuring large in his mind. Two months of married life was all they'd had together. Just two lousy months, during which she and Jimmy had barely seen each other. How the heck was she going to cope with the situation? Did she know already? He had no idea. Hell, as Jimmy's skipper and best friend, he might even be the one given the responsibility of breaking the news to her?

The same tangled mess of thoughts kept on revolving around and around inside Stafford's head. There was no escape from them.

Somewhere in the small hours of the night, the tears that he had been fighting so hard to hold back, finally found a release.

FOUR

MARCH 1962

The strident voice of Stafford's fourteen-year-old daughter reached him clearly from the hallway. 'The mail's here, Dad!'

With all the exuberance of youth she then burst into the lounge clutching a handful of letters. Sifting through the assortment of envelopes, she placed one carefully on top before handing them over.

'It's an airmail from England,' she told him. 'I wonder who it's from? Are you going to open it first?'

Stafford grinned. 'Do I have any choice, Connie?'

Although not showing it, his own curiosity was close to that of his daughter's. Thoughtfully, he tore open the envelope and began to read. Connie, watching his face closely, saw him frown.

'What does it say, Dad? Is it bad news?'

The reassuring smile he gave her did not quite come off. 'No, it's nothing to worry about.'

'So why are you frowning then?'

'You're too nosy, young lady. That's your trouble.' He raised a hand playfully, as if about to smack her.

Giggling, she jumped back out of his reach. 'I was only asking.'

Still curious, the young girl remained where she was as her father fell silent for a moment or two. Eventually he said: 'Do you know where your mother is?'

Connie sighed, raising her eyes to the ceiling as if despairing of the older generation. 'She's gone next door to Mrs. Laing's house for their coffee morning. She goes there every Saturday, don't you remember?'

'Oh, of course. She usually gets back around noon doesn't she?

The young girl nodded.

'Look, be an angel, honey. Go and do something that doesn't make too much noise for half an hour, will you? I need to think for a while.'

'Aren't you going to tell me who the letter is from?'

'No. I am not.' The words came out very deliberately.

Connie sighed. 'Okay. I'll go and see my friend Sandy. She's got a new Elvis LP she wants me to hear.'

'Just don't play it too loudly then. Think of their neighbours.'

'You're a real square sometimes, Dad,' Connie accused him with mock seriousness. A cheeky grin then appeared. 'But I reckon you're okay, all the same.'

Before Stafford could respond to this, she skipped quickly away.

***

He waited until hearing the front door slam before reading the letter once again. Everything came back to him in vivid detail as he scanned the single page. Not that he was ever likely to forget. How could he?

It was eighteen years almost to the day since K for King had flown its final mission. If time had finally managed to ease the anguish and sense of guilt, it was only superficially so. Even now the bad memories were never far from the surface; all they ever needed was a little nudge to flare up again. This letter was more like a violent kick.

The years fell away as the memories took a firmer grip.

Following his discharge from hospital there had been a short spell of sick leave, then it was straight back to operational flying. No allowances of time were made for his mental recovery. The stigma of LMF, an officially created term standing for 'Lack of Moral Fibre' and probably created by someone who had never seen real action in his life, was something that all RAF squadrons were desperate to avoid.

At least there had been no more trips to Berlin. He'd flown the two remaining missions required to complete his tour of duty like a robot, not even able to remember what his new bomb aimer and rear gunner were called. They were just faces to him. Even the remains of his old crew must have found him a remote character. But at least they had all survived the war, and that was the most important thing.

After this, he'd never flown on operations again. Someone higher up must have said something. At the end of his tour they simply handed him the Distinguish Flying Cross and posted him off to a training squadron where he'd spent the rest of the war as an instructor.

When peace and eventual demob came around he wasted no time in returning home to Canada. After all that had happened he was only too happy to put the Atlantic between himself and the scene of so many painful memories. Maybe a few thousand miles of ocean would help to wash away some of the guilt, he'd told himself.

It didn't, of course. But something else – or rather someone else – did help to make a difference. Her name was Alice, and in true storybook fashion she was the girl from next door. Unknown to himself, she had long carried a secret torch for him. Soon after his arrival home he discovered that during the war years she had spent many hours with his parents, constantly asking of his welfare and eventually revealing to them the depth of her feelings. Both his mother and father had always been fond of the girl anyway, so they were only too happy to dabble in a little matchmaking. Not that they had to dabble very hard. He and Alice were married within eighteen months of his return.

Right from the very beginning she had been a good listener. Bit by bit he told her the whole story, something he had not even discussed in very much detail with his parents. For long periods he'd unburdened himself on the poor girl, and through it all she'd remained attentive and sympathetic, inevitably chipping in with just the right words of understanding. By the time Connie was born it appeared that, outwardly at least, he had finally purged himself.

Shortly after the birth, Alice suffered a womb infection that effectively ruled out the possibility of any more children. Perhaps because of this, Connie was spoiled a little too much. Not that he minded. She was still a good kid with a surprisingly sensible head on her shoulders.

Unlike many other pilots returning from the war, he had no desire to follow a career in civil aviation. Any form of flying would only perpetuate the very memories that he was trying to escape from. Life as the branch manager of an insurance company in his home town of Brandon could hardly be described as exciting, but it was pretty secure. And it paid fairly well. Besides, he felt quite sure he'd experienced all the excitement and drama he could handle in one lifetime.

Exactly how he felt now while reading the letter for a third time was rather more difficult to decide.

Seventy-nine Squadron were to hold an inaugural reunion on the second weekend in June. It would be taking place at one of their old drinking haunts, The Compton Manor Hotel in Wetherditch, Yorkshire. Please would he respond as soon as possible stating numbers. It was signed by Doug Short.

Stafford leaned back in his armchair and closed his eyes. A mental picture of all the good times he and his crew had enjoyed in the pub came back to him. But that was before ...

He couldn't go. Absolutely not.

The decision was final. Even so, now that the memory had been sparked, it was impossible not to wonder what had become of all the other guys. Doug was obviously still going strong, but what about the rest? Phil Thomas, for instance. Was he back in New Zealand receiving the very same letter and debating whether or not to make the long journey?

And Geordie? The last he'd heard of him he had been back on flying duties again. That was in early '45. Then there was Hughie Smith and the youngster Pete Cowley. What were they doing these days? There were so many tantalizing questions.

On top of these guys, there was also Jimmy's widow to think about. How had Barbara coped with things? Had she re-married? Not long after leaving hospital he'd made a special trip down to London to see her. Not that he'd achieved anything. Neighbours told him that she'd gone to stay with her mother for an indefinite period. There was no forwarding address, and they had no idea if she would be returning. Despite several further attempts, he had never managed to make contact with her.

He was still sitting in his chair pondering the past when Alice returned from her coffee morning. Although just two years younger than himself, in his eyes she still had that 'girl next door' look. He doubted very much that this would ever change.

'Hi, honey,' she said on entering the room. Her face then clouded. 'You look troubled. What's on your mind?'

He let out a small sigh and handed her the letter. After reading it, she sank down into the chair opposite. Her voice was very soft.

'What do you think? Are you planning to go?'

'How the heck can I? The truth is, I couldn't have screwed things up any worse that night even if I'd tried to. Do you think anyone really wants to see me again?'

'They must do,' Alice pointed out. 'Otherwise, why would this man Doug Short have written to you?'

Stafford conceded this point. 'Okay, you may be right about that. I guess what I really meant was – can I face any of them?'

'But they were your friends. You went through so much together.'

'Sure. Even so …'

'What about this man Geordie you told me about? It seems to me that you two would have a lot to catch up on, what with you saving his life.'

'I didn't save his life. All I did was put the aircraft down.'

'It was how you put it down that counts.'

'Okay. But even if you are right, you're still missing one very important point.'

Alice shook her head. 'Oh no I'm not. I know exactly how close you and Jimmy were. Like brothers, I think you said.'

'More like twins,' Stafford corrected.

He let out a deep sigh. 'It's been eighteen years. If I go, it's sure to dig it all back up again. Maybe even worse than before.'

'Or get rid of it once and for all,' Alice pointed out softly.

She reached across to take hold of his hand. 'Let's face it, Mike. No matter what you try to pretend, I know how badly it still affects you. I'm not saying forget all about Jimmy, but for goodness sake, you did what you thought was right at the time. You can't spend the rest of your life making apologies to the dead. Remember Jimmy as the close friend he was and all the good things you shared. That's what he'd want more than anything. This reunion could be your big chance to make that happen.'

'You really believe that?' There was an incredulous note to his voice.

'Yes, I do'.

She gave his hand a squeeze. 'How many times have you heard people say: "I went back there years later but it wasn't the same." Usually that's said in a negative sense, but it can work the other way too.'

The pressure from her fingers grew. 'You might find that by actually facing up to Jimmy's ghost, you'll be able to see things in a different way. I know you can't change what happened that night, but you sure as heck can change the way you remember it.'

She released his hand and sank back in her chair, as if exhausted by the intensity of her reasoning.

Stafford regarded her with a mixture of surprise and deep affection. Never before had she spoken out in such a strong manner on the subject. One look at her face told him how much she cared and loved him. His peace of mind was her only motive. He quickly reminded himself what a lucky guy he was to have her as his wife.

Moved, he found himself saying: 'Okay, honey. No rash decisions, but I promise I'll think about it. I can't say any more than that right now.'

Alice smiled. 'That's all I'm asking.'

The look on her face said that she was now sure her husband would make the trip. Even if he didn't know it just yet – she did.

***

Siggi opened the front door of her apartment, threw off her jacket, and with a loud sigh sank into the nearest armchair. It had been a long day.

The apartment was both spacious and well furnished. As the personal assistant to the chairman of the largest advertising agency in West Germany, her salary allowed her to live in a more than comfortable style. She had worked and studied hard to attain this professional status, and for nearly three years now had been reaping the rewards of her efforts.

At thirty-eight years old she knew that she was still a very attractive woman. Certainly her figure had remained good, and men were forever complimenting her on her long dark hair and exceptionally large eyes. Not that she ever allowed any of them to get close to her. Yes, she had made use of some influential admirers from time to time in her climb up the corporate ladder, but none had ever gained anything much from her in return. In the business world she was always highly efficient, but never would she trust a man sufficiently to share her personal life with him.

The loss of her father on the Russian front had been bad enough, but that terrible morning she watched her dear mother's body being lifted from the ruins of their house had been the bitter end. From that moment on she made a conscious decision to become a much harder person. The old, easy going and tender-hearted Siggi had died along with her mother that day, replaced by a cynical and embittered veteran of the Berlin blitz.

At first she and her sister had clung to each other for comfort. They moved to Hamburg together to escape the memories, which turned out to be an incredible stroke of good luck. When Germany became divided, they at least escaped the iron rule of the communists.

But despite their closeness, she found Astrid coming to terms with the realities of post-war life far more easily than she ever could. Any scars on her sister seemed to fade and then virtually disappear after just a couple of years. Siggi could still remember her horror when, in 1948, Astrid started going out with a British soldier. She did everything she could to break up their relationship, but in the end all she succeeded in doing was driving a huge wedge between herself and the only person in the world she had left to truly care about.

And then came that fateful day when Astrid made her decision. 'I'm going to marry him,' her sister had told her. 'I know you don't like the idea, Siggi, but please try to be a little happy for me. No matter what you may think, Terry is a good man.'

And what had she done in response? She'd blown her top completely. A terrible row followed. She'd said unforgivably cruel words. Within a week Astrid had moved out of their home and they had not seen each other since that day. That was thirteen years ago.

A few months after Astrid's departure she heard from a mutual acquaintance that the marriage had taken place and the couple were now living somewhere in England. That was all. Not knowing how else to react, Siggi made a determined effort to reshape her life. All of her energies were now directed into attaining success in the business world. Nothing else mattered. There *was* nothing else to matter.

Now she had achieved that success. But for several months recently there had been the same unsettling thoughts sneaking their way into her mind. There was still an emptiness within her. What more did she want? Deep down inside Siggi knew the answer only too well, even though she could not bring herself to fully acknowledge the truth.

While trying to relax in the armchair, the same mood came over her yet again. Like so many times before, it seemed to creep up and take her by surprise. One minute she would be reflecting on some work-related matter, the next, Astrid was right there in the room with her. Quite frequently on these occasions they would be small children playing happily together in a world full of innocence. At other times they were young adults providing all the support they could for each other during those terrible war years. There was no logic or order attached to her sister's appearances. But the questions they inevitably created were always the same.

Had Astrid's marriage worked out? Did she have any children now? And most importantly of all, did her sister ever think of her in the same way? After all the years of shutting Astrid from her life, Siggi was becoming uncomfortably aware that blood was indeed much thicker than water.

As always during these bouts of melancholy, she tried to push such sentimental thoughts aside. What was the point of dwelling on them? Even if she wanted to do something about the situation, she wasn't able to. Her sister could be anywhere. Irritated with herself, Siggi shook her head in an effort to clear her mind.

At that precise moment, the telephone rang.

She picked up the receiver. 'Hello.'

There was no answer, though the sound of breathing could clearly be heard.

'Hello,' she repeated, her irritation growing.

'Siggi.' The voice was soft and hesitant, almost a whisper.

She recognised it immediately. 'My God – Astrid!'

Apart from the breathing, there was silence once again. But the breaths had noticeably quickened.

'Astrid, answer me. Don't hang up,' Siggi found herself shouting.

A click on the line said that her sister had done exactly that.

'Damn! Damn! Damn!' she cried.

Furiously she banged the receiver rest up and down, at the same time knowing it to be a pointless action. Tears of frustration welled up in her eyes. After all these years. To be so close and then ...

She tried to calm herself and think logically. What on earth had made her sister call, especially at that exact moment? Could it be that there was some kind of telepathic connection between them? Had the power of her own thoughts actually transmitted itself to wherever Astrid was? If she had achieved this once, perhaps she could do so again?

Desperately clutching at this straw, Siggi concentrated as hard as she possibly could. She found herself literally shaking with the effort.

'Please ring me back, Astrid,' she repeated over and over again. She clenched her fists tightly, as if this might somehow add extra power to the message. Her fingernails bit deep into her palms, drawing blood.

The telephone remained silent.

It must have been well over an hour before Siggi finally gave up. Drained beyond belief, she began to cry. Quietly at first, but soon great sobs shook through her entire body and the tears ran freely. For herself – for what she had become – and for all the lost years with her dear sister. She knew now beyond any doubt that she could never rest until she had set things right between them.

Somehow, she had to find Astrid.

***

Sleep was impossible. Siggi lay in bed tossing and turning, her mind a tangle of emotions.

How on earth would she set about tracing Astrid? True England was not a particularly large country, but there were many millions of people living there. And her sister's married name of Johnson was one of the most common surnames of all. Could it be more difficult?

She switched on the bedside light to see the time. It was three o'clock.

Then the telephone rang again.

The sudden loud noise in the stillness of the night made her jump. For an instant she couldn't move. Breathlessness overcame her. It had to be Astrid again – it just had to be. Surely no one else would be calling her at this time of night?

The phone rang a second time, galvanizing Siggi into action. Throwing back the sheets, she leapt out of bed and raced through to the lounge.

'Keep ringing,' she cried out, her hand groping for the light switch.

As she snatched up the receiver her hands were shaking so much that she very nearly dropped it. 'Don't hang up on me again, Astrid,' she yelled into the mouthpiece. 'I love you.'

The sound of crying came down the line. And then she heard her sister's voice.

'I love you too, Siggi.'

***

They were still talking half an hour later. Stupid things – sentimental things. It didn't matter. Both were full of tearful remorse. Both of them wanted to forgive and forget.

Yes, Astrid was still happily married. 'You have a young niece,' she told Siggi. 'You must come over and meet her soon.'

'I will…I will. Anytime.' Siggi was ecstatic. 'Just tell me when.'

'How about early in June? Would that suit you? Terry is away for a couple of weeks on business then. We can spend lots of time together.'

'That would be perfect,' Siggi agreed. 'I'll make the arrangements at work as quickly as possible.' She paused before adding: 'By the way, you haven't told me where you are living yet.'

Astrid laughed. 'How stupid of me. We're in Yorkshire. It's a lovely little town called Wetherditch.'

***

Doug Short sighed, removed his spectacles, and ran a hand over tired eyes. The mountain of correspondence piled on his desk was proof of how successful his idea for a squadron reunion had been. The response had exceeded all of his expectations.

He smiled to himself. Would he really have started this thing if he'd known in advance how much work was going to be involved?

It was a rhetorical question. Since being forced into early retirement with a serious leg injury, he had needed something to occupy his time. And what better way than to organise this meeting of old comrades? It was a true labour of love.

His surroundings were also conducive to the task. Living on his own in a quiet Cotswold cottage ensured that there was little else to make demands on him. He was his own person, and had quite deliberately chosen this solitary life in preference to that of a family man.

Replacing his spectacles, he once again cast an eye over the list of acceptances so far received. They amounted to over seventy percent of all those squadron members known to have survived. Tracking some of them down had been a difficult task, but with masses of time on his hands he had succeeded in most cases. A few had so far escaped the net, but he was still trying. A new batch of advertisements announcing the event had recently been placed in relevant magazines and newspapers. Former comrades were contacting him all the time.

The telephone rang yet again. This could be another one, he thought.

'Hello. Doug Short speaking.'

Surprisingly, it sounded like a young man, possibly a teenager, on the line. He had a London accent. 'It's about this reunion you're arranging. There's something I want to know.'

'Just ask me. That's what I'm here for.'

'Do you know if Mike Stafford will be there?'

'Yes, as a matter of fact he is coming. I received a letter from him confirming this only yesterday.'

There was a short pause.

'By the way, who am I speaking to?' Short asked.

There was no reply. The caller hung up, leaving Short with just the dialling tone buzzing in his ears.

FIVE

Unlike New Zealand's capital city of Wellington with its frequent low cloud and high winds, the friendly little town of Tauranga was blessed with a beautiful climate. Most of the residents would quickly agree that it was a very pleasant place to live. In the summer months large numbers of visitors came to enjoy the warm sunshine and beaches of the area, while the waters around the resort were renowned for their big game fishing opportunities. Boats to suit just about every kind of requirement were always available for hire, along with the equipment and expertise of the local experts.

Amongst this group of game fish specialists, Phil Thomas was widely recognised as being one of the best. After spending much of his war service days in the air, the majority of his working life was now spent on the water. There were times when, with a wry sense of humour, he wondered if somewhere deep inside him lurked a phobia against remaining on solid ground for too long.

This may have been a source of mild amusement to Phil, but he was sharply aware that his wife, Donna, viewed their life here together in a very different light. To her, Tauranga seemed to have become little more than a place to escape from. Her increasing complaints about their limited lifestyle, his own lack of ambition, and just about anything else she could think of at the time, combined to cast a disturbing cloud over Phil's otherwise contented world. They had only been married for less than two years, but already he was beginning to question his judgment. Why the heck, after so long as a single man free to do exactly as he pleased, had he suddenly decided to marry a girl fifteen years younger than himself?

Despite the fact that he was always in big demand during the summer season, Phil knew that he could never earn enough as a fisherman to satisfy Donna. As far as he was concerned, they were going along nicely already. His house was nearly paid for, and as long as he was bringing home sufficient money to feed and clothe them both, plus put a little aside for a rainy day, what else was needed? But Donna seemed to want far more from life. As far as she was concerned, he should sell both his house and boat and take her back to her former home of Auckland. For her, life away from the city had long since lost its novelty.

'You could earn three times as much there,' she was constantly telling him. His response was always the same.

'Maybe that's true, Donna, but this is where I was born and raised. I'm happy here. She'll be right if you give it a bit longer.'

'She'll be right,' she'd mimic. 'That's your bloody catchphrase.' Hearing these three short words irritated her beyond belief.

They'd met when she was on holiday with a couple of girlfriends in nearby Mount Maunganui. Blazing hot sunshine coupled with clean white sand and palm trees had probably given everything an idyllic feel from her point of view. He had been posing for a photograph on the beach with some tourists and the giant marlin they'd caught that day when she first approached. He was wearing just a pair of old shorts, causing her to make some flip comment about his muscular, deeply tanned body. Flattered, he made an equally complimentary remark about her body's most attractive features.

Once the affair started, he quickly found himself falling for her in a big way. She was sexy, and amazingly good company. Even though there had been no shortage of brief flings with other girls who came to the area for a beach holiday, when Donna said she could hang around at his place for the entire summer if he wanted her to, he began to think that perhaps there was something to be said for a steady kind of relationship after all. By the end of the summer season the attraction was so great that he was even ready to ditch his confirmed bachelor status. They were married in July.

For the first six months of their marriage everything was fine, and she continued to tell him how much she loved their new life together. Any qualms Donna might have felt over settling in Tauranga were probably smothered by the intense passion they continued to share in the bedroom, Phil realised. But little-by-little the city girl in her began to re-establish itself, and soon after that a sense of dissatisfaction set in.

At the start it was just little things. Odd remarks here and there hinting at her feelings. Soon though, probably due to him not taking her remarks as seriously as she expected him to – Phil was quite ready to recognise his own part in the breakdown – the rows developed into something more significant. And as the frequency and intensity of these rows increased, so both of them found themselves automatically hardening their stances. These days, Phil considered sadly, perhaps it was time to accept that it had been a classic case of marrying in haste and repenting at leisure.

Although the problems usually revolved around the same old subject of them moving to Auckland, for the last month there had been a new topic of disagreement. This had arrived in the shape of Doug Short's letter.

Phil read the invitation and knew immediately that he would love to go to the reunion. Many times he had thought with nostalgia of the old crew. An opportunity to see them all again and find out how they were getting on was irresistible. It would mean spending a large lump of his carefully saved nest egg built up over ten years, but hadn't he been putting the money aside for just such a purpose?

For several days he kept these thoughts to himself, waiting for the right time to raise the subject with Donna. The only problem was that the right time never seemed to present itself. Eventually, he just took a deep breath and told her anyway after dinner one evening.

Her reaction was predictable. She exploded.

'You can't be serious,' she told him. 'You want to spend our entire savings on a trip to the other side of the world just to meet up with a bunch of guys you haven't seen for eighteen years. Are you bloody mad?'

It would have been different if there had been sufficient money for her to go along with him. A visit to England, especially London, had long been a dream of Donna's. But there wasn't nearly enough cash in the kitty for two, and she knew it.

There followed four weeks of rows, broken only by silences of deafening proportions. He tried hard to explain to Donna how much the reunion meant to him. That after all the things he and the guys had gone through together, there would always be an unbreakable bond. Time and distance didn't come into it.

Despite Donna's moods, Phil posted off his acceptance letter anyway. All the same, he did begin to feel that he was being selfish over the matter. Maybe he could make it up to her in some other way. A special present of some kind perhaps? He would think of something.

Their latest silence had been dragging on for three days. It was Donna who finally broke it by confronting him as he came in from work that evening.

'I take it you're still planning to go to this reunion of yours,' she said.

Phil kicked off his boots and sighed. At least she was talking to him again. But was that really good news? The last thing he felt like at present was another argument.

'Well are you?' she persisted.

'Look, we've talked it over a thousand times,' he said wearily. 'It's something I've just got to do. I was hoping you could understand that.'

To his utter amazement, her expression then softened. She actually smiled at him. 'Maybe I'm beginning to, Phil.'

For a few seconds he was too stunned to reply. Could he actually believe his ears? And when was the last time she had smiled at him like that?

Donna waited, clearly pleased with the impression she was making.

Phil was now noticing other things. Her blonde hair, more often than not these days pinned up any-old-how, was now tumbling freely down over her shoulders. Instead of the usual baggy tops, she was wearing a tee shirt that had to be at least two sizes too small. It strained to contain what he used to jokingly describe as her port and starboard radials. To complete the picture, the shortest pair of shorts imaginable showed that Donna's legs were still amongst the best in town.

Phil swallowed hard as she arched her back at him, the action producing even greater thrust from her port and starboard assets. It was obvious to him now what her game was. Yes, it had been a long time. And yes, he did still have strong feelings of love for her, in spite of everything. But did she really imagine that one session of sex was going to change his mind over making the trip to England?

He said as much.

She looked hurt. 'I'm only trying to make things better between us,' she told him without a trace of anger. 'Don't you believe me?'

'Let's get this straight, Donna. You're saying that you honestly don't mind if I go?'

'If it means that much to you, I reckon I can live with it.'

A huge sigh of relief slipped out. He grinned at her. 'So what the heck have we been arguing over for the last month?'

Moving closer, she pressed herself against him. Only briefly though. She moved back, wrinkling her nose. 'For Christ's sake, Phil. Go take a shower.'

A sharp reply rose up, but she silenced him with a look. 'And then perhaps we can forget about dinner for a while.'

There was something in her eyes that suggested dinner might be forgotten altogether. Phil decided that he would make it a very quick shower indeed.

***

They had still not eaten by the time the sun came up next morning. Alongside Donna in bed, Phil reflected that it had not been this good since their first few months together. The recent troubles between them now felt almost worthwhile.

Donna was still asleep. Gently, he moved back the tangled mass of blonde hair obscuring her face. Her mouth was set in a contented little smile.

Right now, he too felt contented. But that didn't alter the fact he would have to get up soon. There was a lot to do today, and anyhow, he was starving. Perhaps he'd knock up some breakfast for the pair of them.

Careful as he was, the bed moved as he slid out, causing her to stir. He was in the act of pulling on his trousers when her eyes opened. She gazed at him and gave a lazy smile.

'Come back to bed. Just for five minutes.'

He hesitated, but not for long. Five more minutes wouldn't make much difference. The trousers were discarded once again.

'No, Phil,' she said as he moved in close. 'I just want to talk.'

He looked at her sharply. 'You haven't changed your mind have you?'

'No, of course not.'

'Thank Christ for that. I don't want to go back to the way we've been recently.'

She kissed him lightly on the cheek. 'Neither do I.'

'So what do you want to talk about?'

'Oh, I don't know. Anything you like. Why don't you tell me about the friends you're going to meet? I'd like to know more about them.'

Phil had a vague idea that he was being led somewhere. She had never shown the slightest interest in any of the guys before. Even so, he did as she suggested. While speaking, he could feel his eagerness to meet up with them all again building to even greater heights. It should turn out to be one hell of a bash.

He talked for several minutes before she interrupted. 'You really are looking forward to this so much, aren't you?' Her eyes shone as if sharing his expectancy.

'You can't know how much.'

He paused, suddenly feeling awkward. 'Look, I know it seems like I'm being selfish by going off on my own. I'd take you with me if we could afford it. You know I would. But I'll make it up to you in some other way, I promise. She'll be right.'

Donna smiled. 'I don't want anything. Just make sure you enjoy yourself. That's all that matters to me.'

'That's not fair. You deserve something for understanding. Just think about what you'd like and let me know?'

She laughed, as if dismissing the subject. 'Okay then. Why don't you get up and make me a cup of coffee? How does that sound?'

***

For the next week Donna did all she could to make Phil feel good about the trip. Never once did she ask for anything in return. His happiness was apparently sufficient for her.

By the end of the week he was completely in love with her all over again. This was the girl he had originally married. It was incredible how something that at first had threatened to be the final breaking point in their relationship, in the end was bringing them back closer than ever. Life could be strange sometimes, but he always reckoned that certain problems had a way of sorting themselves out if you gave them enough time.

They had already agreed that it wasn't worth him making the long journey for anything less than three weeks. Even this had been Donna's suggestion. He'd have settled for a far shorter stay if she'd demanded it.

Tomorrow was Thursday, and the flight left from Auckland that morning. Allowing for the fact that New Zealand was twelve hours ahead of Britain, he would arrive in plenty of time.

He was packing a suitcase when Donna wandered into the bedroom. 'Nearly done?' she asked.

'I reckon so,' he said, laying out his meagre collection of shirts. 'Jeez, Donna, I can't remember the last time I had to wear a collar and tie for anything.'

'Probably our wedding,' she suggested with a smile.

'You could be right about that.'

There was a pause, then he added: 'I'm going to miss you, sweetheart.'

'Me too.'

'What will you get up to while I'm away?'

She looked at the floor. Her voice dropped to a whisper. 'I don't know. Nothing much I guess.'

He was immediately contrite. 'You know I'm feeling bad about leaving you behind. I keep asking you to let me do something to make it up.'

Her mouth formed into a brave little smile. 'That's not necessary.'

'Too damn right it's necessary. Come on, Donna. There must be something. You name it. Anything you want.'

'Anything?'

'You heard me. Anything at all.'

'Okay. Seeing as how you insist.'

She took a long deep breath. 'I want us to go and live in Auckland.'

He saw a couple of tears running down her cheek. Suddenly, she threw her arms around his neck.

'I've tried to settle here,' she cried. The tears rapidly multiplied. 'I've tried hard, but I just can't do it. I want to go home.'

Phil realised in a flash the trap he had fallen into. She clung to him, sobbing, and he didn't have a damn clue what to say to her. Anything, he had promised so rashly. But this wasn't anything. This was *everything*. Everything as far as he was concerned, at any rate. All of his friends, his roots, his very livelihood that to him was a way of life and not some ordinary job – they were all here in Tauranga.

His silence drove her on. The words tumbled out.

'You promised me, Phil. You can't go back on your word now. I only want what's best for both of us. You could sell the house for quite a bit, and the boat. Your mate Gavin said he'd take it off you anytime you wanted to sell. We'd have plenty enough to make a new start.'

Her body pressed hard against him, a reminder of the superb sex they had both recently been enjoying.

'We've discussed all this before ...' Phil began, hesitant at first.

His voice then firmed. 'No! This isn't something I can decide on just like that. I'm sorry, Donna.'

'You promised,' she repeated, an edge creeping into her voice.

'Yes, but I didn't mean this.'

'So you won't even think about it?' Port and starboard radials desperately backed up her argument as they flattened themselves against his chest.

'Can we talk about this when I get home?'

She quickly seized the initiative once more. 'So you will discuss it then?'

He sighed. 'Perhaps.'

All he wanted to do was end this conversation. Why had she brought it up now of all times, just as he was preparing to leave? It was important to him that they parted on good terms tomorrow morning.

She seemed to sense what he was thinking. 'So if you're prepared to talk about it when you get home, why not now?'

He placed both hands on her shoulders and eased her away from him. He couldn't think properly when she was so close.

'Because there's nothing new to say on the subject,' he said. 'All I need is some time to think.'

A light of hope sprang into her eyes. 'So now you'll think about it. That's wonderful. When? While you're in England?'

Phil was quick to see the light at the end of the tunnel. At least here was a temporary way out of this conversation. 'Sure. Why not? If that's what you want.'

'You know what I want.'

He sighed again. 'I'm not promising anything.'

'But you already have,' she reminded him.

At this point, a change came over her. It was as if, having pushed matters this far, she'd decided she may as well go for broke. Her voice rose.

'You think about things in England, Phil. But if you come back with the wrong answer, I'm leaving you. I'll go back to Auckland on my own. I'd rather we do it together, but either way I'm going back.'

He stared at her for several seconds. 'You mean it, don't you?'

'I mean it, all right. I've had all I can take of our life here, always counting the pennies. When did we last dress up and go anywhere nice together, tell me that?'

Phil was forced to admit that their life was hardly one great social whirl. The occasional party or barbecue sure, but that was about all. His work took up most of his time. Early in the morning 'til late at night in the peak season. Weekends too. But that was what being a fisherman was all about.

'It costs money to go to the sort of places you want,' he pointed out defensively.

'Exactly!' There was triumph in her voice. 'And you'd have a darn sight more of it if you took a job in Auckland. I know plenty of people there who would give you a good start.'

And that, Phil knew, took them right back to the same old stalemate. Except this time, an ultimatum was being issued. No more *'she'll be right'* if he wanted to save his marriage.

At almost any other time recently he would have told her to go if that's what she wanted. The last year or so together had hardly been great. But she'd played it smart. His conscience was now giving him hell. He could not put their rejuvenated sex life out of his mind either.

What the heck was he to do? She was still staring at him, waiting for a response. He had to say something.

'Okay, Donna. I promise I'll give it some serious thought while I'm in England. But can we drop it for now?'

She took a pace backwards, shaking her head in amazement. 'I'm talking about leaving you, and you *still* want three weeks to think things over. Well that shows how much you bloody well care about me.'

If perhaps her earlier tears had been contrived, there was no doubting that those now flooding down her face were genuine.

'Bastard!' she shouted as a parting shot before storming from the room. The door slammed behind her.

'Oh shit,' Phil murmured.

***

His anticipated final night of passion before leaving turned into nothing more romantic than a few fitful hours on the front room settee with their mongrel pup Dag for company. He felt like hell when the alarm clock went off at 4.00am. Gavin would be round to drive him to Auckland in less than an hour.

He showered, dressed and made a cup of coffee, creating enough noise in the process to wake anyone. There was still no appearance from Donna. The door to their bedroom remained firmly locked. With only a few minutes to spare, he was determined to make one final effort.

He knocked loudly on the bedroom door. 'Can you hear me, Donna?'

'I should think they can hear you in England,' she responded almost immediately. From the sound of her voice, she had been awake for quite some time.

'I'm leaving in five minutes. Open the door and at least let me say goodbye to you properly.'

'Goodbye.'

'Is that it? For crying out loud, I can't hang around for much longer.'

Even as he spoke, he heard Gavin's pick-up arriving outside. Trust him to be early.

Donna heard it too. 'Time you were going,' she called.

'Look, I don't want to lose you, sweetheart. Are you sure there's nothing else you want to say to me before I go?'

'We said it all last night.'

A sudden rush of anger gripped him. 'Well bugger you then. If that's how you want to play it, I'll see you in three weeks' time.'

She made no reply.

He gave the door a sharp kick – a vent for his frustration. There was no more he could do in the time remaining. Crossing the lounge, he snatched up his suitcase and stepped outside to meet Gavin.

As the first leg of his dream holiday began, Phil could not remember the last time he had felt quite so miserable.

SIX

Stafford's Vauxhall Cresta purred smoothly along the quiet Yorkshire country road. The big car had been expensive to hire, but he considered the money to have been well spent. It was a pretty long drive from London to Wetherditch, so he may as well do it in comfort. The trip was costing a packet anyhow; a few extra pounds wasn't going to make very much difference.

Though still over twenty miles away from his destination, several familiar landmarks were already cropping up: the River Ouse and an ancient ruined castle were just two of the sights he had regularly viewed from the air when returning to base during daylight hours. Even the massive greenhouse situated in the middle of nowhere was still standing. He never did discover what kind of crops they grew in it.

He had come alone. Alice insisted that he did. *'This trip is all about you, Mike,'* she'd told him. *'It's your past you'll be dealing with. Connie and I would only get in the way of that.'*

As usual, she was right. His current life had no part in the tangle of memories and emotions that would surely be waiting for him in Wetherditch.

'Another time maybe,' he'd told a dismayed Connie. 'And I promise to bring you back a whole stack of presents.'

The young girl, totally unaware of her father's tormented background, found her disappointment hard to hide. Nevertheless, by the time he was ready to leave she was reconciled to remaining at home.

She gave him a big kiss and told him: 'Come home safely, dad.'

He laughed at her serious expression. 'Of course I will.'

What had made her say such a thing? he'd wondered at the time. It wasn't as if he was going anywhere dangerous.

Wetherditch was drawing nearer. While passing an old mill, he suddenly caught his breath. A hard kick to the heart forcibly reminded him that this was the very spot over which he had ordered Jimmy to bale out. For a moment or two he felt a sickness rising up from his stomach. Then, amazingly, the nausea was replaced with an almost serene calmness. It was as if his old friend was actually sitting in the passenger seat alongside him. Never during the last eighteen years had Stafford experienced anything like it. Jimmy's voice was so clear in his head as he began recalling their long past conversations. It might just as well have been 1944 all over again.

A heavy bump shook the Cresta as it strayed off line and the nearside wheels ran over a grass verge on the roadside. For several seconds the vehicle shuddered and bounced as Stafford struggled to correct the mistake.

'*Steady – steady,*' the bomb aimer's calm voice told him when he'd finally regained control.

There was nothing malicious or reproachful about the experience. Quite the opposite in fact. Jimmy's presence was bringing only the good times back to mind. But there was something else too. Stafford had a strange sensation that his old friend was asking something of him. A favour of some kind. Frustratingly, what that favour might be wasn't being made clear, even though everything else was coming through vividly.

It was still no clearer when a large and colourful roadside hoarding announced that the Compton Manor Hotel was just two hundred yards ahead. All conversation ceased and the seat beside Stafford suddenly became empty once again. Reality kicked in with a rush. He shook his head. Hell, he must have been driving almost in a trance for the last few miles. Thank God there had been very little other traffic around.

But everything had felt so real. And what made the episode even more unnerving was the normality of it all. There was still absolutely no sense whatsoever of having experienced anything out of the ordinary. Why should that be?

He shook his head a second time before turning off the road.

***

The Compton Manor Hotel was situated about a mile outside of town. Once a home to local landed gentry, it had been converted into a licensed hotel just before the start of the war. More recently a public restaurant had been added, quickly building a reputation for quality food at reasonable prices.

The hotel was set well back from the road in its own expansive grounds. Leaving the Cresta in the already crowded front car park, Stafford paused briefly in his approach to regard the ivy-covered façade of the building. It had changed little in the years. The large bay windows, the terrace on which he and Jimmy had so often sat while sharing a few beers, and the two imposing marble pillars framing the short flight of steps leading up to the entrance were all exactly as he remembered them. Even the gigantic lion's head knocker was still hanging from the solid oak doors, its polished brass features snarling defiance.

Inside the foyer, a dark red carpet led up to the reception desk. The same aged oil portraits, each one depicting a member of the wealthy Compton family who had once lived in this mansion, still adorned the walls. In fact, apart from the new carpet and a refurbished reception desk, everything else here was also pretty much unchanged.

That didn't include the receptionist herself, of course. Eighteen years ago she would most likely have still been in diapers, Stafford considered. Her eyes, heavy with mascara, swept over him. She gave a bright, professional smile.

'Good afternoon, sir. Can I help you?'

'I'm here for the squadron reunion' he told her. 'The name is Stafford.'

After consulting a typewritten list she smiled again, this time with more warmth attached. 'Ah yes! I had a feeling you might be one of the reunion party. I thought straight away that you looked like a pilot.'

To Stafford, who in his time had seen pilots of just about every size and description, it was a curious remark. 'So what exactly is a pilot meant to look like?' he asked with mild amusement.

This threw the girl. 'Oh...I don't know. Something like you do, I suppose.'

He gave a small laugh while signing the register. 'Then it's a darn good job I didn't join the army instead.'

The receptionist handed him his room key, together with a plain brown envelope with just his name hand-written in an untidy scribble across the front. 'Someone left this at the desk for you earlier today,' she said.

Stafford was on the point of tearing the envelope open when a loud voice called out from the other side of the large foyer.

'Skipper!'

There was no mistaking the broad Newcastle accent of Geordie Heatley.

Shoving the envelope into his back pocket, Stafford walked quickly over to meet the man. All his doubts over making the trip seemed to dissolve in an instant as he shook the gunner's hand.

'Hey, it's good to see you, big fellow. And you can cut the skipper bit out. Mike will do fine.'

They chatted away for several minutes exchanging details of their present lives. Geordie then stepped back to survey the Canadian.

'You haven't changed much at all, man,' he said. 'Hardly a touch of grey hair. And you're still about the same weight from what I can see.' He patted his own expanding waistline. 'Not like me eh.'

At that moment Doug Short appeared in the doorway behind Geordie. He approached with a welcoming smile on his face, his left foot dragging in a pronounced manner.

He held out his hand. 'I'm so glad that you could make it, Mike.' His eyes searched Stafford's face as if looking for something that might, or might not, be there.

'I'm glad to be here, Doug,' Stafford assured him. He glanced down at the other man's leg. 'What happened?'

Short gave the limb a slap and grinned self-consciously. 'Just a stupid accident. I'm quite used to it by now.'

It was obvious that he did not wish to enlarge on the matter.

Geordie nodded toward the main bar. 'I don't know about you guys, but I reckon it's time for a drink.'

'An excellent idea,' Short agreed. He patted Stafford on the shoulder. 'Come on, Mike. Everyone you'll remember is already in there.'

For an instant the comment was like a slap across Stafford's face. Everyone except Jimmy, he wanted to say. The bitterness quickly passed.

Short, realising his poor choice of words, shifted uncomfortably. His discomfort only partly lifted as Stafford gave him a grin.

'Sure, Doug. Let's go and meet the guys,' he said.

***

'Are you ready yet?' Astrid's voice carried easily up the stairs to Siggi's bedroom.

'Two minutes,' Siggi called back. She gazed into the dressing table mirror while putting the finishing touches to her make-up. Not too much. Just a touch of lipstick and a dab of rouge. That was all she needed.

Her first week in England had flown by. Tonight she and Astrid were going out for a celebration dinner together. Astrid's husband was away on a business course, so most of their evenings up until now had been spent at home with her sister's young daughter. That had been fine, but this evening would make a nice change for both of them. Astrid deserved a special night out to mark their reunion, and Siggi was going to make sure that she had one. It would be her treat.

She took one final look at herself in the mirror. The new dress she was wearing had been purchased on a recent shopping trip to York and was quite a departure from her usual wardrobe of severe business suits. Astrid had played a large hand in the choice.

'You've still got a terrific figure,' her sister had told her. 'Why not show it off a little?'

Well, the dress certainly achieved that all right. But was it really her? Siggi doubted it very much. Nonetheless, she felt compelled to wear it anyway, if only for Astrid's sake. Flicking her long hair back over her shoulder, she headed for the bedroom door.

Halfway down the stairs she heard the front doorbell ring. Their taxi had arrived.

Astrid gave her young daughter a kiss before leaving. 'We won't be very late,' she told the baby sitter. 'You know where we are if you need us.'

'Where to, ladies?' the taxi driver asked as they got into the cab.

'The Compton Manor Hotel,' Astrid told him. 'Do you know where it is?'

The man laughed. 'I certainly do. I took the wife there for our anniversary dinner last week. It's a nice place. You'll enjoy yourselves.'

***

After a few initially uncertain minutes, Stafford soon found himself being drawn ever more into the spirit of things. Just about everyone he'd expected to see was here. Even Phil Thomas had made the long trip from New Zealand. There were so many hands to shake and so much to talk about.

It turned out that Geordie was now a wealthy man. A small building business he'd started with his brother soon after demob had really taken off. Land speculatively bought for a knock-down price had rocketed in value. He now employed more than a hundred full-time workers and a small army of sub-contractors. Not that this new found wealth had changed his character very much. It was clear that Geordie was still very much the same down-to-earth kind of guy he had always been.

Just once did the big man display a more sombre side. Although happily married, his young daughter had been stricken with polio. As he spoke of her life trapped in leg irons, his usually loud voice dropped to a near whisper. The jovial mask momentarily slipped, revealing the anguish that existed in an otherwise happy and successful life.

The moment passed. His large hand descended heartily on to Stafford's shoulder. 'Hey, I'm sorry, Mike. This is meant to be a happy occasion. Come on, have another drink.' He was his old self once again.

Phil Thomas, who Stafford remembered as being by far the most relaxed member of the crew, came across as being unusually preoccupied. The Canadian put it down to simple tiredness and the crossing of too many time zones. The guy would be fine tomorrow.

Pete Cowley, always considered the baby of their team, was a true revelation. It seemed that he was still working hard to preserve his Peter Pan image. Amongst the mass of conventional short haircuts, his chosen style certainly stood out. Thick and curling down well below his collar, the length of his hair raised almost as many comments as the guitar he had slung over his shoulder when first arriving.

Along with Doug Short, Pete was one of the few present not now married. After leaving his home on the Isle of Man he had moved to Liverpool and was now full of stories about some kind of musical revolution he imagined was taking place there. Most present at the gathering considered him as being a shade eccentric but good for a laugh.

Even though the majority of veterans were now family men, many of them, like Stafford, had decided to come without their wives. By early evening the relatively small group of women who were attending had discreetly formed a little hen party of their own, leaving their husbands free to reminisce loud and long about the old days. Tomorrow night's dinner and dance, they knew, would be an evening far better suited to couples.

One notable exception to this tactful separation of sexes came in the shape of Hughie Smith's wife. A large woman in both physique and presence, there was never any possibility of Gloria Smith being excluded from anything. She sailed freely between the various male groups, an apologetic looking Hughie following closely behind her.

'I used to be in show business you know,' she announced to all and sundry shortly after invading Stafford's table. There quickly followed a claim that she had once shared a dressing room with someone who had gone out with Bob.

'Who the heck is Bob?' asked Pete Cowley on behalf of just about everyone.

'Why Bob Monkhouse of course, darling,' Gloria gushed. 'And you can take it from me, he's an absolute sweetie.'

'That woman drops names like we used to drop bombs,' someone murmured as Gloria finally moved off in search of new admirers. Hearts went out to the hapless Hughie still dragging along in her wake. He was a mere shadow of the man they had once known.

For two hours now Stafford had been taking in all of these developments. Not that he had forgotten about Jimmy. But as in the car earlier, the feelings he was experiencing were warm and friendly. His friend did not blame him for his tragic mistake: that was the message coming through loud and clear. Already he was gaining more peace of mind than he could ever have hoped for. Alice had been so right to suggest he come here.

There was just one worrying aspect. As before, he could not get it out of his head that Jimmy was asking something of him. But no matter how hard he tried, he could not seem to grasp what that something was. Perhaps he should go somewhere quieter for a short while, he considered. That way, he might be able to make a bit more sense of things.

'I'm going into the other bar for a spell,' he told Doug Short quietly.

Concern appeared in the navigator's eyes. 'Are you feeling all right, Mike?'

'I'm fine, Doug. Honest I am. I just fancy a few moments on my own. I'll be back in no time.'

Despite this assurance, he could feel Short's worried gaze following him as he moved away.

The small cocktail bar close by was almost deserted. The young barman looked particularly bored as Stafford purchased a whisky and dry ginger and then selected a table in the corner. After the babble of noise he had just left behind, the almost library-like hush in here was a relaxing change.

Only a very occasional smoker, he lit a cigarette and tried to gather his thoughts. Maybe all this weird stuff about Jimmy was just his imagination working overtime? He'd never had much faith in things like ghosts and spirits, so it was hard to imagine that he was actually receiving any kind of spiritual communication from beyond the grave. On the other hand, if Jimmy's voice was indeed nothing more than his own mind playing tricks, what the heck was this favour his old pal seemed to be asking for? It was even harder to believe that he would have invented a problem like this for himself. And certainly not without a clear idea of what that favour involved.

He took a drink from his glass and sighed. No amount of thinking seemed to be helping. He decided it was time to challenge fate head on.

Come on then, he silently demanded to whatever forces may be listening. How about some proof that I'm not going crazy? I don't care what it is, just make something happen. Let's get things started.

***

Siggi paid the taxi driver, including an extra one shilling as a tip. 'Would you pick us up from here at ten-thirty?' she asked. The man confirmed that he would.

She turned to Astrid. 'Let's have a drink first, shall we? Our table is not booked for another half an hour yet.'

They headed toward the main bar. 'Goodness,' Astrid remarked as they looked inside. 'It's so busy tonight. There must be something special going on.' She nudged her sister and gave a small giggle. 'Look at all those men.'

Disapproval crossed Siggi's face. 'Men!' she muttered. 'For all the trouble they cause, the world would be a far better place without most of them.'

'Well you may think that way, but one of them helped to produce the young niece that you seem to care about so much,' came the gentle response.

Astrid's point was conceded with a frown. 'I suppose so.'

'See, there's another little bar over there. That looks to be quieter.'

They entered the cocktail lounge. 'There, I told you so,' Astrid declared.

The young barman's bored expression lifted as he saw the two new customers enter. His eyes lingered particularly on Siggi. 'Yes, ladies,' he said with a bright smile.

'Two glasses of dry white wine please,' Siggi told him.

At the sound of her German accent his smile immediately froze. An ironic laugh slipped out.

'Is something the matter?' Siggi demanded.

'Nothing at all, madam.' His face was now deadpan.

'Then why do you laugh like that?'

The bitterness that Siggi had been trying so hard to suppress came to the surface and began to control her. 'Perhaps it is because I am German. Is that it?'

'No, madam.'

Astrid tugged at her arm. 'Don't get upset. I'm sure he didn't mean anything.'

But Siggi was in no mood to be diverted. Fixing the barman with an icy stare, her voice became very loud.

'You listen to me, young man. You do not even remember the war. I do. If you had lived through all of the bombs that fell on Berlin, and lost both your mother and father because of the madness, then perhaps you might be a little more understanding. The German people suffered every bit as much as you English.'

'If you say so, madam.'

'I *do* say so.'

The barman's voice suddenly had a lot more of a London accent in it than before. 'In that case, the best thing you can do …' he began.

***

Stafford listened incredulously to the German woman's words about the bombing of Berlin. If this was the sign he was waiting for, it was hardly what he'd expected. He could see from the barman's face that the young guy was on the point of losing his temper. The tightly compressed lips and narrowing eyes were a plain warning. Rapidly, he rose up from his chair and moved to the far end of the bar.

'Another scotch here when you're ready,' he called down the counter.

It did the trick. The barman was cut off in mid-sentence. Both he and the woman were sufficiently distracted to take the immediate heat out of the situation.

'Be right with you, sir,' the barman responded, his professional voice back in operation.

In stony silence he poured the two glasses of white wine. While this was being done, Stafford noticed both women glance at him curiously. They seemed to sense the purpose of his interruption. The one who had not been involved in the debate even flashed a tiny smile of gratitude in his direction.

His own drink was then placed before him. Stafford dug a hand into his pocket. With a flash of embarrassment, he discovered that he had run out of ready cash.

'I need to change some travellers' cheques,' he told the barman. 'Can you put this drink on my bill? I'm in room twenty-one. The name is Mike Stafford.'

At the sound of his name, just for an instant something hostile appeared to register on the young man's face.

He then nodded politely. 'Very well, sir,' he said.

***

Both sisters watched Stafford as he returned to his table. 'I think he's American. That or Canadian,' Astrid whispered. 'I wonder what he's doing here?'

Although displaying an outward indifference, Siggi was also finding herself unaccountably interested in the man. Exactly why this should be was a mystery to her.

'He's quite good looking too,' Astrid continued in the same low voice.

Siggi gave her a reproachful look. 'You are a married lady with a beautiful child. You should not be talking like that.'

'I was only saying. Anyway, you're not.'

'I'm not what?

'Married.'

Siggi slapped her thigh in a gesture of exasperation. 'Please do not start that again. I've told you before, the very last thing I need in my life is a man. I'm perfectly happy as I am, thank you.'

'As you wish,' Astrid said.

***

Stafford was well aware that the two women were talking about him. He was also pondering uneasily on the outburst he'd overheard. Surely this German woman could not possibly realise that many of those who'd played a hand in the destruction of Berlin were gathered here in this very hotel? Himself included.

While on operations he had always closed his mind to this sort of thing. There was a job to be done, and each man simply got on with it. Virtually all aircrews firmly believed that what they were doing would shorten the war by many months and save countless lives in the process. Naturally, there was always the possibility of innocent civilian casualties during any raid, but it was not healthy to dwell on such matters. You just hoped that your bombs would find the correct military target and any other casualties were kept to a minimum.

He glanced once more in the women's direction. From the look of it, they were preparing to leave. Could it be that they were heading into the main bar? The possibility disturbed him. If one immature barman could so easily upset this German woman, how the heck would she react to a room full of Bomber Command veterans? She must be spared that, if at all possible.

Without having any clear idea of what he planned to do, Stafford followed the women at a discreet distance. They paused in the reception area, as if to get their bearings. The one who had been involved in the argument then swung around unexpectedly. She looked straight at him.

'Are you following us?' she demanded.

He felt colour rise to his cheeks. 'Of course not.' To justify himself, he said the first thing that came into his head. 'The truth is, I was looking for the restaurant.'

The other woman smiled. 'That's what we're looking for as well. I think it's somewhere along that corridor. Yes, there's the sign look.'

Stafford hesitated, but they seemed to be waiting for him to make the first move. This is crazy, he told himself. Now he knew they were no longer heading into the main bar, there was no need to concern himself any more. Anyhow, the guys would be wondering what had happened to him.

'After you,' Siggi prompted with a thin smile.

For some unknown reason, Stafford found himself heading down the corridor: Siggi and Astrid followed.

The maître d'hôtel greeted them at the restaurant door. 'Good evening, sir. Do you have a reservation?'

Uncomfortably aware that the two women were immediately behind him, Stafford smiled apologetically. 'I'm afraid not. Does that matter?'

'I'm very sorry, but on a Friday evening a reservation is essential.'

'That's okay. I'll get a bar snack instead.'

Stafford turned to leave but found Siggi blocking his path. 'Just one moment,' she instructed. She spoke with the maître and then turned her attention back to him.

'You can dine with us if you do not mind sharing a table with two German ladies.' It was said almost as a dare.

She regarded her sister. 'Is that all right with you, Astrid?'

Astrid's mouth dropped open in surprise. 'I've no objections.'

'And you?' Siggi asked a still bemused Stafford.

Circumstances seemed to be overtaking him. What the heck was he getting himself into? Every instinct told him to leave.

It was with a sense of utter amazement that he found himself saying: 'Thank you. I'd be happy to join you.'

SEVEN

The dinner proved to be excellent, more than justifying the hotel's reputation. Also, conversation between the three of them had so far gone much better than Stafford could have dared hope for. Both women's English was excellent. Astrid for the obvious reason of her marriage, while Siggi explained that fluency in English was a necessary requirement of her job. To that end she had spent considerable time at evening classes attempting to master the finer points of grammar.

Up until now Stafford had managed to steer the conversation away from his own background as much as possible. Sharply aware of how difficult it could turn out to be if either woman were to discover the part he had played in the bombing of their home city, he'd encouraged them with a series of open-ended questions to talk about themselves. Astrid spoke of her family and life since moving to England, while Siggi's main topic was her career in the rapidly developing world of advertising.

There was one moment of concern for Stafford when, while they were halfway through their main course, Hughie and Gloria Smith entered the restaurant. Gloria, it appeared, was determined to dine in grand style that evening. The bar buffet organised by Doug Short was not to her taste: a point that she was making loudly to her embarrassed husband. As if to emphasize her determination to dine in this particular restaurant, with or without a reservation, the red chiffon scarf adorning her throat was thrown dramatically back over her shoulder as she fronted up to the maître d. The man, so much in control earlier, was now clearly intimidated. Nervously, he consulted a large, leather bound book.

To Stafford's dismay, a supposed late cancellation magically provided an opening for the Smiths. He prayed that they would not spot him and come over. Introductions could prove to be very difficult indeed, disastrous even if Gloria continued to be so tactless. To his enormous relief, the couple were eventually escorted to a table some distance away from their own. Even so, from that point onwards he found himself periodically making apprehensive glances in the Smith's direction.

After the dessert plates were cleared away, Astrid produced a packet of cigarettes from her handbag. These were offered around and there was a short lull in the talk as everyone lit up.

Siggi was the first to speak.

Her question came out of the blue. 'And how about you, Mister Stafford? We have told you a great deal about ourselves, but apart from your name and the fact that you come from Canada, we know very little about you.'

For almost the first time, she smiled. 'So tell me now, what dark secrets are you hiding?'

The suddenness of her question threw Stafford. Yet again he found himself wondering why on earth he had allowed a situation like this to develop? He should have been much firmer. But earlier it had been as if some irresistible force was guiding his actions.

He shrugged in a dismissive gesture, his answer deliberately vague. 'Well, to be honest, I don't reckon there's much interesting to say about me. I'm just an insurance salesman – very boring.'

Siggi's eyes searched deeply into his own as she spoke. 'Somehow that does not fit the image I see. It is hard to imagine that you have always been a man content to spend his life in an office. Please do not try to fool me.'

She then hit him with the question he had been dreading. 'Tell me, what did you do during the war? Were you perhaps a man of action?'

He hesitated for what felt like a very long time before answering. 'I'm sorry. I was just remembering what you said to that young guy in the cocktail bar. Maybe it's better if we forget any talk of those years.' He had no wish to lie, and was now stalling for all he was worth.

After considering his reply, Siggi gave a brisk nod. 'Yes, perhaps you are right. Even so, I must admit to being curious. I have a strong feeling that there are...how do you say?...hidden depths to you.'

Astrid hurriedly cut in. 'I think he has a point, Siggi. It is not good to drag up all those bad memories. You should know that better than anyone.'

'I'm sorry. I will probe no more on the matter.' Siggi paused before asking: 'Are you married, Mister Stafford?'

Happy for the diversion, Stafford confirmed that he was. He spoke warmly of Alice and Connie, and their home in Brandon, Manitoba. Now more relaxed, the time began to race by. It was with some surprise when he heard Astrid proclaim that it was already quarter past ten.

'Our taxi will be here in fifteen minutes,' she told him.

Siggi stood up. 'In that case, I shall go quickly to what you Canadians call the powder room.'

Astrid watched her disappear through the restaurant door before turning to regard Stafford. Her voice was soft. 'I want to thank you for what you did earlier in the bar. If you had not stepped in the way you did then I am sure there would have been a nasty scene. My sister is so much more volatile than I am. She finds certain things very hard to deal with.'

'I wasn't aware that I had done anything.'

'Oh yes you are, Mister Stafford.'

She hesitated before continuing. 'Siggi has a tendency to over-react. That much must be obvious to you. Also, she can be rather too assertive at times. But I want you to know that she never used to be this way. It was only after our mother's death that she changed. Before the war she was such a happy person, always so full of fun and ready to laugh.'

Stafford found himself asking the question that had been troubling him all evening. 'So how exactly did your mother die?'

Astrid's face suddenly clouded over. As she spoke, her voice trembled slightly.

'I will never forget the date. It was on the twenty-fourth of March, nineteen forty-four. They say a thousand bombers came that night. It was terrible. The noise...the fires...and death everywhere. Our house was hit and mother was buried in the cellar. She had a heart attack and died before anyone could dig her out. Siggi and I watched them bring up her body.'

Much as he tried, Stafford could not prevent a reaction from showing on his face. It was the same night. The very same night that Jimmy had died. It could even have been his very own bombs that were responsible for destroying their house. And here he was chatting away to this woman as if the cause of her distress had nothing to do with him.

Astrid misread his expression. 'Did you lose someone close too? Perhaps also in a bombing raid?'

'No. Well not in the sense you might imagine. Someone did die, but ...'

His voice trailed off. This was becoming far too painful from every angle.

She was instantly contrite. 'I'm sorry. I reprimanded Siggi earlier over bringing up the past, and now here I am doing exactly the same thing.'

A poignant look came over her. 'No matter how much we try to forget what happened during those terrible years, it seems that the memories are never very far away from the surface.'

With perfect timing the waiter arrived with the bill, helping to ease the melancholy mood. 'I'll settle this,' Stafford offered. 'I insist.'

Astrid smiled. 'You're very kind. But first please check to see if they will allow you to sign for payment. You have no money with you...remember?'

What with all else going on, the lack of ready cash had indeed once more slipped his mind. Stafford felt a touch foolish for having to be reminded of this fact. As luck would have it, the waiter agreed that the meal could be put onto his hotel bill, saving him any further embarrassment. He was in the act of signing the receipt when Siggi returned.

She seemed to take offence at his gesture. 'I clearly stated that this evening was to be my treat,' she told Astrid. 'Besides, I was the one who booked the table. The bill is my responsibility, not his.'

'Mister Stafford is only being a gentleman,' Astrid pointed out. 'I think the very least we can do is thank him nicely.'

For a moment it appeared that Siggi had no intention of letting the matter drop. Then, in a remarkable switch, she actually smiled at him. 'Yes, I am being rude. Please accept my apologies and gratitude. Naturally though, I will expect an opportunity to return the compliment.'

Stafford was baffled by her sudden change of attitude. But whatever the reason for it, there was not a chance of him repeating this experience. Once had been a big enough mistake. His eyes flickered briefly again in Hughie and Gloria's direction before answering. His tone was firm but polite.

'I appreciate the offer, but I wouldn't dream of imposing myself on you a second time. It's been my pleasure.'

'Nonsense.' Siggi's voice was now full of Teutonic authority. 'I insist.'

'Well, the fact is, I'm rather booked up. I'll be spending tomorrow evening with some friends, and after that I won't be around here for very much longer.'

'Ah yes. Your friends. They would be the ones from number seventy-nine squadron, I presume?'

Her words hit him like a physical blow to the face. His mouth dried up, making him temporarily unable to speak.

'So I was right!' Siggi declared. She smiled again, but this time it was a cold, accusing gesture.

'What on earth are you talking about?' Astrid demanded.

Siggi turned toward her sister. 'If you take a look at the notice board a little further along the corridor you will see that number seventy-nine squadron of RAF Bomber Command are holding a reunion here this weekend. Mister Stafford is attending this, I would imagine.'

She swung back to face him. 'That is so?'

He sighed. 'Yes, that's true. I'm just sorry that you had to find out this way. It's the very thing I was trying to protect you from. I realised how much our presence here would upset you.'

The words sounded inadequate, even to himself.

'Protect us?' Siggi repeated, her voice rising. 'Why on earth would you wish to do that?'

Her tone then quietened and became heavily ironic. 'Oh, I understand now. Perhaps you also thought you were protecting us from the Nazis when you were dropping your bombs on Germany. In truth, it was all for our own good. Was that the way in which you saw it?'

Much as he felt great sympathy for the two women, Stafford could never feel ashamed of the part he had played. Huge numbers of men from Bomber Command had lost their lives fighting the tyranny that existed in wartime Germany. Somebody had to stop Hitler, otherwise millions more would have suffered.

'We did what had to be done,' he said. 'Please don't ask me to apologise, because I can't. At the same time, that doesn't mean I'm not deeply sorry for all the innocent people who suffered. None of us wanted it to happen that way.'

He looked at the two women before him: one shocked and saddened, the other full of accusation. At first he expected Siggi to launch into another tirade of bitterness, but instead she appeared to suppress her emotions.

She spoke very slowly. 'Please tell me something. Were you personally involved in the air raids on Berlin during nineteen forty-four?'

He could not lie. 'Yes, I was.'

'How about on the night of –?'

'Twenty-fourth of March,' he completed for her. 'The answer to that is also yes, I'm afraid.'

Siggi glanced at her sister.

'I told him about mother,' Astrid said in a hushed voice.

Siggi put her hand to her forehead and closed her eyes. Nobody spoke as she remained like this for several seconds.

To the Canadian's astonishment, she then said: 'I was serious when I suggested that we dine together again, Mister Stafford. There are many things I feel that I should discuss with you, but now is obviously not the right time. Shall we say Sunday?'

Astrid started to say something, but was silenced with a movement of Siggi's hand.

'Well?' she demanded of Stafford.

'I really don't think ...' he began.

'Do you not think that you owe me at least a few more hours of your time? Is that asking too much?'

'I can't honestly see what good might come out of our meeting again.'

'Not for you perhaps, but it would mean a very great deal to me. For that reason alone, you must surely see your obligation.'

She then became far less assertive. Some of her carefully concealed vulnerability even began to show through. 'I am now asking you this as a favour, Mister Stafford. If we can talk seriously together – if I can only understand you and what you did a little more – then there might just be a chance of wiping away some of the bitterness and pain. I feel very strongly that fate has provided this opportunity. Please do not deny me.'

It was her final few words that brought a sudden flash of awareness to Stafford. This *was* a fated meeting. Hadn't he come to Wetherditch seeking a similar release from the past? Maybe the circumstances were different, but the pain she was referring to hurt just as much whichever language you spoke. For the very first time he felt more than just sympathy for Siggi. He was beginning to understand her need.

His eyes shifted over to Astrid. Although there was still a trace of shock on her face, there was also something else. Was it a silent plea to accept?

He swallowed hard as the decision was made. 'Very well,' he said. 'What time on Sunday would suit you?'

***

Many of the old wartime songs were now undergoing an alcohol-enhanced treatment when Stafford returned to the main bar. It quickly reminded him that, with the exception of Pete Cowley, the vast majority of the squadron's veterans had never possessed very much in the way of musical talent.

Doug Short spotted him and came over immediately.

'You've been gone a long time, Mike,' he said. 'I was becoming concerned.'

'I'm fine, Doug. I just got a little side-tracked. Nothing for you to worry about.' He stifled a yawn. Suddenly he was feeling weary. The long journey and unexpected events of the evening had worn him down.

'If it's all the same to you, I reckon I'll turn in,' he continued.

Short nodded understandingly. 'That's a good idea. I'll be doing the same thing myself soon. There are still a hundred and one things for me to sort out in the morning.'

It was obvious to Stafford how much the man had put into organising this reunion. Even now he was fretting over details, praying that the event would pass smoothly. This was reflected in his next words.

'You *are* glad you came, Mike?'

'Sure.'

'I'll see you in the morning then.'

Stafford smiled. 'But not too early huh.'

He passed through the lobby and began to climb the stairs, unaware that a pair of eyes were watching his every move.

They contained nothing but hostility.

EIGHT

Stafford woke refreshed just before eight o'clock.

Despite his tiredness when turning in, well over an hour had passed before he'd finally managed to fall asleep. Try as he might, he could not get his encounter with the two German women out of his head. All the things that Astrid had told him while her sister was away from the table, followed by Siggi's disturbing mixture of hostility and vulnerability on her return played out over and over in his mind. Then, just as he was beginning to think that sleep would never come, it all faded away. Nothing intruded further and his sleep was dreamless.

In the cold light of morning, fresh doubts about the wisdom of meeting up with Siggi again quickly began to form. He tried to shrug them off. There was a distinct feeling that he was involved in something beyond his control. Just go with the flow, he told himself. He was here for a special reason; that much was now becoming clear. Everything would become apparent in time.

While getting dressed he felt something buried deep inside the back pocket of his trousers. It was the letter handed to him by the receptionist when first arriving at the hotel. He'd forgotten all about the darn thing. The plain brown envelope suddenly assumed an air of great mystery. Frowning, he tore it open.

The short note was written in an untidy, almost childish scrawl.

I want to talk to you about how Jimmy Knight died. Meet me in the car park at eleven o'clock tonight if you've got the guts.

There was no signature.

He stared at the blunt message in disbelief. His eyes flicked over the page several more times just to make sure that he had not misread anything. He had not.

Who the hell could have written such a thing? Anger began to take over. Nobody had the right to send him something like this. Not that it had achieved anything. Whoever was responsible would have waited in vain last night. But would they attempt to contact him again?

Deep in thought, he finished dressing and went downstairs. There was now a different girl behind the reception desk, but he approached her anyway.

'Someone left this for me here at reception yesterday,' he said, showing her the envelope. 'Do you know who delivered it?'

The girl shook her head. 'I'm sorry; I only work here at weekends. You'll have to speak to Shirley, and she won't be back on duty until Monday morning.'

Frustrated, he moved on to the self-service dining room for some breakfast. He found Geordie sitting alone, tucking enthusiastically into a huge plate of bacon, sausages, eggs and fried bread. Settling into a chair opposite his friend, Stafford watched five slices of toast and marmalade rapidly follow the same route as the jumbo-sized fry-up. His own chosen breakfast of cereal and a single boiled egg felt positively Spartan by comparison.

'You're a bit quiet this morning,' Geordie remarked as his last piece of toast disappeared. 'Is everything okay?'

Stafford hesitated for a moment before producing the note. 'What do you make of this?' he asked. 'It was left for me at the reception desk yesterday. I didn't get around to reading it until this morning.'

Geordie's eyes flicked over the brief message. He frowned. 'Who the bloody hell would write this? No one from our lot, that's for sure. If anyone had something to say they'd do it to your face, not bugger around with stupid notes.'

Stafford nodded. 'That's what I figured.'

His friend handed back the sheet of paper. 'Look, if there's some kind of trouble going on – if there's anything I can do – just let me know.' He shook his head in disbelief. 'What kind of idiot would want to rake up all that stuff again after so many years anyway? Nobody here blames you in the least for what happened to Jimmy.'

'Obviously someone does,' he said quietly.

Geordie's huge hand reached across the table to grip Stafford's arm. His rugged features were full of regard. 'If it wasn't for you, I wouldn't be here right now. I owe you my life, Mike. No one's giving you a hard time while I'm around.'

In spite of his concerns, Stafford could not resist smiling at the big guy. He was solid as a rock, and always said exactly what was on his mind. His words about Jimmy made a big impact. Here was one person whose true opinion would never be masked by simply saying the right thing.

'Thanks, pal,' he said.

'So what are we going to do about this note?' Geordie asked.

Stafford was quick to pick up on the 'we' his friend used. 'I can't see how we can do anything unless they contact me again.'

'Have you asked at reception?'

'Yeah. The girl who took the message isn't back here until Monday morning.'

'Maybe we could find out where she lives?'

'I don't think we need to take it that far.'

His friend was about to respond to this when the public address system crackled into life. 'Telephone for Mister Michael Stafford,' a woman's voice announced.

Geordie frowned. 'Were you expecting a call?'

'No. I told Alice I'd ring her tomorrow, but apart from her, I don't think anyone else knows I'm staying here.'

'Perhaps it's your mystery man then?'

Stafford rose from his seat. 'There's only one way to find out.'

'Do you want me to come with you?' Geordie asked.

'I reckon I can handle it okay.' He paused before adding: 'I promise I'll let you know if there's any kind of trouble brewing.'

'Aye, you make sure you do that,' the big man responded.

***

He elected to take the call in his room. Convinced that whoever was on the line was also responsible for the note, he wanted as much privacy as possible. He took a long look at the receiver before picking it up.

'Hello. Mike Stafford speaking.'

To his surprise, it was a woman's voice that answered. More than that, it was a voice he felt he should know.

Her tone was hesitant. 'I don't know how to start,' was all she said at first.

'Well you can start by telling me who you are?' He was in no mood for guessing games.

'Don't you know? It's Barbara.'

'Barbara?'

'Jimmy's wife. You must remember. You were the chief witness at our wedding.'

Stafford closed his eyes for a moment. Of course it was her. He could identify the voice easily now. How many more surprises were there in store for him on this trip? She was the last person in the world he was expecting to hear from.

He put this thought into words.

'Look,' she said. 'Don't think for a minute that I've called you for a friendly chat about the old times.'

He was mystified. 'So why are you calling me?'

There was a long pause before she replied. 'It's about my son – *Jimmy's* and mine.' She placed an extra heavy emphasis on his old friend's name.

This was getting to be too much. Stafford could barely believe what he was hearing. 'Jimmy's son,' he repeated a little stupidly.

Her voice lifted to an unnatural level. 'I was pregnant when he died. Didn't you ever consider that possibility?'

'Not really. Sure it's possible. But Jim never said a word to me about it.'

'That's because I made him promise not to. We wanted to keep it a secret for as long as possible.' She hesitated before adding: 'Come on, work it out for yourself. I was already two months gone when we were married. Why the hell do you think we rushed into it so quickly?'

'I'm sorry. I didn't even think,' Stafford said, still trying to come to terms with this latest development.

'Well you better start thinking about it now, because our son is up there somewhere in Wetherditch. And he's certainly not come to shake your hand.'

In a flash, the origin of the mysterious note became obvious. The existence of this had slipped momentarily from his mind in the wake of Barbara's startling revelation.

'You better tell me more,' he told her.

She seemed to calm down. 'Alan – that's his name – is what you might call disturbed. It's mostly my fault, I can't deny that. Ever since he was a small boy I used to tell him how you were responsible for his father's death. Back then he even had this game where he'd make little plasticine models of you and then squash them flat with his fist. *"He's like Daddy now,"* he'd say to me.'

She paused, perhaps for dramatic effect. Stafford said nothing. He wanted to. The image she had just described made him feel slightly sick. But what could he say at this stage that would make sense to a woman who obviously detested him?

Barbara continued. 'By the time I realised exactly what I'd done and how badly Alan's mind was affected, it was too late. Several doctors tried, but nobody could do anything with him. As he got older he started getting into trouble with the police. It was just little things at first, but the special school the authorities sent him to made him even worse. He wouldn't learn anything, and was all but uncontrollable. These days, even I can't talk to him. He still believes I'm the one who wanted him sent to that awful place where they beat you for every little mistake.'

A small crack in her composure revealed the depth of her heartache. 'I'm his mother for God's sake. How could he believe that? I've never remarried. He's all I've got in the world.'

Once again Stafford remained silent, allowing her time to gather her thoughts.

When she spoke again, the crack had been papered over. Her words were precise. 'To Alan you're a figure of hate. For years he's dreamed of taking some kind of crazy revenge on you.'

'And my coming back to England has given him that opportunity.'

'Exactly. He left London nearly two weeks ago.'

If it had not been for the note, Stafford would have struggled to believe that things were as serious as she suggested. As it was, he began to hear loud warning bells.

'Have you got any idea what Alan plans to do?' he asked. 'What did he say to you before he left?'

'Nothing other than the fact that he was going up there to sort things out, once and for all. That could mean almost anything with a person like him. It's impossible to tell. I tried to find out more, but he just told me to mind my own business.' She sighed. 'He does have his more sensible moments though. There's a small chance he might try just talking to you at first. If he does make contact, you must speak to him otherwise I'm terrified of what his reaction would be.'

Stafford decided to say nothing of the note, and the meeting that he had failed to show up for. There was no point in worrying her further. Not until he knew more.

'Have you told anyone else about this?' he asked. 'The police perhaps?'

His question alarmed her. 'No! The police mustn't be involved.'

'Why not? You said yourself how uncontrollable and disturbed he is. He could be a danger to himself as well as me.'

Her voice became even more desperate. 'If you go to the police they'll lock him up in a proper prison this time. I know they will. That would be the finish. I doubt I'd ever see him again.'

'But he hasn't done anything wrong yet,' Stafford pointed out.

She was almost sobbing by now. 'Alan's already been in trouble with the courts several times since leaving his approved school. He's been told he's on his very last chance.'

Her anguish was getting to him. Even so, he couldn't leave things the way they were.

'So what do you suggest? You think I should just hang around and wait for him to try something crazy? I'm sorry if I sound hard Barbara, but I'm the one who's sat in the hot seat here.'

'Find him and talk to him,' she pleaded. 'He might just listen. You're the only person who may be able to make him see things differently.'

Stafford could not contain an ironic laugh. 'How the heck did you work that one out?'

'Can't you see? You're at the root of all his problems. That means only you can provide the answer. Instead of being just a mental image for Alan to hate, meet him face to face and become a real person to him. Try to destroy the mixed-up picture he has of you in his mind. If you can only explain what happened that night in detail – let him hear it from your viewpoint rather than mine – maybe that will make a difference. Prove to him somehow how close you and his father really were.'

'I tried to talk to you once shortly after it happened,' he told her. 'You'd gone away for a spell, so I left a message with your neighbours. They must have passed it on, but you still never got back to me.'

'I didn't want to.'

'That's what I figured. But if you wouldn't talk to me then, what makes you think I can get through to Alan now after all these years?'

There was another long pause as Barbara sought the right words.

'All I know,' she began slowly, 'is that I loved Jimmy very much. We weren't together for a long time, but for me there could never be anyone else. He was special: a once in a lifetime thing. I saw you as the person who took all that away from me.'

She was interrupted by the unsympathetic sound of rapid pips, arrogantly demanding that more money be placed into the call box. Hastily, she did this.

'Can you still hear me?' she asked after the second of her two coins dropped into place.

'Sure. Carry on.'

'Alan is all I have left now. I know things aren't right between us at the moment, but there's still time. He's not even eighteen yet.' She gave a hollow laugh. 'Can you believe it? I'm asking you – you of all people – to help my son. More than that, I'm asking you to help me. How's that for a twist of fate?'

A twist of fate, Stafford thought to himself. Didn't that just about sum up this whole trip? Everything was piling up on him. It was one damn thing after another.

And then something else emerged from the jumble of thoughts bouncing around in his head. Suddenly it was clear. The feeling that Jimmy wanted something from him. This was it! Somehow he had to straighten out his old friend's son, and the kid's relationship with his mother.

'Not an easy one, Jim,' he muttered almost silently.

Her voice cut in – anxious. 'Are you still there?'

'Yeah.'

'So what are you going to do then?'

He could not ignore her plea. Here was his chance to make amends a little. Nothing could ever wipe the slate completely clean, but at least it would go some of the way.

It was his turn to choose his words carefully. 'I'm not sure how much good it will do, Barbara, but I'll try to talk to the kid. Maybe we can work something out.'

The relief in her voice was enormous. 'It's very hard for me to say this, and I know you're not doing it for me, but thank you anyway.'

'If things get too badly out of hand then I may still be forced to call in the police,' he warned her. 'If Alan is as screwed up as you say, he might try something really crazy.'

She was silent for a moment. 'I understand that. Please, just do your best. That's all I can ask.'

His shock now fully absorbed, Stafford became brisk. 'Have you any idea where he may be hanging out? I need somewhere to start looking. Far better for both of us if I find him before he contacts me –'

He nearly finished the sentence with 'again', but stopped himself just in time.

'I'm sorry, I can't help you with that,' Barbara told him. 'He hasn't got any friends up there that I know of. He might even be sleeping rough.'

'Okay, how about a description? Does he look very much like Jim?'

'Not a lot.' She sounded doubtful. 'He's five foot nine, medium build, and dark brown hair. I think he looks more like my father than Jimmy.'

Stafford tried to picture the man that he had seen only once so long ago at the wedding. Nothing of much use materialized.

'How about scars, tattoos, anything like that?' he asked.

'Not really. There's quite a large mole on the back of Alan's right shoulder, but he would need to be stripped off for you to see that.'

She then became a touch more positive. 'He does stutter a little bit. Not all the time though. Only when he gets very angry or excited.'

As she finished speaking the rapid pips returned, this time sounding even more strident and demanding than before. Barbara allowed herself to be affected by the urgency of their tone. The speed of her speech immediately quickened, as if trying to keep pace with the insistent beat.

'I'm in a phone box,' she stated unnecessarily. 'Hold on a second. Let me see if I've got any more change.'

There was a pause interspersed with muttered sounds of exasperation. She then came back on the line. 'It's no good; I've run out of money. There's nothing more I can tell you anyway. I'll have to hang up now.'

'No!' Stafford told her. 'Give me the number. I'll call you back.'

He was wasting his breath. Their line of communication was broken. The rapid pips were replaced by a continuous monotone.

***

Stafford remained sitting on the edge of his bed for several minutes, trying to appreciate the magnitude of what he had undertaken to do.

There was a screwed-up kid called Alan who could be hiding out almost anywhere, and who in all probability was out to get him in some way. He had very little idea of what the kid looked like, and it was not possible to involve the police. Somehow he had to find this youngster and then attempt to wipe away seventeen years of brooding resentment and hatred just by talking.

It was a hell of a situation. And one certainly not made any easier by the fact that Alan would be feeling more vindictive than ever after his failure to show up for their meeting last night.

What he needed was some help in tracking the boy down. He thought of Geordie. There was a guy he could always rely on. But was it fair to drag the big fellow into this? Perhaps he should try to tackle the situation alone, even if this did mean making things more difficult for himself.

He sighed. One thing was very clear. However he handled matters, he could not give it anything less than his very best shot.

No matter how difficult things became, he owed Jimmy at least that much.

NINE

Geordie came bustling over the moment he returned downstairs. 'Well, what happened?' he demanded. 'Who was it?'

Stafford hesitated for a moment, still unsure whether or not to divulge what he had just discovered. But Geordie's expression quickly wiped away any remaining doubts. There was no mistaking his friend's eagerness to help. There was also a determined look on his face that said, having learned a part of the story, he now had no intention whatsoever of being excluded from anything that followed.

'Let's go over there and talk,' Stafford said, nodding toward some vacant seats in a quiet corner of the large reception hall.

Geordie listened in near silence while Stafford recounted his conversation with Barbara. Only occasionally did he butt in with an expression of anger or surprise. As Stafford concluded, the big man shook his head and gave a loud sigh.

'Bloody hell! It's hard to imagine a lad of Jimmy's turning out like that.'

'I know, but that's what we're up against. God knows what's going on in the kid's head now he thinks I couldn't even be bothered to meet up with him last night. We need to track him down fast. He must be hanging around somewhere pretty close to here.'

Geordie frowned. 'Why don't you try what I suggested earlier? If we can find out where that other receptionist lives, she might be able to tell us something.'

'Yeah, you could be right,' Stafford agreed.

His friend remained where he was while the Canadian moved across the hall to speak once again with the girl behind the desk. Tentatively, he enquired about the off-duty Shirley.

The girl shook her head. 'I'm sorry, sir. We're not allowed to give out staff addresses without their consent.'

Her response was pretty much as he'd anticipated. Even so, he persisted.

'I wouldn't normally ask, but this really is very important,' he stressed, giving the girl a disarming smile.

'I'm sorry,' she repeated. However, this time her voice lacked quite the same firm conviction. His engaging smile was beginning to win her over.

'There must be something you can do,' Stafford said, pressing home his advantage. 'I'd sure appreciate it.'

The girl sighed. Her voice dropped to just above a whisper. 'Listen, I can't give you her address, that would be completely against the rules. But I could perhaps let you have a telephone number.'

Stafford looked suitably grateful. 'Thanks. That would do fine.'

She reached beneath her desk to consult an indexed diary. A number was then written on the back of a business card for him.

'I didn't give you this,' she said in a conspiratorial whisper, sliding the card across the desk.

He flashed her another smile and winked elaborately. 'Didn't give me what?'

***

The number rang for some considerable time. She answered just when he was on the point of hanging up.

Stafford identified himself and she laughed. 'Yes, I know who you are. You're the one who I said looked like a pilot.'

Encouraged by her tone, he joined in with her laughter briefly before continuing. 'Look, I'm real sorry to disturb you like this at the weekend, and I wouldn't be troubling you unless it was genuinely important.' He took a deep breath before plunging in with the purpose of the call. 'Do you remember that hand delivered message you gave to me yesterday when I first checked in?'

'Yes, of course I do.'

'Can you tell me who it was that left it with you?'

Her response was a severe let down. 'I'm sorry, I couldn't say. That's because it was never actually handed to me.'

'So how was the envelope delivered then?'

'Somebody had already put it in with the morning mail before I arrived.'

'I see.' The disappointment was hard to keep from his voice.

The girl spoke again, this time in a slightly more positive tone. 'Now I think about it though, it must have been put there by a member of our staff. One of the temporary seasonal workers living in the staff quarters most likely.'

Stafford's hopes rose. 'What makes you think that?'

'Well, the early morning post is usually delivered at least a couple of hours before I get into work. The night porter collects it from the postman and then puts it in a special tray under my desk for me to sort out later on. Only a member of staff would know that, and it's mostly only live-in staff who would be around the hotel that early in the day.'

'So I should speak with the porter then?'

'Not really. He would have made a special point of telling me about any hand delivered messages for guests, and he never mentioned a word. He does get called away from the reception area pretty regularly though, so the desk is often left unattended for a short while. I suppose any one of the live-in staff could have slipped your message in with the rest of the mail during one of those times.'

This could be a breakthrough, Stafford told himself. If Alan had been smart enough to get himself a job at the hotel then that would give him the perfect cover. He could hang around and bide his time without ever appearing conspicuous.

'Tell me, is there an Alan Knight living in the staff quarters?' he asked.

There was only the shortest of delays while she considered this. 'No. Definitely not. There are only a dozen or so live-in staff at the moment, and I know all of their names. Apart from the manager and head chef who've both got their own special quarters, they're mostly young seasonal workers who come from outside the area. All the permanent staff are locals like me who live in Wetherditch.'

Stafford hesitated before asking his next question. 'Is it possible that any of the seasonal workers may be using a false name?'

'Why would anyone want to do that?' She was surprised at his suggestion.

Steady, Stafford warned himself. He gave an easy laugh. 'Oh, I don't know. Youngsters can be like that sometimes. Maybe they just don't want their parents bugging them. You know how it is these days. They all want to be rebels.'

His laugh was infectious. 'I'm only twenty myself,' she told him with a slight giggle.

'In that case you'll understand pretty well.' He paused before prompting: 'So what do you think? Is it possible?'

'Well...it could happen I suppose. Some of them are employed on a very casual basis.'

'Which ones?' he asked, and immediately bit his tongue. He knew that he had jumped in far too eagerly.

Sure enough, the girl quickly realised that she was saying far more than she should do. A nervous tone came into her voice. 'I'm sorry, Mister Stafford, but I really shouldn't be discussing any of this with you. Please don't repeat to anyone what I've said already.'

He knew that he would now get no more out of her. Even so, it had been a good start. After thanking the girl and assuring her that their talk would remain confidential, he hung up.

Geordie was alongside him the moment he stepped from the phone booth. 'Well? What did she say?'

Now aware that Alan could be almost anywhere in the hotel, Stafford drew his friend toward the large oak doors.

'Let's talk outside,' he suggested.

The hotel's private grounds at the rear were extensive, covering several acres. The pair of them strolled across a huge expanse of lawn, part of which served as a complimentary putting green for the use of guests. A small wooden hut storing the necessary putting irons and balls was clearly open for anyone to help themselves, but no one at this time of the morning was yet choosing to take advantage of the facility.

Stafford brought his friend up to date as they walked across the grass. By the time he had finished, the main hotel building was nearly two hundred yards behind them. Just ahead lay a fairly densely wooded area, coming from which could be heard a variety of birdsong.

Geordie paused, placing a hand to his ear.

'Did you hear that?' he breathed, suddenly captivated by the sounds that were reaching him. 'That last call was a nightjar. You normally only hear them singing at dawn and dusk.'

Stafford regarded him with surprise. 'I never knew you were keen on that kind of thing. How long have you been interested?'

The gentle art of bird watching somehow seemed like an improbable hobby for his robustly down-to-earth friend. It was nightcaps of the liquid variety rather than nightjars that most people usually associated with Geordie.

As if reading his thoughts, the big man grinned a touch sheepishly. 'It's a fascinating hobby once you get into it. I started about ten years ago. Better keep that quiet back at the hotel though; I've got an image to keep up, you know. Can you imagine what some of the boys back there would have to say if they knew?'

Stafford returned the grin. 'Your secret is safe with me, pal.' He gestured toward the woods. 'Do you want to go on a bit further and take a look for your nightjar?'

'Aye. Why not? You never know, you might learn something too.'

They walked on, mostly in silence, as Geordie continued keeping a sharp eye out for a sighting of the normally nocturnal bird. After a few minutes they came to a clearing where a solidly built teak bench seat had been thoughtfully provided.

It was an ideal place to relax and observe the local bird life. Geordie took great pleasure, and no small amount of pride, in pointing out and naming the variety of species that passed in and out of their view. But there was no further sound, much less any sighting, of the elusive nightjar. Eventually, the big man appeared to give up hope. He sighed before looking directly at Stafford and changing the subject.

'Are you sure you want to waste your time going after Jimmy's kid, Mike? I mean, what's the worst he can do? He's not even eighteen yet: just a bairn. He can't be any real danger to you. It's probably all just big talk.'

Stafford sighed. 'Yeah, I know what you're saying. But it's something I have to do. The kid needs straightening out, and I promised Barbara I'd give it my best shot. Anyhow, there's something else I haven't told you yet. It doesn't make a whole lot of sense but ...'

He hesitated, wondering how best to explain his imagined conversations with Jimmy and the promise he'd made to their long dead crew mate. Geordie was a man renowned for his practical attitude. He could usually be expected to be dismissive of anything less than solid fact.

'The thing is –' Stafford continued.

He was cut off by his friend sharply raising a hand to silence him. There was a warning look in his eyes. He spoke in barely above a whisper.

'Don't look now, but there's someone watching us. They're hiding in the bushes over on our right about thirty yards away. I thought I spotted him a few minutes ago. Now I'm sure.'

Stafford rapidly took in this information. His voice dropped to match Geordie's. 'Okay, so what do you reckon on us taking a walk over that way to flush him out?'

'Sounds good to me. But let's make it a quick walk, eh. I want to be sure of catching whoever it is. I don't like being spied on.'

'It might even be Alan,' Stafford suggested. 'After what Barbara told me about him, it kind of makes sense.'

'Even more reason for us to catch him then.'

A faint smile formed on Geordie's face as he rose up from the bench seat. 'Are you ready then, skipper? Bandits at two o'clock.'

Stafford also rose. 'Let's go, buddy.'

'Just to the left of that fallen tree trunk,' Geordie announced as they set off together at something very close to a run.

'I can see him now,' Stafford responded.

They had covered no more than ten yards when the figure of a youth wearing a green combat type jacket and blue jeans wriggled free from the tangle of bushes and began scrambling away. With his back to the pair of them, identification was impossible.

What was plain to see was the rifle the snooper was carrying in his right hand. At present, however, he was clearly more intent on escaping from the two friends than threatening them with this. Even so, the sight of the weapon was sufficient to induce a lot more caution. Geordie held out a restraining arm.

'Hold it, Mike. He can't get far. Remember, there's a river runs right across the back of these woods. Unless he's got a boat parked down there, he'll have to come back this way eventually.'

They paused, both considering the threat behind this new development.

'If that was Alan and he's got a gun, then he could be bloody dangerous,' Geordie remarked, quickly revising his earlier opinion. 'You're right, Mike. He needs straightening out – and bloody fast.'

Stafford nodded in agreement. He thought for a moment. 'There is something we could maybe try,' he said.

Geordie listened as they set off back in the direction of the hotel.

***

The small shed contained nothing more than a rack full of putting irons and a bucket of golf balls. But for the two friends it also provided a handy place to keep out of sight. At the same time, thanks to a small window, they had a good view across the lawn right up to where it met with the wooded area.

If the gun carrying youth did attempt to return to the hotel any time soon, they were almost certain to spot him. Once emerging onto the open area of the lawn, not even a seriously deranged kid would be crazy enough to threaten anyone with a firearm in full view of the main building, Stafford reasoned.

They could be in for a long wait, of course. There was no guarantee that their target would be returning this way, even though he was most likely a hotel employee. But with a wide river and fifteen-foot high boundary walls protecting the rear of the grounds, any alternative route would be extremely difficult to find. There was every reason for them to be hopeful.

Twenty minutes passed – then thirty. By now, a small number of hotel guests were electing to putt a few balls around the course. None so far were members of their reunion party, although the two veterans' apparently settled presence inside the shed did serve to draw a few curious glances from others while collecting or returning their equipment. Not that anyone chose to make a direct comment. Geordie's sheer size and stern expression did not encourage flippant remarks.

The two of them continued to wait.

***

It was approaching noon when they eventually spotted their target cautiously emerge from the extreme far corner of the woods. There was no mistaking his green jacket and blue jeans, nor the awkward manner in which the rifle was held in a vertical position tightly against his side in an effort to minimize its appearance as much as possible. After casting a careful eye over the few players on the putting green, the youth began moving rapidly forward in the direction of the hotel, keeping firmly to the far boundary edge of the lawn.

He was halfway across when he first spotted the two friends bearing down on him. By now it was much too late for him to retreat back into the cover of the trees. His pace increased as he attempted to veer away from them, but his path was quickly blocked. Drawing closer, Stafford now recognised him as the cocktail lounge barman who had upset Siggi so much the previous evening. At the same time, he also realised that the youth fitted Barbara's description quite well. The details she had given him were vague of course, but the possibility that he might have found Alan was becoming stronger.

Forced to pull up, the youth regarded them coldly. The barrel of his rifle lifted toward them a few degrees. It may have been a deliberate threat, although most likely it was no more than a small adjustment of the arm. Whatever the reason, it was too much for Geordie. He took a rapid pace forward. His huge hand seized hold of the barrel, forcing it back down and then sharply twisting the weapon completely away from the youngster's grasp. His victim gasped out in surprise.

'Didn't anyone ever tell you that you shouldn't point guns at people?' the big man demanded. He broke the rifle to give it a cursory inspection. 'Like I thought, it's just a bloody air rifle,' he told Stafford. 'A pretty powerful one though, and even these can still do a fair bit of damage at close range.'

He swung back to the youth. 'Why were you hiding in the bushes spying on us?' he demanded.

The youth's look of contempt evaporated under Geordie's ferocious glare. His east London accent, barely noticeable when working behind the bar, was now very evident.

'Leave it out, will you? Why would I be interested in watching you two? I wasn't doing no harm. I was after a few rabbits, that's all. That's what I've got the gun for.'

'Why do you want to go after rabbits?' Stafford asked. 'Do you like killing things? Is that it?'

'No! Not like what you mean.'

Geordie thrust his face menacingly close to the youth. 'If I thought you were using that gun on any of the birds over there,' he growled.

'No! Like I said, just rabbits. One of the b-butchers in town buys them from me. You can ask him if you don't believe me.'

The two men glanced at each other. The significance of the brief stammer was not lost on them as they remembered what Barbara had said.

'So you're a poacher as well as a Peeping Tom,' Geordie stated.

'I'm not breaking any laws. There's plenty of rabbits there, and no one minds as long as I keep off the proper game like pheasants and that.'

'You don't seem to have had much luck today,' Stafford remarked dryly, noting the lack of any floppy-eared victims on the youth's person.

The youngster ignored this remark, his eyes never leaving the threatening figure of Geordie. Fright turned to bluster. 'Anyway, what makes you think you can push me around like this and steal my things? Just because you're guests and I'm only staff, that don't mean I ain't got rights too.'

Geordie sucked in a deep breath. 'Point this thing anywhere near me again and I'll break it over your head,' he promised before thrusting the rifle sharply back into its owner's hands.

The youth wisely chose not to offer any response to this threat. Limiting himself to a scowl, he muttered: 'I've gotta get back or else I'll be late for my shift.'

Sidestepping the two friends, he began moving on. After only a few paces, he was stopped by the sound of Stafford's voice.

'Hey! Before you disappear, kid. What's your name?'

He glanced back, staring silently at the Canadian. For several seconds deep hostility was all too clearly reflected on his face.

'Graham Walker,' he eventually replied.

'Can you prove that?'

'Why should I? I don't have to prove nothing to you.'

Geordie took half a pace forward but was held back by Stafford's hand on his arm. Neither man made a move to stop the youth as he hurried away back to the hotel. It was a tricky situation, Stafford considered. A lot of people might have cause to stammer slightly when confronted by an angry Geordie. That alone was not sufficient proof that this was who they were looking for. And even if he was Alan, it was pretty obvious that the kid was not going to admit the truth to them.

As the two men watched his retreating back, Geordie summed up both their feelings. 'Can you believe that our Jimmy could have fathered a nasty little shit like that?' he asked.

Stafford did not reply. It *was* hard to believe, but he still had to find a way of proving the kid's identity one way or the other for certain. What's more, if he was to have any hope of achieving what he'd promised to do, he needed to find it pretty damn quickly.

***

Phil Thomas lay fully dressed on his hotel bed, a heavy frown on his face. Not that he was disappointed in any way with the reunion so far. It was great to see all of the guys again. But he was also well aware that he could be paying a very high price indeed for this holiday.

No matter how much he tried to push his problems with Donna to one side, the same thoughts kept returning. He just couldn't get over how she'd allowed him to leave home without so much as a goodbye kiss. Coming after a week when they had got it back together so incredibly well, the coldness of their parting was now hurting him far more than he was willing to admit.

There was no doubt in his mind that Donna meant every word of her threat. But how could he bring himself to leave Tauranga? Okay, he'd promised her 'anything', and that he'd think things over while in England. But the devious way in which she'd gone about extracting that promise from him was hardly fair. Anyhow, a woman's place was supposed to be with her husband. That was the way of the world. Why should it be any different for her?

At the end of the day, the whole thing came down to pretty much one question. Was the amazing sex they shared the only thing the two of them really had in common, or did the relationship genuinely go much deeper than that? After two years of marriage, it felt a bit late in the day to be asking himself such a thing. But even now Phil could not find a completely honest answer. He would have given a hell of a lot to know Donna's true feelings on the matter.

A burst of laughter from the corridor outside his bedroom door broke through his preoccupation. But instead of irritating him, the sounds had a totally opposite effect.

'What the bloody hell's the matter with you?' he asked himself in a loud voice. He'd come here to enjoy himself, not mope around and be miserable. If he didn't start having a good time pretty soon then he'd have blown the best part of his life's savings all for nothing.

It was at this point that Phil made a decision: a decision *not* to make a decision. He would forget all about Donna for the next three weeks. There'd be plenty of time left for soul searching during the long flight home. He immediately felt better. After jumping up off the bed, he was splashing some water over his face when a knock sounded on his bedroom door. Hastily, he grabbed a towel before opening up.

Pete Cowley was standing there, looking more like a teenage rebel than ever. Faded jeans, a tee-shirt proclaiming *'Liverpool Rocks'*, and hair that seemed to have grown a full inch overnight, all added to the image. Only the guitar was missing.

'Don't tell me you've just got up, you lazy sod,' he said, grinning.

Phil winked at him. 'No. But you could say I've just *woken* up.'

Pete looked confused. 'How the hell can you ...?'

'Don't worry about it, mate,' Phil laughed. 'It's a long story, and take my word, it's not something you want to hear about.'

***

Stafford and Geordie walked slowly back to the hotel. Few words were exchanged as they both reflected on their encounter with the young barman calling himself Graham Walker. They reached the car park and paused, each one still pondering the situation. Geordie spoke first.

'Well I reckon he's Alan, right enough," he said. 'The kid's got a stammer, he fits the description, *and* he's got a London accent. What more do you need?' He spread his hands, as if this provided all the conclusive evidence they needed.

Stafford nodded. 'Yeah, you could be right. But before we take it any further, I've got an idea that should prove things one way or the other for sure. We can't do anything until this evening though, and I'll need your help to pull it off.'

'Just tell me what you want me to do.'

Stafford was on the point of explaining the details of his plan when a voice called out to them.

'Ah, I was wondering where you chaps had got to.'

It was Doug Short, standing on the steps overlooking the car park. He came over as fast as his bad leg would allow. 'The coach will be here in about fifteen minutes,' he told them. 'Are you both joining us?'

'The coach?' Stafford repeated.

Short looked a touch confused. 'Haven't I mentioned it to you two yet? Still, it has been a bit of a last-minute arrangement, I suppose.'

He drew breath before continuing. 'As you probably know, seventy-nine squadron is now based at Burton-on-the-Ouse about fifteen miles away. The CO there has invited any of us who are interested to pop over and take a look around the base as his guests. Jolly nice of him, eh?'

Beaming with anticipation, he added: 'Obviously, you don't have to come if you've made other plans, but we'll be back in plenty of time for tonight's bash.'

It was on the tip of Stafford's tongue to say that he would give the trip a miss when Geordie nudged him.

'Sounds like a good idea to me, Mike.' Their eyes met. 'It'll help pass the time nicely. You know, until we can sort out that other business later on. What do you think?'

Stafford acknowledged the underlying message with a rueful smile. Maybe it would be better if he went along. There was nothing more he could do here for a few hours yet, and brooding around on his own for the rest of the day wouldn't help matters.

'Sure, it sounds like a swell idea, Doug,' he said. 'Count us both in.'

***

Doug Short's last-minute arrangement proved to be even more popular than anticipated. Virtually the entire squadron elected to go, making it necessary for a second coach to be hastily summoned. There was a loud buzz of expectant chatter as Stafford and Geordie climbed on board.

In spite of all the other things on his mind, Stafford was also now anticipating the visit with some interest. Time and technology had moved swiftly on. The modern jet bombers currently being used by the RAF were a far cry from the propeller driven Lancaster and Halifax that he and the others of his era were so familiar with. Comparisons would be fascinating.

Just as the coach was about to set off down the long gravel driveway, Stafford glanced casually out of the window. On the other side of the hotel forecourt he spotted the youth claiming the name of Graham Walker leaving the staff quarters. He was now wearing the short white jacket and black trousers of his barman's uniform. Obviously late, he went hurrying into the hotel entrance without even glancing in the coach's direction.

Was this Alan? Stafford asked himself yet again. With Geordie's help, he should be able to discover the answer to that this evening. But identifying the kid was only going to be the start of the problem. If he did turn out to be Jimmy's son, what words could he find that might make a difference to a mind so firmly set against him? It was a situation that demanded the most cautious and tactful of handling. And even then, there was very little guarantee that he would manage to succeed in fulfilling his promises.

For some reason, his sighting of the youth also reminded him of his lunch date with Siggi the following day. Why the heck had he agreed to their meeting again? Didn't he have enough on his plate? This was another situation that he had very little idea of how to handle in the best way. She was clearly a volatile woman, and the whole thing might easily blow up in his face.

Problems were stacking up all around him.

He let out a long sigh as the coach began moving on down the driveway.

TEN

With the same dark hair, large eyes and striking good looks as her aunt, Astrid's eight-year-old daughter, Tanya, was already beginning to resemble a miniature Siggi.

Astrid had always been aware that, when compared with her sister, most people would regard her as being relatively plain. Not that this had ever been a particular source of jealousy. All the same, she was glad for her daughter's sake that it was Siggi and not herself who she had taken after most of all in the looks department. These days appearances seemed to matter so much more, and a pretty face definitely gave a woman an advantage in life. Of course it was unfair, but undeniably true for all that.

It was amazing how quickly Siggi and Tanya had bonded. Maybe their physical resemblance had something to do with this, Astrid had considered on several occasions. But whatever the cause, the pair of them were already responding to each other as if they had been close for most of Tanya's life.

Astrid opened her kitchen door and called out into the back garden. 'Lunch is ready, you two.'

Tanya emerged from the garden shed. 'I was just showing Auntie Siggi my new guinea pig,' she called back. 'We've decided to name him Simon.'

Siggi appeared behind her. She placed a hand on the young girl's shoulder. 'Come, darling. It is good that we don't keep your mother waiting.'

'Mushroom omelettes,' Astrid announced as they sat down around the kitchen table. 'We can have a bigger meal this evening.'

'What time do you think that will be?' Siggi asked.

Astrid shrugged. 'Maybe six o'clock. Is it important?'

'It is just that I was thinking of going out this evening.'

'Where are you going?' Tanya piped up, anxious to be in on everything.

'Don't be so nosy,' her mother told her.

But it was clear from Astrid's expression that she was also wondering the same thing. Several times during the course of the meal Siggi became aware of her sister's curious gaze lingering on her.

Anxious to get back to her new pet, Tanya was finished well before the two women. 'Hurry up, Auntie Siggi,' she pleaded.

'You go on,' she was told. 'I'll join you in a few minutes.'

A short silence developed once the young girl had left them alone. Eventually their eyes met. Astrid said in a quiet voice: 'You're thinking of going back to the Compton Manor this evening, aren't you?'

Siggi sighed. 'Am I so very obvious?'

'You are in this instance.' Astrid spread her hands. 'Why, for goodness sake? You're meeting him tomorrow anyway. What will you achieve by going there tonight? I doubt he would thank you for turning up.'

Her tone then became gentler. 'In any case, you're only going to upset yourself. You know his squadron are having a big party there tonight. Why on earth would you want to see all that?'

'You tell me, Astrid. I don't know.' Siggi's voice suddenly became very small. 'It is just that something inside of me has been stirred by meeting this man. I cannot explain it, but I feel our paths were destined to cross. I should hate him for what he represents, but I do not. Why is that so?'

Anguish formed on her face. 'I don't understand. What is happening to me?'

In an instant the years fell away. For a moment Siggi could see the ruins of Steglitz once more surrounding her. She could feel the rubble beneath her feet – the heat from the fires – the smoke stinging her eyes.

Astrid moved closer to put a comforting arm around her younger sister's shoulder. 'You're changing,' she said. 'That's what is happening. I think you've wanted to for a long time, even if you didn't realise it yourself. Coming here to England and meeting this Canadian has simply helped that change to begin. In a way it was the same for me when I first came to this country with Terry. In the beginning most people were suspicious and unfriendly. But things are different now.'

She gave Siggi's shoulder a gentle squeeze before continuing. 'You can't go on hating everybody who fought on the other side during the war forever. It isn't right to blame every man who ever put on a uniform for all the terrible things that happened. That would be as wrong as …'

Astrid hesitated, searching for a suitably compelling example. 'As wrong as a Jew holding our dear father personally responsible for all the terrible things that happened in places like Auschwitz and Belsen,' she finally stated.

Something close to outrage showed on Siggi's face. 'How can you say such a thing?' she demanded. 'You know that our father hated what Hitler was doing as much as we did. He had no choice about being in the army. He never wanted to kill or harm anyone.'

'Yes, I know. I know these things very well. And of course he had nothing to do with the concentration camps. I only said that to shock you. But that doesn't change other facts. We both know that father helped to fire the big artillery guns during the siege on Stalingrad. Thousands of ordinary Russian people must have been killed or badly injured as a result of something he *was* directly involved in. Very old people would have suffered, not to mention mothers with young children. Would you ever think that the Russians were right to blame our father for their suffering?'

'No! It is not possible to say that he was responsible. Not in the way you are suggesting.'

Astrid's voice was emphatic. 'Exactly! No more than Mister Stafford was personally responsible for the events that led to our own mother's death. Even if it was his very own bombs that struck our house, he was not the one who created the situation. Only the Nazis can be blamed for that, and they had to be stopped. Surely you can see what I am saying?'

This time the silence was long as Siggi digested her sister's words. What Astrid was saying to her was not a new concept. At home in Hamburg she had heard similar sentiments expressed on a number of occasions. Always though she had rejected the validity of the argument. Somehow, it was so much easier to continue being bitter than to forgive.

But now, everything suddenly seemed different. Astrid was living proof that there was another way. She was happily married with a beautiful daughter, and it was impossible for Siggi to deny her own deep affection for Tanya. The simple fact that the child was an English citizen made nonsense of her past beliefs.

The seed of change had been steadily taking root for some time now. That much was obvious. And as Astrid suggested, meeting the Canadian had simply caused that seed to grow more vigorously. From the first moment she had set eyes on the man, there had been a strange kind of awareness that he was destined to shape her future life in some way. When she had spotted him following them into the hotel foyer, that feeling was confirmed as a fact. That was why she had spoken to him. It didn't matter that she had been brusque. Her words had simply provided a starting point for them. Events, as she had known they would, had then taken over.

Siggi's mind had been in turmoil since that dinner. She knew instinctively that Mike Stafford was a good man, and one half of her desperately wanted to accept him as such. Maybe by talking more with him, this alone might be the catalyst to encourage further change in her?

But the darker half of her personality was also strong, steadfastly refusing to accept that this could be so. It was this side that was motivating her desire to revisit the Compton Manor Hotel that evening. There was no thought of making personal contact with the man. She planned merely to observe. If she were to see him enjoying a good time, perhaps getting drunk with all his friends at their party, then, she told herself, he could not be as remorseful as he claimed to be over the loss of innocent civilian lives. It would confirm the dark suspicions: that he and all the rest of them were gathered for no other purpose than to cynically celebrate the damage they had inflicted on Germany.

She felt Astrid give her shoulder another squeeze, breaking into these thoughts. The two women looked deep into each other's eyes. In that instant Siggi knew that her motivation to return to the hotel that evening was for all the wrong reasons. Everything Astrid had said made perfect sense. And yet, despite this acceptance, here she was still searching for a way to destroy what may be her only opportunity to fully come to terms with the past.

Was she mad?

Siggi smiled at her sister. 'Yes,' she said, 'I can see now that you are right. I would be very foolish to go there tonight. I cannot think what came over me.'

Astrid returned her smile. It was tinged with relief. 'That means you can meet him tomorrow with an open mind,' she said. 'I have a feeling that things will seem much better after you two have talked together privately.'

'I'm beginning to think the same myself,' Siggi agreed.

'So what time is he picking you up tomorrow?'

A voice interrupted. 'Who's picking you up tomorrow, Auntie Siggi?' Tanya was standing by the kitchen door, an enquiring look on her face.

Both women stared at her. 'How long have you been there?' Astrid demanded, frowning.

'I've only just got here.' The child turned to her aunt. 'Is he a boyfriend?' she asked with a grin.

'Tanya!' Her mother's voice was stern.

The grin disappeared. 'I'm sorry. But I heard you say Auntie Siggi was meeting a man, so I just wondered. Don't you think it would be nice for her to meet a boyfriend while she's here with us, Mum?'

Astrid was on the point of scolding her daughter further when Siggi cut in. 'There's no need to tell her off. She doesn't mean any harm.'

She then spoke to the child. 'No, he is not a boyfriend, Tanya. We are just meeting so that we can have a talk together.'

'Can I come with you?'

By now Astrid had had enough. 'No you can't young lady. And if we get any more chat from you, you'll be going straight to your room after dinner.'

A protruding bottom lip showed that the message had sunk home.

'Now go back into the garden and see to your guinea pig. Auntie Siggi will come along in a minute.'

Knowing what was good for her, Tanya departed.

'Don't be too hard on her,' Siggi pleaded when the child was out of earshot. 'It is my fault for encouraging her to be too grown up.'

Astrid sighed with mock weariness. 'Children! You should have had one or two of your own by now, you know. Maybe you will soon. There's still time.'

'I think that having a niece like Tanya is quite sufficient, thank you,' Siggi responded a shade too quickly. She felt a hint of redness showing on her cheeks.

Astrid appeared slightly amused by her sister's reaction. 'You still haven't told me what time he's picking you up tomorrow,' she reminded.

'He said he would be here at twelve o'clock.'

'Oh, I see. High noon eh.'

Siggi was puzzled. 'Why do you say that?'

Astrid laughed. 'It's only an expression. Haven't you heard of the film? You know, the long countdown to the meeting at mid-day.'

'Yes, I have heard of it. But … '

'I didn't mean anything in particular. I just have this feeling that tomorrow could be a very important day for you.'

'Yes, I think you may be right,' Siggi agreed. She sighed. 'We will just have to wait and see.'

***

The two coaches arrived back at the Compton Manor Hotel at 5.30pm. Along with everyone else, Stafford had thoroughly enjoyed the visit to Burton-on-the-Ouse. For a few hours he had been able to put all other concerns to the back of his mind and make the most of the hospitality extended to them by seventy-nine squadron's current members. Doug Short was positively beaming with the success of his organised 'extra'.

During the journey back to Wetherditch, Stafford had outlined his plan for establishing the young barman's true identity to Geordie. His friend, who he needed to play a key part, was keen to get started.

Back at the hotel, the two men separated to prepare for the evening's function. It was to be a semi-formal affair, prompting Stafford to take great care with his appearance. He regarded himself in his bedroom mirror. Well-polished black shoes, neatly pressed trousers, clean white shirt complete with a squadron tie, and a smart blazer bearing the Bomber Command crest on the top pocket all combined to provide the look he wanted. He was giving his jacket a final brush when the expected knock on his door came.

'Are you ready?' Geordie called.

Opening up, he saw that the big man was dressed in almost identical fashion. 'It looks like we're both back in uniform again,' he grinned.

Although there was still more than an hour before the dinner was due to commence, they headed downstairs into the hotel lobby immediately. Just in front of the main bar entrance a large placard announced: *'Bar closed for private function'*. They paused by the sign and exchanged a final glance.

'This won't take long,' Geordie said.

He headed off in the direction of the small cocktail lounge. Stafford watched him go for a moment and then entered the main bar.

Being so early, he was not altogether surprised to find the room deserted. He paused to take in the changes. It was clear that a lot of hard work had been put into transforming the bar into a suitable venue for their gathering. Long dining tables, each one capable of seating a dozen people, were covered with immaculate white cloths and set with shining silver cutlery. A giant candelabrum adorned the centre of each table, and place cards written in stylish script lettering indicated where each of the guests would be sitting.

Beyond these tables and the small dance floor, confirming the evening's entertainment, a stage at the far end showed the recent addition of a full drum kit and several other musical instruments in readiness for the hired band's later performance.

Completing these preparations, a temporary podium positioned well away from the stage featured just one upright chair and a small table complete with a microphone ready for use. Adorning the wall directly behind, a large banner proudly proclaimed that tonight was: **79 Squadron's First Reunion**.

Stafford was still taking all of this in when a voice behind him quietly said: 'A penny for them, Mike.'

He turned to see Doug Short sitting on his own in the far corner. Stafford smiled. 'I didn't notice you there, Doug. What are you up to?'

Short looked a little sheepish. 'To be honest, I'm not altogether sure myself. Just thinking, I suppose. After all the months of planning, I can hardly believe that it's finally come together.'

Once again it was brought home to Stafford how much this reunion meant to his former navigator. And the huge amount of work the guy must have put into making it happen.

'Everything will be fine,' he said. 'Why shouldn't it be?'

Rising from his chair, Short limped over toward him. He laughed nervously. 'No reason at all really. Take no notice. It's just me having a silly moment.'

The limp somehow contrived to age the man, making him appear vulnerable. Time had been less kind to Doug than many others gathered here, Stafford considered.

'So where am I sitting?' he asked, more to get away from this depressing notion than out of any great urgency to know.

Short brightened. He led the way over to a table close to the podium. 'I've obviously kept all of the old crews together as much as possible,' he said. 'I'm sitting here next to you on your right-hand side. There's Geordie's place on your left. Pete, Phil and Hughie are directly opposite.'

'But no place for Jimmy, eh Doug.'

The moment the words were out, Stafford regretted saying them. It was okay for him to have had the thought privately: all he'd intended was a brief silent acknowledgement to his closest ever friend. But why the heck had he expressed it aloud? Doug deserved far better than that after all his hard work.

The navigator's face dropped. 'I can't do anything about that, Mike. No more than I could when I visited you in hospital all that time ago. You asked me then if I could bring Jimmy back. Remember?'

'Sure I remember, Doug. I'm sorry. It was a cheap shot.'

Stafford hesitated and then found himself saying: 'I remember something else too. That time I gave the order to bale out. Even Hughie didn't want to go along with it at first. But you as senior officer never once queried the decision. Why?'

'It wasn't my place to. You were the skipper.'

'That doesn't tell me if you agreed with the order or not.'

Short looked him directly in the eye. 'I considered the situation we were in and decided there was a sound logic attached to your decision. I thought that at the time, and I still think the same today. Despite what happened.'

There could be no doubt that Short was being sincere. Stafford recognised this fact and warmed even further to the man.

'You never once gave me a wrong course, Doug. Not in all the ops we flew together. Even when the Gee packed up, your dead reckoning was spot on. We always got home somehow, didn't we?'

For a short while there was silence as both men reflected on those dangerous days when they had relied so much on each other's skills in order to stay alive.

Short spoke first. 'Geordie seems particularly pleased to see you,' he remarked. 'Still, that's hardly surprising when you consider that he wouldn't be here at all if you hadn't …'

He sighed. There was no need for him to complete the sentence.

'Yeah, I've been real glad to see Geordie too,' Stafford responded.

He then glanced at his watch and wondered how his friend was faring

***

With the main bar closed to the public for that evening, the cocktail lounge was far busier than usual. The young barman had given Geordie a brief glare before stiffly serving him with his drink, but other than that there had been little time for him to dwell on the big man's presence.

Settling his large frame onto a bar stool, Geordie spent the next ten minutes or so observing the youth and listening. Now there was a short lull in waiting customers. He caught the barman's eye.

'Yes, sir,' the youth said woodenly, his working accent still very much in evidence.

'I'll have chicken and chips,' Geordie told him, holding out the bar snack menu.

Silently the youth wrote out his order on a pad. He then placed the slip of paper with several others in a pile beneath the optics and handed Geordie the stub. It bore the number seventeen.

'Three shillings please,' he said, his face devoid of expression.

Five more minutes elapsed before a member of the kitchen staff came in to make his periodic check for orders. Now busy once more, the barman simply scooped up the pending slips and slapped them on the man's tray.

'That's all for now,' he said.

With a quick nod, the waiter left the bar. Geordie rose and was only seconds behind him. Once outside, he quickly caught up with the man.

'My order – I want to cancel it.'

'Which one was that, sir?'

Geordie handed him the stub. 'Number seventeen.' He moved in close as the waiter flicked through his pile of orders.

'Number seventeen…chicken and chips. Is that the one?'

'That's the one.'

A large hand plucked the slip of paper from the waiter's grasp. 'I'll take that, just in case there's a mistake,' Geordie told him.

The man looked surprised but did not argue. He shrugged. A scrap of paper was of little importance.

'As you wish, sir,' he said.

Geordie smiled at him. 'Thank you very much.'

***

Stafford was waiting in the main bar as arranged. Doug Short had hurried off several minutes earlier to make some last-minute check, leaving the pair free to talk.

'Did you get it?' Stafford asked.

Geordie grinned. 'No trouble at all.'

He placed the slip of paper on a nearby table. Stafford produced the anonymous note and did the same. Both men spent several moments comparing the handwriting on each.

Stafford nodded as he came to his decision. 'What do you think?' he asked.

'No doubt about it. It's the same handwriting.'

'Yeah, that's what I figured.'

Once in agreement, Geordie became forthright. 'You can't mess about, Mike. We've got to tackle the little bugger straight away.'

'But it's not that simple, is it? Don't forget, I've got to try and win this kid over. I won't manage that by getting too heavy handed with him.'

Geordie remained uncompromising. 'It's your own safety that's got to come first, man. Anyhow, I don't care if the kid is Jimmy's bairn. I reckon a heavy hand is just what's needed here.'

Stafford frowned. 'What are you suggesting?'

His friend's voice dropped a little. 'Look, he'll be busy in that other bar until closing time. Why don't we wait until later and then grab him outside when he comes off duty? Now we've got this proof, it shouldn't be hard to make him admit who he is and what he's up to. We can take it from there.'

Geordie spread his hands as Stafford continued to look doubtful. 'Bloody hell, Mike, we can't make it any worse. Remember, he's got that air rifle. He might have other weapons like a knife as well. If he's as crazy as Barbara says he is ...'

He let the words hang for a moment before finishing off. 'You can't fool around playing Mister Nice Guy. Maybe that can come later. But not yet.'

Stafford knew that his friend was talking sense. Much as he wanted to get this right for Jimmy, he had to think of his own safety too. If only for Alice and Connie's sake. Anyhow, once the kid knew that they were on to him, he might then become a lot easier to handle.

'Okay, Geordie,' he agreed. 'We'll try it your way and see what happens. I just hope to hell it doesn't backfire on us.'

ELEVEN

By nine o'clock the reunion dinner was in full swing. Smoked salmon starters, venison steaks and a lemon meringue dessert had already been devoured with tremendous gusto. Cheese boards and coffee were now being served.

Geordie was busily chomping his way through a huge chunk of Stilton cheese. Whatever else may have been on his mind, it had clearly not affected his appetite. Never much of a wine drinker, six bottles of his favourite Newcastle Brown Ale had served perfectly well as an accompaniment to his meal. Years ago he had been the unrivalled beer-drinking champion of the squadron sergeant's mess, and from the way he was currently going about things, it looked as if he'd still be quite capable of reclaiming that title from any of the present-day members should he choose to. Stafford marvelled at the big man's capacity, confident in the knowledge that he would still be sharp when needed.

On the other side of the table, Gloria's voice rose easily above competition from a host of other simultaneous conversations. As the only female present in K for King's gathering, she was in her element. Hughie sat quietly beside his wife with the careworn look of a man who had seen and heard her theatrical performances many times before, but sincerely wished he hadn't. Every so often a loud burst of laughter sprang from a nearby table, but if any of the humour was at Gloria's expense, she appeared blissfully unaware of the fact.

Phil Thomas, egged on by Gloria, had just stood up to provide a demonstration of the Maori Haka made famous by New Zealand's All Blacks rugby team. He was in the middle of giving his unique take on exactly why this had to be performed with a grotesquely protruding tongue when a waiter approached and spoke quietly to Stafford.

'Excuse me, sir. There is someone in the foyer who would like to speak to you. Can you spare them a few minutes?'

The Canadian was mystified. 'Who is it?' he asked.

'I couldn't say, sir. I was merely asked to relay the message.'

Intrigued, Stafford rose from his chair. Geordie paused eating long enough to glance curiously in his direction. 'What's up? Need any help?'

Stafford gave his friend an appreciative grin. 'No. Everything's fine. I'll be back in a couple of minutes.'

Geordie relaxed and returned to his rapidly diminishing hunk of Stilton.

Standing in the middle of the near deserted foyer, Stafford cast his eyes around. There was no sign of anyone who looked as if they may be waiting for him. A touch irritated, he glanced at his watch. No matter who had sent the message, he would give them only a few moments to show themselves.

He was on the point of returning to the dinner when, to his surprise, the young barman from the cocktail lounge came walking quickly in his direction. The youth moved right up close.

'You and me need to talk some more,' he said in an urgent whisper. Once again his London accent was far more obvious than when working behind the bar.

For a second or two, Stafford's surprise made him unsure of how to respond. 'Shouldn't you be busy in there?' he remarked, nodding toward the cocktail lounge.

The youth was clearly nervous. 'I got someone else to fill in for a bit. There's stuff I need to sort out with you.'

'What kind of stuff?' Stafford asked, deciding to play it dumb until he knew where this was leading.

The air of nervousness increased. 'You think I'm Alan, don't you?'

'Alan who?' It wouldn't hurt to keep the dumb act going for a little longer.

'Do me a favour. You know who I mean – Alan Knight.'

'And you've come to tell me that you're not? Is that it?' Stafford fingered the two pieces of paper in his pocket.

The youth's voice rose. 'Of course I'm bloody not. Do I look like a nutter?'

His eyes flickered around the lobby before continuing. 'We can't talk here. Let's nip outside for a few minutes. You can go and get that big mate of yours if you don't trust me. He can come with us.'

'Just you and me will be fine,' the Canadian told him. He nodded toward the big oak doors. 'Let's go.'

The pair stepped outside into the fading light of the car park. They paused under the branches of an elm tree.

'So talk,' Stafford instructed.

Look, I swear I'm not Alan. He's got a job in the kitchen doing washing up and cleaning the place.'

'So you're telling me you didn't write this?' Stafford thrust the anonymous note under the youth's nose.

''You know damn well I did. I bet you've got that bloody meal ticket as well just to prove it.'

'Sure. It's right here.'

The youngster let out a hollow laugh. 'I sussed out what your mate was up to as soon as the waiter told me he'd grabbed the ticket back. I should have known right from the start. Why would he bother with a bar meal just before that big fancy dinner you lot are having?'

Under different circumstances Stafford might have found this remark almost amusing. It was exactly the sort of thing that Geordie was liable to do if really in the mood.

'If you're not Alan, then why write the note?' he demanded.

'Because he told me to.'

Stafford sighed. 'You're not making sense. Why would he do that?'

The youth raised his eyebrows. 'Haven't you worked it out yet? Alan can't read or write properly. He never learned any of that stuff.'

In a flash, it all added up. Barbara had spoken of a special school that her son had been forced to attend. What were the words she'd used? *'He wouldn't learn anything and was all but uncontrollable.'* If that were the case, then maybe there was some truth in this kid's story.

But even if he was telling the truth, there was still a load of other questions for him to answer. 'So what did Alan say when I didn't show up to meet him?' Stafford pressed.

'He went mental at first. Got into a right rage and called you all sorts of names. Made out he was going to get you big time. Fuck knows what he meant by that. I didn't have the nerve to ask. But then later I said how I'd overheard you and your mate talking about him in the woods this morning. You know, saying you were going to go after him and all that. That put the shits up him a bit.'

Stafford jumped in quickly. 'What we were saying wasn't meant to be a threat. I just want to talk to Alan, that's all.'

'Well, that's not the way he saw it. Said something about his mother must have tipped you off and that maybe it wasn't worth all the trouble he'd get into, especially if you called in the coppers.'

'Where is he now then?'

'He's gone – scarpered.'

'You're kidding me.' Stafford was sceptical. 'When did he leave?'

'Only about an hour ago. He came into my bar and I told him what your mate had been up to with the meal ticket. That was the clincher for him. He reckoned things were getting too hot and that he had to get out straight away. Tell you the truth, I'm bloody glad he's gone. Why should I take all the shit for his problems?'

The youth's mouth formed into a weak smile. He now appeared genuinely frightened. 'I never knew it was going to get like this. All Alan told me at the start was that you had something to do with his old man getting killed and how he wanted to talk to you about it. He made out like you were a real bastard, so I agreed to help him. Anyhow, you don't argue with Alan. Not if you've got any sense.'

He placed a finger on his temple. 'He can be a real head case. I've seen him go crazy just 'cos some bloke looked at him the wrong way.'

Stafford thought for a moment. There was still a ring of truth to what he was hearing. 'So where's Alan headed for now?' he asked.

The youth shrugged. 'Dunno. He just got on his scooter and pushed off.'

'Scooter?'

'You know, one of them Lambrettas.'

'But he must have said something more before leaving?'

'Nothing much. Just that he was going to get the hell out of here before the law got involved. He's probably on his way back to London.'

'Do you know where he lives?'

The youngster gave a small sneer. 'Alan doesn't stay anywhere for very long. He just moves around and dosses down where he can.'

'What about his mother?'

'They don't see much of each other. He just stops at her place when it suits him.'

'Where's that?'

'Somewhere in the East End – around Plaistow way I think. He never told me the address.'

Stafford sighed. That meant Barbara had moved. She had been living in Croydon when he'd tried to see her shortly after Jimmy's death.

'Hey, Mike!'

It was Geordie's voice calling out. He turned to see his friend striding toward them. The big man glared at the youth.

'What's going on? Is this little bugger giving you trouble?'

Stafford held up a restraining hand. 'Easy, pal. It looks like we may have the wrong guy.' He explained concisely what had been said.

As he finished, Geordie turned his attention back to the youngster. 'So where do you fit in?' he demanded. 'How long have you known Alan?'

'We went to school together.'

'The school for difficult kids?' Stafford asked.

The answer came grudgingly. 'Yeah, you could call it that.'

'I knew it,' Geordie declared. 'A right pair of little villains.'

The youth shot him a surly glance before continuing. 'Anyhow, after we left the school we just sort of carried on hanging around together. Alan might be a bit mental sometimes, but he's dead handy to have as a mate if you're in trouble. And I'm useful to him a lot of the time as well 'cos of my reading and writing.' A note of pride crept into his voice. 'Got myself a certificate for that when I was about ten years old. Used to learn a fair old bit in them days. Even got the hang of how to put on a bit of a posh voice if I wanted to.'

'Pity they didn't give you any lessons in how to stay out of trouble,' Geordie muttered quietly.

If the youth heard him, he showed no sign. 'Anyhow, when Alan told me he was coming up here I just sort of came along for the ride. There wasn't much else going on at the time, and I thought it might be a bit of a laugh.'

'And are you laughing now?' Stafford's expression was far from humorous.

'Bloody hell, I didn't know it would turn out like this. Like I said, I thought we were just going to have a bit of fun. Maybe put the wind up you a touch.'

The youth stood there uncertainly as the two men looked at each other. Each had the same thought.

'Okay. You want a laugh? Take your jacket and shirt off,' Stafford instructed.

'What – here in the car park?'

'Just do it,' Geordie growled.

'What for?'

'Because we're telling you to.'

This time the big man's growl was even more menacing. The youth hastily decided to do as instructed. First the barman's short jacket was removed, then the shirt and clip-on bow tie.

'Now turn around,' he was told.

There was no trace of a mole on either shoulder. The light was still good enough for both men to be certain of that.

'All right. Get your clothes back on,' Geordie ordered.

While the youth was still dressing, Stafford fired another question. 'When you were hiding in the bushes this morning, what was that all about? Did Alan tell you to follow us?'

'No, straight up. Like I said at the time, I was just going after some rabbits to try and earn myself a few extra bob.' The youngster hesitated. 'But I knew who you were as soon as I saw you. You gave me your name and room number in the bar when you ran out of cash last night. Remember?'

Stafford nodded. Even though it had not appeared to be very important at the time, he could still recall the youth's fleeting change of expression when he'd identified himself. Now it all figured.

The youngster continued. 'So when I spotted you and your mate sitting there in the woods, it seemed like a good idea to creep up a little closer and have a listen. You know, see if I could pick up anything that might be useful to Alan. It pays to keep him sweet.'

He laughed weakly. 'I thought he'd be chuffed with what I'd done. As it turned out, he hit the bleeding roof. Said I should never have let you see the gun and that I was a fucking idiot for getting caught and attracting attention. But it ain't my fault. I mean to say, you're both old men now. After you never showed up to meet Alan last night, I didn't think you'd have the bottle to do anything, even if you did spot me.'

The rumbling sound now coming from Geordie was a sure sign that he was very close indeed to losing his temper. More than ever he resembled a large and very angry grizzly bear.

Realising the potential danger he was in, the youth backed off a pace or two. Suddenly, he was even more eager to help. He pointed toward an annex building set some distance to one side of the hotel. 'Look, there's the staff quarters. Me and Alan shared a room there. Do you want to come and see for yourselves?'

'We might as well,' Stafford said, glancing at Geordie.

His still glowering friend gave a sharp nod.

The staff quarters contrasted sharply with the opulence of the hotel itself. Shunted well away from the main building, the single-storey concrete block annex turned out to be a warren of small and sparsely furnished double bedrooms. A wireless was playing Radio Luxembourg inside one of these rooms as the trio moved along the single passageway.

The disc jockey's voice carried clearly. 'You're listening to two-oh-eight, your station of the stars,' he announced. At this point, a rush of static interference surged up from nowhere to drown out any further comment from him. When normal service resumed a few seconds later, Elvis Presley was already well into the opening bars of his latest number one hit, 'Good Luck Charm'.

'In here,' the youth said, opening a door at the far end of the passage and showing them into a dingily lit room.

Bare floorboards and two metal-framed beds separated by twin steel lockers might have given the place a barrack room feel had it not been for the general untidiness and thick layer of dust that was settled on virtually everything. The two men exchanged a look of mutual disgust.

'Just what I expected,' muttered Geordie. 'A bloody tip.'

The youngster wisely ignored the remark. 'This one was Alan's bed, and that's his locker,' he told them.

Stafford pulled open the locker door. Apart from a few crumpled sweet wrappers and a badly holed pair of socks, it was empty. His gaze then switched to the inside of the door. Fixed to this with sticky tape was an old black and white photograph. It was a snap of himself and Jimmy standing outside the front of this very hotel.

He drew a sharp breath, remembering instantly when the picture had been taken. They had just completed their thirteenth mission. Glad to get this unlucky number out of the way, the whole crew had come here for celebration drinks. Doug Short had insisted on recording the occasion by taking numerous pictures with his Kodak Box Brownie.

Geordie was also staring at the photograph. 'Bloody hell, man,' he murmured. 'Do you remember that?'

'Sure. Unlucky thirteen.' Stafford gave an ironic laugh. 'Except that thirteen wasn't our unlucky number, was it? We still had a way to go before finding out what that was going to be.'

The big man remained silent while Stafford carefully picked the tape away from the metal surface. Once the photograph was in his hand he gazed at it for several moments, a baffled expression on his face.

'Why do you reckon Alan left this behind?' he asked Geordie.

His friend shrugged. 'Maybe he just forgot. According to laughing boy here, he did leave in a bit of a hurry.'

'Yeah, it's possible.'

Stafford placed the photograph carefully into his jacket pocket and turned to the youth. 'Okay, it looks like you're on the level. But listen up good. You make damn sure you let us know if Alan comes back.'

'Too right I will. I don't want anything more to do with him after this.'

'So you reckon your name is Graham Walker. Is that right?'

'Yeah.'

'Have you got any proof of that?'

Walker rummaged through the mess inside his locker and eventually came up with a dog-eared motorcycle licence. 'Will this do?' he asked.

The licence was indeed made out to a Graham Walker. The signature at the bottom also matched the scrawl on the other two pieces of paper.

'Just one more thing,' Stafford said. 'Where's that air rifle of yours?'

The question seemed to catch Walker by surprise. 'It's not mine; it's Alan's. He's taken it with him.'

'Where did he buy it?'

In spite of his nervousness, Walker grinned. 'You must be joking. He nicked it from somewhere before we left London.'

Geordie had already taken it on himself to start turfing the entire contents of Walker's locker onto the floor.

'Nothing in here, Mike,' he stated.

Methodically, the pair then searched every other part of the room with the same result. Walker watched them without expression.

'Believe me now?' he asked.

Geordie fixed him with a glare that could slice through granite. 'I wouldn't believe you if you told me it'll be getting dark tomorrow night. Not without checking first.'

The two men headed for the door. Walker called after them.

'You're not going to tell anyone about this, are you? I've been straight with you and helped all I can.'

'What do you reckon, Geordie?'

'I think we should wait a while and see how he behaves.'

Stafford gave a grim little smile. 'That's it then. You're on probation.'

'Probably not for the first time,' his friend remarked dryly.

Once again wisely ignoring Geordie's cracks, Walker sighed with relief. 'Thanks. You won't get no more bother from me, I promise.'

Glad to get out of the dirty room, the two men left him sitting on the edge of his bed. He appeared a sorry figure.

***

'I don't reckon you'll be getting any more trouble now,' Geordie stated confidently as the pair made their way back to the main hotel building.

Stafford frowned. 'Maybe you're right, but this isn't how I wanted things to work out. You know that.'

The big man glanced at him, his surprise very much in evidence. 'Look, you can't be bothering about any promises you made to Barbara. You don't owe her a damn thing. Not after the way she poisoned the kid's mind against you.'

'I know. All the same…'

Stafford hesitated. Much as he wanted to enlarge on his feelings, after a quick reflection he decided it would be better to leave out any mention of his weird, séance type experience with their long-dead friend. Geordie was sure to think him completely crazy.

He limited himself to saying: 'The thing is, I guess I kind of owe it to Jimmy to do something. For sure he'd want me to try and help straighten out his boy if I can.'

'I'm not so sure about that, Mike. It hurts me to say such a thing about Jim's kid, but everything we hear about him says he's a right little waster who's not worth your time. Even if you did manage to find him, chances are he won't listen to a word you say. He'll be more likely to try and stick a knife in you or something crazy like that.'

'Yeah, I know,' Stafford conceded. 'But I've got to give it a go, all the same. It's important to me.'

Geordie shook his head. 'Jesus, you're a stubborn bugger. Jimmy wouldn't expect you to risk getting yourself killed.'

There was a lull in the talk while the pair of them passed through the hotel's oak doors and across the lobby. They paused by the main bar entrance.

Geordie gripped Stafford's arm, squeezing tightly. 'Forget it, Mike. The kid's gone and so is the problem as far as you're concerned. There's nothing more you can do. Not unless you're planning to start wasting your time down in London.'

'We'll see,' Stafford told him.

As the two men entered the bar, the hired band was playing their first number of the evening.

***

Just five minutes after the two men had left Walker's room, the door opened once again. Still sitting morosely on the edge of his bed, Walker showed no surprise at the newcomer's entrance.

'I did what you told me,' he said in a dull voice.

'I know. You wouldn't dare do anything else.'

Walker's unease grew. 'What are you gonna do now?' he asked, staring at the air rifle in the other youth's hand.

His question was ignored. Instead, Alan Knight glanced inside his empty locker. 'He took the picture?'

'Yeah.'

Alan frowned but made no comment.

'So what are you gonna do?' Walker repeated.

This time Alan did respond. A grin spread over his face. 'Stafford's booked in here for three more nights. Most of his mates will be going home tomorrow. Now he thinks I'm not around any longer, he won't be on his guard. I'll just hang around for the right opportunity and then ...'

His grin grew wider as he tossed the air rifle on the bed beside Walker. 'You can keep this as a present if you want. I've got myself something much better now.'

Walker knew exactly what it must be that Alan was referring to. He shivered while wondering what the hell he had got himself mixed up in.

TWELVE

Stafford and Geordie made their way through the crowded room back to K for King's table. The five-piece group was making a brave attempt at re-creating the big band sound of Glen Miller. The strains of 'In the Mood', no doubt intended to get everybody in exactly that, reverberated around the room.

Doug Short had now moved up onto the temporary podium. Sitting behind a small table with reading glasses perched on the end of his nose, he was busy sorting through a formidably thick bundle of papers.

'I hope to heck that's not Doug's speech,' Stafford heard one of the veterans remark while passing the man's group.

Once back with the crew, Geordie soon replenished his stock of Newcastle Brown Ale. Satisfied, he leaned toward Stafford.

'It looks like Phil's trick worked then,' he remarked with a grin.

Seeing the Canadian's blank look, he nodded across the room toward the ever-effusive Gloria. With the dinner now completed, she had departed their table and was currently enthralling O for Oscar's crew with her regal presence.

'You know, that Maori dance thing Phil was doing,' the big man explained. 'Isn't it supposed to scare away bad spirits?'

Stafford couldn't help but laugh. 'Yeah, poor old Hughie.' He shook his head in wonderment. 'How the heck did he and Gloria ever get together? He never used to talk very much about her even in the old days. I guess we can all see why now.'

He took a drink from the large whisky Geordie had ordered for him. It tasted good. Far better than the one he had drunk earlier. Maybe his friend was right, he considered. Alan was gone now, and in many ways that removed his sense of responsibility. It wasn't his fault that he had no idea where to find the kid. Anyhow, even if he did somehow manage to track him down in London, what could he be expected to achieve in the short time he had remaining in England?

All this sounded reasonable, but his conscience kicked in just the same. He sighed. Okay, maybe there was still a small chance he could do something. But not tonight. Tonight he was going to follow Geordie's example and enjoy himself.

He emptied his glass. 'Come on, buddy. What do you say to another drink?'

Geordie beamed at him. 'Now that's what I call a bloody good idea.'

***

Once a few couples had led the way, the small dance floor quickly became busy. The twenty or so wives who were attending soon found themselves in popular demand as partners. But whilst most of them were content to wait until being asked, Gloria obviously felt no such inhibitions. She had already commandeered a number of not altogether willing partners. Drinking aside, 'dodging that woman' had become one of the main activities of the evening.

With his injured leg ruling him out of any such physical distractions, Doug Short was content to simply view the results of his long labour from his podium chair. He drank in the atmosphere. The occasion was turning out to be everything he'd dreamed it might be. He felt a happy and contented man.

At 10.30pm, the band took a break.

With this lull in activity, Short had one final contribution to make. Rising to his feet and blowing twice into the microphone to check the sound, he called for order. Slowly the chatter died away and all eyes turned to face him.

He was uncomfortably aware that many here might see this interlude as being a boring interruption to an otherwise enjoyable evening. They would of course give him their attention out of courtesy, but he had already noticed several people glancing at their watches as if about to time him. *'Come on, Doug,'* they seemed to be saying. *'Let's get it over with.'*

He adjusted his reading spectacles, shuffled the large bundle of paperwork in front of him, and cleared his throat before speaking.

'Thank you ladies and gentlemen
There are a few things I'd like to say
So if you'll spare me a couple of minutes
I'll get the formal stuff out of the way.'

He paused to give his audience a brief, apprehensive smile. People began to realise that he was speaking in verse. Looks - some amused, some perplexed - were exchanged. Gloria giggled loudly. Short continued.

'Why this evening means so much to me
Is just as simple as it appears
It's seeing old friendships from way back when
Now being renewed after so many years.'

A small ripple of applause came in support of this sentiment.

'I know what everyone's thinking
Doug's going to talk for ages
Just look at all those notes he's got
There must be fifty pages.'

A number of self-conscious smiles began to form, but it was Short who was now smiling the broadest as he pressed on.

'Well that may be the number
But let me be quite frank
Things aren't always how they seem
Because most of these are blank.'

With the final line of the verse, Short scattered his notes right across the table and onto the podium floor. There was a moment of surprise, then laughter as people saw how he had tricked them. Short held up his hand in an appeal for silence. When it arrived, it was complete. Everybody was eager to hear what he would say next.

When he continued, it was at a slightly slower pace, allowing the sentiment of each word to fully sink in.

'When asked to fight for freedom
You came from far and wide
Every aircrew man a volunteer
Determined not to hide.'

'We weren't the biggest squadron
But my word, we gave our best
Your fortitude and courage
Stood up to every test.'

'Yes, those days may now be past
But the memories still shine
Of the comradeship that we all had
When we were Seventy-nine.'

The previous hilarity had now turned into gratified embarrassment. Without even realising it, Short was working his audience masterfully. He allowed them a few seconds of reflection before continuing at a much brisker pace.

'You know my name is Doug Short
So short I'll keep this rhyme
You don't need lots of words from me
To spoil a damn good time.'

The mass embarrassment was lifting as he finished off with a flourish.

'So let me say in closing
In words that are sincere
Thank you all so very much
And please come back next year.'

'Thank you everybody, that's all,' he concluded.

The whole thing had been so unexpected: so gloriously out of character. To the majority of those present, Short had always been regarded as a man totally set in conventional ways. That he of all people should come out with something so unpredictable made the impact immeasurably greater.

The applause began normally enough. But from there on it just seemed to grow and grow. Soon the clapping became interspersed with loud cheers. Very quickly the room was ringing with sounds of the squadron's appreciation. Not just for the verse itself, but equally for all the months of hard work that the man had put into making this one very special evening come about.

Short sank weakly back down into his seat. Never in his wildest dreams had he anticipated such a reaction. He had hoped for maybe a couple of half-hearted laughs and a polite round of applause at the very most. But this – the appreciation was just going on and on. And to think that he had very nearly lost his nerve at the last minute and delivered a conventional speech instead.

He rose up again, smiling and waving.

'For he's a jolly good fellow,' someone at the back began to sing. Within seconds, everyone else was joining in.

'And so say all of us …. and so say all of us ….'

This final ovation was too much for Short. Overcome with emotion, he was suddenly aware of moistness beginning to cloud his vision. The singing took on a surreal, echo-like quality. And then, to his utter embarrassment, he could feel the trickle of a solitary tear running down his cheek.

His bad leg felt even more useless than usual as he sought to rapidly climb down from his prominent position on the podium and lose himself somewhere.

He did not get very far. The moment he stepped down, a seemingly endless succession of people began shaking his hand and slapping him on the back. He could never remember a time when he had enjoyed anything like this level of popularity. Nobody appeared to notice the tears in his eyes.

The band started up again with a quickstep and slowly the crowd around him thinned. Without quite knowing how he got there, Short suddenly found himself back at K for King's table. Here, he felt slightly more at ease.

'Never again,' he breathed.

The words conveyed their message, but the light in his eyes told a different story. A close observer might even have suggested that they could see him already making plans for the following year's event.

***

'Go on, go and get it,' Phil Thomas urged Pete Cowley.

Ever since the music had first started, Pete had been feeling the itch to play a few songs himself. He knew that most of the others here regarded him as something of an oddball. Maybe he was, he considered. He was nearly forty years old and still trying to live the life of a teenager. But what really got to him was the fact that so many of his old comrades were ready to dismiss modern popular music as rubbish without knowing the first thing about it.

He'd already expressed this thought to Phil several times. The Kiwi had proved far more interested than most in what he had to say. But in spite of this, Pete still badly wanted to prove his point to everyone in general. For the last half an hour he had been toying with the idea of fetching his guitar. His problem was the band. They were hardly the type of musicians who'd play his kind of stuff. Also, they would most likely resent an outsider pushing in on their act.

'Just go and get it,' Phil told him again. 'I'll fix it with the band for you.'

The Kiwi's continual encouragement, not to mention several large drinks, finally gave him the confidence to go ahead. Pete left the bar and returned a few minutes later with the guitar clutched in one hand.

'Did you sort it out with the band?' he asked Phil.

His friend grinned. 'You can go on after their next number. They won't play with you though, so you'll have to do it alone. Can you handle that?'

Although both the lead guitarist and singer with the group he'd formed at home in Liverpool, Pete still had his doubts. He had never performed on his own in public before. Privately yes, but never to a crowd of any size. And certainly not in front of an audience that had no particular desire to hear him anyway.

What the heck? he told himself. He'd never prove his point without taking a few risks.

'Sure I can handle it,' he told Phil with a lot more confidence than he was actually feeling.

***

While Pete waited for the band's number to finish, some of those sat at a nearby table glanced across at his guitar.

'Time to bale out I think, chaps,' the former skipper of S for Sugar suggested to his grinning crew.

Geordie's ears picked up on the remark. Carefully placing down his glass of beer, he ambled over, somehow looking even bigger than usual.

'I reckon it'd be a good idea if you were to give the lad a chance,' he told the S for Sugar crew in general. His expression suggested quite strongly that this was not a polite request.

The grins disappeared and there was much nodding of heads. No one in the group was going to argue with the big Tynesider.

Geordie then bent down and spoke quietly into their skipper's ear. 'And let's hear no more funny cracks about baling out eh.' He nodded toward Stafford. 'Take my point?'

Fortunately, it looked as if Stafford had not heard the potentially distressing remark. Which wasn't altogether surprising as he was by now showing all the signs of a man who had drunk far too much. Nevertheless, Geordie was determined to ensure that there would be no repetition.

S for Sugar's skipper was contrite. 'Sorry, Geordie. I wasn't thinking.'

Satisfied, the big man returned to his Newcastle Brown.

***

The band came to the end of their number. Realising that there was not going to be another dance immediately following, couples began slowly drifting from the floor. A short introduction from the band's leader was made and then Pete found himself being thrust into the spotlight.

Suddenly, his nerve cracked. What the heck had he let himself in for? He was only going to get laughed at by a bunch of people who had no idea what his kind of music represented. Even to his own ears, his voice sounded horribly croaky as he spoke. Blow the preamble, he thought. Let's just get on with it.

'This is a song I wrote with a pal of mine,' was all he said before beginning.

It had been written as an up-tempo number with a strong beat. But as he began playing, Pete knew at once that he could not get anything like the same effect with an acoustic guitar that he would have done with his electric Fender. Also, with no drums and a lack of anyone to harmonize with on the chorus, the whole thing was now sounding horribly thin and amateurish. Too late he realised that his nerves had allowed him to make a bad choice of material.

There was an almost total hush as he finished. Even his K for King crew mates were looking a touch embarrassed. Several *'I told you so'* smirks were apparent elsewhere. All Pete wanted to do was get off the stage.

And then Gloria's voice broke the uncomfortable silence.

'Well I certainly enjoyed it,' she stated in a voice that was more than loud enough to be heard by everyone present. She began to clap.

'Come on,' she commanded everyone. 'Give him some support.'

The K for King crew immediately took up her invitation, Geordie's large hands making twice the noise of anyone else. A trickle of others, if a little reluctantly, began to join in. It was hardly a standing ovation, but to Pete anything was better than that awful silence. 'Bless you, Gloria,' he murmured, taking back everything he had previously thought about the woman. His resolve firmed. He'd show them. Without further thought, he addressed the crowd.

'I know most of you people here think that popular music these days is rubbish. Okay, I can't do anything to change that. But at least give credit to the fact that we are still musicians. Just because you don't like the material, that doesn't mean we've got no musical ability.'

'Prove it then,' someone called out. 'Play something we all know.'

Pete tried to identify who it was speaking, but the lights shining into his face made it difficult.

His jaw set. 'Okay. If that's what you want.'

He spent a few seconds adjusting his guitar strings while trying to think what to play. Finally, with a deep breath, he launched himself into the opening bars of 'April Showers'.

His singing voice was unrecognizable from the previous number. He was now Al Jolson in everything but appearance. If his first choice of song had been poor, this singalong style was perfect. He was only halfway through the opening verse, and already people were starting to tap their feet and sway to the rhythm. He smiled, growing in confidence.

He then became aware that the band's drummer was wire brushing the skins behind him. And then the double bass crept in. So too did a gentle saxophone, the rhythm guitar, and even the trumpet. They were all there.

The performer inside him was now blooming. 'Come on everybody, join in,' he shouted, launching into the final verse. And they did join in. They were loving it.

This time the applause came without any prompting. Maybe not quite to the level of Doug Short's earlier ovation, but pretty damn close.

'More...more,' they called.

He waited until they had all settled down. Everyone waited expectantly to hear what his next number would be.

They were in for a big disappointment.

'So now you know that a lot of pop musicians can play your kind of music just as well as their own if they want to,' he said briefly into the microphone. 'That's all.'

Having made his point he thanked the band and left the stage, a satisfied smile on his face.

No amount of pleading would get him back up there.

***

The hotel management had insisted that the bar be vacated by two o'clock, and with just half an hour to go, many people had already decided to turn in for the night. Only a hard core of around twenty remained, each of them determined to see the evening fully out.

Gloria, naturally, was one of these.

Hughie had long since left her to it, retiring to their room shortly after midnight. His wife continued to flit unabated between the diminishing groups, the very epitome of a social butterfly.

There had been a moment of near panic for Doug Short when she managed to isolate him on his way back from the toilet.

'Tell me, Douglas, why have you never married?' she demanded of him, at the same time thrusting her ample and well-exposed bosom almost directly under his nose.

To the poor man, it felt as though she were challenging his manhood. 'A matter of personal choice, nothing more,' he replied stiffly.

For some unknown reason his reply brought forth peels of outrageous laughter from her. He made good his escape while she was still wrapped up in the amusement of it all.

But in spite of her posturing and overbearing mannerisms, to the K for King crew at least, Gloria did now have one redeeming feature. All of them were aware that, had it not been for her, Pete Cowley would have suffered a humiliating experience. He approached her in one of her rare quiet moments.

'I just want to say thanks for your support earlier,' he said.

Her heavily made-up lips parted in a gracious smile, dazzling in its intensity. 'We artistes must stick together, Peter,' she responded. 'There but for the grace of God, I always say. Goodness only knows how you must have been feeling, you poor darling. I'd have simply died in your position.'

Pete hesitated before asking: 'Did you really like my opening number?'

For possibly the very first time since arriving, Gloria lowered her voice to a mere whisper. 'Perhaps I was a teeny bit less enthusiastic than I pretended. But that's our little secret, isn't it? And I'm sure there are many thousands of young people who would think your song is wonderful, especially when it is given the right kind of production. I do understand about these things, you know.'

Her volume then increased to its former level. 'And I adored the way you switched so easily from one musical style to another. I know talent when I see it, and you Peter my dear have simply oodles of it.'

Before he could respond to this lavish praise, Gloria added: 'Do you have an agent at present?'

'Well, no. Not exactly.'

'In that case I must have a word with mine on your behalf. He has an office in Wardour Street. He may well be interested in you.'

She then checked herself as a wistful expression passed across her face. 'We haven't spoken for quite a while now. It's time I called him again.'

Briefly – so very briefly – there was a look of hurt and vulnerability about her. Pete wisely said nothing.

And then, in a blink, it was gone. Pete even wondered if he had actually seen it at all.

'Of course, one is constantly driven to pastures new,' Gloria explained. 'And one man can only do so much for you, no matter how good he is.'

Seconds later her eye was caught by O for Oscar's former skipper, one of the few attending who had remained in the RAF after the war and made a career out of it.

'You will excuse me now, Peter,' she said. 'I simply must have another word with the Group Captain before he goes to bed.'

Too late the senior officer spotted her coming. His evasive manoeuvre was neatly blocked off.

'Roger, darling!' was all Pete heard before she completely engulfed the man.

***

'How ya doing, Geordie old buddy?' Stafford slurred from his chair.

The big man placed a hand gently on his shoulder. 'Time to go to bed I reckon, Mike.'

'Do you want a hand with the skipper?' Phil Thomas called over. He appeared to be in only slightly better condition than Stafford himself.

'I can manage,' Geordie responded with a grin. 'Just make sure you're all right yourself.'

Anyone who didn't know better would have sworn he hadn't touched a drop all night.

'You're a dag,' Phil told him, wandering unsteadily off in search of a toilet.

It was now just after two o'clock and the bar was virtually deserted. Even the indefatigable Gloria had called it a night and gone to her room, although whether she might have woken Hughie to give him a detailed summary of her evening's conquests was anyone's guess.

'Come on, pal,' Geordie said, his powerful arms effortlessly raising Stafford's twelve and a half stone into an upright position. With the Canadian leaning heavily on him, they made their way up the stairs to the first floor.

There was a short delay while Stafford groped around inside various pockets for his room key. With an exclamation of triumph, he eventually found what he was looking for.

'We had a good time tonight, didn't we, buddy,' he repeated twice while Geordie unlocked the door for him.

'Aye, we did that,' he was assured.

The big man grinned as he eased his friend into a sitting position on the edge of the bed. 'Get your head down and sleep it off,' he said.

Stafford waved an unsteady arm. 'Sure – I'll be fine.'

Geordie's grin grew broader. 'See you in the morning then.'

Leaving Stafford alone, he closed the door gently behind him.

***

Stafford remained sitting absolutely still on the edge of the bed for several minutes after Geordie's departure. Although perfectly aware that he was drunk and should be ready to sleep, his mind would not allow him to.

A deep guilt complex set in. He'd had a good time: far better than ever expected. And that was the problem. Since returning to the party after their talk with the young barman he had barely spared a thought for Jimmy. Had he really reached a point where he was able to forget so easily? That couldn't be right.

Reaching into his jacket, he pulled out the photograph he'd removed from Alan's locker. For several minutes he just stared at the image of his old friend. Then he began to talk. But even to his own ears, what he was saying wasn't making very much sense. This was no good, he decided. Once more he felt inside his pocket, this time producing a pen.

I *will* try to find Alan, he promised himself. That was a solemn pledge to Jimmy. Turning the photograph over, he began writing on the back of it.

It seemed to take forever, but he finally got down what he wanted to say. It was all there. Should his resolve weaken in the morning, he would only need to take a look at this in order to regain his purpose.

Now he could feel the tiredness closing in. He threw off his clothes and was asleep within minutes.

THIRTEEN

For the majority of veterans who were physically capable of making their way down to the dining room in time, breakfast was a muted affair. No one could ever doubt the success of the previous evening, but the difficulties of adapting to post-reunion life were now becoming painfully obvious.

The wives present wore fixed smiles as they regarded the hungover condition of their husbands. They in turn cast envious looks at their unaccompanied comrades, most wishing that they too had attended without their partners in tow. All the alcohol-induced bravado of the previous evening was now sadly missing. No more were they the dominant males re-living their youth and insisting that they would go to bed only when they were good and ready to. In the harsh light of morning it was back to the reality of life as a middle-aged, married man. The look worn by their spouses strongly suggested that they would be reminded of this fact a good number of times throughout the coming day.

Amongst the men, only Geordie appeared to have escaped totally unscathed from the previous evening's excesses. Not only had he devoured his own fried breakfast with his usual gusto, he was now busy helping out others with lesser appetites.

'That's what friends are for,' he grinned, scooping up two rashers of bacon from Phil Thomas' plate.

The Kiwi merely shook his head in wonder.

Stafford was faring little better than Phil. It was only after two aspirins and three cups of black coffee that he felt in any sort of shape to face the day. He lit a cigarette. It tasted foul and was quickly stubbed out.

A glance at his watch produced a groan. It was already well past the arranged time he had promised to ring Alice. Back home it would now be late into the night. She would be waiting anxiously for his call before being able to sleep.

He hurried upstairs to his room where there was another ten-minute delay while his call was booked. At least this gave him some time to reflect.

So much seemed to have happened so quickly. A lot of this he did not plan to trouble Alice with. She worried too much about him anyway. If she imagined that he was under any kind of threat, however remote, she would go out of her mind.

The tone told him that the number was ringing.

'Hello, Mike,' she answered.

He chuckled. 'You knew it was me then.'

'Who else would be calling me at three o'clock in the morning?' she laughed back. 'It's so good to hear your voice. How are things?'

'They're fine. We had a great time last night. All the old gang are here.'

'That's good. But what about …?' She hesitated. 'You know.'

'You were right, honey,' he assured her. 'It's just like you said. Coming back here was exactly what I needed to do. It's hard to believe, but I'm already starting to see things in a whole different way.'

He could picture her smiling as she responded. I'm so glad, Mike. You're not just saying this are you? I've been worried sick in case it didn't work out the way we wanted it to.'

His voice carried the maximum conviction. 'Well you can stop worrying right now. Like I said, I'm fine – top of the world.'

'That's wonderful. So tell me, what are you planning to do with yourself today?'

Her question instantly reminded him of his date with Siggi. Innocent as the arrangement was, he nonetheless felt a sharp pang of guilt.

'Nothing very much. Just taking it easy I guess and recovering from last night.' How he hated lying to her. He felt like a goddamn heel.

'Well make the most of it, you lazy so-and-so,' she laughed.

Her trusting response made him feel even worse. 'I'll try,' he promised. 'Connie is still awake as well. She'd like a quick word with you.'

Glad to get off the subject of his upcoming day, he responded quickly. 'You better put her on then.'

'Hi, Dad,' her young voice shouted excitedly down the line. 'I've never spoken to anyone in England before. Can you hear me okay?'

'I hear you, honey,' he told her.

They talked for well over a minute about trivial things. 'Be sure to come home safely, Dad,' she told him just before handing the phone back to her mother. 'Love you lots.'

The urgency in her voice struck him. She had said something similar just before he'd left Brandon. Although completely unaware of his tormented past, it was almost as if she was sensing that he might get into some kind of trouble while in England. He was still dwelling on this when Alice spoke again.

'When do you think you may be coming back? Have you decided yet?'

He thought of what he hoped to achieve before returning. 'I'm not sure, Alice,' he stalled. 'It could be a little while yet. There are still quite a number of people I'd like to catch up with.'

'Oh...I was hoping we'd see you back home sometime this coming week.' Her disappointment was obvious.

She quickly forced a brighter tone. 'I'm sorry. I'm not being fair, am I? Listen, Mike. You stay over there for as long as you like and have a real good time. I mean, now you've flown all the way to England, it makes sense to get the most out of the trip.'

He did not know what to say. With the problems he was facing, having a good time was the furthest thing from his mind.

'Are you still there?' she asked.

'Yeah, I'm here.'

'I better say goodnight then. It's very late. At least, it is here in Manitoba.'

She waited, hoping for him to say the words. He did not disappoint her.

'Goodnight, Alice. I love you, sweetheart.'

She sighed with contentment. 'I love you too, Mike.'

There was the sound of a kiss being blown down the line followed by a soft click as she hung up.

***

By mid-morning, most of the veterans had either checked out of the hotel or were in the final stages of preparing to. Not a single one departed without making a special point of thanking Doug Short for all his efforts on their behalf and confirming how much they had enjoyed themselves. His avowed *'Never again'* was now totally forgotten.

'Hope to see you again next year,' were his parting words to everyone.

Stafford had provisionally booked himself into the hotel for two more nights, as had Phil Thomas. Doug Short was planning to stay for one more, whilst Geordie, with only a relatively short drive home to Newcastle, said he would hang around with the rest of them until later that evening.

As anticipated, the social event of the morning was undoubtedly Gloria's grand departure. Her emotion charged embraces and barrage of theatrical style kisses left a lingering mark on just about everyone present. Like a true member of the show business fraternity, she remained a larger than life character right up until her final exit: a scene that also involved her especially favoured beneficiary of the previous evening, Pete Cowley.

Already regarded as a bit of an ageing hippie by several of those attending, it transpired that Pete had further lived up to his offbeat image by hitch-hiking his way to Wetherditch, complete with guitar case slung over his shoulder. On hearing of this, Gloria immediately insisted that he travel back home with her and Hughie in their Morris Oxford.

'We live in Southport, Peter darling, so that's not too far from Liverpool anyway. And I'm sure Hughie wouldn't mind one tiny bit in making a small detour for your benefit.'

Hughie merely nodded his agreement. He had remained a grey and virtually anonymous character throughout the weekend. Although never the greatest of extroverts, he now seemed to be doing little more than going through the motions of life. Not once had he opened up to any of his old comrades, and most were left wondering why on earth he had bothered coming at all if that was how he felt. He was last seen behind the wheel of his Morris, driving away with all the reckless enthusiasm of a hearse driver. In total contrast, Gloria, seated beside her husband, waved and blew kisses to everyone through the open car window until completely out of sight. The legacy she left behind was indelible.

After watching this grand departure from the hotel steps, the remaining members of K for King's crew strolled back inside to the reception hall. Mindful of his meeting with Siggi, Stafford cashed thirty pounds worth of his travellers' cheques at the desk. Up until now he had been careful to keep details of this meeting strictly to himself. Now, when he mentioned to the others that he was planning to go out for a large part of the day, Geordie's disappointment was evident.

'I'm meeting up with an old friend for a pub lunch,' Stafford told him. 'You know the place, the White Rose Inn up on the moors. But don't worry. I should be back here by four o'clock at the latest.'

Geordie gave him a lopsided grin. 'I wondered why you were all smartened up. If I didn't know you were a happily married man, I'd start to think you were meeting a woman.' He sniffed the air. 'Aftershave, freshly polished shoes, and a clean shirt. Are you sure you're not up to something?'

His friend's remark was clearly meant only in fun, but it struck Stafford quite forcibly. Even though he'd not been particularly conscious of making any special effort at the time, he now realised that he had indeed gone to more trouble than might be expected given the circumstances. The brand new pair of slacks and very best sports jacket was proof of that. Why should he have taken so much care? Once again he reminded himself that this meeting with Siggi had not been his idea, and was certainly not a date in any real sense of the word.

After making a slightly awkward denial to Geordie's playful accusation, he glanced at his watch. 'It's time I was on my way, guys,' he stated.

'Be good, skipper,' Phil Thomas called after him as he walked through the hotel doors to the car park.

While unlocking the Cresta, the usual addition to Phil's well-worn phrase ran through Stafford's mind. *'And if you can't be good, be careful'*, might be quite appropriate given the circumstances. His words to this highly sensitive German woman would certainly need to be very carefully chosen, and right now he had no idea of what he planned to say to her. Or of how she might react to whatever he did eventually come out with.

***

Siggi had also gone to a fair amount of trouble over her appearance for their meeting. In her case however, it had been quite deliberate. Her freshly washed long dark hair contrasted beautifully with the simple yet attractive white summer dress that she had bought the day before especially for the occasion. Her usual slight touch of make-up, plus a lightweight pink cardigan and stylish shoes completed the picture. She looked much younger than her thirty-eight years and was well aware of the fact.

Astrid felt positively plain as she surveyed her sister. 'You look nice,' she remarked pointedly.

'Do I detect a note of disapproval?' Siggi asked. 'Maybe you think I should have dressed more conservatively for our meeting?'

'Well – now you mention it.'

'I have dressed this way for a very good reason.' Siggi smiled knowingly. 'It is quite possible that Mister Stafford will be feeling apprehensive about our arrangement. In that case, a more severe appearance on my part would only inhibit him further. And as I wish for him to talk honestly and openly, that would not do at all.'

'I see,' Astrid said slowly.

'If on the other hand I can create a relaxed and sociable atmosphere, he will be more inclined to open up to me and speak from the heart. Appearances can say a lot, and mine today says that I am approachable and very willing to listen to what he has to say.'

'It is also telling me that you are attracted to him.' Astrid remarked. 'Don't forget that he is a happily married man. You must remember how fondly he spoke of his wife and daughter during our dinner together?'

Siggi let out a scornful laugh. 'How can you say that? Never have I been seriously attracted to any man in my life. A couple of teenage crushes many years ago perhaps, but nothing more. You can be certain that I have no intention of starting such foolishness with Mister Stafford.' She made a sharp movement with her hand. 'The fact that he is married is of no consequence to me.'

Her sister was on the point of saying something further when Siggi glanced out of the lounge window. A large car was just pulling up outside the house.

'He is here!' she stated. 'And right on time as well.'

Tanya, who had also been watching out of a window from the adjoining room, called out to them.

'I'll answer the door.'

Before either woman could stop her, she was greeting Stafford on the doorstep. Her eyes quickly appraised him. 'Hello. I'm Tanya. Have you come for my Auntie Siggi?'

He smiled. 'I guess I have.'

She returned his smile. 'You better come in then.'

***

Siggi appeared just as he was closing the door behind him. He relaxed a little, noting immediately that there was no visible sign of hostility in her manner. In fact, on the surface at least, she now came across as an altogether far less formidable and demanding character than the one he could recall from their previous encounter. With a sharp stab of guilt, he also realised that she was looking absolutely gorgeous.

He briefly wondered if he should compliment her on the way she looked, but quickly decided against such a move. It wouldn't do for him to get over-familiar at this stage. She could easily take it the wrong way and become offended.

He limited himself to a pleasant greeting. 'Hi there. It's nice to see you again.'

He went on to explain his plan for them to share a pub lunch on the moors. The suggestion seemed to go down well.

Siggi then clapped a hand to her forehead. 'I am so stupid. I have left my handbag upstairs,' she told him. 'Could you please excuse me for just one moment?'

As soon as she disappeared up the steps, Tanya tugged his sleeve. 'Can I ask you something?'

'Sure.'

Her voice dropped to a whisper, forcing him to bend down to catch what she was saying. 'Can I come with you and aunt Siggi? I've never been to a pub before.'

He was on the point of explaining that she was far too young for such places when he remembered the large garden that this particular pub used to boast. Back in the old days it had been unusual for pubs to cater for children in any special way. But at the White Rose Inn they had made a point of doing so, even going so far as to set up a slide and couple of swings at the back to help keep the young ones happily occupied while their parents enjoyed a drink. Apparently, according to his copy of the latest 'North Yorkshire Tourist Guide', these family type facilities still existed. What's more, the Sunday lunch served there was now widely acknowledged as being the best value for money in this part of the county.

He thought a little further. It promised to be a pleasant sunny afternoon, and the young girl would probably enjoy the amusements provided while he and Siggi talked. Also, on a more practical note, having a child with them might easily help to break down any remaining awkwardness between Siggi and himself. In spite of her apparently friendly welcome, she was still a German woman with strong and highly personal reasons to resent his role during the last war.

'We'll ask your aunt when she comes back downstairs,' he said. 'If it's okay with her, then it's okay with me.'

Tanya was delighted. Siggi was immediately accosted on her return.

'Mister Stafford says it's okay if I come with you.'

'Hey, hang on a minute,' he jumped in. 'I said it was okay if your aunt agreed. That's not quite the same thing.'

'Pleeeese,' Tanya implored.

The two adults looked at each other. Stafford shrugged. 'It's up to you.' He went quickly on to explain about the play garden for children and how they would still have the opportunity to talk privately.

Astrid, alerted by her daughter's loud pleading, emerged from the kitchen. 'I've told you before, you can't go,' she scolded Tanya.

But by now the young girl had won over her wavering aunt. 'That's all right,' Siggi said. 'She can come along with us if she wants to.'

Astrid sighed deeply while giving her daughter a reproachful look. 'In that case, just make sure you behave yourself. And don't go getting into any trouble.'

'I won't, mum,' Tanya promised.

***

Stafford had certainly been right about one thing. Tanya's presence did indeed help to break down any initial awkwardness. The youngster kept up a near constant stream of chatter from the rear seat of the car, firing questions at both adults and in the process making general conversation pleasantly easy.

The green and attractive Yorkshire countryside also contributed to Stafford's sense of ease. He loved the rural atmosphere. Some of his happiest childhood memories came from the time spent at Clear Lake in Manitoba, a national park where he and his parents had regularly spent their summer vacations. With traditional log cabins set in the surrounding woods; fascinating wildlife, including chipmunks that would eat food directly from your hand; and the calm waters of the lake to swim in or boat on, every day had been an adventure of some kind.

'How far now?' Tanya asked yet again, breaking into his brief reverie.

'Not far. Just a few miles.'

'How many swings have they got? Did you say there was a slide there as well?'

Siggi laughed. 'She never stops talking, does she?'

As her face lit up, he once again thought how attractive she looked. The atmosphere between them had become so relaxed that it almost felt as if they were on a family outing together. This was a very far cry from what he had anticipated. Good in one respect, but still a touch disturbing. Things were almost too natural.

The road began to rise as they climbed up onto the moors. There was now an altogether more austere look about the countryside. Lush green meadows gave way to an undulating sea of heather. There was a sense of power and history attached to the land here. Stafford could almost see Heathcliff from the classic novel Wuthering Heights striding majestically across the horizon. Even Tanya seemed a little bit awed by her surroundings. With her eyes investigating every part of the landscape, she lapsed into a temporary silence.

The isolated pub came into view.

'Is that it?' the young girl cried out, breaking her silence.

'That's it,' Stafford confirmed.

They arrived to find the place already busy. Stafford's perception of a family outing was further increased when Tanya grabbed hold of his hand and led him eagerly in search of the play area. There was no doubt that the young girl had taken a big shine to him. He too felt drawn, and could see a lot of his own Connie in her when she had been Tanya's age. He briefly wondered what Astrid's husband was like.

It turned out that the play area in the back garden had been much enlarged since he had last seen it. There were now climbing frames, a sand pit, and several new types of ride. In no time at all Tanya was happily making new friends with some of the other children already there.

He and Siggi selected a rustic style table twenty yards away. From here they were close enough to keep an eye on the child, but still have sufficient space for privacy. It was after ordering a round of drinks and roast beef dinners that their eyes met. An unspoken message transmitted itself. It was time to begin the real talk.

Despite this mutual acceptance, neither of them was quite sure how to start the conversation. An awkward silence followed.

Finally, Stafford said gently: 'We don't have to do this, you know. I understand if you've changed your mind.'

'No – no. I want to. I just thought that it would be easier than this to make a beginning.'

'Why don't you tell me about your family?' he suggested.

A sad yet fond smile slowly formed. And then the words began to flow. She spoke first of how her father had been sent to the Russian Front and had died there during the terrible winter in January 1943. This was followed by accounts of the struggle to continue some semblance of normal life as the bombs continued to fall on the devastated city of Berlin. But most of all, she talked about her mother and how close they had always been. A solitary tear ran down her cheek as she recounted her desperate journey back home to Steglitz, only to discover that her surviving parent had also become a victim of the war.

She reached into her small shoulder bag for a tissue, brushing the tear irritably away. 'I am sorry. I promised myself I would not do this.'

To Stafford, there seemed little he could say at this point. He restricted himself to an understanding nod.

'The thing is, Mike, in spite of whatever else you may think, none of my family wanted the Nazis to win. We all hated what they were doing as much as you did.'

She then corrected herself. 'Well, there was an uncle of mine who supported Hitler, but he was the only one.'

It did not escape Stafford's attention that this was the very first time she had addressed him by his Christian name.

'What happened to your uncle?' he asked.

Her mouth set in a firm line. 'He was totally brainwashed. When Germany fell and Hitler shot himself, he decided to take the same way out as his beloved Fuhrer. The shame of losing the war was too great for him.'

'And what about the other members of your family? Obviously I know about Astrid, but what happened to the rest of them?'

'There are few others left alive now. We have some cousins on my father's side trapped in East Germany, but neither Astrid nor myself have heard from them in many years. For all we know, they could be dead.'

It was a sad story. Stafford found himself deeply moved. Instinctively, he reached out to touch her hand. 'I'm sorry to hear that,' he said.

The moment he uttered these words, they seemed to stick in his throat. For a second or two he feared that she would come back with a biting response. And who could blame her? She must surely still see him as one of those responsible for inflicting much of the misery. Sorry must sound like the worst kind of platitude.

But if such a stinging reaction had crossed her mind, she managed to hide it well. It quickly became clear that, whatever Siggi's purpose in meeting him, she had certainly not come to drag up old recriminations. This in itself was an enormous relief.

He suddenly became aware that his hand was still resting on hers. Embarrassed, he moved it away, but there was no trace of annoyance on her part. She simply gave him a wistful look.

Then she became brisk.

'And now I want to hear your story,' she told him. 'You also have memories of the war that cause you pain. I'm right, am I not?'

'Yes.' His voice was very soft.

'I knew it! Please tell me. Did it perhaps happen during one of your air raids?'

The full irony of their situation was forced home to him. 'Yes. The very same one that you lost your mother in. March the twenty-fourth, nineteen forty-four.'

She merely nodded. 'It is fate. Everything about our meeting is fate.'

Their roles were now reversed. Stafford was the one struggling to find the right words and Siggi becoming the prompter.

'Somebody died?'

'My best friend. But he didn't die because of anything the Germans did. At least, not in a direct way.'

She frowned. 'So who was responsible then?'

Up until a couple of days ago he would have unhesitatingly heaped the blame for Jimmy's death entirely on himself. But since his arrival back in Yorkshire, things were becoming increasingly blurred. Something strange was happening to his mind. Had he been playing the martyr all these years for something that, in truth, had always been out of his control? Perhaps if he told Siggi the story exactly as it happened, with no bias whatsoever, her spontaneous reaction might just spell out the final truth of the matter. In many ways she was better qualified than anyone he knew of to give an honest opinion.

He lit a cigarette, his first since stubbing out the one he'd failed to enjoy at breakfast time. This time it tasted a whole lot better.

Hesitantly at first, he began to talk.

***

Shortly after Stafford's Cresta arrived at the White Rose, a Lambretta scooter followed them into the car park.

There had been a few times when Alan thought he might have lost touch with their car. His scooter lacked the speed of the big Vauxhall, especially on some of the steep hills they encountered. But he had been lucky. As he'd rounded a fairly sharp bend he just caught a glimpse of them in the distance turning into the pub. A couple of seconds later and he would have missed the manoeuvre completely.

From where he was now parked he had a good view of the pub's rear garden, enabling him to keep a careful watch on Stafford and the woman. Sitting astride his machine, he took in everything that was going on. He noted the young girl come briefly over to their table to claim her drink before returning to join the other children in the play area. After that, it soon became clear that the two adults were involved in some very deep kind of conversation. Their attention to each other barely wavered, and they gave every impression of planning to be here for some time. There was little Alan could do but wait.

Exactly what he was waiting for wasn't all that clear. A chance to get his revenge - yes, of course. But where and when that chance might turn up remained to be seen. Perhaps the right opportunity wouldn't come along at all today. But if it did, he was determined to seize it.

There was one thing he was absolutely certain of. He was not going to take a chance on ending up in prison. A powerful gut feeling told him that, some time before Stafford returned to Canada, fate would provide him with a risk-free opportunity to even things up. That was surely the justice he was entitled to after waiting for all these years.

Alan's eyes narrowed as he continued watching. It wouldn't have been quite so bad if Stafford had cared enough to meet up with him on Friday evening. He knew the bastard had got his message because he'd watched the receptionist hand it to him. But the bloke obviously didn't give a shit, and that confirmed everything he'd ever been told.

Up until then he might just have been prepared to think that the stories he'd got from his mother were a bit exaggerated. But not any longer. Some weird sense of duty to the father he'd never known had forced him to offer Stafford the benefit of the doubt and a chance to explain. But that offer had been chucked back in his face. Now the bastard deserved everything that was coming.

Alan climbed off his scooter and wandered over to a seat by some trees. From here he could still see everything, and had the advantage of looking a lot less conspicuous. The young girl playing with the other kids caught his eye again. Could she be the key? He wondered who she was and what she meant to Stafford.

The idea of maybe making use of the girl was quickly dismissed. She looked far too nice to risk harming. The truth was, he had always wanted a little brother or sister of his own - someone who would look up to him and be grateful for the way he protected them. But just like everything else in this bloody life, that too had been taken away from him. Just the same as having a proper dad had been.

His gaze returned to Stafford: the cause of all his problems. A man who had claimed to be his father's best friend, but who couldn't even spare a few minutes of his time to explain the truth of how he died. That could only mean he had no real defence to offer. He was as guilty as his mother had always said he was.

He thought of her back down in London. Why had the stupid cow warned Stafford about him coming up here? It made no sense. But it must have been her who had tipped him off. No one else knew where he was, or what he was planning. No one apart from Graham Walker, and he wouldn't have dared say a word.

So why had his mother done it?

A fresh thought then sprang into Alan's mind, bringing with it a spurt of vicious anger. Maybe she actually wanted him to get caught and locked up again? Now it was starting to make sense. She'd done it to him once before and got him sent away to that bloody prison they called a school. Well he wasn't going back anywhere like that again. She could forget any idea of that. His anger grew. If you couldn't trust your own mother to do what's right for you, who the hell *could* you trust?

He forced her from his mind. There would be time to have all that out with her later on. Right now, he needed to concentrate on Stafford.

Alan thought of his newly acquired weapon and smiled. One way or the other, sometime very soon, Stafford was at last going to get everything he deserved.

FOURTEEN

For the last hour Geordie had spent his time strolling around the hotel grounds with the few other remaining veterans, most of whom were in much need of the gentle exercise and fresh air to help clear their muddled heads. Not so the big man. It was now one o'clock and he was thirsty. Just a couple of quick ones, he told himself, mindful that he would be driving home to Newcastle later that day.

His suggestion to the others that they should join him was greeted largely with looks of disbelief or plain nausea. Only Phil Thomas, now recovering a little and determined to uphold Kiwi honour, went along with the idea.

To Geordie's exasperation, they found the main bar closed. It appeared that the clean-up operation after last night's dinner was taking longer than anticipated.

Because of this prolonged closure, the small cocktail bar was once again busy. Geordie noticed immediately that, instead of Graham Walker, there was now a much older barman on duty. Several customers were waiting to be served, making it a lengthy wait before the man worked his way around to himself and Phil.

'Where's the other barman today?' Geordie asked as their drinks were finally served. 'Is it his day off?'

Walker's replacement raised his eyes to the ceiling. 'I wish I knew. I'm having to work his shift for him.'

'You mean he should be working here right now?'

'That's exactly what I mean. And I'm not happy about it, I can tell you. I was planning on going out this lunchtime.'

'Someone must know where he is,' Geordie pressed.

'I don't know about that. All I know is that I've been dragged in here to do a shift that isn't mine. Blooming kids! You can't rely on them.'

He was still muttering as he moved away to serve the next customer.

Geordie took a large swallow from his glass before turning to Phil. 'Give me a couple of minutes, pal. There's something I want to check out.'

'Hey, you're not giving up already, are you?' the Kiwi taunted. 'If you can't finish your drink, just say so.'

But Geordie was already striding toward the door.

Once outside the hotel he headed straight for the staff quarters. Two youths hanging around in the corridor there gave him a curious glance as he strode past them and onwards into Walker's room. Curious they might have been, but neither one questioned what he might want. One look at the big man's determined expression was enough to deter any enquiries.

It took only a few moments to confirm what Geordie suspected. Walker's locker was now as empty as the other one inside the dingy room. It looked as if he had followed Alan's example and also skipped town.

The big man strolled thoughtfully back to the hotel. Did this second disappearance mean anything much? Probably not, he decided. The kid had looked pretty shaken up by the time they'd finished grilling him last night. He was unlikely to relish the prospect of any further questioning, particularly if he thought the police might be getting involved. Just like Alan, Walker must also have a bit of a record to have ended up in the same approved school. It wasn't such a big surprise that he'd decided to follow his friend's example.

Geordie nodded slowly. This appeared to be the logical answer. All the same, he could not shake off a slight feeling of uneasiness. He considered telephoning the White Rose Inn and attempting to inform Stafford of this new development. Only after a few moments of thought did he finally decide against such a move. He could end up looking pretty foolish. Mike would only draw the same conclusion as himself. Anyhow, it didn't seem fair to interrupt the skipper's lunch date with his mysterious friend. Especially after he'd got himself all dressed up for the occasion.

Geordie smiled at this final thought and quickened his pace. He had an unfinished pint to attend to.

***

The big man was at least half right in his assumptions. Graham Walker *had* left Wetherditch because he was frightened. But the reason for his alarm was not quite what Geordie imagined.

Alan was going to do something completely crazy: Walker was now certain of that. And if the shit was going to hit the fan, he had no intention of being anywhere near Wetherditch to cop some of it. These days, the mad bastard was getting just too dangerous to know. Bloody hell, unlike Alan, he'd already had his eighteenth birthday several weeks ago. And at that age they could bloody well hang you for murder, even if you didn't actually do anything yourself. You could get the rope just for being with the person who did do the killing. Although only a kid at the time, he could well remember everyone in the East End talking about that kind of stuff when they'd hung Derek Bentley back in the early 1950s. And there was no guarantee that Alan wouldn't go so far as murder either. The state he worked himself into sometimes, he was crazy enough to do anything.

As he left the city of Sheffield behind him, Walker opened up the throttle of his 250cc BSA motorcycle. He would head for the south coast, Brighton maybe, and lose himself down there for a while. Getting a job in one of the big hotels should be easy at this time of year.

***

Siggi listened attentively as Stafford recounted the whole painful story. Never before had he spoken so graphically about that fateful mission, not even during his long discussions with Alice. When talking with her, the details had come out little by little over a long period of time. And even then some of the more alarming aspects of life in those heavy bombers had been conveniently omitted.

Not so now. Every tiny detail of the mission was re-lived in stark reality. Only once during the telling did Siggi display any outward sign of emotion. When he spoke of the moment their bombs were released over Berlin, her face visibly tightened. What was going on in her head, he couldn't even guess at. But she made no comment and the tension thankfully soon appeared to pass.

By the time he had finished Stafford was mentally drained. It was all there, laid out bare before her. What would her reaction be now? He searched her face, looking for signs of condemnation.

It was an eerie sensation for him. Here he was seeking absolution from a near total stranger on a matter of intense personal anguish. He wondered if this was how Catholics felt when confessing their sins to a priest.

Siggi remained silent and in thought for an agonizingly long time. Then, just when she seemed to be on the point of delivering her verdict, the waiter arrived with their meals. Stafford silently cursed. There was nothing he could do for the present. Whatever she was about to say was now stifled by the outsider's presence.

'We'll finish this later,' she said as the man set down the plates.

Her eyes then darted over toward Tanya. She summoned the girl with a wave of her hand before turning back to Stafford.

'Yes, later,' she promised.

***

By the time they had finished eating it was approaching two o'clock. Throughout the meal, as before during the drive out to the pub, it was Tanya who did most of the talking. With many other children Stafford might have found this constant chatter becoming a touch irritating after a while, but Siggi's niece had a cheeky charm and energy about her that was hard to resist.

The waiter approached their table with the bill.

'I will pay this,' Siggi told the man. 'Just wait one moment please.' She reached for her handbag, waving aside Stafford's protests. 'I insist,' she stated. 'It is my turn, remember?'

Stafford could see from the determined look on her face that it would be a waste of time protesting. While Siggi searched through the variety of unfamiliar coins inside her purse for the correct money, Tanya tugged at his arm.

'Are we leaving now?' the young girl asked.

'It looks like it,' he told her.

'We don't have to go home yet, do we?'

'I hope not.'

That was true. Still nervously waiting for Siggi's response, he needed to hear what she had to say before they set off on the drive back to Wetherditch.

He caught her eye just as she was passing over the last of her coins to the waiter. 'How do you fancy a walk on the moor before we head home?' he suggested. 'It's a nice day, and I'm sure Tanya will enjoy the chance to run around for a bit.'

Just as he'd anticipated, the young girl was instantly enthusiastic. Siggi also agreed. She seemed to sense quickly enough what was on his mind.

With the bill settled, they returned to the car. After only a few minutes of driving, Stafford pulled the Cresta over onto the side of the road.

'This looks like a good spot,' he said.

Once out of the car, the rugged wildness of their surroundings became even more apparent. Mile after mile of rolling hills stretched as far as the eye could see. Only the occasional cluster of trees or large rocks scattered randomly about broke an otherwise never-ending tangle of heather, bracken and grass. The purple flowers of the heather, although not yet in full bloom, were sufficiently developed to lend a small variety of colour to an otherwise almost unbroken carpet of dark green.

It was obvious that many others before them had stopped at this same point to stretch their legs and sample the unique atmosphere of the North Yorkshire Moors. A well-trodden track beginning not far from the road edge led directly out across the moorland, although exactly how far it continued for was impossible to tell from where they were standing. The snaking trail was soon lost from sight in the undulating terrain.

'Don't go too far in front,' Siggi told Tanya as the young girl skipped ahead of them.

The sun was warm and there was a pleasant light breeze. They wandered on for several minutes making nothing but small talk. Although eager to complete their earlier conversation, Stafford had no wish to appear over-anxious in re-introducing the topic.

After encountering yet another gentle slope, he could see that although the track veered off to the right, Tanya had moved across in the opposite direction to where a number of large, prehistoric looking stones were strewn about the ground. It was a kind of Stonehenge in miniature.

'Don't go any further,' Siggi called out to her. 'Wait for us there.'

The girl waved in response and selected a long, flat stone to sit on.

Whatever their purpose, the clustered stones had obviously been there for a great number of years. Heather and grass sprouted freely between every available gap, while large patches of furry moss grew on many of the surfaces.

'I think you have a good idea,' Siggi smiled at Tanya after catching up. Sitting down beside the girl, she removed her fashionable shoes with a sigh. 'That is better. These are not the very best for walking in such places.'

Stafford grinned apologetically. 'I'm sorry. I should have realised.'

Tanya, restless as ever, jumped up. 'Do you mind if I look around for a while, auntie Siggi? I promise I won't go very far.'

This was exactly what Stafford had been hoping for. He looked at Siggi.

She caught his glance and flashed a brief smile of understanding.

'Please be careful then,' she told her niece.

'I will,' a happy Tanya called out while skipping away.

Both of them watched her in silence for a short time. The girl, already lost in the world of the young, moved eagerly about seeking new things of interest.

It was during this lull that the sound of approaching aircraft first reached them. Within just a few seconds it became a huge roar as a trio of RAF jet fighters – possibly those super-fast new Lightnings, Stafford considered – raced directly overhead. His eyes tracked the aircraft until they had faded just as rapidly into the opposite direction.

'They must be out training from one of the stations close by,' he remarked awkwardly.

He sat down beside Siggi feeling a shade uncomfortable. It was hardly a perfect moment for the RAF to be staging a fly-past.

As if prodded into speech by the aerial display, Siggi got down to business. 'So, we can talk at last.' She looked him directly in the eye. 'You wish to know if I consider you to be of blame for your friend's death? That is the truth of it – yes?'

Her forthright manner threw Stafford. At no point had he presented such a question to her. At least, not directly. Yes, he longed to know her true feelings on the matter. Suddenly, it was more important than ever for him to discover what she thought. But he'd never imagined she would be quite so blunt about it as this.

She appeared to read his thoughts. Her approach changed.

She smiled gently. 'It is strange, Mike, but I feel I know you very well. We both agree that we were destined to meet and that we are here to help each other. After listening to your story, perhaps I can now provide you with some of that help.'

She paused briefly before continuing. 'I am not one of those who was with you on your plane, nor am I your close family seeking to spare your feelings with soft words. But as we both know, I too have painful and bitter memories from that night that refuse to die. Therefore, in a way, maybe I can be both objective *and* subjective.'

It was true. There was an almost reassuring logic to her reasoning. No one could possibly be better qualified to pass an honest opinion. But Stafford was far too tense to return Siggi's smile. Far too apprehensive of what she might have to say next.

'So please, carry on,' he said.

In the blink of an eye she reverted to her forthright former self. Her first words were not at all what he wanted to hear.

'You ordered your friend to jump, and he died because of that order.'

He wasn't sure if this remark was being put to him as a question or a statement. Not that it made much difference. Either way, his response was still going to be the same.

'That's how it was. No doubt about it.'

'And because of this you have carried the guilt with you for eighteen years?'

This time it was definitely a question. His voice was quiet. 'I guess so.'

She shook her head slowly several times, as if in deep sadness. 'How can an intelligent man like yourself be so very stupid? You made an honest decision: one designed to possibly save a number of lives, not just your friend Jimmy. Then, because something that is completely beyond your control goes wrong, you rush to place all the blame on yourself.'

Apart from the rather blunt accusation of being stupid, this was not a particularly new angle being put to him. Similar words had been said several times before.

'Yes, but ...' he began.

She stopped him with a sharp movement of the hand. 'Yes but nothing. What about the person responsible for packing your friend's parachute? If there is any blame to share out, do you not think they deserve to take a large part of it? It seems to me that they could not have done their job very well. Which makes it their mistake that was the direct cause of your friend Jimmy's death. Please, just think about that for a short while.'

Stafford was shocked. This was not a line of thought he had cared to even consider before. 'But you can't blame the girls who packed our chutes,' he protested. 'We knew every one of them personally. The safety of aircrews was always the most important thing in the world to them.' He shook his head. 'No, any fault was more likely to be with the materials the chute was made of, not the way it was packed.'

'If so, then who was responsible for checking the quality of those materials? Somebody must have been.'

'How the heck would I know? You could carry on blaming people all the way down the line.'

'Exactly! So what makes you and your actions any more significant than those of all of these other people? You must accept that, one way or another, the parachute was faulty long before you even took off that night. And if your plane had not been damaged, someone else would have used that same parachute on another day and died instead of Jimmy.'

She gave a hollow laugh. 'While we are talking about it, why do we not blame the fighter pilot who attacked you as well? If he had not fired his guns at your plane then there would have been no need for anyone to jump out. So there! It was the Germans at fault all the time, you see. You have been making a martyr of yourself all these years for nothing.'

She glared at him, as if defying him to contradict her.

Taken aback by the sheer forcefulness of her argument, Stafford felt incapable of making an immediate response. She was right when she had referred to *'soft words'* from those close to him. Everyone had always handled the subject with kid gloves. He hadn't asked or expected them to act this way, but their concern for him invariably made tactfulness the keyword.

The contrast with Siggi's approach was a revelation. But was it sufficient to cut through where those others had failed? He wasn't yet sure. There was so much new to consider.

He was still reflecting on her words when Siggi jumped to her feet in alarm.

'Tanya!' she cried out. 'Where is she?'

***

After the jets had passed over, Tanya glanced in the adult's direction. It looked as if her aunt was once again in deep conversation with Mister Stafford. Briefly, she wondered what they were talking about.

A movement to her right then caught the corner of her eye. Something brown and furry scuttled through the heather. A rabbit perhaps? The prospect of seeing one of these in its natural surroundings filled her with joy. Her eyes strained to catch another glimpse. Yes, there was some more movement about twenty yards away. But before her eyes could focus properly on the fast moving bundle of fur, it disappeared into a small hole set in the hillside.

It was only when Tanya moved up close to the hole that she realised it was far bigger than she'd imagined. Thick layers of straggling grass, weeds and heather had grown over what was in fact quite a large opening. An opening that was certainly big enough for her to clamber through.

Dropping to her knees, Tanya peered inside. It was dark, and there was a mouldy kind of smell that she did not like very much. She wrinkled her nose before pulling aside some more of the tangled foliage obscuring the way in. The extra daylight now shining through showed her that this was much more than just a rabbit hole she had found. It was more like a tunnel that seemed to go back for quite a long way. She glanced across at the two adults. They were still talking and paying her little attention.

Tanya's curiosity finally got the better of her. There wasn't any harm in her having a quick peek inside, she told herself. It looked as if there was enough room for her to fully stand up once through the opening, and she wouldn't go on very far.

Memories of the story 'Alice in Wonderland' that she had finished reading only a few weeks ago began to form. In an exciting kind of way she was now copying Alice's adventure. If only the rabbit she was following had been a white one, it would have been almost exactly the same. She took a tentative step into the hole. Was she really going to find something strange and enchanting in here?

She paused after only a few paces. The way ahead was looking very dark. Also, she could feel the ground starting to dip sharply away from her. It was time to go back. There was no adventure to be had in this nasty place after all.

A small scratching sound made her pause. Was this her rabbit? She strained her eyes into the gloom ahead. Yes, she could make out something now. The shape then scuttled forward a short distance, allowing her to see it much better.

Tanya gasped with horror. This was no cuddly rabbit but a ferocious looking rat. It was huge, easily the size of a rabbit, but nothing else was the same. The creature's eyes were shining brightly in the gloom, staring wickedly at her.

She wanted to scream and cry out for help, but fear was stopping her. A loud noise might make the rat even angrier than he already looked. She remained frozen to the spot while the thing circled slowly around her, as if to block off her way out of the tunnel. She turned to face it and the creature darted forward a few small paces, baring its teeth and making a terrifying hissing sound.

Sheer terror jerked Tanya back into movement. She must get further away from this horrible thing. With no thought in her head for anything but this, she scrambled desperately backwards a few paces. Here, the ground began sloping down even more sharply. In her haste, her foot slipped. Then her leg collapsed and she tumbled over completely. Carried on by her own momentum, Tanya continued rolling down the incline. Just before screaming, she imagined that she could hear Auntie Siggi calling out her name.

With tears streaming down her face, she plunged ever deeper into total darkness.

FIFTEEN

The barman standing in for Graham Walker picked up a couple of empty glasses from the counter. 'Time gentleman please,' he called.

He moved to the end of the bar close to where Geordie and Phil were positioned. Still brooding over his lost lunchtime, he set about rinsing the glasses in a small sink beneath the bar.

Phil grinned at the man's obvious bad grace. 'I'd say he's not a happy guy,' he whispered to Geordie.

Despite the softness of his remark, the barman still picked it up. He glanced at the two men. 'I'm not. And Graham Walker will be unhappy as well when I get hold of him.'

'You can forget about that,' Geordie responded. 'He's packed his bags and gone back to London, just like his mate.'

The glass washing ceased as this information was considered. 'Ah well, Walker's no big loss.' The barman then frowned. 'But that mate of his you're talking about is still around. I saw him here just this morning.'

Geordie's heart gave a small jolt. 'You can't have,' he said.

'Well, I think it was him.' The barman was now looking a little less certain. 'I only caught a quick glimpse, but that kid is the only one I know of working here who rides around on a blue Lambretta scooter. Noisy flipping things they are.'

'What time did you see him?' Geordie demanded. He leaned across the counter, at the same time slapping a hand hard down on the surface.

Startled by this sharp reaction, the man took an involuntary pace backwards. 'I was just on my way in here. It must have been around quarter to twelve I suppose.'

He hesitated before adding: 'I passed that friend of yours. You know, the Canadian gentleman. He was driving out of the main gate around the same time. The scooter followed just behind him.'

'Bloody hell!'

Without adding anything more to his exclamation of anger, Geordie raced from the bar, leaving both Phil and the barman looking totally bemused.

***

'Tanya!'

Siggi's eyes frantically scanned the landscape as she called out the young girl's name for a second time.

'Where is she, Mike? Why is she not answering?'

Stafford could see that the woman was making a huge effort to control her rising panic. He placed a reassuring hand on her shoulder.

'Take it easy. She can't be very far away. I saw her no more than a couple of minutes ago.'

'So where is she then? She cannot have just vanished.'

Siggi called out again. The moor swallowed up the sound of her voice and offered nothing in return.

'Come on,' Stafford told her, pointing to a spot a short distance ahead. 'That's roughly where I saw her last. We'll start looking over there.'

With no better idea to offer, Siggi followed him.

'What now?' she demanded as they surveyed the deserted area.

'We'll split up. You look in that direction, I'll try this way.'

'Look for what?' Already there was growing despair in Siggi's voice. She swept her arm around in a wide arc. 'If Tanya was close to here then surely we would be able to see her?'

'Listen,' Stafford said patiently. 'She *has* to be somewhere pretty close by. There's no time for her to have gone very far.' He frowned. 'You don't think she's hiding somewhere and playing games with us do you?'

Siggi glared at him. 'Of course not. She knows better than to worry me like that.'

'In that case, I reckon she's most likely fallen down somewhere and hurt herself. It would be hard to spot her in some of this thick undergrowth.'

Although hugely agitated, the logic of this got through to Siggi. Making an enormous effort to steady herself, she began searching the area, moving in a zig-zag fashion through the heather while constantly calling out the girl's name.

Stafford set off in similar style in the opposite direction. For Siggi's sake, he was trying not to let his concern show too much. The kid had probably tripped over and hit her head on something hard. That was the only reason he could imagine for her not answering their calls. He prayed that she was not badly hurt.

It did not take long for him to spot the entrance to the tunnel. There were clear signs of the overgrowth obscuring the hole having recently been pulled aside. Stafford bent down by the opening and peered into the gloom. Although unable to see very far inside, he sensed that this was only a small beginning to a significantly large excavation. He called out the girl's name into the darkness, the slight echo coming back to him as good as confirming this supposition.

This time, he did receive a response. 'I'm down here, Mister Stafford,' a tiny sobbing voice drifted back to him almost immediately. It sounded like it was coming from quite a long way inside.

He let out a huge sigh of relief. 'Are you hurt?' he asked.

'I've twisted my ankle and I can't walk properly.'

The distress in the young girl's voice tugged at his heart as she continued: 'It's dark, and there's a horrible big rat somewhere. I'm frightened. Please come and get me out of here quickly.'

His first reaction was to press forward immediately and hope to somehow find her in the darkness by the sound of her voice. Then he remembered the torch he had in the car. It would be crazy to go rushing inside this tunnel without a light, and it would take only a few moments for him to get one.

'Can you hold on for just a couple more minutes while I fetch a flashlight?' he called back.

Tanya did her best to sound brave. 'Alright, but please don't be very long.'

He turned away from the tunnel and saw Siggi rushing over toward him, her little shoulder bag slipping down over her arm in her haste to discover exactly what it was that had captured his attention.

'Have you found her?' she gasped, almost totally out of breath. 'Is she in there? Is she safe?'

Without waiting for a reply, she tried to step past him.

He moved to restrain her. 'Take it easy. Tanya's safe. She's twisted her ankle, that's all. But you can't go in there yet; it's too dark. I'm going to fetch a flashlight from the car. Once I've got that, we'll have her safely out in no time.'

Siggi seemed to go limp with relief. He dropped the arm that was restraining her. 'Don't move from this spot until I get back,' he instructed. 'The kid's a little bit frightened, so talk to her. Let her know that you're still here for her while I'm gone.'

He set off as rapidly as the bumpy terrain would allow, covering the five hundred yards back to the car far faster than he would have thought possible. Breathing heavily from his run, he unlocked the driver's door.

Fool, he thought as he found himself having to stretch right across in an almost horizontal position to reach the glove box on the far side. If he hadn't been in such a damn hurry he would have thought to open the passenger door instead. To make matters worse, the catch on the compartment was stiff, forcing him to shake it several times before it yielded. Finally grasping hold of the torch, he headed back across the moor.

In his haste to leave the car, he failed to notice the wallet that had slid free from the inside pocket of his jacket. It now rested on the floor directly in front of the passenger seat.

***

Siggi fully intended to do exactly as Stafford had instructed and stay where she was. One look into the suffocating gloom of the tunnel convinced her that this was the very last place on earth she would wish to venture inside.

Eighteen years had passed since the bombs had fallen on Berlin, but the claustrophobia and terrible fear of being buried alive remained all too real for her. Even while she was still in the open air and full glare of daylight, the dark walls of the interior seemed to be reaching out in an attempt to close in around her. The black hole was like the mouth of some monstrous vacuum cleaner seeking to suck her bodily into a world full of her very worst nightmares.

She called out to Tanya in a voice that, despite all her efforts to control it, shook badly.

'I'm here, darling. Don't worry, we will come to get you out very soon.'

***

Tanya was sitting on hard rough ground, her back resting against what she imagined to be the side of the tunnel. The darkness was total. She had no idea of what her immediate surroundings were like, or of how much room there was for someone to come inside to rescue her. Her ankle was throbbing with pain and she could already feel it swelling up over the top of her shoe.

She chewed on her bottom lip, fighting hard against her fears. She was just about to reply to aunt Siggi when she felt something brush against her legs. It could only be that horrible rat again. It was too much for her.

She let out a terrified scream.

***

Tanya's scream reverberated down the tunnel, striking Siggi full in the face. She had no idea what might have caused her niece to cry out in such a frantic way. The only thought instantly rushing through her head was that she must do something to help the little girl.

Stafford had only just left her, so it would probably be several minutes before he returned. Siggi knew for certain that she couldn't wait that long for him. Tanya needed someone beside her immediately. All thoughts of her personal fears had to be smothered in the face of this emergency.

'I'm coming, darling,' she called out, hesitating only briefly before bending low and forcing herself into the gloom.

The first few yards were not so bad. The tunnel height quickly increased, but so too did the darkness, and with it, all of Siggi's deep-rooted demons. 'Go away!' she told them savagely under her breath. For Tanya's sake, she was determined to fight her fear with everything she had. She slowed to a cautious walk, her fingers groping for the side wall of the tunnel. Using this as a guide for further progress, she drove herself on.

She took yet another blind step forward and was horrified to find no ground there for her foot to land on. Thrown completely off-balance by the unexpectedness of the steep incline, Siggi lurched forward, stumbling ever deeper underground. Her feet were running away with her as she struggled to prevent herself from falling over completely. There was nothing but total darkness ahead. Her every instinct was to cry out loud in terror. She clamped her teeth hard together in an effort to contain the cry. Tanya must not realise – not for one single second – that she too was terrified. She tensed, preparing herself for the painful crash to the ground that must surely be coming any second now.

But suddenly the way ahead became level once again. Her momentum slowed and her balance was restored. Breathing heavily, she muttered a quick prayer of thanks to have escaped serious injury. Then her right foot pressed down hard onto a sharp pointed stone. The initial pain was intense, and this time a small cry did slip out. Only now did Siggi become aware that, aside from the already badly torn nylons she was wearing, her feet were still bare. So great had been her concern since Tanya's disappearance, the lack of shoes had not even crossed her mind until now. Even so, she could not allow the discomfort to distract her any further.

She gritted her teeth for a second or two before calling out. 'Talk to me again, Tanya. Let me know where you are.'

'I'm over here,' the soulful reply carried back.

Her voice sounded quite close. But which direction was it coming from? Since her stumble, and in total darkness herself, Siggi felt completely disorientated. Her hands reached out, searching for the hard comfort of the guiding wall. But the wall wasn't there any longer. At least, it wasn't where it should be. Panic was rising sickeningly close to the surface, threatening to gain the upper hand.

She fought back the nausea. Tanya must not get the slightest hint of her fright. She *must* keep her head. With a rush of relief her groping hands finally brushed against a solid surface. She moved in close to the wall, almost hugging it with relief.

Steady now, she told herself. Just take one careful step at a time. Tanya can't be very far ahead.

She had moved just a few tentative paces further along when, from somewhere just above, a light began shining directly into her face, dazzling her with its brilliance. She shut her eyes to keep out the stinging rays. Then she heard Stafford speaking her name.

Only after opening her eyes once again did she realise her mistake. Somehow she had lost her sense of direction. For the last few paces she had actually been heading away from Tanya and back toward the tunnel entrance. Her relief at seeing Stafford was tempered by a feeling of complete inadequacy. How on earth could she have become so confused?

He placed a comforting arm around her shoulder. 'Are you okay?' he asked. There was no reproach in his voice for her having been so stupid. His presence immediately gave her strength.

'Yes, I'm all right. But Tanya. She screamed with fright and I ...'

'So let's go get her then.' His understanding tone said that no further explanations were necessary. For both of them, saving Tanya was the only thing that mattered at present.

The torchlight showed Siggi that the shaft here was around six feet wide and much the same in height. This allowed her several inches of headroom, but he was being forced to lower his head slightly. A few rotting timbers lining the walls and roof were scattered about, but they looked far from convincing.

The powerful torch beam swung forward, and almost immediately picked out the terrified girl about twenty yards further ahead. Tanya's tear-stained face regarded them both with a mixture of pain, uncertainty and relief as they approached.

'I'm so sorry,' she began. 'I didn't mean to --'

Siggi dropped to her knees and threw her arms around the child. 'Thank God,' she breathed, cutting the apology short.

Stafford also knelt down, shining the beam on Tanya's injured ankle. It was badly swollen. She gasped with pain as he tenderly made an examination of the damage.

'What is this horrible place?' Siggi asked. Her eyes darted nervously about their surroundings.

'It must be an old mineshaft,' Stafford told her. 'Probably nothing more than a small exploratory tunnel from the last century that's been completely forgotten about.'

'A coal mine?'

'No – iron ore. A hundred years ago iron was big business around here. Then the seams ran out. They've all been pretty much abandoned since the twenties.'

'And dangerous places like this are just left open for innocent children to wander into,' Siggi exploded, her raised voice sounding louder than ever in the confined space. 'A person could die down here, and no one would ever know.'

She hugged Tanya tighter than ever.

'Come on, let's get out of here,' Stafford told them.

He handed Siggi the torch before scooping Tanya up into his arms. She was light and presented no problem. Through her pain the young girl even managed to give him a tiny smile.

'This should get you off school for a few days, young lady,' he grinned in an effort to lighten the atmosphere.

Siggi led the way, constantly shining the torch ahead to see where she was going and then back for Stafford to follow.

A small glimmer of light from the tunnel entrance was just beginning to show ahead when the sounds of the returning RAF jets reached them. Siggi's hand went to her mouth and she stopped dead in her tracks. The noise reached a crescendo as the aircraft passed directly overhead. But this time it was not just the screaming jet engines. This time they had something more to deliver.

Like angry claps of thunder, the sonic booms reverberated down from the sky. With her free hand now covering her eyes, Siggi began to shake. A small part of her brain was telling her the true reason for these explosions of sound, but that did not matter. For her, the similarity was just too frightening to bear. All the terrible memories from those countless grim hours spent sheltering underground as bombs rained down all over Berlin came rushing back to her – vivid in detail.

'No – no – no,' she murmured over and over.

Even after the sound of the jets had faded away, she still remained rooted to the spot. Her eyes met with Stafford's and she could see he understood the mental hell she was going through. Tanya too, was for the moment awed into silence.

The hush was broken by a creaking sound from overhead. Seconds later a trickle of earth and tiny stones showered down on Siggi's head. They ran through her hair before settling ominously on the ground by her feet.

The effect on her was electrifying. She screamed: a frantic release of all the pent-up dread that had filled her ever since entering this hellish place. Wildly she brushed at her hair to remove any lingering trace of the debris, while at the same time furiously shaking her head.

It was as if her scream added to the impetus of the roof fall. A huge section of sandstone and shale on the roof closer to the exit began to groan and shift. It hovered there for several moments, defying anyone to dare pass beneath it. Then the entire mass came crashing down, all but blocking their only route to freedom. A thick, choking cloud of dust rushed back down the tunnel toward them.

There was a lot more yet to fall, that much was obvious. And Siggi, petrified with fear, knew that she was standing directly in the firing line.

***

Sheer terror had rooted Siggi to the spot. Stafford saw this in a single glance. He took a few rapid paces back down the tunnel before placing Tanya gently on to the ground.

'I know it's going to hurt, but you've got to get yourself further inside as fast as you can,' he told the little girl. 'I won't leave you alone, I promise.'

With amazing maturity, the youngster began doing exactly as instructed. 'Save Aunt Siggi,' she implored while limping along as best she could.

Stafford returned and snatched the torch from Siggi's hand. With one arm around her waist he tried to hustle her back along the shaft. But her feet were still barely moving. Another cracking sound above them was followed by more loose stuff sprinkling down on to their heads.

'Move it,' he shouted in Siggi's ear. 'Do you want to be buried alive?'

As he'd intended, his words went straight to the heart of her greatest nightmare, shattering her trance. In an instant her eyes lost their glazed look. Her feet began to match his own rapid pace.

They caught up with Tanya. Siggi reached down to touch the girl but Stafford pushed her on. 'Keep moving,' he instructed. 'I'll take care of Tanya.'

All of his old authority of command in an emergency situation – a quality uncalled on throughout the long years of self-doubt and recrimination – was now instinctively taking control. In one swift movement he scooped Tanya up with his right arm. The torch in his left hand showed their way forward.

Another large fall crashed down horribly close behind them as they hurried ever deeper into the mineshaft.

SIXTEEN

Geordie's patience was wearing thin. 'Come on. Come on,' he muttered into the telephone mouthpiece.

A look at his watch said it was now well over five minutes since the girl at the White Rose Inn had told him to hold on while she made a few enquiries.

At last her voice came back on the line.

'I'm sorry, sir, but it appears that the person you're trying to contact has already left the premises. One of our waiters definitely remembers serving a gentleman who he believed was quite probably an American or Canadian. He was with a lady – another foreigner – German he thinks. There was also a young girl of around eight or nine years old with them. Would that be the Mister Stafford in question?'

Not having any proper idea of who his friend was spending the day with, this last piece of information did not help Geordie very much.

'Was the man wearing a navy-blue jacket?' he asked.

'I couldn't say, sir. I didn't see him myself. Only the waiter did.'

The girl gave a lengthy sigh, a sure sign that this game of 'hunt the customer' was beginning to bore her. 'All I can say for certain is that nobody here responded to the public call we put out for your friend,' she added. 'I'm afraid that's the best I can do. We will be closing very shortly.'

The tone was final. Realising that he would get no more help from her, Geordie hung up. As he did so, Phil Thomas came across the hotel lobby.

The Kiwi grinned. 'I've never known you to leave a drink behind before. Was it something important?'

Geordie did not waste time with details. 'Aye. Chances are, it's *bloody* important,' he said. 'Especially for Mike.' He jerked a thumb toward the exit. 'I need to go out and warn him. Do you want to come with me?'

'Sure. But what's it all about?'

'I'll explain in the car,' Geordie told him, leading the way rapidly out.

***

Alan rose slowly from the kneeling position he had been in for the last fifteen minutes. He brushed the clinging bits of heather from his clothes, a deep frown forming. He was now certain that fate had taken a big and unexpected hand in matters. Exactly how big a hand would only be discovered by taking a closer look. With eyes fixed firmly on the hillside point into which Stafford and the woman had disappeared, he moved cautiously forward.

***

Earlier, after waiting just long enough so not to be obvious, Alan had followed their car as it left the pub. He wondered if Stafford was taking the woman and young girl home already. A gut feeling told him that wasn't the case. That if he was patient, his opportunity for revenge would still come about today. There was now a growing certainty over this.

In spite of that certainty, he was still taken by surprise as he swung the Lambretta into a long sweeping bend. The Cresta had pulled up and was parked on the side of the road less than one hundred yards ahead.

He braked hard and did a U-turn.

Safely back on the blind side of the corner, he parked his machine beside the edge of the moor. Strapped securely to the scooter over the rear seat and spare wheel rack was a long canvas sports bag containing all of his personal belongings. From this, Alan removed his most recently acquired possession.

Having already seen several years of service on the fairground circuit, the rifle was far from new. But it was still in good working order, and the .22 rounds it fired were perfectly capable of killing a man providing the target was not too far away. As he'd anticipated, the sights on his chosen weapon were set a little bit out. That didn't matter. After investing ten shillings in four further goes on the 25-yard range with the same rifle and looking closely at the results on each cardboard target handed to him afterwards, he quickly learned how to compensate for this slight misalignment.

'Like your guns do you, boy?' the villainous looking man running the attraction had grinned while relieving him of his last half crown.

It was expensive, but worth it. After secretly making a small identifying scratch on the wooden stock of his chosen rifle, he returned to the travelling fair's current site on Wetherditch Common the following morning a couple of hours before daybreak.

At this hour, apart from a few small security lights, the entire site was in darkness. There was no sign of movement coming from any of the caravans the fairground people used for accommodation. With the rifle range itself constructed mainly of plywood panels and canvas sheets, breaking in was easy. Inside, all the rifles were chained together and secured to a hefty concrete weight by a tough looking padlock. But the padlock wasn't the weakest point. As he'd already noted, that was the relatively flimsy chain itself, and this soon parted with the help of metal cutters taken from the hotel maintenance man's toolkit. Before leaving, he grabbed some .22 rounds from a box and made sure that his chosen rifle's magazine was fully topped up. He knew from experience that the fairground people were unlikely to report the theft of just one small item to the authorities. Encouraging contact with the police was not their usual way of doing things.

With the stolen weapon tucked under his arm, Alan began moving in a wide arc across the moor, continuing on this path until the Cresta came back into view. Here, he immediately dropped to the ground.

All three passengers had now emerged from the car and were heading out onto the heathland. The young girl led the way, with the other two following at a more leisurely pace. He remained motionless for several minutes, content to watch. From the way they were dressed, he could not imagine them walking for very far.

He was right. They soon stopped by a cluster of large stones or rocks. Stafford and the woman sat down together on one of these stones while the little girl wandered off to play a short distance away.

Alan's eyes remained on the adults. Once again they seemed to be involved in a deep conversation, but it was impossible to hear what they were saying. His curiosity rising, he wriggled forward snake fashion through the long heather and grass until he was no more than thirty yards away. They both still had their backs turned to him.

The woman suddenly called out, alarm in her voice.

'Tanya!'

Her loud cry carried easily. Tanya must be the young girl, Alan realised. His eyes darted over to where he had last seen her. There was now no sign. How the heck could she have disappeared so quickly?

He ducked his head low as Stafford's eyes began sweeping round in his direction. He heard the woman call out the little girl's name a second time. His mind was now racing. How would he react if the two of them came over this way and discovered his hiding place? All his anger was directed toward Stafford himself, and the thought that he might have to kill the woman as well had not entered his head. He sighed, unsure of the answer. The only good thing was that the little girl was somewhere well out of the way at present. Harming her would definitely be more than he could handle.

Risking a quick glance up, Alan relaxed as he saw the two adults were now moving directly away from his hiding place. Very soon after that they separated, but his eyes remained on Stafford. Every word his mother had said about the bloke kept repeating itself inside his head. He could feel the anger and hatred taking an ever more powerful grip. No one knew better than himself how uncontrollable his temper could be when roused. He had a crazy impulse to rush forward and blast the bastard where he stood, just like in the war movies.

Common sense regained control for a short while. Wait for the right moment, he told himself. You'll know it when it comes along. Fate wouldn't allow him to be caught just for doing what was right.

He continued watching as Stafford paused to bend down low. Alan could see that he was kneeling alongside what looked like a fairly large hole dug into the slope of the hillside. Stafford called the girl's name into this opening. No reply reached Alan, but he knew there must have been a response because he then heard Stafford asking the girl if she was hurt. The woman joined him a few moments later, and something was said between them about a twisted ankle and a torch in the car. Stafford then set off at a fast run back toward the road.

There was nothing Alan could do for now but carry on waiting.

He was still watching Stafford's retreating figure when the woman called out.

'I'm coming, darling,' he heard her say.

Despite her reassuring words, she hesitated for what looked to be a few fearful seconds before crouching low and working her way inside the dark hole. Within moments it had swallowed her up completely, telling Alan that the excavation must go in much further than he'd first thought.

This was beginning to look promising. If the woman remained out of the way until Stafford returned, he would be sure of having a clear shot with no risk of a witness. Once the shot had been fired, he could be away in a matter of seconds. Even if she did re-appear out of the hole in time to see him running off, it would still be impossible for her to identify him properly. In no time at all he'd be back on his scooter and speeding off in the opposite direction.

But first of all he needed to get a bit closer, just to make sure of the job. Still keeping low in case Stafford chanced to look back in his direction, he moved forward to the cluster of stones where the Canadian had been sitting a few minutes earlier. Two of the largest rocks provided perfect cover, and a narrow gap separating these gave him a direct line of fire to the right spot on the hillside.

He was a pretty good shot anyway. From here, it would be almost impossible to miss.

A grim smile formed as he spotted Stafford heading back across the moor. After all the long years of waiting, his moment of revenge was almost here. Of course he would be suspected – his mother would most likely try to drop him in it as soon as she heard about the shooting - but the coppers could think what they bloody well wanted. All he needed was a bit of time to get clear of the area. After that he'd wipe the rifle clean and dump it somewhere well out of sight. Nobody would be able to pin a damn thing on him.

Stafford was now coming into range but moving quickly. With great care, Alan lined up his target. He was tempted to try a head shot, but quickly decided against taking the risk. The body was a much bigger area to go for. The rifle barrel centred on Stafford's chest.

A trickle of sweat ran slowly down Alan's brow and directly into his eye, destroying his aim. A low growl of irritation slipped out as he used a finger to wipe the stinging fluid away. Get a bloody grip, he told himself. If he didn't get this done quickly, the chance would be lost.

Once again he concentrated on his target. The moment of revenge he'd been dreaming of all his life had finally arrived, and now all it needed to settle things was just one little movement of his finger. Just one little squeeze, and then every bit of the hatred would at last be wiped away. The thought that he could finally be free from the rage that was forever screwing up his brain and forcing him to do crazy things made him feel almost light-headed with anticipation.

But first, his father *must* be avenged. Once that was done, there would be no more anger. He would be able to stay out of any more trouble with the law and start a completely new life for himself. Even his treacherous mother would be proud of him eventually.

All the incentives were there, but his finger stubbornly refused to follow the command of his brain. He growled again. This was bloody stupid. He had mentally rehearsed moments exactly like this a thousand times before, and never once had he hesitated. So why was he hesitating now that the real thing was here?

What the fuck was stopping him?

A disturbing thought sneaked into his head. In spite of all his big plans and burning need for revenge, when it came right down to the sharp end of killing, was he really tough enough to do the job himself?

Of course he was, he told himself savagely. He was plenty tough enough. But it was now too bloody late to prove it. Just like the woman before him, Stafford had already disappeared through the opening in the hillside.

Alan's frustration exploded. He pounded the rock face with his fist, barely feeling the pain. 'Shit! – shit! – shit!'

He wasn't sure how long it took for his rage to settle. He took a deep breath and tried to pull his thoughts together. His chance of a witness free killing was gone. After all the panic about the little girl getting herself lost, the three of them were sure to be sticking closely together from now on. Especially if the kid had an ankle injury. When they did eventually reappear they'd get straight back into their car and head for home, no doubt about it.

Which meant he was back to bloody square one again. Like a fucking idiot, he'd screwed up the one golden opportunity he'd always known was coming his way.

These thoughts were interrupted by the sound of the RAF jets returning.

Like overhead explosions, the sonic booms sent a whole mass of shock waves shuddering through air that, up until now, had been unusually still that day. Angry, thunder-like rumblings quickly increased in intensity until they felt like an almost living presence – a huge mass of energy sweeping across the moor intent on engulfing everything in its path. With head bowed, Alan placed both hands over his ears in an effort to protect them against the force.

When he eventually removed his hands the jets were gone. But faint echoes of the sounds left in their wake still lingered ominously over the deserted countryside for a while longer, creating an almost supernatural atmosphere.

Alan shook his head in an effort to shake out the pressure that seemed to have built up inside his skull. He would have to decide what to do next very quickly. He looked again in the direction of the hillside and was astonished to see a large cloud of dust now billowing around the area. It was blotting out any sign of the opening that had been there before.

He frowned. What the hell was going on? Had something caved in? His mind began exploring the possibilities.

If Stafford was buried somewhere inside there, that might mean the job had been done for him? He could walk away with clean hands. Maybe this was what his gut feeling had been all about? Fate had decided to hand out its own punishment to the bastard, with himself here to witness it. While still considering this, Alan heard a fresh rumble of falling earth and stone. The dust cloud intensified, as did his certainty that justice was indeed finally being done. A grim smile started to form.

And then he thought of the little girl once again. His smile immediately faded. The idea of her being buried inside some dark hole out here on the moor made him feel ill. He swallowed hard, trying to force this disturbing thought from his head. He wouldn't get anywhere by being soft. If things had really turned out the way it seemed then he should be celebrating, not trying to find reasons to be miserable.

Gradually, the dust began to settle and the picture became clearer. There was no sign of life on the hillside. In fact, there was no sign of the opening that had been there only a few minutes ago either. Alan got to his feet and brushed himself down. He would have to check this out at closer quarters.

Still clutching the rifle, he moved cautiously forward.

**

It took just a few minutes to confirm that his guesses were pretty much correct. It was as if the shock waves from the jets had caused a long section of the ground beneath the moor to simply collapse in on itself, but without disturbing anything very much on the surface. What looked like a shallow dip now running up a part of the hillside was the only clue as to how big a fall must have taken place below. Lower down the slope, where until a few minutes ago the actual entrance to the tunnel had been, a solid mass of earth and stones now blocked any way out.

Tentatively at first, and then with increasing force, Alan kicked at the fallen soil here with the bottom of his shoe. The barrier it formed felt absolutely solid. But new questions were now forming. Was Stafford already dead and buried? This seemed to be quite possible. But if the man had somehow managed to escape that fate, was there any chance of him digging his way free? Alan made a brief attempt at clawing some of the earth and stones away with his hands to test this possibility. What little he did manage to shift made no impression whatsoever.

He was now convinced that, one way or the other, Stafford was finished. There might be a search party set up some time later when they were eventually missed, but why would anyone come looking for them in this particular spot? And even if someone did, there was nothing to show that they had been buried beneath all of this.

Just as it had done a few minutes earlier, the thought of the young girl dying in such a horrible way then forced itself into Alan's mind. This time it struck much deeper than before. This time he could see her face very clearly. She was *exactly* like the little sister he'd always wanted.

'But she's not your bloody sister,' he muttered angrily. 'She doesn't even know you exist, and she never bloody will.'

Why was there always something to spoil things for him? This was meant to be his big moment. He should be celebrating. Nothing could ever make him lift a finger to help Stafford.

Anyway, they're probably dead already, he told himself. There was nothing he could do, even if he wanted to.

With a major effort, he managed to push the image of Tanya from his head. There was now one final thing he needed to do to make sure that Stafford was never found. At least, not for a very long time.

The man's car was the only clue as to where he was buried. If he shifted the Cresta a few miles further away then there would be nothing to show that Stafford had even stopped here. It might be years before anyone ever dug him up. Alan had learned from experts how to steal a car, so getting into the Cresta and starting it should be easy. With one final glance at Stafford's tomb, he headed for the road.

A grin formed as he approached the vehicle. The keys were still hanging in the lock of the driver's door, saving him the trouble of breaking in. Stafford must have been in such a damn hurry, he'd forgotten to take them with him. This, Alan decided, was another sign from his father. A sign confirming that he was doing the right thing. After tossing the rifle out of sight into the car boot, he slid behind the wheel and started the engine.

The wallet lying on the floor caught his eye. On inspection, he found two fivers and two tenners inside. Another huge slice of luck. It seemed as if everything was going his way for a change.

Shoving the wallet into his back pocket, he put the car's column change lever into first gear and pulled onto the road. There was a small village a couple of miles further on that he remembered passing through on the way out here. Just beyond that was as far as he needed to go. All he'd have to do then was walk back here and pick up his scooter.

By the time anyone started looking for Stafford, he would be far away.

**

'Come on. We've got to keep moving.'

With limestone and shale still crashing down behind them, Stafford urged Siggi ever deeper into the mineshaft. Great sobs and gasps flew from her mouth as she scrambled desperately to keep up with him. But there was little in the way of physical help he could offer her right now. Cradling

Tanya in one arm and with the child clinging tightly around his neck, his free hand was already fully occupied holding the torch steady and picking out their way forward into what would otherwise be complete darkness.

'Please...we must rest for a minute,' Siggi implored. She pulled up, clutching at her side and fighting for breath.

He swung the light in her direction. Her tortured features showed plainly the distress she was suffering. He also noticed for the first time that her feet were still bare and suffering from a multitude of small cuts.

The crashing noises in their wake were now much less frequent and sounded well behind them, suggesting that they were at last clear of the danger area. A brief inspection of the roof in this section confirmed that, for the moment at least, it was looking pretty secure.

'Okay, we'll hold on here for a spell,' he agreed.

With a great sigh of relief, Siggi slumped to the ground.

Stafford placed Tanya down beside her and continued to survey their surroundings. So far the size of the tunnel had remained fairly consistent. It was still around six feet wide but currently a few inches higher, enabling him to stand fully upright and even have a small amount of headroom to spare. A couple of comparatively minor roof falls sounded in the distance behind them. These were followed by a long and significant silence. Could this be confirmation that the shifting ground had finally settled?

The air was thick with dust and foul smelling. Nobody spoke for some time as each of them tried in their different ways to take in the peril of their situation.

Stafford did not need telling that Siggi must be very close to the edge. During her recollections of the war when back at the White Rose Inn she had spoken vividly of the long hours spent sheltering in the cellar of their house along with all the other residents during the regular bombing raids. She had even made a point of saying that everyone's greatest fear back then – a far greater dread than that of dying instantly in a direct hit - was of being buried alive and slowly suffocating, alone and helpless in the dark.

As she'd spoken he could see plainly how deep-rooted this fear still remained for her, even though it was now many years since the war and bombs had ended. Stafford could not even imagine the hellish thoughts that must be going through her head in their present situation.

He adjusted the direction of the flashlight beam slightly in order to get a better look at Siggi's face, but she did not even bother to glance in his direction. Her attention at present was concentrated totally on her young niece sitting on the floor beside her.

This non-reaction told him a lot. He quickly realised that the one slender thread holding Siggi together was her desperate need to be there in every possible way for Tanya. The young girl's eyes, until now fixed on the opposite wall with a bemused and fearful expression, shifted toward her aunt. Instantly, they drew strength from each other. Tanya brushed a hand across her face. Then, in a gesture of mutual comfort, they threw their arms around each other.

'It's all right, darling,' Siggi whispered. 'Don't worry, I am here for you. And so is Mister Stafford. We won't let anything bad happen.'

Both then gazed up at him, a mixture of hope and faith on their faces. Their total belief that he could somehow get them out of this desperate situation brought a lump to his throat. In truth, things were looking pretty grim, though obviously he couldn't tell them that. Much better if he played the situation down as much as possible.

He forced a confident smile. 'Sure, everything is going to be fine. There's bound to be another way out of here somewhere.' He flipped a thumb in the direction they had just come from. 'First off though, I reckon I should go back and take a look at the damage.'

'You're not leaving us here…alone and in the dark.' The alarm in Siggi's voice was clear.

With a great effort, she then steadied herself. 'I'm sorry. Of course you must go. It is the sensible thing to do. But please be careful, and try not to be so very long.' She clung tighter than ever to Tanya.

He left them wrapped in each other's arms.

Moving with great care and constantly checking the state of the roof, he set off. At first there were just relatively small heaps of debris scattered along the way. Gradually however, these increased in size. Then he came to the first major obstacle. It was a solid mass of rubble spread right across the width of the shaft and piled up to within a few inches of the roof.

Standing up on his toes, he directed the torch through this small space at the top and peered along. His heart sank. There was no end in sight. In fact, the gap quickly tapered away to nothing. Beyond this point the tunnel was completely blocked from floor to ceiling. For all he knew, it remained like this all the way back to the entrance.

While shifting slightly to get a better look, his head brushed against the roof. Almost at once he felt movement there, prompting him to jump sharply away. It was as well he did. A large lump of sandstone crashed down, missing him by inches.

Stafford blew out his cheeks. This lucky escape told him better than anything that there was absolutely no possibility of them being able to dig a way out. Even the smallest disturbance here was sure to bring about a lot more falls. The few roof timbers still in place were loose and utterly rotten.

Dejected, he made his way back to the others. What the heck could he say to them? There must be something more he could do? How did you tell anyone, let alone an eight-year-old little girl, that there was a good chance they may die soon?

The answer, of course, was that you didn't. You kept your damn fool mouth shut. Even so, shielding them both from this brutal reality for as long as possible was going to be a mighty difficult job.

He thought of his own family. *'Come home safe, Dad,'* Connie had said to him. Her words had amused him at the time. Well he sure as heck wasn't laughing now. He could feel only relief that she and Alice couldn't see the hellish spot he was in.

His torchlight picked out Siggi and Tanya ahead. They were still sitting in exactly the same position he had left them in. Both pairs of eyes gazed at him expectantly as he approached. Their faith was still holding up.

'I'm going to take a look further along now,' he told them, indicating the as-yet unexplored depths of the shaft. 'It won't hurt to know what's down there.'

His tone reflected no hint of the frustration and distress he was feeling. Nonetheless, he could see from Siggi's face that she was already drawing her own conclusions. She knew as well as he did that the way out he'd just investigated was impassable. He would have told them immediately had it been any different.

She merely nodded to him, doing all in her power to smother any outward signs of having gathered bad news. But Stafford knew she must be screaming with despair inside. Anxious not to be drawn into any further talk at this stage, he kept moving.

After a minute or so he encountered a slow curve to the left. Here, the tunnel narrowed to around four feet and he was forced to crouch much lower than before as the roof dipped alarmingly. It was as though the miners of old had at this point started to give up hope of finding any worthwhile seam of ore. He had a sinking feeling that the shaft was going to peter out completely before very much further.

Within another few yards it did exactly that. The rapid tapering continued until the only way forward was to crawl. Then, just as if somebody had shut off a valve, the shaft came to an abrupt dead end.

Stafford muttered a curse as the sense of failure bit deeply. That was it. There was to be no alternative way out conveniently materializing to save them. It had always been a slim hope anyway. He swore yet again under his breath, this time bitterly cursing the bad luck that had brought about this situation. Of course he didn't want to die down here: nobody would want to. But at least he'd had some kind of life. Why the kid for Christ's sake? And Siggi? Hadn't she suffered enough in the past without it ending this way? Where was the bloody justice in it all?

He scrambled back to a point where the tunnel offered enough space to stand up again. He paused here to weigh up their chances of being rescued. Mindful of the dwindling battery life, he switched off the torch.

Astrid would quickly become concerned when the other two failed to arrive back home on time, so she was sure to be the first person to report them missing. After that, Geordie would be able to say where they had planned to go, and what car he was driving.

The car! That was the key, he realised. Once the Cresta was identified as being his, an organised search of the surrounding area was sure to happen. By then it might turn out to be too late of course, but at least this possibility offered them some small hope to cling to.

He gazed into the black void leading back to Siggi and Tanya, as if seeking to pluck divine inspiration from out of the darkness. Not that he seriously expected any to be forthcoming. What was he hoping for? A blinding flash of light perhaps, followed by some celestial being in white robes appearing to show him and the others a magical way out of here? He gave a cynical laugh at the stupidity of such a thought. Nonetheless, he continued staring into the darkness while weighing up their more practical chances of survival and rescue.

Abruptly, he stiffened, blinking hard. Were his eyes playing tricks on him, or was there just the tiniest glimmer of daylight a short distance ahead? It was impossible to be certain. One moment the light appeared to be there, the next it was gone. This must be a cruel joke played by the senses. Some kind of subterranean mirage perhaps? Even so, right now he was prepared to clutch at any damn straw that was on offer. Sharply aware that switching the torch back on might cause him to lose sight of this faint hope, he picked his way slowly along through the darkness toward the source, real or imagined.

A surge of expectation twisted his heart into a reef knot as he drew closer to the spot. It *was* a light! Not much bigger than a pin prick, but definitely a light all the same. It was flickering down from the tunnel roof. Having now definitely located the exact point, Stafford flicked the flashlight back on.

Embedded into the roof directly overhead he could see the rim of a circular clay lining pipe, roughly five inches across. Wedged in the mouth of this pipe was a large stone, and around the edges of this a collection of much smaller stones and lightly compacted earth. Stafford prodded at the earth with his fingers and almost immediately brought a small amount trickling down. Encouraged by this, he prodded harder. More soil ran out.

Excited now, he could see that this must have been an old air vent. With the bottom section of rough clay lining undamaged and still in place, he could only pray that it continued like this all the way to the surface. If it did, it was a potential lifeline.

After a few minutes of work, the pile of earth by his feet was growing. The pinprick of daylight shining down had also grown into something slightly more significant. But no matter how much Stafford pulled, twisted and struck at the wedged stone, this obstruction refused to budge. Both hands felt sore and bruised from his efforts.

He paused, trying to look at the problem in a different way. The clay lining jutted clear of the roof by about half of inch. Stafford removed one of his shoes and swung the heel in a series of sharp blows aimed at this projecting rim. After three strikes the brittle clay began splintering. Two further blows and a sizeable section close to the edge of the trapped stone flew away. A second piece quickly followed.

This time when Stafford tried pulling down on the stone he definitely felt it move. Only a tiny amount at first, but it was enough for him to redouble his efforts. So great was the pressure he continued applying that, when the obstruction did suddenly break free, his own downward force sent him staggering backwards and tumbling hard into the ground.

But from there on it was easy. The remaining earth trapped inside the vent came down with a rush, much like the final few grains of salt in an egg-timer appear to do. And then – with glorious intensity – there was real daylight. In reality it was no more than a narrow shaft, but to Stafford it was one of the most spectacularly beautiful sights he had ever witnessed.

He let out a deep sigh of relief. At least they would not now suffocate down here. That had been one of his main concerns. Many others, a lack of water being the most pressing of all, still existed. But this was a damn good start.

He peered up through the vent. His eyes, unaccustomed to such direct brightness, stung furiously. It took several seconds before they managed to adjust and he could see what he wanted to know. Yes, the vent was a fairly consistent five inches across and went all the way up to the surface. At a guess he would say they were at least thirty feet down. Maybe a lot more, it was hard to tell exactly. But even after accepting this as a fact, he was still cheered. Now they needed to build on this discovery. If only there was some way they could get a message or small personal item up this vent and onto the ground above. That would make a huge difference to their chances of being found quickly once the inevitable search party arrived.

No idea of how to achieve this sprang readily to mind. Still dwelling on the problem, Stafford headed back to the others.

SEVENTEEN

The village of Scapdale was a good deal busier than might be expected for a Sunday afternoon so early in the summer season. A steady flow of people, the majority of them tourists, wandered along the picturesque main street taking full advantage of the pleasant weather. The village's fourteenth century church provided an historic focal point, while the souvenir shop and aptly named 'Moor Tea' restaurant close by were capitalizing on the unusually warm sunny spell by enjoying a brisk trade.

Sharply aware that even a minor accident in Stafford's car would ruin everything, Alan drove through the village centre with caution. At the same time, he now wanted to get out of this populated area as quickly as possible. It had suddenly occurred to him that some suspicious copper might glance his way and think him too young and rough looking to be driving a top of the range car like the Cresta.

Only when he was well clear of the village outskirts and back on a quiet country road did his concern start to fade. He blew out his cheeks with relief, aware that he had probably been worrying himself for nothing. He had seen no sign of a police presence anywhere in Scapdale. Maybe they thought it was too peaceful a place to bother with very much? Whatever the case, by his reckoning he had now moved Stafford's car plenty far enough away from its original spot. It made sense not to push his luck by hanging on to it any longer than necessary.

Less than half a mile further on he pulled into a small lay-by. This was as good as anywhere, he decided. No other parked vehicles were in sight, and at present there was little passing traffic. Also, the countryside here was very similar to the spot where Stafford was buried. If he or the woman with him had mentioned to anyone that they planned to take a walk across the moor, this was an equally believable place for them to have stopped.

Using his handkerchief, Alan carefully wiped the steering wheel, gear lever, and any other parts inside the Cresta he felt he might have touched. Some people called him Mad Alan, but that didn't make him stupid. With all his personal details held on police records, he sure as hell wasn't dumb enough to risk getting caught out by something as simple as fingerprints.

The wiping completed, he got out of the vehicle and removed the rifle from the boot. After locking everything, he gave a final wipe to all the external handles he had touched. Now he had to face the long walk back to his scooter.

But it was worth it, Alan considered, setting off in the direction of the village. Nobody had seen him dump the car. Everyone would think it had been parked there by Stafford himself. They'd spend hours, maybe even days, wasting their time searching for him and the others around this area. Never in a million years would they guess that the bastard was buried in some remote hole in the ground nearly three miles away.

While walking, his eyes constantly scanned the moor for a safe place to stash the rifle for a short time. He had no way of concealing the thing while carrying it back to his scooter, and being caught in possession of a stolen firearm would be more than enough to get him locked up again. With the busy village rapidly getting closer, he had to lose the weapon quickly before some smartarse started asking him awkward questions. Once he'd retrieved his scooter it would be easy to come back to this quiet stretch of road and pick it up once again.

The sound of an approaching vehicle made him look back. Some distance away was a single-decker country bus heading into Scapdale. Almost without thinking, he dropped the rifle into a roadside ditch and carried on walking. Thankfully, the bus drove straight past the request stop a little further ahead without pausing to drop any passengers off.

As a warning, it was clear. Get rid of the thing NOW. There was no such thing as the perfect hiding place on this part of the moor.

While going back for the weapon, his eyes searched for a landmark in the almost featureless sea of heather and bracken. The best he could spot was an old-fashioned stone marker set low down on the side of the road. Carved into the face of this, the fading letters offered the information: PICKERING 10 MILES.

Taking a line directly away from this stone, he counted twenty paces out onto the moor. At this exact point, he pushed the rifle deep into a thick patch of heather. For a moment he paused to consider whether it might have been wiser to remove the full magazine of seven rounds first. But the weapon was now nicely concealed. It should be safe enough where it was, he decided. And he would be back here to collect it again in little more than an hour.

Satisfied, he headed back to the road.

***

With mouth set in a firm line, Geordie drove his Rover saloon rapidly away from the Compton Manor Hotel,.

'So, are you going to tell me what this is all about?' Phil asked him.

As concisely as possible, the big man explained. Phil's mildly amused expression quickly turned into one of concern.

'But we know Mike's already left the pub,' he pointed out.

'Aye, but he told us he was planning to be back at the hotel by four o'clock, remember. So chances are he's on his way to Wetherditch right now. And if he is, he'll almost certainly be using this road. So keep your eyes skinned for his car. He's got to be warned to watch out.'

Phil frowned. 'This Alan is only a kid you know. Do you really think he'll try something crazy? He could be all talk.'

'After what we've been told about him, do you want to take a chance on that?'

'I guess not.' Phil shook his head. 'Jimmy's son. I can hardly believe it.'

'You're not the only one.'

Both men lapsed into silence, all the time keeping a careful lookout for any sign of their friend or his car. It was Geordie who spoke first.

'Damn!' he suddenly exclaimed.

'What's up?'

'The temperature gauge. It's overheating.'

Almost as soon as these words were out of his mouth, the first signs of steam began showing. By the time they had travelled another hundred yards there was a great cloud billowing in all directions. Still cursing, Geordie pulled into the side of the road and raised the bonnet.

Phil pointed. 'There look! You've got a busted hose, mate.'

He was right. Through a split in the rubber pipe at the bottom of the radiator, a steady flow of boiling water was still escaping. The rapidly expanding puddle on the ground dribbled closer to their feet.

'Damn!' Geordie repeated, this time with even more feeling.

***

The narrow shaft of daylight filtering down through the air vent Stafford had discovered provided only limited illumination over an area just a few feet across. Beyond this little oasis of hope there was nothing but the same pitch-black darkness. All three of them were now sitting closely together on the floor within this small patch of light. The torch remained switched off to conserve what little life remained in the batteries.

He had done his best to sound confident, reassuring them several times that there was certain to be a search party out looking for them well before it got dark.

'With my car being parked so close by, they'll be sure to find us in no time,' he added yet again.

He could see that Tanya believed him. Although obviously in a lot of pain from her ankle, she still managed to muster up a brave smile at his words. The child's resilience and courage, plus her faith in him, humbled Stafford. Subconsciously, he found himself wondering if his own daughter would be so strong under the same circumstances. It was a question he prayed would never have to be answered.

Siggi, although not quite so taken in by his confident remarks, also appeared to be holding up much better than expected. The welcome shaft of daylight, together with the reassuring knowledge that they would at least have an adequate supply of air for as long as they needed it, had produced something of a calming effect in her. All the same, Stafford could not help wondering how long this would last. She was smart, and despite his assurances, other factors would soon become apparent.

Even if his car was discovered fairly soon, there was nothing to mark the exact spot where they were trapped. The moor was a huge place; God knows how long it might take before anyone actually managed to find them. Making matters worse, once the daylight faded, the torch would be of limited use. Siggi would have to face the daunting prospect of spending possibly many hours buried deep beneath the ground in total darkness.

He did not need any reminding that this was the stuff of her very worst nightmares.

Every so often Tanya glanced at him, still obviously believing that he would soon come up with something more to help them. The trouble was, there wasn't a damn thing down here that he could use in any way. If this had been in the movies, he thought dryly, there would be all kinds of tools and equipment conveniently left lying around. Then he, the hero, would brilliantly manufacture a means of escape. But there was no Hollywood scriptwriter around to fortuitously provide these items for him. This was for real – and reality was a bitch.

It would always be possible to light a fire. This idea had occurred to him a long time ago. He had a lighter in his pocket, and they could perhaps spare a few items of clothing to burn? Most of the smoke created by this would probably rise up the vent okay, sending out signals Indian style.

The idea sounded good if you considered it quickly, but in reality it was pretty much a non-starter. They would very quickly run out of things to feed the fire with. And, just as importantly, how could they possibly know when there was someone up there who might see the signals?

He was still searching for another solution when Tanya gave a terrified gasp. She was staring, eyes full of horror and revulsion, at a point directly over to his left.

He followed her gaze. Another pair of eyes glared back at him. Glittering evilly in the half-light, they belonged to the biggest rat Stafford had ever seen. It must have been at least two feet long including the tail. The creature appeared completely unafraid of them as it continued its unblinking gaze. His silently transmitted message came over loud and clear: *'I'm the king down here. You are not welcome.'*

It was a battle of wills, and Stafford was the first to shift his eyes. His hand reached out for a nearby stone to throw at the menacing brute. Then, as his fingers closed over the missile, he hesitated. An idea triggered by the creature in front of him was now beginning to form. Was there a way of getting a message up to the surface after all?

There was no time to enlarge on these thoughts. Before he could get any clear details of a plan worked out, the giant rodent took a couple of paces closer in a clear attempt to further establish his authority.

Siggi too now gasped out in horror. At the same time, Stafford found himself considering how many more of these foul creatures might be lurking in the darkness immediately behind their leader, waiting to see what happened next. For all he knew there could be dozens or even hundreds of them. Any sign of weakness by him now could result in them being overrun by a whole swarm of the things.

With a sharp movement, he threw the stone.

King Rat squirmed sideways, and the missile flew harmlessly past. Even so, this sign of aggression was sufficient to temporarily check him. He glared venomously at Stafford for a long moment before withdrawing back into the darkness. Even in retreat his manner was threatening, the look suggesting quite plainly that he would be returning when it suited him.

Siggi once again had a protective arm wrapped tightly around Tanya when Stafford turned to look at them. 'He's gone, and I don't think he'll be bothering us again,' he told them, not believing a word he was saying.

From the expression on their faces, they had little belief in his assurance either. Siggi appeared to be on the point of saying something when he touched the hem of her knitted cardigan.

'What is this made of?' he asked.

She looked at him as if he had gone mad. Nevertheless, she answered quickly enough. 'It's bri-nylon wool. Why do you wish to know such a thing?'

'Never mind that for now. That's pretty strong stuff, isn't it?'

'Yes...I mean, I think it is.'

He nodded. 'Do you figure you'd be able to unravel some of it for me? You know, so we can make up a long length of cord. Believe me, this is important.'

'Very well, I believe you. But please tell me why I am doing this?' Siggi's curiosity was for the moment overcoming all other considerations.

Tanya was also taking a big interest. 'Have you thought of something to help us, Mister Stafford?' she asked. Now that the rat had disappeared, he could see expectation once more shining in her eyes. Her faith in his ability appeared to be almost inexhaustible.

He smiled encouragingly at the young girl, then briefly explained to them both how much it would help if they could get some small personal item to the surface to show exactly where they were located.

'I've got a hankie with my name on it,' Tanya announced quickly.

In spite of everything, the girl positively beamed with pleasure when he took it from her and declared it to be perfect for their purpose. Siggi was also now far keener to assist. 'I have a lipstick in my handbag,' she said. 'We could use that to write the word help on the handkerchief.'

'That makes it even better,' Stafford told her.

Removing her cardigan, she began picking at the seam with a small nail file also taken from her bag. 'How much of this will you need?' she asked.

'Enough to go all the way to the top, and then some to spare.'

The first length Siggi managed to unpick and hand to him was around six feet long. He tugged at it, testing the strength. As she had said, it was pretty strong. This was soon followed by a slightly shorter piece, which he knotted carefully to the first.

'Keep it coming,' he instructed when she produced a third length. Now that a start had been made, the nylon was unravelling far more easily.

It took a total of fourteen pieces before Stafford was satisfied that he had sufficient length for his purpose. Each knot was carefully inspected a second time before he finally nodded his approval.

'But I still don't see how your idea is going to work,' Siggi said. 'What are you going to use to get the handkerchief up to the top?'

Stafford gave her a tight smile. Here came the crunch. 'Haven't you guessed?' he told her. 'We're going to use that big rat.'

There was a stunned silence. Both Siggi and Tanya visibly shook. He did not need any telling how terrified they were of the creature. He wasn't all that keen on the damn thing himself. But there was more to come. How on earth were they going to react to what he said next?

He took a deep breath before continuing. 'The thing is, you'll have to help me, Siggi. I'm sorry, but there's no other way. It's going to take two pair of hands to make this work.'

Aunt and niece exchanged a look of mutual despair, both appalled at the prospect.

'Can I do anything?' Tanya asked in a tiny, frightened voice.

Siggi firmed. 'No, Tanya. I will do whatever has to be done.' She looked at Stafford, clearly ashamed that she had even hesitated. 'So, how can I help?'

As gently as possible, he explained to her.

***

Everything was prepared. Now, for the easy bit, Stafford told himself with a heavy sense of irony – catching the damn creature. But it wasn't ironic at all, he suddenly realised. This *was* going to be the easy bit. Even if he did manage to get the huge rat briefly under control, there were still a hundred and one other things that could go wrong. Things that depended just as much on sheer luck as careful preparation. But at least they were doing everything possible to help themselves. If his plan worked out then the odds on them being rescued in time would surely be improved.

And if it didn't work out? Well, that was something he didn't really want to think about.

King Rat had made a brief reappearance twice during the last fifteen minutes. Each time, a well-aimed stone sent him scuttling on his way. Now, when his presence was actually required, how much longer would it be before he returned?

Stafford removed what up until now had been his best sports jacket. Carrying the garment with him, he moved away from their small patch of light and a short distance further along the tunnel. He glanced back at the other two just before blending completely into total darkness,. Siggi, pale and tense, responded with a determined nod. Tanya's eyes flicked rapidly from her aunt across to him and then back to Siggi again. The child was doing her best to hide the fact, but he could see that her swollen ankle was causing her a considerable amount of pain.

Although now completely invisible to the others in his new position, Stafford was in fact less than twenty feet away and could still clearly see them as they remained huddled together in the little pool of daylight. With his back against the wall he waited, absolutely motionless and drawing in only the shallowest of breaths.

More than ten minutes passed with no sign whatsoever of his prey. His joints began to stiffen as he continued to retain this unnatural stillness. It was hard to resist the temptation to move around slightly to help ease the discomfort.

Five more minutes passed, seemingly with the length of hours. Then, just as he was certain he would have to shift a little or cramp up completely, he sensed as much as heard a tiny amount of activity down on the tunnel floor. It was coming from uncomfortably close to his feet. Moments later he caught sight of movement at the point ahead where gloom and total darkness merged. Perhaps there was more than one movement? He could not be sure. Whatever, only one shape eventually advanced further on into the pool of daylight to become clearly visible.

King Rat was on the offensive once again.

The giant rodent paused in its advance, its sharp, gleaming eyes regarding Siggi and Tanya triumphantly. It could see that their protector was no longer with them. Inspired by this, the aggressor scurried sharply forward almost to within touching distance of the pair before pausing again. Hideously long claws scratched ominously on the stony ground as if in final preparation for an attack.

The speed of the rat's advance took Stafford by surprise, forcing him to move much more rapidly than expected. Holding the jacket out before him in both hands, he closed in as fast as he could on the brute. A series of enraged squeals and soft squishing sensations beneath his shoes as he rushed forward confirmed the presence of countless more rats lurking just within the limits of the darkness.

Had he not become so confident, King Rat would have had plenty of time to evade Stafford's lunge. As it was, he turned slowly and with almost regal disdain to investigate the cause of the commotion amongst his subjects. This brief delay in reaction cost him dear. Stafford literally threw himself over the final few feet, just managing to cover the giant rodent with his opened jacket before it could dart sufficiently to one side.

He at once dropped to his knees, both hands desperately feeling through the jacket's material in an effort to get a firm grip on the writhing, enraged creature trapped beneath. The king's muffled squeals of rage literally filled the tunnel as he fought ferociously to free himself. After a few moments of frenetic struggling Stafford was sure he had finally managed to get a good hold on the creature, but this quickly turned out to be a mistaken belief.

Somehow the rat twisted out of his grasp. An instant later, razor-sharp teeth sliced clean through the thick material of the jacket's shoulder padding, missing his hand by a mere whisker.

The struggle continued. For a second time he managed to get a good grip on the rat, this time gauging more accurately where the head was. His fingers found a better purchase and closed tightly around the back of the creature's neck. With his other hand grasping it by the buttocks, Stafford rose to his feet. The folds of the jacket fell back as he lifted his arms, fully exposing the snarling, squirming King to Siggi.

'Are you ready?' he called out to her, at the same time shaking the rat violently in an effort to confuse and subdue it. The measure seemed to work, and for a moment the struggling became slightly less frantic.

Her normally large eyes now appeared enormous as Siggi fearfully drew closer, clutching in both hands the makeshift line of nylon created from her cardigan. The very end of this line was already coiled to form the twin loops of a clove hitch knot. A few feet further back from this knot, Tanya's handkerchief had been securely attached, whilst midway between these two points was a deliberately weakened section where a large number of the nylon fibres had been picked away. In theory, this was where the line should break first when put under strain.

'Come on – do it now!' Stafford urged. His fingers were already throbbing from the constant pressure they were being forced to exert.

'Go on, Aunt Siggi,' Tanya joined in, echoing his instructions. Her voice was a strange mixture of excitement and fright.

It was the child's words that gave Siggi the final push she needed. Deliberately averting her eyes from the creature's malignant glare, she steeled herself. With a rapid movement she dropped the looped clove hitch over one of its hind legs and pulled the knot tight.

Her action triggered off a fresh burst of frenzied activity. The giant rat's teeth gnashed wildly at thin air. Its claws searched vainly for something to attack in an attempt to extract revenge for this latest outrage.

'Well done!' Stafford told Siggi. 'Now, quickly, tie the other end of the line around my foot the way I showed you.' The frantic writhing continued unabated; it was now all he could do to retain his hold. The strength of the creature was amazing.

With both ends of the cord secured, Stafford raised his arms right up to the air vent opening. At the same time, Siggi was using his lighter to set fire to one of several tissues taken from her shoulder bag. Each had been loosely twisted along its length to form a spill.

'Bring it nearer,' Stafford urged as the flames took hold. 'Let him see the fire close up.'

With teeth gritted and eyes narrowed into slits, she thrust her arm out to its full extent. The tissue flared only a few inches from the snarling rat's contorted features. It could feel the heat – smell the smoke. Aggression instantly transformed into naked fear. From violently seeking to free itself, the creature now sought to drive itself even further back into Stafford's grasp. Its terror of fire was unmistakable.

As the tissue twist slowly began to burn itself out, Siggi lit another from the embers. Seeing the effect the flames were having was clearly giving her added strength.

Satisfied that the rat was now sufficiently frightened, but for the moment still retaining his hold, Stafford thrust the creature head first up into the air vent. With the opening now temporarily blocked, only the flickering flames of the third tissue provided any light to see by. He held his breath. This was the moment of truth. Once released, the creature had two alternatives. It could run hell for leather up the side of the vent all the way to the surface, or it could stay where it was and continue the fight. He was banking heavily on the creature choosing the first option.

Somehow his aching fingers found the strength to give the rodent one final intimidating squeeze to the back of the neck before at long last allowing his grip to slacken. He immediately withdrew his hands to either side of the vent, at the same time being careful to keep the opened jacket directly below the opening in case the rat did decide to return. Having nearly been bitten once, he had no wish to give the brute a second opportunity.

For a second or two nothing much happened, probably due to the creature's sheer surprise at its sudden freedom. Then a loud scratching sound could be heard as its claws sought to get a better grip on the pitted surface of the clay lining. A moment later the thread looped by Stafford's feet began to travel rapidly upwards.

'It's working!' he exclaimed, dropping the jacket down to his side and peering up at the king's undignified retreat. 'It's damn well working.'

As a little of the daylight shone back down on them again, Siggi and Tanya exchanged hopeful glances. The young girl clapped her hands. 'I knew you'd be able to do it, Mister Stafford.'

Barely were her words out when, three-quarters of the way up, the rat suddenly stopped in its ascent. It was as if pride and anger were now overcoming its fear of the flames. The large head twisted and glared down the shaft directly into Stafford's eyes.

'Quick. Light another tissue,' he urged Siggi.

With shaking hands, she did as instructed.

By the time the flames had taken a hold, the creature was already attempting to turn in the confined space. Stafford tapped the burning tissue on the edge of the vent. Smouldering ashes were immediately sucked in and flew upwards.

This was enough to convince the king that it really was time to abdicate. His newly found resolve disappeared. With one final snarl, he continued his climb. Moments later he reached the surface and disappeared from view. The pink thread continued to follow in his wake before suddenly becoming taut. Stafford felt a small tug where it was tied to his shoe. This was followed by several more.

'Come on – break damn you,' he muttered.

The line suddenly went slack. Had it broken, or had the rat doubled back on itself? It was impossible to tell.

The question was soon answered as renewed tugging, far more violent than before, began. Such was the power, Stafford suspected that the infuriated creature might have now taken the line into its jaws. Whatever the case, there was one more powerful tug followed by a definite springing sensation. Then the line became slack once again. This time there was no doubt. It had definitely broken.

There was only one uncertainty. Had it broken in the intended place? If it had, that would leave Tanya's handkerchief lying on the surface at the end of the pink cord, which in turn would lead directly to the top of the vent. At least, that was the theory. Any doubts he might have about the reality were better kept to himself.

Perspiration ran down his face. Only as he brushed the sweat away from his brow did he realise how rapidly his heart was thumping. Well, he had done all he could. There was now nothing else for it but to wait.

He gave the other two a confident smile. 'Everything is going to be fine now,' he assured them.

EIGHTEEN

Scapdale was still busy when Alan walked back along the twisting main street. Already he was perspiring under the warm sun. On top of this, his mouth was becoming uncomfortably dry.

People passed him by without a second glance. Not that there was any reason for them to act differently, but their lack of interest was reassuring all the same. He noticed a restaurant on the other side of the road and crossed over to look in through the window. The sight of customers enjoying a variety of refreshing looking drinks made him realise how bad his thirst was, and he still had more than two miles left to walk. There wouldn't be any harm in stopping here for a short time, he decided.

Stepping inside, he sat down at the only remaining free table. From here he watched the overworked waitress hurrying to and fro until she finally made her way over to him. She was quite pretty in a way, he thought. Aged around eighteen, her shoulder length blonde hair was tied back with a red ribbon. In spite of the pressure she was working under, she smiled at him in a friendly way.

'What can I get you?'

Alan became aware that he was smiling back at her. This spontaneous reaction surprised him slightly. Simple, pleasant gestures like this were not something he found himself doing very often.

'A large glass of orange juice,' he told her.

'Anything to eat?'

He shrugged. Maybe he should have something? 'A ham sandwich.'

She scribbled his order down on a pad. 'It won't be long.'

As the girl made to move away, Alan could not prevent himself from saying: 'Do you mind if I ask you your name?'

She hesitated a second before answering. 'No, I don't mind. It's Sue.'

This time there was a slight air of uncertainty about her smile. Having answered his question, she hurried off.

He leaned back in his seat trying hard to relax. Things couldn't have worked out much better, he kept telling himself. Stafford had finally got what he deserved, and at no risk to himself. He was completely in the clear. He couldn't bring himself to feel much sympathy for the woman with Stafford either, but it *was* a bloody shame about the little girl. She definitely didn't deserve to die.

He shook his head in an attempt to clear it of this disturbing thought. He couldn't allow the little girl's bad luck to spoil his own moment of triumph. Everything that had happened that afternoon was down to fate. The truth was, things would have worked out exactly the same way even if he hadn't been there.

Much as Alan kept telling himself this, his mind wouldn't settle. The kid was called Tanya, he recalled. Maybe she wasn't dead after all? There was no way of knowing anything for sure yet. Once again he could clearly see the child in his mind's eye, trapped but still alive inside that black hole, frightened and crying, praying that someone would come to their rescue.

Suddenly, it was all too much to think about. Why, whenever something went right for him, was there always something else to spoil it? He raised a hand to the side of his head and could feel a pulse beating heavily in his temple. *Leave me alone,* he wanted to shout to no one in particular. *There's nothing I can do to change things, even if I wanted to.*

His order arrived. The unexpected sound of the small tin tray dropping on to the table made him jump. The waitress was immediately apologetic.

'I'm sorry, I didn't mean to startle you. You must have been miles away.'

He looked at her, almost afraid that she could read his thoughts. 'Yeah, I suppose I was.'

'Is anything the matter?' she persisted, studying his expression. 'You look a bit upset about something.'

'I'm okay,' he told her, forcing Tanya completely from his mind.

The kindly, enquiring look on Sue's face was unsettling. People didn't usually give a shit how he felt. Yet this girl – a total stranger – was concerned for him. Why was that? Confused, he turned away from her and took a bite from his sandwich, realising almost immediately that this might be mistaken for a snub. He was right.

'Just let me know if you want anything else,' she said, apparently losing interest and moving away.

Alan took a mouthful of orange juice, at the same time allowing his gaze to follow the girl as she continued tending tables. Inexplicably drawn, he continued in this way for several minutes.

In a subconscious movement, his hand moved to his back pocket. With a sense of surprise he felt Stafford's wallet. He had forgotten all about it being there. This was something else he'd have to ditch pretty soon. But before doing that, now would be a good time to take a proper look inside. It would give him something to do other than watching the waitress.

Placing the wallet on his lap below the table, he flicked through the contents. There was the thirty pounds he already knew about, but nothing else of much interest. Only a zipped compartment remained to be investigated. He felt inside.

With a huge jolt he realised that he was holding his father's photograph: the very one he had deliberately left stuck to his locker door to remind Stafford of the man he had murdered. Without quite knowing why, Alan turned the photograph over.

He blinked with surprise at the drunken scrawl written all over the back. A feeling of frustration quickly grew. Not for the first time in his life he realised how difficult things could be when you couldn't read and write properly. What the hell had Stafford written down here? Time after time his eyes ran over the words, desperately trying to make some sense of them. He could vaguely recognise some letters, but others were a complete mystery. It didn't help that the writing was so bad. Even he could recognise what a terrible scribble it was.

The waitress was close by, heading for the kitchen. Without thinking, Alan called out her name.

She paused in mid-stride. 'Yes. Can I get you something else?'

Alan hesitated briefly, but an overwhelming need to know the truth of these words easily outweighed all other considerations. 'Could you do me a favour please?' he asked.

She became slightly guarded. 'What would that be?'

'Please, if you'll just come here for a moment, I'll tell you.'

Like smiling at strangers, using the word 'please' was a rare occurrence for Alan. Now he'd used it twice within a few seconds.

'I'm rather busy at the moment,' Sue told him. 'Unless it's very important ...'

'It is! At least, it is to me.'

She frowned, but then moved closer. 'All right. How can I help?'

Normally, he didn't give a damn what people thought of him. But for some reason Alan did not want to admit to this girl that he was unable to read. The fact that Stafford's writing was so poor made it a little easier for him. Laying the photograph face down on the table, he smiled awkwardly.

'There's something written on the back of this picture, but the writing's so bad and squashed up, I can't work out what it says. I was hoping you could help?'

Relaxing more, Sue bent down to take a closer look. For several seconds she concentrated on the scribble. Then she began to read aloud.

'This is a solemn promise to my old pal Jimmy.'

She paused to give him an enquiring look, as if asking who the Jimmy in question might be. He frowned but said nothing in response, merely motioning with his hand for her to continue.

Haltingly, the girl continued reading. 'Now I know about Alan, I understand what it is you want me to do.'

She paused again to look at him. 'Is this making any sense to you?'

Alan nodded, although in truth it was making very little sense at all. But the reference to himself was clear enough. Now, more than ever, he needed to know everything that Stafford had written.

'Go on. Finish it,' he said.

'Okay.' Her eyes returned to the photograph. 'I swear to you, Jim, I'll do everything I can to help your boy and make things right for him. God bless you, old buddy.'

Sue lifted her gaze. 'It's signed by someone called Mike, I think.' She shrugged. 'That's it.'

Confusion was raging inside Alan's head. His voice was barely a whisper. 'Are you sure you read everything the right way?'

'Yes. Absolutely.' She appeared alarmed at his stunned reaction. 'Do you want me to read it again?'

He shook his head. 'No. Thanks for your help.'

Her eyes continued to study his face. She was on the point of saying something further when an impatient voice called out.

'Miss! We're still waiting for our bill over here.'

She gave Alan one final look. 'I'll come back over to you in a few minutes if you like.'

He made no reply. In fact, he had hardly heard her at all. Sighing, she hurried away to continue with her work.

***

Alan barely moved for over ten minutes. His eyes for most of this time were locked rigidly onto Stafford's scribbled promise to his father. On several occasions he sensed the waitress glancing in his direction, but he gave no sign to her of wanting anything further.

Although sitting virtually motionless, his mind was racing all over the place. Nothing that was written here could ever be enough to excuse Stafford for what he had done all those years ago. This was the thought that passed through his mind for about the tenth time. And just like all the other times before, it sounded straightforward enough at first. But suddenly things weren't quite so cut and dried. What if the bloke wasn't as guilty as his mother had always told him? The words Sue had read out didn't sound anything like those of a coward who only cared about himself. Maybe that wasn't proof of anything on its own, but it was the closest Alan had ever come yet to hearing Stafford speak up for himself.

Could his mother have been mistaken? Or worse than that, even been lying to him all his life?

He swore under his breath. This was all bollocks. How could he just shove aside a lifetime of belief? Stafford must have written this when he was pissed up on the night of their party. It was nothing more than his way of trying to ease a guilty conscience. He probably didn't even remember having written it the next morning. If the bloke was genuinely on the level then he would have turned up for their meeting on Friday evening. If he'd done that, then perhaps all this other stuff would never have happened. Stafford only had himself to blame for the way things had turned out.

Backwards and forwards the mental debate raged, relentlessly increasing the pressure inside Alan's head. This was not a new sensation for him. Something similar always seemed to happen when he didn't know what to say or do next. Usually it was much easier just to lash out and hit the nearest person or object rather than try to find a better answer. At least it got rid of the headaches more quickly. And anyway, he'd always quite enjoyed having the nickname of Mad Alan. It helped to keep most of the other kids frightened of him.

He turned over the photograph and looked again at his father and Stafford standing side by side, both of them with big smiles on their faces for the camera. Even though he fought against it, he knew then that his doubts were winning the inner argument. For all he knew, Stafford might still be a total bastard, but ….

Why the fuck did there have to be any buts?

Alan could not hold back a low growl of frustration. His very reason for being the way he was – or, as some of those bastards at the approved school had put it, *his excuse* – was being taken away from him. Without Stafford to hate, he'd no longer have someone else to blame for all the crazy things he'd done in the past. And if there was no one else to blame, everything he did from now on was going to be all down to him. The good things, and the bad.

He began to think the unthinkable. There was always a small chance that Stafford and the others might still be alive. Even at this late stage, should he do something to help try and save them?

But that meant putting himself at risk. The coppers were just waiting for him to step out of line again. He had to look after number one. And it wasn't as if he was the one to blame for the mess Stafford was in.

The pressure in his head was becoming unbearable. His protective shell was cracking. Like a bad dream that refused to go away, another image of Tanya suddenly appeared. Once again she was tearfully begging for help.

His help?

Was she really still alive? How could he ignore that possibility any longer? Would it turn out to be his fault if she died some time later on?

There were too many questions. He couldn't think straight. His brain was exploding.

Mindless of his surroundings, Alan shot up from his seat. His voice filled the restaurant as he shouted out in an attempt to free himself of the mental torment.

'Okay! I'm g-going back. I c-can't do no more than that.'

A stunned hush fell over the small restaurant. People were staring. Then the girl Sue was standing beside him. Her face was full of concern.

'What on earth's the matter?' she asked softly. 'You look terrible.'

Her voice jolted him back into the real world outside of his head. Reaching into Stafford's wallet, he thrust one of the five-pound notes into the girl's hand.

'Thanks for helping me; k-keep the change,' he told her, only now aware that his hated stammer was back.

She looked at the note in utter astonishment. 'Five pounds! The bill only comes to one and ninepence.'

Alan did not hear her. He was already on his way out of the door.

***

He hurried back as fast as possible to the abandoned Cresta, all the time thanking his lucky stars that he hadn't yet thought to throw away the keys. He'd meant to, but like the wallet, he'd forgotten all about them being in his pocket.

The first thing he needed to do was return Stafford's car to where it was originally parked and make it look as if it had never been moved. After that he should be able to phone the police without risking very much. All he needed to tell them was that he'd been walking on the moor and that he'd seen the cave-in happen when the jets flew over. He'd show them exactly where to start digging, then push off quick on his scooter before any awkward questions started.

Much of the way back was up a steep, twisting hill, and it took him nearly twenty minutes to reach the Cresta. By that time the sweat was pouring down his face. Quickly, he unlocked the vehicle and jumped behind the wheel. The engine started first time.

After doing a rapid U-turn, he set off back in the direction of the White Rose Inn.

***

'Try it now,' Phil called from beneath the raised bonnet of the Rover.

Sitting in the driver's seat, Geordie started the engine as instructed. After a few moments of steady running Phil's voice sounded again.

'It looks like she's holding. Give her a few more revs.'

The big man trod on the accelerator and the engine noise increased to a roar. He held it there for several seconds before letting it return to a gentle tick-over.

The bonnet slammed shut and Phil appeared at the driver's window. 'That should be okay for a while.' He grinned. 'Like I always say, it's bloody amazing what you can do with a bit of insulating tape and a few drops of recycled beer.'

For once, Geordie was not in the mood for any light-hearted remarks. 'Jump in,' he snapped. 'We need to get moving.'

He drove at a brisk pace, but steady enough for them to take note of everything they passed. A signpost told him that they were now two miles away from the village of Scapdale.

They continued on their way in silence. Geordie grim-faced and determined, glanced across at Phil. He could see that the Kiwi, although remaining watchful, was still a little sceptical about the whole business. And maybe Phil was right? Maybe a seventeen-year-old kid, no matter how wild he was, wasn't going to be any serious kind of threat to Mike? But Geordie for one wasn't prepared to bet his old skipper's safety on that. He knew from what he'd seen back home in Newcastle that teenagers these days were becoming a lot more aggressive and dangerous. And this kid Alan was reckoned to be more out of control than most of them.

The car swept around a right-hand bend and there, less than a hundred yards ahead of them, was a Vauxhall Cresta. From this distance it looked to be exactly the same model and colour as the one Stafford was driving.

'Put your foot down and let's have a closer look,' Phil suggested.

Even as the Kiwi spoke, the big Rover was already surging forward and closing the gap.

'It *is* Mike's car!' Geordie exclaimed when getting close enough to read the registration plate.

'But it sure as heck isn't Mike driving it,' Phil added.

The Rover's horn blared aggressively as Geordie pulled out to overtake.

***

The sudden blast of noise from behind startled Alan. His eyes flicked up to the rear-view mirror. The car bearing rapidly down on him was already close enough to identify the driver. Panic immediately took hold.

The car disappeared from his mirror as it pulled over to the far side of the road in an attempt to overtake. Alan glanced back over his right shoulder. The big guy and another of Stafford's mates were both gesturing furiously at him to pull up, and they did not look as if they were in the mood for just talking. The driver, especially, looked as if he wanted to beat the hell out of him.

There was nothing left to do but try and outrun them, at least until he could think more clearly about how to deal with the situation. Alan felt his hands shaking as he swerved across in an attempt to prevent the other car from getting alongside. He then pressed the accelerator to the floor. In no time, the Cresta's speedometer shot up to seventy miles per hour.

The hill leading directly down into Scapdale was now only just ahead, and it was obvious that he was still not losing his pursuers. Once in the village he would be forced to slow right down, maybe even stop completely if someone got in his way. Yet again he glanced over his shoulder. The big guy was shaking his fist and had a face on him like thunder.

Alan's eyes returned to the road ahead just a fraction too late. A fairly sharp bend in the road immediately ahead – not a problem at a slower speed – rushed up far too quickly at him. Frantically, he braked and spun the wheel, in the process completely over-steering. He was out of control and could feel the back end of the car swinging across. The Rover behind him came briefly into view. Then it was lost again. Which way was he pointing now? What should he do? Both questions quickly became meaningless. The car was rolling over.

Alan held his breath and wondered if he was about to die.

***

Geordie could see the accident coming a mile off. With the bend rushing closer, he braked hard. It was obvious that the kid was going way too fast to make it all the way around. The Cresta skidded violently, twisted and then rolled over completely after dropping into a shallow ditch on the side of the road.

The battered vehicle had already come to rest the right way up again by the time he and Phil jumped out of the Rover. Both of them began running over to the wreckage. With much less weight to carry, Phil was the first to arrive on the scene. It took three vigorous tugs from him before the driver's door finally opened, giving a loud screech of protest as it did so. By then, Geordie had caught up with him. The pair of them gazed for a moment at the bloodied figure of Alan, now sprawled right across the front bench seat, his head and shoulders propped up by the passenger door.

With a snort, the big Tynesider reached past Phil in an attempt to get at the youth. 'Come on. Stop pretending you're hurt.'

Phil tried to restrain him. 'Hang on, mate. I reckon he *is* hurt. Pretty badly too. He might have even bought it.'

Geordie eased back as common sense prevailed. 'Aye, you could be right,' he muttered.

Phil reached down to pick up Alan's wrist, feeling for a pulse. 'No, he's still alive,' he finally announced. 'But he's out cold, there's no doubt about that. We better not try to move him before the medics get here.'

This was not what Geordie wanted to hear. 'So how the bloody hell are we going to find out where Mike is?' he demanded. 'Any damn thing could have happened to him, and this little sod is the only one who can tell us what's going on.'

It was a problem that Phil appeared to have no ready answer for. A passing car pulled up a few yards away, saving him the trouble of admitting this.

The driver leaned out of his window. 'Do you want me to call an ambulance?' he called across. 'There's a phone box a short way ahead.'

'Aye, do that,' Geordie responded. 'And while you're about it, you can tell the police to get here too.'

NINETEEN

Sue removed her waitress' apron with a sigh of relief. It had been a demanding few hours and she was glad to have finished her shift. Now, thankfully, another girl was taking over for the rest of the day. She exchanged a few moments of small talk with her replacement before leaving by the restaurant's back entrance. Propped up against a wall here was the ageing bicycle she used for travelling to and from work. Living as she did on a small farm well away from the village centre, the bike was more than useful. Especially with the local bus service being so infrequent.

Pedalling slowly through the village, her mind turned once again to the strange youth who had come into the restaurant a little earlier that afternoon. And the tip he had given to her – nearly five pounds! That was as much as she normally earned in an entire week.

But it was not the huge tip that was occupying most of her thoughts. Although the lad had been a bit rough looking, and a Londoner judging from the way he spoke, there was still something about him she'd quite liked. She couldn't forget the stunned look on his face when she'd told him what the writing on the back of that photograph had said. The words were certainly a bit unusual, but even so, there was nothing in them that might explain his astonishing behaviour shortly afterwards. What on earth had made him shout out like that and then go rushing off out the door as if there was some terrible emergency? It was all very disturbing.

She began to ponder more deeply on the matter. She had told the boy her name when he'd asked her, but he had not given his in return. Was he the Alan that the writer had been referring to? Although there was no reason why she should feel responsible for causing his distress, a small part of her was stubbornly clinging to the idea that she must have been.

Why did he have to pick on her? Anyone in the restaurant could have read out those few words for him. Despite the untidy way they were scribbled, they had not been so very difficult to understand. Which made his excuse about not being able to read them for himself sound pretty weak. All the same, he must have been telling the truth. No one could have faked such a powerful reaction. Not if they had already known what the words said.

Sue shrugged in an effort to break this unsettling train of thought. The lad was gone now, so there was no reason for her to keep thinking about him. If he did come from London like she supposed then he was probably just another visitor to the area who she would never see again. It was pointless to let him play on her mind.

She cycled steadily on, leaving the village centre behind. The road became steeper as she began to encounter the lower slopes of Squire's Hill. As usual at this point, she dismounted and began to push the bike.

While rounding the last bend before the top, she immediately caught sight of the battered car on the edge of the moor ahead. She caught her breath. It looked like a very nasty accident. Several people were standing beside the crashed vehicle, and through a large hole in the windscreen where most of the shattered glass had fallen out she could see the head and shoulders of a figure still trapped inside. Her first instinct was to press on and mind her own business. There were already enough people gathered around to do whatever needed to be done.

On a whim, she changed her mind. There might still be something useful she could help with? She crossed the road. Drawing closer, she could now see that there was quite a bit of blood on the trapped person's face.

Her pace quickened. It wasn't – it couldn't be – surely not?

But when still several yards away, she knew for certain that it *was* the same boy. She pulled up sharply, staring in horror. Her mind immediately flashed back yet again to when she had seen him rushing wildly out of the restaurant. She could picture the scene more clearly than ever now. In truth, he had looked to be half out of his mind with some kind of inner turmoil.

And all because of a few innocent sounding words.

Had those words helped to cause this accident?

While standing there, stunned and still trying to comprehend what part she may have played in all of this, Sue sensed someone approaching.

'Do you know him?'

Her eyes shifted over toward the big man who had positioned himself directly in front of her. His words came out half as a question, half as an accusation. His tone was intimidating.

'No, n-not really,' she stammered.

'But you *have* seen him before,' he persisted. 'I can tell from the way you were looking at him.'

Before she could respond, a second man joined them and spoke to the first. He sounded as if he might be Australian.

'Ease up, Geordie. You'll frighten the poor girl to death.'

The big man let out a deep sigh and ran a hand over his brow. He then turned back to face her and forced a smile. 'I'm sorry. I didn't mean to sound so rough.'

His friend chipped in. 'It's just that a good mate of ours has gone missing, and that's his car over there. The kid inside must have stolen it.'

'And he's the only one who can tell us what's happened to Mike,' the one called Geordie finished off. 'So if you do know anything about him that can help, for Pete's sake please tell us.'

His urgency got through to her. 'Well, he did come into the restaurant where I work,' she began nervously. 'All I did was …'

She broke off, suddenly remembering the signature on the back of the photograph. 'Did you say that your friend's name was Mike?' she asked.

Geordie nodded. His expression became even more intense. 'Aye, that's right. Mike Stafford. Why are you asking that?'

She ignored his question. 'How about the names of Jimmy and Alan? Do they mean anything to you?'

The two men exchanged startled glances. But before either one of them could question her any further, a blaring siren announced the arrival of an ambulance. A police motorcyclist followed closely behind.

'Why don't you go and deal with those guys,' the one who sounded like an Australian told Geordie. 'I'll carry on here with …'

He paused to look at her.

'Sue,' she told him.

Probably realising that his friend's more relaxed approach was better suited to getting all the information they wanted quickly, Geordie reluctantly agreed.

'I'll be back,' he promised before striding away.

***

The ambulance carrying the still unconscious Alan was just setting off when Geordie returned. He was closely followed by the motorcyclist police constable.

The big man wasted no time. 'Well?' he asked.

Phil was equally brisk in replying. 'You remember that photograph you told me about – the one Mike found stuck on the door of the kid's locker. It looks like Alan has got his hands on it again. Apparently Mike wrote some sort of promise to himself on the back. The kid got Sue here to read it out for him.'

Geordie immediately faced her. 'So what did it say? What did he write?'

He could see her wilting slightly under the intensity of his gaze and tried to soften his expression. She seemed to firm herself anyway. Soon, she was going through the whole story once again for his benefit.

It was the constable who spoke to Sue first as she neared the end. He was taking notes.

'Tell me again please, Miss. What were the words the injured youth shouted just before rushing out of your restaurant?'

'Okay, I'm going back. I can't do no more than that,' she repeated.

'You're sure that's exactly what he said?'

She nodded. 'I can still hear him saying it.'

Geordie's frustration was reaching new heights. 'But where?' he demanded of no one in particular. 'That's the bloody question. Where was he going back to?'

He did not need it pointing out to him that, if he'd only followed the Cresta discreetly instead of charging in without thinking, Alan might have led them straight to where Mike was.

The constable spoke again. 'Is there anyone else you know of who may still be with Mister Stafford?' he asked.

Geordie remembered what he had been told over the telephone by the girl at the White Rose Inn. 'There might be a woman, German perhaps,' he said. 'And a young girl of around eight or nine years old. I don't know either of their names.'

At the mention of a child, the constable's expression of concern deepened. He quickly wrote down the details.

'So what are you going to do to find them?' Geordie demanded, desperate to get some kind of action going.

'I'll get on to the station right away and make a report bringing them up to date. After that – –'

This was too much for the big man. 'Make a report!' he exploded. 'How the bloody hell is that going to help? What we need now is a search party, not everything writing down in bloody triplicate.'

The policeman sighed. 'It's not like that. I understand how you feel, but until we get all the details properly together and – –'

Once again Geordie interrupted him. 'Look, I've already told you what this kid's like. He's got some mad idea in his head about wanting revenge. We already know he's taken Mike's car, so who's to say he hasn't done something a whole lot worse as well.'

He waved an irate hand. 'You make your report if you want to, I'm going to start my own bloody search party.'

'And where do you plan to start?'

'How the hell do I know? Somewhere...anywhere. Anything's better than just standing around doing nothing.'

Geordie turned his attention to Sue. 'You're sure Alan didn't give any clue that might tell us where he was heading for?'

She shook her head. 'But I think I can understand what he meant a bit better now. It was as if he knew he'd done something wrong, and he wanted to go back to where it had happened to try and put things right.'

'Maybe we're not too late?' Phil suggested. 'Whatever Alan's done with Mike, if he thought he had enough time to go back and fix things, then maybe we've still got long enough to do the same.'

'Aye, you could be right,' Geordie agreed. He jabbed a finger in the direction of Scapdale and the White Rose Inn beyond. 'When we ran into

Alan, he was heading that way. So I figure that's where we need to start looking. We'll drive along this road and see if we can spot anything.'

He grabbed Phil's arm. 'Come on, pal. Let's get moving.'

'I'll get things organised as quickly as possible,' the constable promised. 'Just be sure to let us know immediately if you find anything.'

'You can count on that,' Geordie told him.

***

With Scapdale now behind them and the Rover travelling at a steady thirty miles per hour, both Geordie and Phil's eyes scanned the moor that stretched out on both sides of the road. So far, apart from a few other cars overtaking them, there had been little sign of anyone, let alone Stafford and his companions.

Phil was the first to say what they were both feeling. 'This is a hell of a long shot. If Alan really has done something to harm Mike, then we're hardly likely to find him just driving around up here.'

There was a sharp edge to Geordie's response. 'Have you got something better in mind?'

'Well, we could try going straight on to the White Rose. I know it's well past closing time now, but there's always a chance there might be someone still there who can remember seeing him. Maybe we'll pick up a lead if we poke around hard enough.'

Geordie frowned. 'Aye, that's not such a bad idea, I suppose.' He put his foot down and the big Rover quickly gathered speed.

They swung around a slow bend at fifty miles an hour. The road had barely straightened out when, without the slightest warning, he slammed on the brakes. Caught unawares, Phil was jerked forward, catching his elbow painfully on the face of the dashboard.

'What the flaming heck did you do that for?' he demanded, rubbing the sore joint.

Ignoring Phil's discomfort, Geordie pointed behind them. 'Look there. Just on the edge of the moor. A Lambretta by the look of it! And it's a blue one.'

He reversed the car to where the scooter was parked. Both men got out and looked carefully around. There was no sign of anyone nearby who might be the owner.

'We've no time to mess about, man,' Geordie stated. It was all the justification he needed for his choice of action. He began rifling through the contents of the canvas bag strapped to the back, searching for anything that might positively identify the machine as belonging to Alan.

A collection of unwashed clothes was quickly dragged out and strewn in an untidy heap on the ground. Phil picked up a pair of jeans and began searching through the pockets. Geordie, meanwhile, produced a large pair of metal cutters from somewhere at the bottom of the bag. He stared curiously at the hefty implement for a moment or two before tossing this aside too.

'I've got something here,' Phil told him.

The Kiwi held up a book of matches. The Compton Manor Hotel name and crest was printed large across the front flap.

'Not perfect, but that's good enough for me,' Geordie declared.

'We best call the cops,' Phil told him. 'That constable said to let them know if we found anything.'

'Aye, let's get things moving. We'll ring them from the White Rose. It's only a couple of minutes further on.'

'The place will be closed remember,' Phil pointed out. 'There's no guarantee anyone will be around to let us inside.'

'In that case, I'll just have to let myself in.'

It was clear from Geordie's expression that he meant exactly what he'd just said.

***

The clock was showing 5.30pm when Astrid felt the first flutter of genuine concern. She had expected Siggi and Tanya to be back some time ago. They'd only gone out for lunch, and her sister had said quite clearly that she did not want to be late home.

Stop being so silly, Astrid told herself. It's a nice afternoon, so they've probably stopped off somewhere on the return journey to make the most of the sunny weather. She wondered what Siggi had said to the Canadian. Had they talked very much about the war? That, after all, was meant to be the reason for their meeting. Or so Siggi claimed. But there was no doubt that Mike Stafford was a good looking and charming man.

Astrid then had another thought. Suppose their talk had gone badly? What if Siggi had said some terrible things and offended the Canadian so much that he'd abandoned her? Not knowing the area, her sister might easily get lost.

This idea was quickly dismissed. He was far too much of a gentleman to do anything like that. No matter what her headstrong sister might say to him, Astrid was certain that Mike Stafford would always act in the correct manner. Besides, there was Tanya for him to consider as well.

She prayed that her daughter had not got into any mischief while with them. There were definitely times when she could be far too inquisitive for her own good. From nowhere, a yearning to give her child a hug came over her. Astrid had no idea what had suddenly brought on this feeling, but whatever the cause, the need to give Tanya that cuddle was now very strong indeed.

Once more she looked at the clock on the mantelpiece. If they were not home very soon – silly or not – she would have to do something.

***

The landlord of the White Rose Inn was rudely woken from his afternoon nap by a loud and persistent banging on the front door. Whoever it was, they were obviously not going to go away. Muttering to himself, he pulled back the two large bolts securing the entrance.

'What do you want?' he demanded of the two men standing outside. 'We're closed until seven o'clock.'

'Not any more you're not,' Geordie told him.

TWENTY

Yet again Astrid glanced apprehensively at the clock on the mantelpiece. It now showed 6.30pm. She jumped up out of her chair and began pacing up and down the length of the living room.

After less than a minute of this, she stopped. Her mind was made up. The situation was now well past the *'being silly'* stage. If Siggi was planning to be this late home, she would most definitely have telephoned to put her mind at rest.

Astrid had no idea how the police would react to her calling them. It wasn't as if her sister and daughter had been missing for a particularly long time. In fact, at the moment they were only a couple of hours or so later than expected. She could end up looking very foolish indeed, especially if the pair of them were to arrive home immediately after she'd made the call.

'So what?' she said aloud. Looking foolish was the least of her concerns.

She picked up the telephone.

***

Stafford watched as Siggi shifted her leg slightly in an effort to ease the cramp that was obviously starting to set in. The action must have done some good because it drew a sigh of relief.

Considering what she had gone through in the past, she was still holding it together far better than he could have hoped for. The way she'd managed to smother her fears and help him deal with that huge rat had been amazing. He would never have been able to do it without her. Now, hopefully, their success in getting Tanya's handkerchief up to the surface would be sufficient to sustain her for a while longer. Whatever happened in the short term – no matter how fortunate they might be – there was not going to be any quick way out of this place.

Tanya, quite incredibly under the circumstances, had fallen asleep. The girl's breathing was deep and steady, indicating that she was out for the count. Her last words before dropping off had displayed her undying faith in his ability to get them out of this situation.

'We'll soon be safe now,' she'd told Siggi, as if sensing her aunt's own fears. 'Mister Stafford's fixed it.' Her eyes widened. 'I don't know anyone else who could have caught that huge rat. Not even Dad.'

'Sure he could have,' he'd grinned at her.

What impressed him more than anything about the young girl was her courage. He knew that the injury to her ankle must be pretty damn painful, yet there had not been a word of complaint from her. Some kid, he considered. For her sake, far more than for himself or even Siggi, he prayed that they would be discovered in time.

Siggi caught his eye. 'She's fast asleep,' she said.

'That's probably the best thing for her right now.'

There was a pause, then: 'Mike ...'

By now he was becoming more used to her addressing him by his first name. 'Yes,' he answered, noting her hesitant manner.

'Forget it. It is nothing.'

'Come on. Spit it out.'

A nervous smile crossed her face. 'Some English expressions are so horrible. You make it sound as if I have been sick.'

Stafford made no comment. It was obvious to him that this little aside was nothing but stalling on her part. Whatever it was she wanted to say, it was not coming easily.

She tried again. This time the words came in a rush.

'I am frightened, Mike. I mean *really* frightened. Now that Tanya is asleep, do you think that I could ...?'

She stopped, almost as abruptly as she'd begun.

Not that she needed to say anything further. Her need was perfectly clear. When awake, Tanya had been acting as a shield between Siggi and her own fears. The necessity to put on a brave face for her niece's sake had her almost believing she could handle the stress of the situation. But now, temporarily deprived of that crutch, she was in desperate need of some support herself.

He raised an inviting arm in response to her unfinished question. 'Sure you can,' he said gently.

Taking great care not to disturb Tanya, Siggi eased over a short distance and slid gratefully up close to him. As his arm dropped protectively around her, she placed her head on his shoulder.

'Danker, thank you,' she murmured. 'I don't want to talk. Not yet, anyway. Just let me be next to you for a short while please. Make me feel safe, even if we are not.'

In the silence that followed, Stafford could feel the tension in her body slowly easing away.

***

Half an hour passed without a word being exchanged. After a while, Siggi became so still that it was easy to imagine she too had fallen asleep. Then, quite suddenly, she raised her head and spoke. Her voice was very quiet.

'I was wrong, Mike. So very wrong. If I am to die here, at least I understand that now.'

He looked at her seriously. 'No one is going to die down here. Trust me, they'll find us soon enough.' The firmness of his tone was convincing.

He paused before asking: 'Anyhow, what were you wrong about?'

She let out a long sigh. 'Life in general – men in particular.'

'That's a mighty big subject to be wrong about.' There was just the trace of a smile on his face.

'Yes, maybe that is so. But the war years changed so many people's way of thinking. All the hardships we faced. The grief of losing ...'

She stopped herself in mid-sentence, shaking her head. 'But of course, you know all this as well as I do. Forgive me. For a moment I was forgetting about your friend Jimmy. It is always so easy to think that only one side suffered.'

The mention of his friend's name brought back to Stafford the very reason for his return to England. Since this underground drama had begun, it was hardly surprising that Jimmy had not entered his thoughts. But now memories of his old friend were forming once again. For the first time ever he felt capable of looking back on K for King's final mission with calm objectivity. Once again, there was this weird sensation that Jimmy was close at hand.

Siggi's voice interrupted these thoughts. 'You have become silent. Are you troubled by something?'

'No. I'm fine.'

'You were thinking about your friend, were you not? Perhaps I should not have spoken about him?'

'That's okay. I'm glad that you did.' He hesitated. 'That stuff you said about the way Jim's parachute was packed. Did you really mean all of that?'

'Of course.' For a moment her voice was once again full of Germanic authority. 'I would not have said such a thing if it were not the truth.'

He gave an uneasy laugh. 'It's just that I've never considered an angle like that before.'

'And that is what makes you so special. So much a man of honour.'

'I don't understand.'

She sighed. 'Can you not see? Many men in your position would have automatically looked for someone else to at least share the responsibility for Jimmy's death. Even people with genuine blame to carry will often try to lay it elsewhere. The fact that you did none of this tells me all there is to know about you.'

An embarrassed Stafford did not know what to say. Siggi, having made her point and seeing it register, also chose to remain silent.

After a short while she glanced up at the air vent. Her eyes followed the pink cord down to the small rock around which it was now tied.

'It will be dark in a few hours,' she said, almost to herself.

Stafford gave her a comforting squeeze. 'You said yourself that Astrid is sure to have reported us missing by now. So that means there's every chance they'll find us before the light goes. And if they don't, it's bound to be very soon afterwards.'

Her big eyes looked directly into his. 'How much do you honestly believe that? I want you to tell me the truth.'

He held her gaze. 'I'll show you how sure I am. I'll bet you the price of a slap-up meal that we get out of here safely. How about it?'

Her voice shot up. Once again her German accent became far more pronounced than usual. 'You wish to make bets with me at a time like this? To gamble with our lives?'

The penny then dropped. 'Only you can win this bet. If I win it means that ...'

Her voice tailed off and she could see that he was grinning at her. 'Now you make jokes with me. What is it about the British that makes them think a joke is the answer to adversity?'

'Canadian,' Stafford corrected. 'British grandparents yes, but I'm Canadian if you don't mind.'

She flicked a hand. 'British – Canadian – Australian. What is the difference? In so many ways you are all the same.'

Stafford decided that this was not the best time to debate with her over such a controversial statement. Instead, he contrived to appear repentant.

'Look, what I said just now. I'm sorry. That was just my way of showing you how little I'm concerned,' he explained.

The apology worked. 'I am sorry also,' Siggi told him. 'I know that you have done everything you can. I am frightened, that is all. Not only for myself, but for Tanya and you also. I want to share your confidence. I am trying very hard to but ...'

Once again, her need was obvious. Probably without even realising it, she was appealing to him for something more than just words. Without thinking, Stafford kissed her gently on the lips.

He was immediately stunned by what he had done. At first, Siggi also appeared to be shocked. But then her fingers dug into his shoulders, urging him not to pull away.

You're a married man, for God's sake, Stafford told himself. A happily married man who loves his wife dearly. What the hell was he doing? What had he started? He must back off right now before things went any further.

Siggi's fingers squeezed again, begging him not to.

'Please,' she whispered.

Despite all the warnings and pangs of conscience, Stafford knew that he must respond. He kissed her again, this time with far more intensity.

As their embrace ended, he assured himself repeatedly that he was not being unfaithful to Alice. That he was only doing this to provide temporary comfort to a frightened woman. Because of that, his actions didn't really count in the same way.

But there was a hollow ring to this excuse. Even dirty and dishevelled, Siggi was still a very attractive woman. Hadn't he acknowledged this to himself several times already? So, were his motives entirely unselfish?

His head was beginning to spin as he struggled with the uncertainty of it all.

***

Siggi too, was trying hard to understand what was happening to her. Just to be kissed like this was an almost forgotten experience. The last time it had happened was during the early days of the war. It was a young soldier called Karl who she had been fond of. Like her father, he too had died on the Russian Front.

She knew that what she was doing was wrong. Mike Stafford was a fine man who had a loving family, and she would never seek to destroy this for him. But at this moment she needed to borrow him for a short time. His family need never know about it, and this was the only way she could ever hope to get through their ordeal.

'Kiss me again please,' she said softly.

She felt only slight resistance from Stafford before he did as she asked.

***

At first, only a single patrol car containing two constables turned up at the White Rose in response to Geordie's telephone call. The big man was outraged at this scant turnout and made no bones about telling the constables exactly what he thought.

But from then on matters began moving rapidly. With no sign of Alan recovering consciousness any time soon, more police were drafted in to track down and question staff from the White Rose Inn who had been working that lunchtime. A waiter was found who remembered serving the group. It was the second time he had been asked about them, he told the officer. Being so soon after the war, he was unlikely to forget serving a German woman, especially one in the company of a Canadian. Almost as an afterthought, he added that he'd overheard them planning to take a walk on the moor after leaving the pub.

Astrid's call to the police added even more urgency to the enquiry. With news of a missing child rapidly spreading, everyone was now eager to offer information they imagined might be useful. Amongst these, a young couple from Scapdale returning home after enjoying lunch at the White Rose remembered seeing a Vauxhall Cresta parked on the moor edge. They were able to show officers approximately where that had been. The woman explained that the new Cresta model was a car her husband longed to own himself. When driving past it and seeing no one about, he had even made a light-hearted remark about coming back later and taking it home.

For the last half an hour, Geordie and Phil, together with four police constables, had been searching the moorland close to where the Cresta had been sighted. But manpower was still very limited, and the dense undergrowth of the moor did not offer much help. Any clues that might be around would be very easy to miss.

Although desperate not to put his concerns into actual words, Geordie was beginning to fear the worst. He knew better than anyone how resourceful his old skipper could be. Unless he was dead or badly injured, Mike would have found a way of contacting someone by now. Geordie was sure of that. The fact that the search party hadn't yet turned up any bodies hidden amongst the heather offered just about the only crumb of consolation.

More police were now arriving. Amongst them was the motorcycle constable that he and Phil had spoken to at the scene of the car crash. They both approached the officer.

'Any news on the boy Alan yet?' Geordie demanded. 'Has he woken up and said anything?'

The constable shook his head. 'He's still unconscious. With a double fracture of the skull, he could be out for some time apparently. And even if he does come around any time soon, they say he's most likely going to be concussed and confused. There's even a possibility of brain damage. They can't tell for sure yet.'

'Bugger!' Geordie exclaimed.

Phil could add little to that.

'It's bad enough when anyone goes missing up here on the moor,' the constable remarked. 'But when there's a young child involved …'

He sighed and shook his head as the full depth of his concern momentarily showed through.

Quickly, he became the professional policeman once more. 'I do have some good news for you though. We'll have a lot more help arriving here soon. There's a bus load of experienced officers already on its way up from York. Many of them are off-duty volunteers. The local farmers are also in the process of rounding up anyone willing to help.'

'Aye, that's good,' Geordie responded. 'We'll be needing everyone we can get if we're going to start spreading the search. We've already covered this part of the moor pretty much.'

The constable gave a dry laugh. 'Believe me, you haven't even scratched the surface yet. Let the people who know this area well get on with it.' He spread his hands. 'Besides, we've nothing else to go on at the moment. Obviously every officer for miles around has a description of all three missing persons, and they'll be keeping a sharp lookout for them. But until we know differently, all the evidence says that this is the area where we need to keep looking.'

Geordie placed a hand firmly on the policeman's shoulder. 'And what does all the evidence say about the outcome? You must have seen cases like this before.'

'I really wouldn't like to guess at this stage.'

The officer then glanced to one side as another police car pulled up. 'Here's the Inspector,' he said. 'He'll be wanting to speak to me.'

Breaking free from Geordie's grasp, he moved quickly away.

***

The constable had been accurate in his assessment. By 8.00pm, large numbers of volunteers, both police and members of the public, were gathered on the moor. Even Geordie was forced to concede that he had been way off the mark in his earlier outburst. Everything humanly possible was being done. Long sweeping lines of searchers carefully picked their way across the ground on both sides of the road. Progress was slow and meticulous as countless pairs of eyes searched for any small clue that might help.

Shortly after 9.30pm, just as the daylight was beginning to fade, Geordie heard a shout go up away to his right. He and Phil exchanged rapid glances before running over to the source. A large, ruddy-faced local farmer was holding up a pair of woman's shoes.

'I found them by these rocks here,' he said.

With darkness imminent, an even greater sense of urgency developed as Geordie and Phil joined the rush of volunteers now concentrating their search on the area immediately around this cluster of large rocks.

Only a couple more minutes passed before a large mound of newly settled soil and stones set directly in face of the hillside was discovered. A freshly dug grave was the first thing that sprang naturally to mind, although no one was yet willing to suggest such a thing openly. Geordie swallowed hard. He was feeling close to tears as a squad of policemen with shovels began digging.

Another shout went up, this time from one of the police reinforcements drafted in from York. 'Over here, Sarge.'

Accompanied by several officers, Geordie ran further up the hillside toward the man, fear and hope battling inside him for supremacy.

'It's got the little girl's name embroidered on it,' the constable said. 'There's a message too.' He held up the handkerchief for everyone to see. Although slightly smudged, the large capital letters written in red lipstick were still clear enough to read. They spelled out the single word: 'HELP'.

'And there's a line of something attached to it,' the officer continued.

Geordie was way ahead of him. His eyes were already tracking the pink cord as it ran away through the heather.

Without hesitation, he followed its path.

TWENTY-ONE

Tanya stirred before opening her eyes. She could feel her ankle throbbing quite painfully. Automatically, her hand felt for Auntie Siggi, who she was expecting to be immediately beside her. Alarm briefly flared as her fingers failed to make any contact. Her heart gave a little jerk of uncertainty, forcing her back into the wide-awake world much faster than usual.

Her eyes then fell on Siggi just a few feet away. Tanya's uncertainty faded as rapidly as it had formed. For a frightening few seconds she had imagined that she was all on her own, but with the reassuring sight of her aunt and Mister Stafford close at hand, she relaxed.

It was only then that Tanya realised how closely they were holding on to each other. It was just like mum and dad did sometimes. This puzzled her, especially after what her aunt had told her before. *'I do not have a boyfriend or husband because I have no wish for one.'* she had said several times during their talks together. Well, it certainly did not look like that now.

Tanya gave a small cough. Both heads swung in her direction.

***

'Oh, you are awake,' said Siggi. Her embarrassment was clear.

Stafford rapidly took in the young girl's puzzled expression, at the same time wondering if she was aware that he was a married man. He decided not. There was no trace of condemnation on her face, only uncertainty and surprise.

Casually, he removed his arm from around Siggi's shoulders. 'Your aunt was feeling a little cold without her cardigan,' he explained.

'I see,' Tanya said. There was even a small hint of disappointment in her voice.

Siggi, more composed now that this explanation had been accepted, wriggled over closer to her niece. 'How is your ankle feeling?' she asked, switching the conversation.

Her ploy worked. Tanya gingerly ran her fingers over the swelling and produced a brave smile. 'Maybe it's a tiny bit better.'

Stafford was on the point of making some encouraging remark to the girl when he checked himself. Instead, he got quickly to his feet and positioned himself directly beneath the air vent, listening closely.

The other two stared at him. 'What is it?' Siggi asked.

He waved a hand to silence her. 'Hold on a minute.'

He remained absolutely still, straining to catch any further small sound. Were his ears playing tricks on him, or had he really picked up the faint sound of a man's voice drifting down from the surface? He did not want to say anything to the others just yet. It would be cruel to raise false hopes.

Siggi and Tanya were now as still as he was. Despite his restraint, there was already expectation on their faces. Again he felt that he heard something. This time there might even have been more than one voice.

A short period of total silence followed. Should he call out? he wondered. Still anxious not to speak until certain, he tilted his head to one side, at the same time lifting himself up onto his toes. His ear was now only a couple of inches away from the small opening overhead.

He had barely shifted into this new position when he picked up a light scratching sound. Before he had time to move, a small shower of dirt came sprinkling down, some of it falling directly into his ear. Instinctively, he stepped back a pace to shake this out. He was still attempting to clear the dirt away when a voice boomed down through the vent. In spite of its muffled quality, he would recognise it anywhere.

'Mike! Can you hear me? Are you down there?'

The relief that surged through him was a painful but beautiful thing. He glanced across at the other two. Both appeared to be momentarily stunned. Tanya recovered first. She threw her arms around her aunt.

'I told you,' she cried out. 'I told you Mister Stafford would save us.'

The young girl's reaction seemed to unlock Siggi's own numbed emotions. She hugged Tanya for all she was worth. Words still refused to come for her, but Stafford could see that the flood of tears she had steadfastly been holding back all this time were now on the point of bursting free.

Sobbing, but at the same time laughing, they clung to each other.

Geordie's voice called once again, this time with more urgency. 'Mike! Can you hear me, man?'

Swallowing down the lump in his throat, he was at last able to respond.

'Geordie,' he called back up, his voice croaky. 'It's sure good to hear your voice, buddy.'

These were all the words he could manage for the moment.

***

By 10.30pm, Astrid was going out of her mind with worry. She had been unable to contact her husband Terry on the telephone, and there was no one else she could share her agony with. Something terrible must have happened to her little girl and sister, but so far the police had told her nothing.

The sudden ringing of the doorbell caused her to jump. She glanced out of the front room window. Standing on the step outside was a constable. There seemed to be a stern expression on his face that instantly spelled bad news. Quite suddenly, the rapid thumping of Astrid's own heartbeat was loud in her ears.

She raced to the door, yanking it open.

'Please tell me what is happening?' she demanded before the officer even had time to speak.

His expression relaxed. All of a sudden he was wearing a reassuring smile. 'We've located your daughter and sister,' he said. 'They are both safe and well at present.'

Astrid felt herself swaying. For an instant the man became a blur. 'Thank God,' she breathed.

She was barely conscious of the constable stepping forward to support her. Large hands took her weight. 'You better sit down for a minute,' she heard him say.

He guided her back into the front room and lowered her gently into an armchair. Only when she was comfortably settled did he begin to tell the full story.

***

The initial euphoria of being discovered was now wearing off for Stafford as he began to recognise the potential dangers that they still faced. A safe escape for them was by no means a certainty yet. There were still countless tons of earth and stone to be shifted first. And all the time any digging was going on, there would be a very real danger of further cave-ins almost anywhere inside the shaft. He glanced quickly up at the tunnel ceiling. Perhaps even here, directly below this life-giving air vent that they had no choice but to stay close to. Judging from her expression, Siggi had also begun thinking along similar lines. Only Tanya remained brightly optimistic.

He was still dwelling on these problems when a voice he did not recognise called down the vent. 'Hello, Mike. Can you hear me?'

He acknowledged the man's call and the voice continued. 'My name is Roy Adams, and I'm in charge of this rescue operation. First, let me reassure you all down there that I've organised many such underground rescues before. This one should be a piece of cake.'

'A piece of cake.' Stafford had not heard that expression since the war. It meant that something was going to be very easy, and was a popular saying amongst RAF aircrew, particularly fighter pilots. It was not rare for them to be heard using it immediately before flying off to their deaths.

Keeping this thought strictly to himself, he called back up. 'Is there anything we can do to help?'

'I'm just coming to that bit. The most important thing is that we protect both you and your air supply from any further falls that might occur.'

Stafford frowned as he heard his earlier fears being put into words. He shot a quick look at the other two. In the tiny amount of daylight still filtering down, he was sure he detected a slight tightening of Siggi's features. She also made a point of drawing Tanya closer than ever to her. But on the surface at least, there was little other reaction.

Adams continued. 'We've been rather lucky in one respect, what with this air vent being a little bit wider than some I've seen in the past. What we plan to do is drop you down some short steel sections. These will bolt together much like a Meccano set. The idea is for you to build the framework of a cage that you will be able to shelter inside. How does this sound so far?'

'Yeah, it sounds pretty straightforward,' Stafford told him. 'And in case you're interested, I did have a Meccano set when I was a kid. I used to make all kinds of stuff with it.'

'That's good. Then it should be easy for you, Mike. After you've put the framework together, we'll then let you have some rolls of canvas. You can spread these out over the frame to act as a guard against dust and small debris.'

'You make it sound like camping,' Stafford remarked.

A throaty chuckle sounded. 'That's the spirit. How are the ladies?'

Before he could answer, Tanya spoke up. 'We're all right thank you, Mister Adams.'

Stafford smiled to himself. Now feeling safe, the kid seemed to be treating the whole thing as an exciting game. Even the pain from her ankle wasn't getting in the way of her enjoying this new adventure.

Siggi however, appeared less comfortable. 'Ask him for another torch,' she said in a loud whisper. 'The daylight is nearly gone.'

He conveyed her request adding: 'And how about a flask of coffee too?'

'The coffee is already on its way over. As for the light, I've got two torches here beside me that I'm going to drop down to you right away.' Adams paused. 'Now, apart from that, is there anything else you need?'

'Only a bath.'

Once again Adams chuckled. 'I don't think we can quite manage to squeeze a bath tub down. Still, a nice long soak can be something for you to look forward to.'

There was a breezy confidence about the man that inspired belief, Stafford reflected. But of course, keeping their spirits up was an important part of his job.

Adams completed his instructions. 'When everything is assembled and ready, then we'll slide an air-line down the vent. Make sure that the end of this goes right inside the cage. This way, your air supply will be protected no matter what.'

Stafford could not resist asking: 'How long do you reckon it will be before you get us out of here?'

'We've got some heavy earth-moving equipment arriving soon. Once that's working, it shouldn't take too long.'

Other than that, Adams refused to be drawn. With a cheery: 'See you later,' he set off about his business.

***

Just as Adams had stated, the short, right-angled steel sections resembled an oversized Meccano set. Holes drilled at regular intervals enabled each piece to be easily bolted to the next. With Siggi and Tanya both eager to help by holding the torches, Stafford set to work. By the time he was finished he had erected a structure eight feet long by four feet wide. There was enough height to sit comfortably upright.

Next, he spread the canvas lengths over the framework, fixing these securely in position by means of more bolts through strategically placed eyelets. Just a small flap was left loose for entry.

'All set, guys,' Stafford called up to Geordie and Phil, who had been taking it in turns to offer an almost continuous stream encouragement and advice.

Adams must have been nearby, because it was his voice that responded. 'The digger is here now, Mike, so we can get started as soon as the air-line is in place. Any final questions?'

'No, I don't think so.'

'Okay, just give three hard tugs on the line when you're safely in position. Once we get that signal, we'll start digging. All you have to do is sit there and relax. But one important thing. Do not under any circumstances come out of the shelter until we tell you to. Understand?'

'Absolutely,' Stafford said.

'She'll be right, Mike,' Phil's nasal tones told him.

'Aye, just hang on there a short while longer,' Geordie added.

Before Stafford could respond, someone began to feed down a hard rubber hose. Adams had already assured him that oxygen would be regularly pumped down to them through this. He grabbed hold of the end and fed it in through the cage's entry point. With the three of them safely inside, he gave the hose three hard tugs and then secured the flap.

By torchlight he regarded the other two. He noted with a sense of apprehension that Siggi was now looking far from good.

***

Even while watching Stafford construct their shelter, Siggi had still somehow managed to keep her nerves under tight control. Then she saw the air-line snaking its way down to them. Memories of the very worst kind came rushing back. She could well remember a disturbingly similar line going down through the ruins of their Berlin house. It had done nothing to save her mother. Was she now destined to die in a similar way?

Once inside their makeshift shelter, the terror clawing away at her immediately intensified. In such a tightly confined space she was feeling utterly trapped. It was now taking every tiny bit of her willpower not to scream out loud. Mike was talking to her, but the words he was saying were barely registering. What she wanted more than anything else was to cling to him again and feed off his strength. The more she dwelt on this, the more she needed him.

Tanya touched her hand, making her jump slightly. She gazed at her niece. I must be strong, she told herself. Tanya must not get any hint of how I'm truly feeling.

'Can I cuddle up again?' the young girl asked.

'Perhaps we all should,' Stafford quickly suggested.

Siggi knew instantly that, however much she might be fooling Tanya, she was not concealing anything from the Canadian. He was more than aware of what she currently needed, and he was doing as much as he could to help her. But it would never be the same as before. She could tell from his eyes that a huge love for his wife would not allow a repeat of their earlier intensity. The guilt inside him was already far too strong.

Even so, he *was* still offering her something. The three of them drew together. Siggi's hand found Stafford's and she squeezed it fiercely.

She had absolutely no intention of letting go.

***

Even after several hours, the team of rescuers were still hard at work. With temporary lighting running from two large generators, the small section of ground they occupied stood out like a well-illuminated oasis in the middle of an otherwise formidably dark moor.

Contradicting his outward show of breezy confidence, Roy Adams was proving to be a cautious and meticulous man. Because of this, progress was slow. Every yard of the way was carefully plotted, and although the mechanical digger did its fair share, much of the way forward still had to be done by hand. Every possible precaution to avoid fresh falls was taken, with shoring being set up along both sides as they advanced. The mountains of earth and stone piling up testified just how much of the hillside had already been removed. It was almost as if a major new road was being cut directly through the slope.

Astrid, after being driven to the scene in a police car, had spent what felt like an eternity just waiting and watching the progress. Although constantly receiving assurances that all three were safe, not being able to speak to Tanya was driving her crazy. At first she had wanted to grab a shovel and start digging herself. It had taken some time to convince her that she would be far better off leaving the work to those better suited to the task, and that she may well prove to be more of a hindrance than a help. Now, all she could do was wait and pray. Her mind was returning to that terrible morning in Berlin. She knew that Siggi's mind would be dwelling on this too. Dark thoughts and a powerful sense of déjà vu prevailed.

Whenever called upon to dig, Geordie and Phil worked non-stop. Doug Short had joined them some while ago, and although unable to effectively use a shovel himself, he had contributed to the cause by relaying messages and providing refreshments to the sweating workers.

Hovering in the background of all this activity, unsure exactly why she was even there at all, stood the young waitress, Sue. Like Astrid, she too could do nothing but simply wait.

***

At a signal from Adams, the digger driver switched off his engine and climbed down from the machine.

A babble of excited voices sounded as the head of the rescue regarded the result of this latest excavation. From what he could see they had at last reached the end of the main blockage. The way ahead from here on looked to be reasonably clear.

In a moment, Geordie was at his side. 'Is it safe to go in there now?' the big man demanded.

Adams did not reply immediately. Compared with the wide-open pathway that had already been carved out, the way leading even deeper into the hillside was now narrow, dark and lacking any kind of new support. He viewed it with a fair degree of suspicion, torn between his natural caution and a desire to complete the rescue without unnecessary delay.

Clearly impatient for an answer, Geordie repeated his question.

'I'm going to take a closer look first,' Adams told him. He unclipped a powerful flashlight from his belt and switched it on, adding in a loud voice: 'I want everyone else to stay well back. And for Pete's sake don't let anyone start that digger up again while I'm inside.'

He moved cautiously forward, inspecting every step of the way. By his calculations the cage was still a good thirty yards ahead.

Totally engrossed in his survey, he failed to hear another figure coming up behind him. Not until Geordie's huge hand dropped on his shoulder was he aware of the presence. Taken by surprise, he jerked back.

'What the hell are you doing here?' he demanded. 'Get back with the others.'

Geordie shook his head. 'Sorry, pal. It looks pretty safe to me, so I'm going in.' He had already equipped himself with a torch of his own.

Adams could feel his anger rising. 'What the hell makes you think you're an expert all of a sudden? You haven't got a clue what to look for. If you go lumbering around in there you could easily bring the whole damn lot down.'

He glared at Geordie. 'If you want to kill yourself, that's okay. But think of your friend and the other two with him. It could take us hours or even days to get them out if you mess this up.'

Geordie shrugged. 'Fair enough,' he said. 'You can come along with me and keep an eye on things. At the first sign of trouble we'll go back.'

'You don't seem to understand --' Adams began.

He was cut off. 'Let me tell you one thing I *do* understand. Mike Stafford saved my life eighteen years ago. I owe it to him to make sure he gets out of danger as quickly as possible.'

Geordie's expression hardened. 'So, are you coming with me or not?'

Adams could see that he was determined go on alone if necessary. For him to physically restrain such a big man would be impossible. His only other option apart from calling for police assistance was to continue on with Geordie and try to minimize the danger.

'Very well,' he reluctantly agreed. 'But I'll lead the way. Keep your head well down away from the roof, and make bloody sure you don't touch anything.'

'You're in charge,' Geordie told him.

At that particular moment, Adams very much doubted the truth of this.

***

As they progressed, Geordie was forced to stoop increasingly lower in order to keep his head clear of the roof. At nearly six inches shorter, Adams had no such problem, but his constant backward glances at where the big man had passed showed his continuing concern.

They stepped around several smaller mounds of fallen debris along the way, but there was no sign of any further major falls. Geordie guessed that they must now be very close to their objective.

Eyes that had spent countless hours searching the night skies for the smallest sign of enemy fighter planes then suddenly picked out a dark silhouette ahead.

'Look,' he told Adams. 'Up there.'

The far more powerful beam of Adams' flashlight swung forward, catching the canvas covered cage full in its glare. The two men closed in.

With a huge grin on his face, Geordie reached down to tap on the canvas flap covering the entry point.

'Anyone at home?' he called out.

TWENTY-TWO

Still carrying Tanya in his arms, Stafford blinked as the five of them emerged from the gloom of the tunnel. Spontaneous applause and cheering immediately broke out. Suddenly, people were all around them, their voices combining to create an almost deafening babble of noise. Everyone seemed to have a word of encouragement or congratulations to offer.

A camera flashbulb exploded somewhere close to his face. For the first time since being rescued, he saw Geordie's expression of pleasure fade.

'Take that bloody thing away,' his friend growled, waving an arm at a pair of men he presumed to be from the press.

'Tanya! Siggi!'

Astrid came bursting through the mass of people. Stafford placed the young girl gently on to the ground.

'Here comes your mum,' he grinned.

A worried frown appeared on her face. 'She won't be angry will she?'

He shook his head and laughed. 'I don't reckon so.' To him the kid looked more apprehensive now than at almost any stage of their rescue. With the danger now past, he found this quite amusing.

Tears of relief and happiness streamed down Astrid's face while hugging her daughter and sister. Siggi was crying too. Then they all started talking at once.

'Mister Stafford was amazing, Mum,' Tanya said for the third time.

He placed himself discreetly a little apart from this emotional family reunion and quickly became engulfed by more well-wishers. All of them wanted to shake his hand. Geordie, helped by Phil and Doug Short, finally managed to form a protective shield around him.

'Give the guy some room,' Phil pleaded.

A police sergeant approached them. 'There's an ambulance waiting to take the three of you to hospital,' he told Stafford.

He signalled for a couple of his men to clear a path through the crowd. A burly but cheerful looking constable scooped Tanya up into his arms, and with Siggi and Astrid following closely behind, they were all ushered along the same route.

'We'll follow you in the car,' Geordie called out.

Stafford looked back, but already his friends were lost somewhere in the muddle of people.

***

Continuing to remain on the fringe of the crowd, Sue watched the rescued group being led away to the ambulance. Although she kept telling herself that it was ridiculous, she could not shake off the feeling that matters were not over yet and that she somehow still a part to play in this drama. But if she did have another part to play, she could not for the life of her imagine what it might be.

Glancing at her watch, she saw with a sense of shock that it was now nearly three o'clock. She thought of her parents. She had told them she'd be spending the night at a friend's house, and she hated lying to them. But it was as if an irresistible force had drawn her here in order to witness the rescue. Her parents would have gone mad if they'd known she was alone on the moor at such an hour, even though half of Yorkshire's policemen were close at hand.

Geordie and Phil passing nearby caught her eye. There was also another man with them who she had not seen before. He was walking with a heavy limp. Without thinking, she approached the group.

'Excuse me,' she said.

It was Phil who responded. 'Hey, I didn't know you were here.'

He turned to Doug Short. 'This is the young lady who told us about Alan being in her restaurant.'

Short gave her a friendly smile. Geordie also acknowledged her, but it was obvious that he was anxious to be on his way.

'Where are you going now?' Sue asked. She was aware that her question might sound nosy, maybe even rude. But it popped out just the same.

Geordie looked pointedly at his watch before answering. 'To the hospital at Scarborough. That's where they're taking Mike and the other two.'

'Oh – I see.'

Sue knew that this was almost certainly where the boy Alan would also be. She had already spent a lot of time debating on whether to attempt visiting him there. It was stupid, she supposed. She had no idea what he was really like, but the feeling she was at least partly responsible for him having his accident persisted. There was also the fact that everyone else seemed to be so much against the boy. Yes, he had stolen a car, and that was wrong. But sometimes young lads did silly things just to show off. From what she had seen of Alan, he seemed to be nice enough. Okay, there was a lot of stuff going on she knew nothing about, but she was convinced he could not be as bad as all these other people were making him out to be. He might even be grateful to have a friend around for support when he recovered consciousness.

Geordie made to move on. Sue wanted to ask him if she could travel with them in his car. It was at least twenty miles to the hospital: much too far for her to be cycling at this time of night. But as she looked at the big man, she swallowed back the words. He obviously had little time to be bothering with her problems right now. Besides, he was hardly likely to be sympathetic if he discovered that it was Alan she wanted to visit.

With an inward sigh, Sue kept her thoughts to herself.

The group began walking away from her.

**

After moving on for only a few yards, Doug Short paused. There had been something about the look on the young girl's face that struck a chord. He was sure that she'd been silently pleading with Geordie for help of some sort. But as almost everyone knew, whilst his former comrade undoubtedly had a heart as big as a house, perception was far from being one of his strongest qualities.

He called after the other two as they pulled ahead. 'My car is over this way. You chaps carry on and I'll catch up with you both at the hospital.'

He then turned and limped back toward Sue. He gave her a friendly smile to put her at ease before speaking. 'I don't want to appear a nuisance, but I got the impression just now that there was something else on your mind. Would you like to tell me about it? You never know, perhaps I might be able to help.'

His gently spoken words had the desired effect, even though she hesitated and shuffled her feet for a few seconds before replying.

'Well, the truth is, I was just wondering if I could go with those two friends of yours in their car. You know, to the hospital.'

In a flash, it all made sense to Short. Having already been told the full story by the other two during their long wait on the moor, he was well aware of Sue's encounter with Alan, and of how she had suggested to Phil that she felt in some way responsible for causing Alan to crash the car.

He smiled to himself. The two youngsters would be pretty much the same age. He did not doubt Sue's feelings of guilt in the slightest, even though they were entirely unjustified. But was there also a little bit of teenage hormones at work here?

He regarded Sue more closely. She appeared to be a pleasant enough young lady. Should Alan regain consciousness fairly soon, perhaps her visiting him might not be such a bad idea? Mike still had an enormous job on his hands if he was going to succeed in getting through to the boy. So, if there had indeed been a mutual spark between the two youngsters, getting them together again might just help to prepare some of the ground. Alan could certainly use a friend at present, and it was amazing what a little bit of female influence could sometimes achieve.

'Why don't I give you a lift there myself?' he told Sue.

***

After placing Sue's bicycle inside the boot, the two of them climbed into Short's car. Like Geordie, he too drove a large, three-litre Rover. Once settled into the passenger seat, Sue gave him a quizzical look.

'I'm not trying to be funny, honestly I'm not. But how do you manage to drive a car with only one leg working properly?'

He gave her a rueful grin. 'It's an automatic.' Noting her puzzled expression, he added: 'There isn't any clutch you see. Everything is done with just my right foot. There's what they call power steering as well. See here? I can turn the wheel easily with just one hand.'

'I've never heard of a car like that before.'

'There's not many of them about at present,' Short agreed. 'But there will be in a few years' time, take my word for it.'

After this exchange they fell silent. Two miles passed before Short spoke again. He picked his words with care.

'Tell me, Sue, what did you make of Alan? What is he really like?'

She showed surprise at his question. 'I thought you and your friends all knew him. At least a little bit.'

'We know *of* him, that's all. None of us have ever actually met the boy.'

She hesitated, a defensive look developing. 'It's not really for me to judge what sort of person he is. We only talked for a few minutes.'

'But obviously enough for you to want to visit him at the hospital.' Short raised an eyebrow.

She sighed. 'All right. If you must know....yes, I liked him. He had a nice smile and seemed quite friendly at first, even though I could see he was already troubled about something. He even asked me my name. But after I read out that stuff written on the back of the photograph it was like I'd told him something terrible. He changed completely. He became really upset.'

She frowned heavily. 'I couldn't help worrying about him. Especially after he went running out of the restaurant the way he did.'

'And now you feel that what you did may have contributed toward him having his accident?'

Her voice was very small. 'I don't know. Maybe. I feel all mixed up at the moment.'

Short decided that it was in everyone's interests for Sue to know the full story as soon as possible. There was a danger that she might feel a whole lot differently about Alan once she knew more about his troubled background, but that was a risk he would have to take.

'I think I'd better explain a few things to you,' he began.

***

After a general check-up and a precautionary anti-tetanus injection, Stafford was given a clean bill of health. He stepped out from behind the screens and saw Siggi sitting alone nearby in the hospital's general waiting area. She gave him a tired smile as he approached. She too had received similar treatment, and sticking plasters covered the worst of the cuts to her feet. Although now reunited with her shoes, she remained for the moment bare-footed.

'Tanya is still having her ankle looked at by the doctor,' she told him. 'Astrid is with her.'

She had barely finished speaking when Geordie and Phil came through the swing doors. Geordie carried two large mugs of coffee.

'I expect you could both do with these,' he said.

His offerings were gratefully accepted. But Stafford had much more than just coffee on his mind. The bits and pieces of information he had so far gathered about Alan's involvement were deeply disturbing. This was the one part of his story he had withheld from Siggi, and she knew nothing at all of the boy's existence. When she was called back into the treatment room a few minutes later, he seized his opportunity to discover more.

Between them, Geordie and Phil related everything they knew. But even after listening to them, there was still so much that did not make sense. He could only guess at the missing pieces.

Alan must have been watching while he and the others were on the moor. This appeared to be the only logical answer. He must have seen all three of them become trapped in the mine and then moved the Cresta in order to confuse the search parties that would invariably be out looking for them later that day.

But even that didn't tell him why, only shortly afterwards, the kid had decided to bring the car back again. It was hard to believe that a few drunken words scribbled on the back of an old photograph were sufficient reason for such a dramatic change of heart. Surely there must have been something more than that motivating him?

Whatever the case, one fact was horribly clear. At one stage Alan had wanted to make certain that all three of them, including an innocent young child, died down there in that mine. How much hate must be eating away inside of the kid for him to attempt something as cold-hearted as that?

It was a question that Stafford was not sure he wanted to discover an answer to.

He passed a hand over his brow. He was overpoweringly tired; his mind was becoming a jumble. He needed some sleep before attempting to work things out any further.

As if sensing his need, a nurse approached. 'The doctor would like you and Miss Hoffman to remain here and rest for a few hours before leaving,' she told him. 'Your beds will be ready for you in about five minutes.'

These were the most welcome words Stafford had heard since first being rescued. 'Thank you,' he said.

Raising a hand to his mouth, he did his best to stifle an almighty yawn.

***

'Have you seen anything of Doug?' Geordie asked Phil as they walked together toward the hospital exit. 'I thought he said he was going to follow us here.'

Phil frowned. 'Yeah, that's right. I wonder where he is?'

After a few more paces, Geordie pulled up. Digging into his pocket, he produced his car keys and held them out to Phil. 'Why don't you go on to the car and wait for me there?'

'You're not going to start looking for Doug are you? He probably just changed his mind and went to bed.'

'No, it's not Doug I'm thinking about,' Geordie told him. 'But there is something else I want to sort out while I'm here.'

Phil yawned. After the late drunken session on Saturday evening, and then spending most of the following night on the moors, bed now seemed the only sensible place to be. Not for the first time, he marvelled at the big guy's stamina.

'What are you planning?' he asked.

'Never mind, it's not important. You just go on. I shouldn't be long.'

Phil shrugged, too weary to pursue the matter any further. He accepted the car keys and continued on his way.

***

Short was not a fast driver. By the time they arrived at the hospital, Sue had heard the entire story. Everything was covered. How Jimmy had died; everyone's surprise when discovering that he had a son; and finally, how a mixed-up Alan had set out to take revenge on this man called Mike who she had yet to meet.

While listening to all of this she had deliberately said very little. She needed time to let it all sink in properly.

Short parked the car and switched off the engine. 'So, what do you think?' he asked her. 'Do you still want to go inside and try to see him?'

Sue chewed furiously at her bottom lip, her mind struggling to accept that the friendly boy she had spoken to at the restaurant was the same person who had spent time in an approved school for violent behaviour, and might even be capable of actually killing someone. People like that did not exist in her little world of cream teas and rural family life.

Suddenly, her mind was made up. It could not all be true. She did not doubt Short's sincerity, but there must be another side to the story he didn't know about. And if there was, she wanted to hear it directly from Alan if possible.

'Yes, I do still want to see him,' she said, her voice now firm. She looked Short directly in the eye before adding: 'It's hard for me to believe that Alan is as bad as you and all the others seem to think.'

She tensed, fully expecting a display of annoyance from the man. Although he had been nice to her up until now, he was still one of those ganging up on Alan. To her utter surprise, he smiled at her instead.

'That's what I was rather hoping you would say,' he told her.

She tried to smile back. 'I don't understand.'

Short twisted in the car seat to face her better. 'Jimmy meant a very great deal to all of us, especially Mike. They were the best kind of friends you can imagine. And in spite of what you may think, Mike still wants to help the boy if he's allowed to. He feels very strongly that he owes his old comrade at least that much.'

Sue began to get the picture. But it was a picture she was finding it hard to see herself fitting into very easily. 'And you honestly think I can act as a sort of go-between for them? Is that it?'

'You could put it like that, I suppose.' Short raised his forefinger to emphasize his next point. 'The thing is, I have this feeling that you've already made an impression on the lad. Yes, it may only be a reasonably small one at present, but given his history, even that is a major achievement. From everything I've been told, smiling, being friendly and asking people their names is not the kind of behaviour that is normally associated with Alan. Quite the opposite in fact.'

She frowned, but said nothing.

Short continued. 'What we need to do is try to break down this wall of hatred that Alan has built around himself. As I've already told you, Mike is blameless, and there is absolutely no reason on earth why the boy should feel the way he does. I can only imagine that his mother has badly distorted the facts of the matter.'

'And you think he'll take any notice of what I say? Especially if it goes against what his mum has told him.' A nervous laugh slipped from Sue's mouth. 'We hardly know each other. For goodness sake, he might not even remember me. Didn't you say there was a chance he could be brain damaged?'

Short nodded slowly. 'If that turns out to be the case, then there's little any of us can do. But if he isn't – and please, let's try to think on the positive side – then he's going to need an awful lot of help. Without that help, the way Alan is going, he will almost certainly end up spending a very long time indeed in prison. Do you want to see that happen?'

'No! Of course I don't.'

'Then you'll do what you can to help prevent it?'

'I – I really don't know if I can.'

Even as she spoke, Sue realised that she had little choice but to agree. She had been unwittingly sucked into this affair, and now the whole thing was engulfing her. If she just walked away at this stage, she would never be able to discover the real truth. Apart from any imagined sense of responsibility, curiosity was also now playing a major part in her thinking.

But how could she possibly find the right words? She had only just turned eighteen herself and had little experience of the real world.

He seemed to read her thoughts. 'Never underestimate the female touch,' he said gently.

Sue sighed. 'All right. I can't promise you anything, Mister Short, but I'll try. I'll do my best.'

***

They located Alan's ward without too much difficulty. Short drew the Night Sister aside and spoke to her quietly, bending the truth slightly.

'The young lady with me is the lad's girlfriend. Do you think it is possible for her to see him for a few minutes?'

The middle-aged nurse cast her eyes in Sue's direction and appeared satisfied with what she saw. For a brief moment their eyes met in a woman-to-woman understanding.

She diverted her attention back to Short, a sympathetic smile replacing her earlier cool efficiency. 'I'm afraid he's still unconscious at present, although that could change at any time.'

The woman beckoned to Sue, who came over. 'I really am sorry, my dear, but there are rules I have to stick to. Visits at this time of night, especially by people who are not close family, are simply not allowed.'

She spread her hands. 'If you were a blood relation or something, maybe then I could have allowed you to stay by the bedside for a little while. But seeing as ...'

Short jumped in. 'Well how about just a quick look, Sister? Surely that wouldn't do any harm? And you can see how worried the poor girl is.'

Once again the woman looked at Sue. She sighed. 'Very well, a quick look then. But that's all, I'm afraid.' She indicated a door close to her office. 'Alan's got this room to himself for the moment. That's just until he's off the special observation list and we've a free bed in the main ward.'

With the sister hovering closely behind them, the pair stepped inside the small room. They gazed in silence at the figure in the bed.

Short found himself trying hard to see something of Jimmy in the boy's features. Maybe there was a slight likeness around the mouth, he decided. But nothing appeared to stand out as being remarkably similar. What certainly did stand out quite clearly was the large bald patch on the top of Alan's head where the hair had been shaved away. An ugly row of black stitches crossed this area, while scattered about his face were a number of small cuts, probably caused by flying glass from the broken windscreen. Both of the boy's arms rested exposed on top of the bed covers, the right limb with a drip feed inserted into it. His breathing was regular.

Short glanced across at Sue. He saw her swallow hard, but her eyes remained firmly fixed on the boy.

It was the sister who spoke first. 'We had the police in here earlier checking up on his condition,' she said.

There was no mistaking the question posed in her tone. This told Short that she knew little yet of the circumstances surrounding her patient's accident, He reacted with a casual shrug.

'I expect they just wanted a statement about the car crash. You know how keen the police can be on paperwork these days.'

The sister nodded and let the matter drop. She allowed them a few more moments inside the room before saying: 'I'm sorry, I think you should be leaving now.'

For the first time since entering the room, Sue took her eyes away from the bed. 'Please, let me stay just a little longer,' she pleaded. 'You did say that he could wake up at any time.'

Her reaction pleased Short. So far, all his assumptions about the girl were proving to be correct.

The sister shook her head. 'I'd love to say yes, my dear, but I'd get shot if Matron or one of the doctors were to come along and find you in here.'

Her tone then brightened. 'I'll tell you what I can do. There's a patients' recreation room two doors up along the corridor. You can wait in there if you promise to keep quiet. That way I can let you know if his condition changes.'

Sue smiled with gratitude. 'Thank you,' she said.

The two of them found the room in question easily enough. Various magazines and board games were scattered across a large table, while an old but comfortable looking settee offered the possibility of snatching some sleep. Short watched as Sue settled down on this.

'I'm going to leave you here for a little while,' he told her. 'I want to see if I can find out what's happening with Mike and the other two. Will you be all right on your own until I get back?'

'Yes. Of course I will.'

She then looked at him seriously. 'I think you are a very nice man, Mister Short. You seem to be thinking of other people all the time.'

Taken aback by this unexpected remark, he blinked at her. Compliments like this from a young female were something he was far from used to handling. With an embarrassed smile, he left the room as quickly as his bad leg would allow.

***

Despite her tiredness, Sue found it impossible to sleep. After half an hour she ceased trying and got up from the settee.

She chewed hard on her bottom lip while wandering around the room. Now that she had learned all the facts, the enormity of what she'd agreed to do was frightening. Why on earth had she allowed herself to become so involved? A long sigh slipped out. Whatever the reason, there could be no going back now. Not until she had at least spoken to Alan one more time. Only then would she be able to make a proper decision. And even after that, there was still her promise to Mister Short to consider.

The memory of Alan unconscious in his bed returned to her. She could see him clearly with that tube sticking out of his arm and those horrible looking stitches on the top of his head. These were what troubled her most of all, she realised. In her mind, the possibility that he might have suffered serious brain damage was now looking to be even more real than before. No matter what he might have done, he did not deserve to end up like that. She ran a hand quickly through her hair, as if this action might help to push such awful thoughts from her mind.

It did not.

Maybe another quick glance into Alan's room might help to settle her mind a little, Sue considered. She wouldn't actually go inside. Just a peep through the window in his door would be enough. If she were to see him still sleeping soundly, perhaps then she would be able to relax more and get some rest herself?

Stepping out of the recreation room, she glanced up and down the corridor. It was deserted. She tiptoed back toward the ward. His room was now only a few yards ahead. She heard the rustle of some papers coming from the night sister's office, but no one came out to challenge her.

Peering through the circular shaped window in Alan's door, she saw that he was lying in exactly the same position as last time. She blinked. Or was he? Surely his arm without the tube in it had been in a different position the last time she'd looked. A sigh slipped out. She was being silly. People moved about in their sleep all the time.

And then, just as she was on the point of returning to the recreation room, Alan's head rolled over so that he was completely facing her. His eyes were wide open and staring directly into her own.

So great was her shock, Sue could not quite hold back a small gasp. Her first instinct was to immediately tell the Night Sister the news.

But something held her back.

Without having the faintest idea why, she instead pushed at Alan's door and stepped inside the room.

TWENTY-THREE

With Phil gone, Geordie spent several minutes just pacing around the near deserted hospital corridors. He was well aware of how impulsive he could be at times. Because of this, he wanted to feel sure that he was going about things in the best way before acting. But in his book there were never many shades of grey. Right was right, and wrong was always wrong. Wrong needed to be dealt with in a firm manner. These days, many of the so-called authorities were becoming way too soft.

Much earlier he had made enquiries about Alan and learned of the small private room he was currently occupying. Now all Geordie could think about was whether or not the kid had recovered consciousness yet. If he *had* recovered and still had his wits about him, then there was only one person who was going to have the first crack at sorting him out. Even if a good old-fashioned slap was currently out of the question, the kid still needed a scare thrown into him. That was vital before a bunch of namby-pamby social workers and psychiatrists got to work making half-baked excuses for his behaviour. Once that happened, Mike wouldn't stand a chance of putting him right.

He ceased his prowling and stood still for a while. It would be daybreak soon. Maybe he should go and take a look at Alan right now, before the hospital started getting too busy again. It wouldn't do any harm just to stroll past his room. If it turned out that the kid was still unconscious, then obviously he'd have to leave matters until later. But if he was now awake and understood what was going on ...

Geordie shrugged. He'd do whatever needed to be done when he got there.

***

Sue stepped tentatively into Alan's room and closed the door behind her. His eyes watched her every movement.

She paused a little way short of the bed. He did not utter a word as she continued staring into his face, searching for some clue as to his condition. Was his brain functioning normally? she asked herself. Was he even capable of communicating?

Her questions were soon answered.

'Where the bloody hell am I?' he said in a barely audible whisper. There was no hello. No sign of recognition.

Sue's spirits sank; this was not a good start. But she had to make allowances. He was bound to be confused, so this reaction was only to be expected. Even if his brain was undamaged, the car accident would still be the last thing he'd remember.

'You're in hospital,' she told him in a voice only slightly louder than his.

Alan's brow furrowed with deep lines as he tried to unscramble his thoughts. Sue sensibly said nothing. At last he spoke again.

'You're the girl from the restaurant, aren't you...Sue?'

A small stab of pleasure spurted through her. He had remembered her name. 'Yes, that's right,' she said.

Her pleasure was short-lived. His next words saw to that. 'What the hell are you doing here?'

His aggressive tone took all the stuffing out of her. 'I only came to ...'

'To what? Take the piss? Make sure I'm not going to run away? Who sent you in here?'

She could feel the colour rising on her face. 'No one sent me. Not in the way you think. I came to help you if I can.'

'Bollocks!' His voice was starting to get a little louder.

'Please! Will you stop swearing at me. You're making me nervous. I didn't think ...'

Her words froze as she heard the sound of footsteps coming out of the nearby office. She tensed, waiting for an angry night sister to come storming into the room. But the footsteps continued in the opposite direction. Sue imagined that the woman must be making a routine inspection of the main ward.

Alan continued glaring at her for a few moments longer and then appeared to soften a little. 'How can you help me?' he said. 'I'm in the shit, aren't I?'

This conversation was not going anything like the way Sue had imagined it might. She tried to steady herself.

'You only stole a car,' she told him. 'They can't hang you for that.'

He made no reply, so she tried again. 'You were going back to that mine on the moors, weren't you?'

This did get a reaction. Alan tried to raise himself up from the pillows but fell back again. He grimaced with pain. 'How do you know about any of that?'

'They found your scooter. After that they started searching the moor all around there.'

'The little girl? And Stafford and the woman? Did they find them?'

Sue nodded.

'Alive?'

'Yes. They're all safe.'

Once again Alan lapsed into silence while digesting the news. But it was clear that his mind was working furiously.

Gaining a little in confidence now that they were communicating, Sue repeated her earlier question. 'You were going back to help them, weren't you? It was because of what was written on that photo. I saw the effect it had on you.'

'You don't know anything,' he muttered.

'I do,' Sue persisted. More words slipped out before she could stop them. 'I know all about you and the trouble you've been in with the police. And about your father and how you've got it all wrong about Mike Stafford.'

She knew immediately that she had said the wrong thing.

'Who have you been talking to?' he demanded. 'And what the fuck has any of this got to do with you? Just bugger off and leave me alone.'

Sue's confidence instantly drained away. 'I'm sorry… I didn't mean to upset you. I just thought that if….'

'You heard what I said. Bugger off!'

Her eyes stinging with threatened tears, Sue turned to leave. She had taken only one pace toward the door when it swung open.

The huge bulk of Geordie glowered at them both.

***

The big man had been close to changing his mind over paying Alan a visit. Perhaps he was being a bit hasty, he considered. Maybe Mike would not thank him very much for interfering. But he was, after all, only trying to help his friend.

In the end he settled for a compromise, promising himself that he would do nothing more than look. That wouldn't do any harm, and he needed to know for his own peace of mind if the kid had woken up yet. Perhaps the little shit was even feigning unconsciousness now to delay the consequences of his actions. A sneaky look when he wasn't expecting it might catch him out.

Geordie peered through the door window, and in an instant all of his intended caution evaporated. The kid was not only awake, he was also talking to that girl from the restaurant. What the devil was she doing here with him?

Reason and Geordie parted company. He pushed his way forward.

***

He paused immediately inside the door, scowling at both of them. In Sue's eyes, his massive presence seemed to almost fill the room.

She glanced across at Alan. She could see that he was quite badly shaken too. Neither of them spoke.

'So you're Jimmy's son.' Geordie's voice was full of contempt.

He moved closer. 'You don't look so tough now, do you?'

At last Alan managed to speak. 'What do you w-want?' The words came out as little more than a nervous croak.

Geordie gave him a mirthless smile. 'I reckon it's more a case of what *you* want, sonny. Which by my way of thinking is a bloody good slap.'

Amazed at what she was doing, Sue glared at the big man. 'Leave him alone. He hasn't done anything wrong,' she said.

He shot her with a withering look in return. 'Hasn't done anything wrong,' he echoed. 'How would you know what the little sod's been up to?' A suspicious look sprang into his eyes. 'Then again, maybe you *do* know. Why are you here? Have you been helping him to cook up some clever story to get him out of trouble?'

'No – of course not!'

Sue could now feel herself shaking. 'Mister Short asked me to talk to him, that's all. He thought I might be able to help.'

Her mention of Short's name seemed to take a little of the steam away from Geordie. He frowned at her. 'Are you trying to tell me you came here with Doug?'

'Yes, that's right.'

'So where is he then?'

'He's gone off somewhere to see about your friend.' Sue waved a hand in agitation as the stress made her momentarily forget the name she needed. 'You know, the one who was trapped in the mine. Mike – Mike Stafford.'

He looked at her for what felt like a long time, as if unsure whether or not to believe what he was hearing.

Suddenly, all the hostility she had been forced to suffer since entering this room was too much for Sue. First of all it had been Alan, and now this man Geordie. The tears she had been struggling to hold back burst free with a rush.

'Why are you being so horrible?' she sobbed.

He gave a loud sigh, but did not answer her. For several seconds she could hear nothing but the sound of her own crying. Irritated with herself, she quickly wiped away the clouding moisture from her eyes. Amazingly, as Geordie came back into focus, she could see that all of his anger seemed to have drained away. And then she realised that, big and tough as he was, he had no idea at all of how to handle a crying woman. There was a far less confident air about him now. Perhaps even thinking twice and regretting his actions?

Sue was still trying to take in this remarkable change of character when the door flew open once again. The Night Sister's eyes flashed from Alan to her, and then settled on Geordie.

'What on earth is going on in here?' she demanded. Her voice rang with authority and controlled anger.

Geordie began to say something, but she cut him off.

'Out!' she commanded. 'Get right away from here immediately or I shall call the police.'

Sue opened her mouth, but was also silenced by an imperious wave of the sister's arm.

'You too, young lady. Out – out – out! You should be ashamed of yourself after the consideration I showed to you earlier.'

Although still being hustled, Sue paused long enough to throw a glance back in Alan's direction. 'I'll try to see you again later on,' she promised.

Though he looked directly at her, he did not reply. His expression gave nothing away.

A large hand then landed with surprising gentleness on her shoulder. 'Come on, lass, we better leave before we get into any more trouble.'

Not understanding at all why Geordie had suddenly become so considerate, she allowed him to usher her from the room.

***

They paused in the corridor, just outside the recreation room. You've done it again, you stupid bugger, Geordie reproached himself. Another bloody cock-up.

He regarded the forlorn figure of Sue. It still wasn't clear to him what Doug had put the girl up to, but whatever it was, it would surely have been done with the best possible motive. He prayed that he had not destroyed matters for them.

'I'm sorry if I upset you,' he said as gently as possible. 'I know I shouldn't have gone barging in there like that. I don't always handle things the right way, you know.'

He saw the surprise on her face as she listened to his meek sounding apology. But after a moment's hesitation, she gave the hint of a smile.

'I shouldn't have been in there with him either,' she pointed out.

'So Doug drove you here, did he?' he asked after a brief pause.

Sue nodded. 'He was really nice to me.'

'Not like big bad Geordie eh?'

'Oh – I didn't mean ...'

He laughed. 'Don't worry about it.'

He glanced past her and saw Doug Short limping along the corridor toward them. 'Talk of the devil,' he said.

Short's pace quickened as he spotted them. He arrived a little breathless. 'Is everything all right with you two?' he asked immediately.

Geordie assumed his contrite expression once again. 'I think I might have messed things up a bit for you, Doug,' he admitted.

Short eyed him closely. 'Nothing that can't be put right, I hope.'

The big man took a deep breath and explained what had happened. Sue chipped in with her side of the story.

'I don't know if Alan will even allow me to talk to him again,' she concluded.

'But you *will* try?' Short asked her.

'I have to. I can't leave things like this.'

'Good girl. I knew from the moment I saw you that you had character.'

While Sue blushed, Geordie brightened. 'How about we have something to eat?' he suggested. 'There's a place I know not far from here that does a fantastic early morning fry-up. The full works. I don't know about you two, but I'm starving. Phil's sure to be as well.'

'No one can think properly on an empty stomach,' he added, seeing Short still frowning at him. 'We'll make it my treat all round.'

'I am hungry,' Sue admitted.

'Very well,' Short agreed. 'And after that I'll drive you home, Sue. We can talk some more on the way.'

***

Siggi woke from her sedated sleep at 4.15pm. For a few panicky moments she began wondering where she was. Then her eyes took in the details of the hospital ward and it all came flooding back to her.

She shivered as the memory of being trapped in that awful mine shaft returned. Without Mike's support she would have gone completely out of her mind, there was no doubt about that. He was the most amazing man she had ever met. Up until now she would never have believed that such decent men still existed.

An already familiar feeling of bewilderment crept up on her as she once again tried to analyse what had happened between them. In truth, it had been nothing but a few comforting kisses. So why did she continue to feel as if they had shared something far more special than that? Neither of them would have behaved in such a way had it not been for the extreme circumstances.

However, the uncomfortable truth was, she had been the one who had instigated everything. Siggi knew that her greatest fear was of him now deeply regretting those few shared moments. If that were true, then he may soon begin to regard her in an altogether different way. Possibly out of embarrassment and loyalty to his wife, he might even refuse to see her again?

Without fully realising why, she knew that this would hurt her far more than she could ever imagine.

TWENTY-FOUR

Confined to his bed, Alan stared bleakly at the ceiling of his hospital room. In spite of the strong medication they were giving him, the headaches still kept returning. But at least they had their advantages. For two days now he had been using them as way of stopping the police from pestering him with awkward questions. Since he'd woken up they'd made three attempts to interview him. Each time his doctor had sent the constables away, saying that he was still too mentally confused. Alan knew that this tactic couldn't delay their questions forever, but with so much else on his mind, he sure as hell didn't want to be facing all that kind of crap just yet.

At least the little girl Tanya had been rescued safely. He was feeling strangely good about that. As for the other two, he didn't give a toss about them any longer. If it hadn't been for the girl being there, he would never have changed his mind about leaving them to rot on the moor.

A long sigh slipped out. Okay, at first he *had* been confused by what Stafford had written. But now he'd thought about it some more, it wasn't possible for the bloke to be totally innocent. There was too much evidence against him, and a few words scribbled on the back of a photo couldn't change that. All the same, Alan was starting to suspect that his mother might have exaggerated the true story a bit as well. Why she would want to do that over something so serious was hard to work out. All he'd ever wanted from her was the honest truth. Now, with everything so screwed up and his mind telling him different things at different times, he didn't know what the hell to think.

He swore, realising that he would probably never get to know the real story. It was all right for Stafford to turn up now claiming he wanted to be friends and all that old bollocks. If he was so full of good intentions, why hadn't he bothered to show up for their meeting on that first night? That was the thing that really stuck in Alan's mind. His determination grew. Even if there was one small part of him that still wanted to talk to the man, there was another far more powerful part that kept saying forget it. Stafford had had a bloody lucky escape. The bloke should just be grateful for that and piss off back to Canada.

Whenever his thoughts reached this dead-end point, he found his mind invariably turning instead to the young girl Sue. How the heck had she become so involved in all of this? What was in it for her to start showing concern and speaking up for Stafford? She'd been pretty quick to jump to his defence as well when that big bloke from Newcastle had come barging into the room.

He frowned, his mind returning to his first meeting with her at the restaurant. It was stupid, but back there for a short time he'd felt something different. It wasn't just in the way that you normally fancied some girl – he'd actually liked her as a person as well. It was as if she'd somehow charmed him.

Charmed? He'd never used a bloody word like that in his life before.

What was the matter with him? She was probably one of those weirdo do-gooders who got their kicks out of going around helping people. He was kidding himself if he thought she might have any proper feelings for him. Most girls he'd fancied before had run a mile as soon as they found out he'd been in trouble with the police for violent behaviour.

But she knew all about that, and yet she'd still come to see him?

A second sigh slipped out. Whatever Sue's reasons for coming, he was now feeling a whole lot of regret over the way he'd spoken to her.

He wondered if she'd come back again. She had said she would, but that didn't mean a thing. People made all sorts of promises they had no intention of keeping. And he *had* treated her like shit.

The clock on the wall told him it was 6.00pm. Through the window in his door he could see a steady flow of people passing by on their way to visit other patients in the main ward. A few peered curiously in at him through the glass.

'Piss off,' he murmured, scowling back at them.

A wave of self-pity suddenly washed over him. All these visitors were coming to see someone, and what did he get? Nothing but bloody coppers. His mother sprang to mind once again. After constant questions from the hospital staff, he had finally given them her name and address as his next-of-kin. Not that she would give a toss. She was the one who had warned Stafford about him being up in Wetherditch, hoping to get him arrested. That showed how much she cared about anything.

He found himself wishing – even longing – for Sue to walk in through the door once again. But the flow of arriving visitors soon trickled out. Only the brief sound of a young child's voice drifted into his room. For no reason that made any sense to Alan, the regular line from a children's radio programme he used to listen to what seemed like a hundred years ago sprang to mind. It came just before the daily story.

"Are you sitting comfortably? Then I'll begin."

Well he wasn't sitting comfortably. He was most un-bloody-comfortable. And nothing was about to begin for him. Nothing good anyway.

He closed his eyes and tried to shut out the whole damn world.

***

The room clock was showing just after 7.00pm when Sue peered through the window, then quietly entered Alan's room. The door swung open with just the faintest of creaks. She trod softly over to his bed, noticing first of all that the drip feed tube had now been removed from his arm. Did that mean he was recovering well?

It looked as if he was asleep. Should she wake him? she wondered. Her hand reached out to touch his shoulder, but at the last second something made her pull back without making contact. For a moment she hovered there, feeling that this could be a sign for her to leave. Things might be difficult enough without aggravating him further by disturbing his rest.

Just as her nerve was failing, he opened one eye. Then the other. With a rush of relief she felt that he was pleased to see her.

His mouth formed into a shape that just might have passed as a smile. 'I heard you come in. I thought it was the nurse.'

'I hope you don't mind me visiting you again,' she said.

'I'm glad you did.'

This was exactly what she needed to hear. Sue relaxed a little. 'So am I now.'

There was a pause before Alan said: 'What made you come here the other day? No bullshit. Give me the truth.'

Sue did not know where to begin. To gain herself a little extra time, she made more fuss than necessary out of sitting down on a nearby chair before replying.

'I don't know really. I think it must be because I was worried about you. I thought it might even be my fault that you had your accident. You know, because of that stuff I read out. Anyone could see how much it upset you.'

He studied her face for several seconds, as if searching for any trace of insincerity. 'That's all? No other reason?'

Sue shifted a little under his prolonged gaze. 'Not in the beginning,' she said.

'But after that, someone got at you, didn't they?'

'No. At least, not in the way you mean.' She could feel indignation rising. 'You make it sound like everyone is ganging up against you.'

'Well aren't they?'

'No! Why do you keep thinking like that?'

He made no immediate reply. Eventually, he sighed. 'Okay, when you were here before you said you knew all about me? What did they tell you?'

Sue realised that she was now getting to the difficult bit. If she said the wrong thing, he could easily become upset again. But all her carefully planned lines were disappearing from her mind, leaving her with only a vague idea of what to say.

'I know what happened to your father,' she began, bracing herself for another outburst.

The anger did not come this time. 'What else?' was his only response.

'And how you've always thought that Mike Stafford was to blame for him getting killed,' she continued.

'Are you trying to tell me that he wasn't?'

'That's what everyone says, and I believe them.'

'Not everyone. My mother says different, and she should know well enough.' There was a deeply cynical note to his voice.

'Maybe she was mistaken.'

'How the hell can you be mistaken about something like that? Anyway, she was told exactly what happened by --'

He stopped abruptly.

Sue leaned closer. 'Who told her? What did this person say?'

'Nothing. It's not your business. I don't want to talk about it.'

Although her curiosity was now high, Sue could see from his face that it would be a bad mistake to press matters.

'You know Mister Stafford wants to help you if he can,' she said after a suitable pause.

Alan's face tightened. 'He didn't bother coming to see me last Friday night like I asked him to. Why should I bother with him now, just so he can try and ease his conscience?'

'It's not like that. And he never got around to reading your message until Saturday morning. That's why he didn't come to meet you.'

'It's easy to say that. How do I know it's true?'

Sue slapped her thigh in frustration. 'Don't you want to believe anything?'

'Okay, what if I do go along with what you're saying? I've still never had a father like most other kids have, and that's all down to Stafford. He was the one in charge that night. He was the bloke giving the orders. All the talking in the world won't change that.'

Sue could not understand how Alan could keep his mind so firmly closed.

'You're not being fair,' she said. 'I spent a long time talking to Mister Stafford yesterday. And I've talked with three other people who were there on the plane with him. They all say the same thing. He only did what he thought was right for his crew.'

Alan glared at her. 'You don't know what you're talking about.'

'Don't believe me then. Just speak to them yourself and hear what they've got to say.'

'No! If I talk to anyone it'll be to Stafford. I'll tell him to his face what a bloody liar he is.'

There were now clear signs of Alan's old anger beginning to return. Sue rose slowly from her chair. This was becoming too much for her. 'You just don't know how stupid you're being,' she remarked quietly.

'Don't call me stupid. I don't like it when people do that.'

'Well try doing something sensible for a change then. Listen to what I'm saying.' Even as she was speaking, Sue saw more warning signs forming on his face. She sighed, adding: 'Maybe it's best if I come back when you're in a better mood.'

'Don't bother. I don't know why you've come 'round here sticking your nose in my business in the first place.'

His sharp reaction struck deep. 'If that's how you feel, I'll leave you alone altogether then,' she told him.

There was nothing more she could say. Walking over to the door, she hesitated for a moment to glance back. His face was flushed red with anger.

'Go on! Get out of here,' he told her. 'Go and f-find another mug to mess around with so you can f-feel good about yourself.'

With a shake of her head, she continued on her way.

***

Ten seconds after Sue walked out, Alan's anger finally exploded. His swearing continued for several minutes.

The rage he could feel inside was now physically painful. It was a pain made far worse by the hard knowledge that it was himself that the anger was being directed against.

Stupid, she had called him. And even though he had always reacted badly to anyone calling him this, she was right. He *was* stupid. A stupid fucking idiot. He'd really screwed things up this time, and there wasn't a hope in hell of her ever coming back to see him again. What was it inside of him that made him say shitty things to her all of the time?

Gradually the anger settled down to a more manageable level. But the mystery of why he kept pushing Sue away remained.

He was still trying to find an answer to this when, half an hour later, the object of all his hatred walked into the room. Directly behind Stafford, with that worried frown on her face that Alan had seen so many times before, came his mother.

***

Alan's head dropped back down onto the pillow.

'Bloody hell,' Stafford heard him mutter.

He glanced at Barbara. It had been agreed between them that she should be the first to speak.

'Hello, Alan,' she offered.

He raised his head a little to look at her. His eyes shifted briefly in Stafford's direction. 'I might have known *he'd* be hanging around somewhere, but what are you doing here? I didn't ask for you to come.'

The hurt caused by this greeting showed on Barbara's face. 'You're my only child. Did you really think I'd leave you here on your own when you're like this?' She moved a little closer to him.

'On my own?' He let out an ironic laugh. 'Suddenly everyone in the world wants to come and see me. It's like Piccadilly bloody Circus in here.'

Stafford gave a discreet cough and cast a gaze toward the door.

Barbara shook her head. 'No, that's all right. I'd rather you stayed.' She appeared unsure of herself and grateful to have him there for support.

'Did he send for you?' Alan asked her, once again flicking his eyes in Stafford's direction.

'No, we just happened to meet here in the hospital. I came as soon as I heard about your accident because I thought you might need me.' Her hand reached out to touch his arm lightly. 'In spite of what you think, Alan – no matter what you may have done – I do still love you. Can't you see that?'

If he did, Alan gave no sign of it. His features froze into an impassive mask, stating quite plainly that he had nothing more to say to her.

She turned to Stafford in a silent appeal for help.

It was time to take a direct approach, he decided. This wasn't the perfect moment. But left as it was, this conversation was going nowhere.

'Your mother and I have had a long talk,' he began. 'There are some things you need to know.'

At least this drew a response. Alan's eyes shifted.

'Like what? Like how she warned you that I was coming up here to see you. She probably told you I was a nut case. Right?'

'Well you *have* been in a fair bit of trouble. She's worried about you.'

'I can look after myself. I don't need you. Or her.'

'Please,' his mother begged. 'Hear what he's got to say. It might help.'

Alan's voice rose. 'For crying out loud, will everyone stop trying to help me. I don't need no bloody help.'

'So you don't want to know the true story of what happened to your father,' Stafford said quietly. 'Maybe that's not important to you any longer.'

Alan turned his head away from both of them. This time his voice was little more than a whisper.

'I already know the truth, don't I? Do you think I'd believe anything *you* tried to tell me?'

Barbara moved around to the other side of the bed in order to gaze into her son's face. She crouched down so that her eyes were level with his. 'You only know what I told you when you were little.'

She took a long deep breath before continuing. 'What I said then might have been wrong. I don't know for certain – not yet anyway. But it might have been.'

'Wrong! How could it be wrong?' Alan's voice began rising again. 'The bloke who told you all about it was there when it happened wasn't he? Why would he lie about something like that?'

For a moment Stafford struggled to take in the boy's words. There must be some mistake, he told himself. He looked sharply at Barbara. 'What the heck does he mean by that? Who was there? Who spoke to you? You never mentioned any of this to me before.'

She struggled to meet his gaze. 'I didn't want you to know. Not yet. Not until I'd sorted things out in my head.'

'Who spoke to you?' Stafford repeated. What he was imagining couldn't possibly be true. But he sure as hell wanted to hear what she had to say.

Slowly, Barbara raised herself from her crouching position and sank down into a nearby chair. She sighed. 'It was one of your old crew. He came down to London and told me everything that happened that night.'

Her accusation hit Stafford with an explosive force far greater than any bomb he had ever carried. What he was hearing was unbelievable.

'Told you what?' he demanded. 'All that bullshit you gave me earlier. I thought you'd made all that up. That you'd imagined it because you needed someone to blame and hate.'

His tone softened a little. 'I know how hard you took Jimmy's death. We all did. Sometimes grief plays strange tricks with the mind. People end up believing what they want to believe.'

She shook her head sadly. 'No tricks. No imagination.'

'So who was it? Give me a name.' Stafford now felt in need of a seat himself. Alan's eyes bored into him as he dropped onto the edge of the bed.

A stubborn look came over Barbara. 'It's not for me to say. Not until I know for sure who's telling the truth.'

'Sod that,' Alan snapped at her. 'Tell him…tell me. Why have you always kept it a secret?'

'No!' She regarded both of them resolutely. 'I'll tell you everything else that happened, but no names. Not yet.'

Stafford had little choice but to agree. 'Okay, have it your way. Let's hear the rest of it.'

What she had said so far was all garbage anyway, he kept assuring himself. Even so, he found himself listening intently. Alan too, remained silent.

She began softly and hesitantly. 'When Jimmy died, yes, I took it hard. Harder than you can ever imagine. I was just two months married and pregnant. Who wouldn't feel angry and cheated in that situation?'

Her voice gathered pace and volume. 'And when I asked the War Office for more information on how Jimmy died, do you know what they said?'

Stafford knew very well. No details of operations would have been disclosed, not even to close family members. They would be given nothing more than the hard facts. Missing in action or confirmed dead was the usual limit of things.

'They were very sorry, but they couldn't give me any further information,' Barbara continued. 'Any medals due to him would be posted on at the appropriate time.' She trembled with indignation at the memory. 'I didn't want their damn medals. I wanted my husband. And if I couldn't have him, at the very least I wanted something more than an impersonal telegram from someone I didn't even know.'

Her resentment was still rising. 'Killed in action! What did the heck did that tell me? He could have been shot – burned – anything at all. And how come all the rest of you on the same plane got back home alive? Why Jimmy, I kept asking? Can you imagine how I was feeling at the time?'

Stafford nodded slowly. 'Sure. I know how it was.'

'Do you?' Barbara retorted. 'You might have been his best friend, but you weren't married to him. You didn't sleep with him. And you damn sure weren't carrying his child.'

She paused to look at Alan, as if remembering her son as a baby. Stafford saw the boy shift uncomfortably under her gaze.

He waited while Barbara wiped a hand irritably across her eyes. Then she continued. 'In the end I decided to try and find out what happened another way. I would have contacted you, but you were away somewhere on sick leave at the time. So I tried the others instead.'

'The other guys from the crew?'

'Yes.'

This was all news to Stafford. No one had ever mentioned a word to him. But looking back, that was hardly surprising given his mental condition at the time.

He frowned. 'Go on.'

'The first four I tried weren't any good at all. One of them was still in hospital under intensive care, and the other three wouldn't tell me anything when I telephoned them.'

He jumped in quickly. 'Which ones were they?'

Barbara looked at him sharply. 'Come on. Credit me with a bit of intelligence.'

'Sorry.' He felt embarrassed at having asked. But at least he knew for certain that it wasn't Geordie who she was attempting to incriminate.

'So that meant there was only one of your lot left. He was my last chance. I could hardly believe it when he agreed to meet me.'

'And you're saying that's how you got hold of that cock-and-bull story you gave me just now?'

'Can you prove it's not true?' Alan butted in.

Barbara snapped back at her son. 'Just shut up for a minute and let me finish will you?'

He blinked in surprise at the sharpness of her rebuke, but remained silent.

Barbara returned her attention to Stafford. 'Yes, that's where I got it from. Almost as good as straight from the horse's mouth you could say. But there's a lot more to the story than what I've told you so far. And believe me, you don't come out of it very well.'

'What more could there be?' asked Stafford. 'You've already accused me of panicking under pressure. And of having Jim physically forced out of the aircraft. That's a lie for a start. Okay, I'll admit he didn't want to jump at first, but that was mainly because he thought he should hang around and take his chances with me. I couldn't let him risk that.'

He shot Alan a quick glance. The boy was staring, stone-faced at him.

A flash of uncertainty showed on Barbara's face. She quickly firmed herself. 'Please let me finish, then we can talk about your side of the story.'

His mouth set into a firm line. 'Go ahead.'

Barbara continued. 'I was told you had a man on board who was too badly injured to bale out. It seems like you were planning for everyone, including yourself, to abandon the plane and leave him to it. You said he didn't have much hope of surviving anyway. Jimmy argued with you and said he would rather try to land the thing himself than leave his crew mate to die. You lost your temper, and that's when you ordered two of your other men to force him out before jumping themselves.'

She gave a humourless laugh. 'Whichever two they were, it's easy to see why they wouldn't talk to me when I asked them to.'

Stafford could take no more. 'This is bullshit!"' he exploded. 'All lies.'

He turned to gaze at Alan. 'Is that what you've believed about me all these years?'

The boy's grim expression did not change. 'She hasn't finished yet,' was all he said.

There was more? How much worse could it get? Stafford agonized. None of his crew would ever have said anything like this. It was all too crazy for words. He had to fight back the urge to tell them his own version of events immediately. But better he heard the whole goddamn thing first before trying to defend himself.

Barbara saw his hesitation. 'When you were told that Jimmy's parachute hadn't opened properly you lost your nerve completely and didn't have the guts to jump out yourself. That left you with only one choice if you were going to save your own skin. You *had* to attempt a landing. It wasn't anything to do with being a hero and wanting to save your injured man.'

'No! That's not the way it was!'

Stafford could not contain himself any longer. Shaking with pent-up frustration and anger, he shifted his attention to Alan. 'You want the truth, son? Well I'm going to give it to you. Blow by blow as it really happened.'

'Maybe you should let me tell Alan your side of the story,' Barbara suggested.

'Not a chance. The kid's going to hear it straight from me. But I'll tell you one thing before I even get started. Jimmy was the very last man on board to leave the aircraft. No one else could possibly have seen or heard what happened between us at the end. I don't know who you spoke to, Barbara, but they sure as hell weren't there when Jimmy went out.'

She frowned, as if reluctant to concede any further ground. 'I've already admitted that some of the facts I was told might possibly be wrong. What more do you expect from me after just one talk together? Total forgiveness? There's nothing to prove that what you've told me today is true. All I'm doing now is repeating what was said at the time by one of your own lot.'

She shrugged. 'Maybe he was telling the truth. Maybe you are.'

Stafford was bemused by her attitude. 'But why now? Why begin to doubt things after eighteen years? All the damage has already been done.'

To his surprise, her face began to colour up slightly. 'I don't know. Like you said just now, I suppose I wanted something or someone to blame and hate. You were it at the time.'

'At the time, sure. I can understand that. But how about now?'

There was a long pause as Barbara attempted to find an answer to his question. She took a deep breath before speaking any further.

'If you must know, seeing you here today has made me remember just how close you and Jimmy actually were. I keep saying to myself that, if you had really done all those things the way I was told, surely to God I'd be able to see it in your eyes. No one can hide that much guilt, can they?'

Her hands began to move around in an agitated manner. 'Oh hell, I don't know what to think any longer. Why on earth did you have to come back here again?'

Her gaze shifted to the floor. Suddenly, she looked drained of all emotion.

Ignoring his mother's distress, Alan fixed Stafford with a grim look. 'All right then. Forget about her now. If you still want to talk, let's do it. Let's see if you can make *me* believe you.'

Stafford could see from the challenging light in the boy's eyes that this was going to be one of his toughest battles yet.

TWENTY-FIVE

Stafford spread his hands as he concluded. 'So that's it,' he said. 'No matter what else your mother may have been told, that's the honest to God truth, Alan. It's up to you now which story you choose to go along with.'

He had been talking almost non-stop for close to fifteen minutes, spelling out in clear detail everything that had happened during the critical moments of K for King's final mission. Despite being offered several opportunities to make some kind of comment during the telling, Alan had chosen to remain stubbornly silent throughout. Every now and then Stafford spotted the boy frowning briefly, but that aside, his expression remained a mask of disbelieving hostility.

Barbara too, had said little. Apart from an occasional brief reaction to some point or other he was making, she had spent most of the time studying her son's face. Twice she reached out to touch his hand. Both times, Alan drew away from her.

Even now, with everything on the table, the boy's silence persisted. His eyes stared straight at Stafford, cold and unfriendly. Was this a cover for confusion, or was the kid simply using this silent treatment as a weapon against him? It was starting to feel pretty much like the second option.

Still ignoring Stafford, Alan's gaze suddenly shifted over to his mother. 'Do *you* believe him?' he demanded.

After only a short hesitation, she answered in a low voice. 'I don't know for certain yet, but maybe I'm starting to. I can remember when --'

Alan's voice, loud and incredulous, cut her short. 'You're going to take his word for it? Just like that?' He let out a hollow laugh. 'So what are you saying to me? Sorry, son, but all those things I told you when you were a little boy was just a load of crap. Never mind if it screwed your head up. Mummy will kiss it better.'

'Please, Alan. I never meant to do anything that ...'

Barbara's speech faltered. No adequate words would come as her eyes moistened.

Heedless of her distress, Alan shifted his attention back to Stafford. All thoughts of continuing with the silent treatment were clearly forgotten. Anger was the only emotion driving him now.

'You want to know what I think? All right! I think everything you've told me so far is a load of crap. It's easy for you to come in here and change the story to suit yourself. Where's the bloody proof? What you need to do is bring me this bloke from your crew who she met up with. Stick him right here in front of me and let me hear the bastard admit he told my mother a pack of lies.'

Alan let out an empty laugh and his voice dropped. 'Can you do that? If you can't, then forget it. We've got nothing more to talk about.'

Stafford met the boy's challenging look. 'You know that's not possible. I don't know who this mystery guy is any more than you do. In fact, the way I see it, I don't figure he ever existed.'

His accusing words hung heavily in the room, dragging Barbara right back into the centre of things. Suddenly, she was the person now standing in the dock.

'Well? Was he real?' Alan demanded. 'Or was that all bullshit as well?'

'Of course he was real,' Barbara told him. 'Stop looking at me like that? Do you think I would have lied to you about something so serious?'

Alan kept the pressure on. 'So go on then, tell us. Tell us his name?'

'I think you should,' Stafford added. A sick feeling was developing. But if he had truly been betrayed by one of his crew, then he needed to know who it was.

Or did he?

Tears were now forming on Barbara's face. She produced a handkerchief and began dabbing at her eyes.

'I never lied to you, Alan,' she said. 'I told you exactly what he said to me. If that was wrong, forgive me. Please God forgive me.'

'Just tell us who it was.'

She took a deep breath, still hesitating.

'It was Hughie Smith,' she finally told them.

***

For a brief moment Stafford imagined that he might actually be sick. He swallowed hard, forcing back the bile. There was a foul taste in his mouth.

'Hughie Smith?' he repeated.

Barbara nodded. 'I swear to you it's the truth.'

Only Alan appeared to be pleased about the revelation. There was a look on his face that was very close to triumph. 'There you are,' he stated. 'Now all you've got to do is bring this Smith bloke back here and make him admit what a lying bastard he's been. You were his skipper, so that should be easy enough for you.'

The mocking tone in his voice barely registered with Stafford. A large part of him was doing all that it could to reject what he'd just been told. It was almost impossible to believe that Hughie would have betrayed him with such a damaging pack of lies.

Yet could he be so certain? Recollections of how his former flight engineer had been at their weekend reunion – grey and anonymous with barely a word for anyone – were already forcing their way into his thinking. If there had been one member of the old squadron who had looked out of place, it had been Hughie. Like everyone else there at the time, Stafford had put the man's subdued behaviour down to the fact that he had been completely overshadowed, not to mention hugely embarrassed, by his wife's outlandish behaviour.

Now though, little things were starting to take on a much greater significance. Not once could he remember the man looking him directly in the eye. More than that, there had been times when he'd got the distinct impression that the guy was trying to avoid him altogether. Thinking about it, he could not recall a single occasion when Hughie had spoken directly to him unless pretty much forced to.

Even so, it still made no sense. What reason could Hughie possibly have had for inventing such a story? Sure, he'd never taken much part in the off-duty camaraderie that the other guys in the crew shared, but that didn't mean anything. At thirty-five, Hughie had been at least ten years older than everyone else on board apart from Doug, and he was already a married man when joining them. It was hardly surprising that he didn't have quite the same all-out enthusiasm for dance halls and pubs. Even so, it was safe to say that the pair of them had never seriously fallen out over anything. Certainly nothing serious enough to justify such a vicious stab in the back.

Stafford forced his mind back to the present. 'There's got to be a mistake somewhere here, Barbara,' he said.

She shook her head. 'There's no mistake. I met him when he came down to London. We even had lunch together.'

There was no trace of deviousness on her face. Her words were spoken with total conviction. If this was an act, Stafford considered, it was an incredibly convincing one.

He was still trying to clear his thoughts when Barbara spoke again.

'If you can't accept what I say, why don't you go and talk to him yourself?'

Her suggestion made obvious sense. At the same time, Stafford had a sudden urge to get out of the room. Maybe then he'd be able to see things more clearly? He got to his feet and began heading for the door.

'I'll leave you two alone to talk things over,' he said.

Alan's voice stopped him when he had moved only a couple of paces. 'Are you going to see this Hughie bloke or not?'

He turned and nodded. 'Yeah, I'll head over to his place first thing tomorrow morning. I need to get to the bottom of this as much as you do.' A frown formed. 'But there's a limit to what I can do. Even if Hughie did mislead your mother, I can't force the guy to come here and admit anything if he doesn't want to.'

For a long moment Alan simply stared at him. 'Yes you can,' he finally said. 'You can get whatever you want if you need it bad enough.'

If only that were true, Stafford thought.

'We'll see,' he replied. 'But whatever happens tomorrow, I'll be sure to come back here and tell you about it. That's a promise.'

Alan nodded. After hesitating for a moment, he reached beneath his pillow. 'You better have this back before you go.'

Stafford had already decided not to bring up the subject of his missing wallet for a while longer. His surprise at its sudden appearance was only half pretence.

'I was wondering when I might see that again,' he said.

'So now you know. I've taken back that picture of you and my old man, and there's a fiver missing. Everything else is still in there.'

He accepted the wallet from Alan, not knowing quite what to say. To thank the boy would have sounded all wrong and patronising beyond belief. In the end, he restricted himself to a brief nod that could have conveyed almost anything.

'Don't think I'm doing you any favours,' Alan continued. 'I've already had the coppers in here three times. I don't want them finding that thing on me. Know what I mean?'

Stafford could read the underlying message very clearly. 'I can't remember it ever being missing,' he said.

For an instant he thought he detected a look of grudging respect on Alan's face. Encouraged by this, he held out his hand.

The boy's look hardened. His offered handshake was ignored.

'You ain't my best friend yet,' Alan told him.

***

Hughie Smith had been alone ever since Gloria had taken the train down to London a day and a half ago.

'I simply must go to town and see some old friends,' she'd informed him. 'You can expect me back some time over the weekend.'

After driving her to the station, he returned to an empty house. In this solitary state, he had been brooding for the last thirty-six hours.

Sitting in his favourite armchair, Hughie sighed deeply. So keen had Gloria been to get away, she had failed to detect even a hint of the distress currently eating away at him. But this was hardly surprising. For several years now he had been living his life with all the enthusiasm of a condemned man. On the surface, he would have appeared to be little different than usual.

At the beginning, it had been so much easier to bury his feelings of guilt. Like so many of the RAF flyers during the war, he'd conditioned himself to blank out all memories of lost colleagues. Allowing thoughts of those killed in action to linger in the mind would have made it impossible to carry on with the job. And after the war was over, he'd simply continued with this same method of self-induced amnesia to conveniently forget how he had deliberately maligned his old skipper. There were still the occasional flashbacks and flickers of remorse, but mostly the guilt was kept securely tucked away in a corner of his mind marked '*Do not disturb*'.

Things had remained like this until about five years ago when, purely by chance, he spotted Doug Short in Manchester. His old crew mate was limping along a busy main street in the centre of town. His first reaction was to call out. He actually did so once, but his voice was lost in all the traffic noise. He looked to cross the street to where Doug was, but then stopped himself.

Of all the people he had ever known in the RAF, Doug was by far the most perceptive. Talking about the old days would be unavoidable, and a great deal of their conversation would inevitably involve Mike Stafford. This was the very last thing Hughie wanted. A man with Doug's insight could easily pick up on the fact that any mention of their old skipper's name was making him uncomfortable. All kinds of awkward questions might be put to him. Suddenly alarmed and fearful, he instead hurried away in the opposite direction.

Small as this incident was, it was still sufficient to spark a major change in Hughie. Bitterly ashamed of his own cowardice, he was now finding it ever more difficult to push aside the memory of his betrayal. The outrageous lies he had told about Mike Stafford steadily grew into an almost unbearable burden of guilt. As his depression deepened, so he became increasingly incapable of sharing his shame with anyone. Gloria tried on numerous occasions to get to the root of his problem, but he rejected her on every occasion. Gradually, they grew further and further apart. He could hardly blame her when she once again began embracing the show business world. Her unfulfilled yearning for stardom, long ago abandoned in favour of married life, became an all-consuming passion for the second time around. And who was he to dare tell her that she was many years too late?

Doug Short's posted invitation to the reunion in Wetherditch came like a bolt from the blue. Nothing in this world would make him attend, he told himself, fully intending to destroy the letter. But instead of doing this immediately, he had stupidly left the envelope lying on top of the bureau. There was no one to blame but himself when Gloria picked it up and read the invitation.

She was immediately enthusiastic over their attending, seeing the occasion as yet another opportunity to promote herself. It had long since become apparent that the entertainment world was not exactly holding its breath for her comeback as a dancer or actress, but to Gloria it was still a case of simply getting out there and making new contacts. Any kind of social gathering offered the possibility that maybe, just maybe, somewhere amongst the guests there might be a theatre talent scout or a TV producer. Hughie had tried repeatedly to tell her that no such people would be attending in Wetherditch, but she would have none of it.

'How could you possibly know what your old friends are doing these days?' she'd demanded. 'I admit that the chances are small, but it's an established fact that you make your own luck in show business. All I need is just one small break.'

From that point on, he'd stood little chance. He tried putting forward every imaginable excuse for not attending, but she placed him under relentless pressure. Finally, Gloria telephoned Doug Short herself and accepted on his behalf. It was done, and unless he wanted to endure months of retribution, there was little choice but to go along with the arrangements. All he could do now was pray that Mike Stafford would not be making the long trip over from Canada.

Almost inevitably, his prayer was not answered. The entire weekend was a personal nightmare. Even though he made every effort to avoid his old skipper, there was a limit as to how much he could separate himself without attracting unnecessary attention. As it turned out, Stafford's mere presence in the hotel became sufficient to leave him feeling like the very worst kind of traitor. Even when the reunion was all over, there was still no immediate escape. For the majority of the drive back to Southport, Pete Cowley, encouraged by Gloria, talked endlessly about the many hair-raising moments they had survived on board K for King. By the time he and Gloria eventually arrived home, the sense of guilt was unbearable.

It was whilst listening to the news on the BBC Home Service the following day that he first heard about the rescue on the moor. The huge sense of shock over this was still sinking in when the report ended with the devastating words: *'Police are also waiting to interview a seventeen-year-old London youth, Alan Knight, in connection with the incident. He is at present in hospital after sustaining head injuries in a car accident. His condition is said to be stable.'*

Memories of his wartime meeting in London with Barbara instantly came flooding back to Hughie. This time, the incriminating details cut deeper than ever before.

***

He met Barbara as arranged in the Lyons Corner House on Tottenham Court Road. Almost immediately she produced a shock by informing him that she was pregnant. Whether she was using her condition as a form of emotional blackmail and an extra inducement to tell her what she wanted to hear was hard to tell. But if it was, the ploy worked. She went on to say that, if the child turned out to be the boy she was hoping for, she planned to call him Alan after Jimmy's father.

It was after they'd finished eating their lunch that matters started getting seriously out of hand. Hughie began by depicting Stafford as having made a panicky decision that none of the crew really wanted to go along with. Jimmy's reluctance to jump was particularly stressed to Barbara, although not her husband's close friendship with the skipper being the main reason for him wanting to stay on board. Nor did he make any mention of Jimmy's subsequent acceptance of the situation.

The anger his words provoked anger in Barbara was far greater than Hughie could possibly have imagined. So violent was her reaction that she actually began to frighten him.

She had no way of knowing that the truth was very different. Within the squadron, Mike Stafford had earned himself enormous respect for the way in which he had put his own life on the line to save Geordie. Of course, no one was crass enough to offer this opinion to his face because of what happened to Jimmy. But the respect was there all the same, and it was this constant exposure to hearing his skipper's flying skill and courage being praised that fuelled Hughie's spite. Before his meeting with Barbara he had naively considered that he could somehow redress the balance by telling her his own mildly distorted version of events, and that she would merely come to regard Stafford in the same less-than-heroic light that he did.

But the whole thing rapidly got out of hand. After listening to his story, Barbara quickly began placing her own interpretations on events. Soon she was wildly exaggerating everything he had told her. Worse than that, she began putting entirely new and unintended words into his mouth: terrible accusations that had no basis of fact whatsoever. And because of her anger, he had been too cowardly and weak to set the woman straight. As soon as an opportunity presented itself, he made a hasty excuse and left her still sitting there.

The look on her face as he walked away would live with him forever. But even then, he knew that it would have been immeasurably worse had she known the true reason for him choosing to talk to her.

That was a secret he would keep with him until the grave.

***

After hearing the radio news broadcast, it was not difficult for Hughie to piece things together. A son christened Alan must indeed have been born. It was a simple matter to work out that he would now be seventeen, nearly eighteen, years old. The boy, fuelled by the hatred passed on by his mother, must have come seeking revenge on the man he wrongly held responsible for his father's death. Quite possibly he had already played a significant part in placing Stafford and the other two with him in danger. There appeared to be no other possible explanation for why the police would wish to interview him.

Sweat trickled down Hughie's face. It had all started with a few small lies. What in God's name had he set in motion?

He shifted in his chair to find a more comfortable position. After his long hours of solitude, he knew that he must finally unburden himself. Now, while Mike Stafford was still in the country. His telephone was beside him on a small coffee table. He had placed it there some time ago as a symbol of what he must do. All that was required was to pick it up and dial the number. He had told himself this more than a dozen times already.

Once again his hand reached out to the instrument. This time, he actually made contact.

'The Compton Manor Hotel. Can I help you?' a woman's voice responded.

'Is Mister Michael Stafford still staying there?' he enquired.

'Yes, but he is out at present. Can I take a message for him?'

Hughie said that there was no message and hung up. He ran a hand over tired eyes, in many ways relieved. To try and discuss such a delicate matter over the telephone was not the way to do things. Why on earth had he imagined it was?

A letter – that was the answer. A letter that not only owned up to everything, but also made at least some attempt to explain why he had behaved so unforgivably. There would be repercussions of course, but that didn't matter so much after all these years. What was important was the urgent need to set the record straight before something possibly even worse happened.

Rising from his chair, he went to fetch a pen and some paper. He must do it straight away, before he lost his nerve.

***

It was approaching 10.00pm by the time Stafford arrived back at the Compton Manor. He made straight for his room and called Geordie, who had returned home to Newcastle early that morning.

The big man was as shocked and disbelieving as himself over Barbara's allegations. 'Hughie would never have said anything like that,' he stated.

It was only when they both began to analyse the man's behaviour at the reunion that doubt began creeping into Geordie's voice.

'So what are you going to do about it?' he asked.

Stafford sighed. 'There's only one thing I can do; I'll have to try and talk to him and get his side of the story. I'm planning to drive over to Southport first thing in the morning. Phil's letting me use his car.'

'Why don't you take Phil with you?'

'No, this is something I have to handle on my own. Just me and Hughie, face to face.' He sighed again. 'If Barbara's shooting me a line, it's going to be awkward as hell explaining things to the guy.'

'But say it does turn out to be true,' Geordie pressed. 'What will you do then?'

Stafford gave a mental shrug. Right now, he did not have the faintest idea. 'I'll worry about that possibility when it happens,' he said.

Both men remained silent for several seconds. Geordie spoke first. His voice had a much softer tone than usual.

'You know something, Mike. If Alan has grown up believing all this bullshit he's been getting from his mother, maybe it's not so difficult to understand why he's turned out the way he has. Something like that would mess up most kids.'

Stafford could not help smiling to himself. Geordie the psychiatrist was a new and unlikely role for his friend. All the same, he was right in this instance. Alan needed a break – that was all. He was sure of it. Any son of Jimmy's had to have something good going for him.

They talked for a few minutes longer. 'Keep me in touch,' Geordie concluded. 'I've a bit of business to sort out here tomorrow, but after that I can be free for a few days. I'll come back down there on Thursday morning.'

'I'll look forward to that,' Stafford told him.

***

The clock on the mantelpiece had just finished striking midnight when Hughie eventually completed his letter. Half a dozen other sheets of paper, all badly crumpled and scattered across the bureau's writing surface, gave testimony as to how difficult it had been for him to find the right words. At last he felt that he had got somewhere close to the mark with this latest attempt. Whatever the case, it was the best he could manage in the time available. It would have to do.

He gave it one final reading. Yes, everything was there. What he had told Barbara; why he had chosen to lie to her; and most importantly of all, a true and honest account of events on board K for King that would fully exonerate his old skipper. After placing the letter in an envelope, he addressed it to Mike Stafford, c/o The Compton Manor Hotel, Wetherditch. Once a postage stamp had been found, he left the house and walked slowly to the corner of the street.

Standing immediately in front of the post box, the envelope in Hughie's hand suddenly seemed to weigh a ton. For a moment or two it required all of his strength just to raise his arm high enough to reach the opening. Then there was a soft rustle as the letter dropped down amongst the other mail inside the box. The deed was done. He walked back to the house with a mechanical tread. His letter would not be collected until the following morning, but the essential part was now completed.

Once back indoors, Hughie destroyed his previous attempts at writing the letter. He then sank into his armchair, reflecting on what he had done.

And what he intended to do next.

His life was a total mess: there was no doubt about that. And it was certain to become an even bigger mess once his letter was delivered. He knew that, when the crunch came, he would never have the guts to look Mike Stafford in the eye. He'd already taken a coward's way out by writing to him rather that admitting everything in a face-to-face meeting. Twice he had tried to screw up enough courage to say something at the reunion and failed miserably on both occasions. What sort of man was he? Were it not for the fact that three innocent people, including a young child, had very nearly suffered an awful death, he might even now still be concealing the truth.

On top of all this, his marriage was broken beyond repair. When he thought about it seriously, he could never understand what Gloria had seen in him in the first place. She had been a truly beautiful woman when they'd first met back before the war, and far better catches than himself were pursuing her. He couldn't blame her in any way for the breakdown of their marriage. Life with someone like him for the last five years must have been hell for a woman of Gloria's extrovert nature. She needed a husband with vigour to match her own, not someone who never wanted to go out anywhere or do anything even mildly exhilarating.

It was a hard fact to be faced, but their life together could only deteriorate even further now that he'd finally managed to clear his conscience. Their marriage had been childless, so he could not even use this as a reason to soldier on. The outlook was too bleak to contemplate. He still loved Gloria, but she deserved something a damn sight better than more years of misery with him.

The idea that he might choose to end it all had been ticking away at the back of his mind ever since returning from Wetherditch. Hearing about the narrowly averted disaster on the moor had simply hastened the process along. It was probably while attempting to write Stafford's letter that the decision was definitely made. Hughie knew that all he was doing now was justifying that decision.

He rose slowly from his chair. Show some guts for once in your life, he told himself. If he carried on like this he'd talk himself out of it again. It was time to actually do the deed, not just think about it.

He found a torch in its usual place in the kitchen. With the same mechanical step he had used when returning from the post box, he made his way to the small shed at the bottom of the garden. A coil of rope was hanging on the wall there. It seemed ideal for the purpose. He wasn't a heavy man – quite small in fact – so it should take his weight easily enough. His hand shook as he grasped the coil, the mere feel of it bringing home sharply the stark reality of what he intended to do. This seemingly innocent length of rope was to be the instrument of his death.

He remained frozen in this position for perhaps ten seconds before pulling the rope quickly from its hook. It would not do to dwell on matters. Moving with more urgency now, he returned to the house.

Should he leave a note for Gloria? he wondered. Another long letter was out of the question; it would take him far too long to complete. By the time he'd managed to get down on paper all of the things he wanted to say to her, he would almost certainly be starting to lose his nerve. He racked his brain for something suitable to write. Something brief, yet which still expressed exactly how he felt.

Eventually he wrote: *To my dearest Gloria. Many years ago I did something that I have always been deeply ashamed of. That alone is bad enough, but I have recently discovered that the consequences of my past mistake are now having serious repercussions for an old friend and comrade who I hold in the very highest regard. Let me stress that none of this has anything to do with you my darling, or our relationship. Everything that has happened, I have brought upon myself.*

I love you dearly, but cannot bear to live with the guilt I am carrying any longer. I pray that you find the happiness you deserve.

He signed it: 'Your loving husband Hughie.'

He read the short message twice, knowing that it was grossly inadequate. But what else could he say in so little time? While placing the note on the kitchen table, he felt a lump form in his throat.

The length of rope lay nearby on the same Formica surface. Like a snake, it appeared to slither invitingly closer to him. He snatched it up, fingers squeezing hard in an attempt to crush out this imagined life. A bead of sweat fell from his forehead, leaving a tiny puddle on the shiny table top. Both hands began cramping from the sustained pressure they were exerting. He released the grip.

Only after flexing his fingers for several minutes was he able to fully restore the circulation. He then set about fashioning a crude noose, managing this with surprisingly little difficulty. It was all done in less than ten minutes. And now for the final act, he acknowledged. It would be final in every way.

Leaving the kitchen, he climbed the stairs methodically one step at a time. Once on the top landing, he tied the end of the rope securely around a stout newel post and returned downstairs. He glanced briefly up at the noose, now dangling directly above the front hallway. From the cupboard under the stairs he removed a pair of wooden steps and positioned these beneath the noose. Everything was set. Hughie climbed the steps and slipped the noose around his neck. He let out a short, nervous laugh. One could almost describe it as being a comfortable fit.

Trembling now, he cast his eyes downwards. By his calculations, he would drop roughly two feet before the rope tightened. He had often heard suicide being described as a coward's way out. Well, that phrase must have been created by someone who had never actually stood in this position, because right now he was having to call on every last ounce of his courage.

His trembling increased. Would it hurt much? How quick would it be? Would the cord take his weight without breaking? There was no way of knowing any of these things. Not until it was too late. He firmed himself with the theory that, with a bit of luck, his neck would snap immediately and separate itself from the spinal cord. Wasn't that how the professional executioners did it? They often claimed that this method was quick, easy, and virtually painless.

This was his final thought. Please God, let it be quick and easy!

Hughie kicked away the stepladder and dropped into the unknown.

TWENTY-SIX

Determined to make an early start, Stafford was out of bed and dressed by 6.30am. He was on the road to Southport just half an hour later.

It was mid-morning by the time he located the quiet little cul-de-sac that Hughie lived in. The house itself turned out to be a well-maintained detached property with a recently cut front lawn surrounded by colourful flowerbeds. The one rather odd feature was the fact that the curtains in all of the downstairs windows were drawn. Stafford frowned, trying to think of a reason why this should be.

The wrought iron gate opened silently on well-oiled hinges. He paused by the front door for several moments, rehearsing yet again how he planned to open what was certainly going to be an incredibly difficult conversation. Even now he could not fully accept what Barbara had told him. Not until he had heard it from the man's own mouth. With a deep sigh, he finally grasped the knocker and gave two sharp raps. The noise echoed loudly throughout the house.

Stafford waited for nearly a minute. There was no sound of activity coming from inside. Nothing at all to suggest that anyone was at home. He glanced once more at the closed curtains. Perhaps he should have telephoned beforehand to save himself an unnecessary journey, but he had wanted to catch Hughie in an unprepared moment if possible. That way he was far more likely to see the truth of the matter on the man's face. More in hope than expectation, he knocked again, this time even louder with three solid strikes.

There was still no response. As a final gesture before returning to the car, Stafford crouched down to peer through the letterbox.

Almost the very first thing he saw was a pair of well-polished black leather shoes. They were swaying slightly from side to side.

***

An ambulance and a police constable arrived fifteen minutes later. Not that either of these would be of much help to Hughie now, Stafford considered. The guy was dead, and had been for several hours from what he could see.

When first forcing his way into the house he'd clung to the hope that there might still be a chance. It was this thought that sent him hurrying straight through into the kitchen in search of a knife. But the moment he cut Hughie down he knew it was too late. It was only when returning the knife to its drawer that he spotted the note to Gloria resting on the kitchen table. One glance at the message told him almost everything. Although it did not confirm Barbara's accusations in precise detail, he knew now that she must have been speaking the truth. There was no other explanation for the wording. Even so, it saddened him enormously to think that Hughie had felt it necessary to kill himself over the matter.

'What the hell made you think this was the way?' he asked the corpse, now stretched out on the hallway carpet. 'There was no need. We could have worked things out somehow.'

The questions from the constable that followed did nothing to ease his sense of frustration.

'Who are you?' the policeman demanded.

'Mike Stafford.'

'Why were you visiting the deceased?'

'It was a social call.'

'Do you know of any reason why Mister Smith should want to take his own life?'

'No, I don't. You've got the note he left behind. Read it again and work it out for yourself.'

It was question after question. Almost an hour later they were still dragging over the same ground. Stafford was upset enough without any more of this. His exasperation finally boiled over.

The constable looked young enough to be his son. 'Listen to me closely,' he told the officer. 'I'll go through this with you one more time. I just came here to visit him; he's an old friend of mine from the RAF. I got no reply when I knocked on the door, so I looked through the letterbox to check that everything was okay. He was hanging there. So what the hell did you expect me to do? Yeah, I kicked the goddamn door open. No, I didn't stop to see if he was still alive before cutting him down. There didn't seem to be a whole lot of point in talking to the guy about it first.'

The officer looked at him impassively. 'And then you called us immediately? You're absolutely certain that you didn't move or touch anything else apart from the telephone and the kitchen knife?'

It was the young man's air of indifference toward Hughie's death that was pushing Stafford to the limit. 'How the hell am I supposed to remember that?' he demanded. 'Strange as it might sound, I had other things on my mind at the time.'

He strode over to the battered front door. 'You've got my statement and you know where to contact me. I've told you everything I can, so now I'm on my way.'

'Don't forget that you will be required by law to attend the inquest,' the officer reminded him. 'You'll be informed of the date within the next few days.'

Stafford did not reply. He left the house and climbed into Phil's car. Neither the constable, nor his recently arrived two colleagues, attempted to stop him.

Moments later, he was on his way back to Wetherditch.

***

With nothing else to help pass the time while Stafford was in Southport, Phil decided to go fishing. He caught a bus to Scarborough, hired a small boat, and spent the afternoon in isolation afloat.

It came as no surprise to him when he reeled in several extra-large sea bass within the first hour. But as a professional fisherman, it *was* a novel experience to find himself returning his catch to the sea. Today was not about the fish themselves. It much more about being able to relax and unwind in a familiar environment.

At least, that had been the idea. But as the day progressed Phil found himself thinking increasingly of Tauranga and his own boat. And then, almost inevitably, of Donna. At first he tried to put her from his thoughts, reminding himself that he had already decided to forget all about their personal problems until actually embarked on the long flight home. It wasn't that easy however, and the ultimatum she had given him would not go away. His present surroundings were making him realise more keenly than ever how much she was asking him to give up. Could he really throw it all away, even to save his marriage?

Back on shore, Phil still did not have an answer. Or maybe he did, but was not yet ready to acknowledge it as being a firm decision. He caught the bus back to Wetherditch and once more closed his mind to the subject. There were more pressing matters to consider at present. He was due to meet Mike in the hotel bar that evening. He wondered how the skipper had got on in Southport. Could Hughie really have been capable of telling such lies to Barbara? And if it turned out to be true, how was Mike planning to handle the situation?

These were the questions that were now uppermost in his mind.

**

Stafford was unsure which of the feelings were hurting him the most. Was it the deep sorrow over Hughie's pointless death, or was it his own sense of failure in being forced to return to Alan empty handed?

The short note Hughie had left behind would not be available to anyone, not even Gloria, until after the inquest. Not that the note alone would be sufficient to achieve much anyway. It would take a whole lot more than a few vague references about Hughie's past to convince Alan of anything. Maybe he would be able to come up with a better way of explaining things to the boy by tomorrow, but given his present lack of ideas, there appeared to be little point in returning to the hospital before then.

He took another drink from his glass. The neat scotch was going down smoothly. Sitting alone in the Compton Manor's near deserted cocktail bar, he began recalling his first encounter with Siggi and her sister in this very same spot. That had been only five days ago.

Five days? Right now, it seemed more like five years.

He'd come to Wetherditch hoping to relax and put his mind at rest. Instead of that, it had been just one drama after another. How could so much have happened in such a short space of time? And the hell of it was, things were far from over. There were still all kinds of complications he needed to find a way of dealing with before feeling free to head back home.

He hadn't seen or heard from Siggi since their rather awkward parting at the hospital on Monday afternoon. It was clear to both of them that they still had a good deal of unfinished business to discuss. At the same time, it was also obvious that they needed a short breathing space away from each other. Rather lamely, he'd promised to call her very soon without stating when exactly.

Their moment of intimacy, although innocent in its purpose, continued to trouble his conscience. It wasn't that he'd wanted to back out of his promise to her, but since then nearly all of his time had been taken up with trying to straighten things out with Alan. And now, on top of that, there was this lousy business with Hughie.

He drew a deep breath. Alice would go out of her mind with worry if she knew even half of the story. A feeling of guilt came over him. He must call her again very soon, but this evening was not a good time. No matter how much he tried to conceal his troubles, she would sense something was wrong just from the sound of his voice.

By the time Phil wandered into the bar, Stafford was already on his fourth whisky. He finished this and quickly ordered another, together with a beer for the Kiwi. He bought a pack of cigarettes at the same time. Hell, he needed another smoke no matter how foul it tasted. As concisely as he could, he related to Phil what had happened in Southport.

His friend's face was grave while absorbing the news of Hughie's suicide.

'How are you going to be able to fix things with Alan now?' he asked when Stafford finished up. 'From what I can see, you've got nothing left to work with.'

Stafford shrugged. 'Convincing Hughie to play along the way Alan wanted was always going to be a thousand-to-one shot anyway.' He gave an ironic laugh. 'But like you say, all I've got left now is a whole lot of nothing.'

The whisky was suddenly hitting him. He lapsed into a brooding silence.

Phil frowned. 'I know you better than that, Mike. You must have come up with something else. Some other plan?'

'Sure I've got another plan, and this time it's a great one.'

A forced grin appeared on Stafford's face. 'To hell with it all for a few hours, that's what I say. Tonight I'm aiming to make the biggest damn hole I can in that whisky bottle over there.'

He raised his glass. 'Let's face it, sitting here having a few more drinks can't possibly make things any worse than they are already.'

***

With the night-time lighting in his room dimmed down to the lowest possible level, Alan stared moodily into space. Although it was nearly midnight, there was no hope of any sleep for him yet. It had been a shit day in every respect.

Yesterday had been so different. Even though he'd managed to remain hostile on the surface, Stafford had still managed to get through to him. Face-to-face, the bloke didn't act or talk anything like he expected him to. For the very first time in his life he had heard a totally different story about the way his father had died. And much as he'd started off by wanting to rubbish Stafford's version, all the time it began sounding more and more like the real thing. Maybe those words Stafford had written on the back of the photograph were starting to influence him again? But if the bloke *was* telling a pack of lies, then he was a bloody expert at it. Even his own mother had admitted that she was starting to believe him.

But all that was yesterday.

Today he'd spent hour after hour trying to imagine what Stafford might be doing. Had he managed to get the truth out of this Hughie Smith bloke yet? Were they, possibly right at this minute, both on their way back to the hospital to give him the proof he needed? All through the day, the words Stafford had said just before leaving kept repeating themselves in his head.

'Whatever happens tomorrow, I'll be sure to come back here and tell you about it. That's a promise.'

Yeah – some fucking promise! All evening he'd waited for the bloke to show up. All for nothing! It was just like the first time back at the hotel.

Alan could hardly believe that the bastard had come so close to making him think he was on the level.

'Don't be so impatient,' his mother had told him as the hours passed by. 'He's probably been held up and will come in tomorrow instead.' That was crap. Just like Stafford's whole story. Everything he said must have been one big trick just to keep him quiet until the coppers were allowed to get their hands on him.

Now he thought about it like that, it was all suddenly making sense. They *were* out to get him. The same two coppers as before had been back here this afternoon, and this time the doctor had let them loose on him. Straight away they started talking about his record, and how they had more than enough charges to make sure he went inside for a long time.

'We can wait, son. We'll be back,' they told him when he refused to say anything to them.

It was all one big bloody conspiracy.

The whole lot of them were in on it: Stafford – his mother – even the doctors and nurses who were supposed to be looking after him. Maybe even Sue as well after the way he'd spoken to her? Like Stafford, she hadn't bothered to come back to see him again either.

Well they could all piss off.

He'd teach every one of them not to take him for a mug.

***

Stafford woke with a dry throat and a slight headache, but the hangover was far less severe than it might have been. In spite of his stated intention, tiredness had overcome him before a seriously damaging amount of whisky could be consumed. He was up in just enough time to catch the final serving of breakfast. Before he even considered what move to make next, there was now a large hole in his stomach that was demanding to be filled.

He was passing through the hotel lobby on the way to the dining room when the receptionist called out.

'Mister Stafford! There's a letter here for you.'

It was the same girl who had been on duty when he first checked in. She smiled her *'How's our local celebrity this morning?'* smile at him. 'It came with this morning's post,' she added.

While taking hold of the envelope he was reminded of that first morning when she had handed him the note from Alan. Forgetting about that had been the start of so many problems. Well, he would not be making the same mistake again. Although this letter could not possibly have such far reaching consequences, he would read it soon anyway.

But breakfast first, he decided.

Although hardly a Geordie-size meal, he ate surprisingly well. Only after the plates had been cleared away did he take a closer look at the envelope. The handwriting had a vaguely familiar look about it. His eyes moved to the postmark.

Southport! Although the ink was slightly smudged, it definitely said Southport. And the handwriting. He could remember now. It was the same as the entry he'd seen in the hotel visitors' book when confirming Hughie's address.

He sat rigidly upright. For several moments his fingers seemed to lose their coordination while seeking to tear open the envelope. The paper finally yielded to his fumbling, leaving a jagged rip across the back. It *was* from Hughie. His name and address were written clearly in the top corner of the first page.

A sudden awareness of how significant the contents of this letter might turn out to be gripped Stafford. He paused for a moment, moving his eyes away from the page. In some ways he was almost frightened to read on. Afraid that what followed might not be what he wanted to see.

He quickly realised what a pointless delaying tactic this was. His gaze moved back to the page and he began reading Hughie's neat, fussy little script.

***

Dear Mike

This is the fifth time that I have attempted to write this letter, so perhaps you will be able to imagine how difficult I am finding the task. If you do not understand at this stage, then you most certainly will do when you have read what I have to say. I should have spoken to you over the weekend, but I could not bring myself to do so. Since then however, circumstances have changed. Now, no matter how great my shame, it is vital that I speak out.

In the light of recent events, it is quite possible you are already aware that Jimmy's wife Barbara was pregnant when he died, and that she now has a teenage son called Alan. I believe that the boy is currently in Scarborough hospital following a car accident.

Barbara contacted me shortly after Jimmy's death. She was in a highly emotional condition and wanted details of how her husband had died. To my eternal shame I lied to her, placing the blame for his death squarely on your shoulders. I cannot bring myself to repeat the exact words I said. In truth, they are a little blurred after all these years. What I can say beyond doubt is that I portrayed you as being weak and cowardly, which we both know is a total fabrication. Never at any time did you panic, and I clearly heard Jimmy eventually agree to bale out of his own free will. At all times you acted as a responsible skipper who displayed great courage and concern for his crew.

I can hear very clearly what you will now be asking. Why then did I relate such a different story to Barbara? Well, I can tell you now that my reasons for this were very real to me at the time. It is only in more recent years that I have come to realise how shallow and self-absorbed they really were. I will attempt to explain.

When you gave the order to jump, I don't mind admitting that I was badly frightened. I never did trust those parachutes they gave us, and although your decision was made in our best interests, I would still have much preferred to stay and take my chances with you on the landing. Like almost everyone else in the squadron, I regarded you as the very best pilot we had.

It was only when I got to the rear exit point and clipped on my chute that I realised I must have picked up Jimmy's pack by mistake. I knew straight away because the serial number was different. It was just one of those stupid things that can sometimes happen. You remember how Jimmy threw his chute on to the floor close to where I'd dropped mine? Don't ask me why, but after realising my mistake I very nearly came back to change packs with him. What matters of course is that I did not. This fact has haunted me ever since.

Things only came to a head when I discovered that Jimmy hadn't made it. His chute – my chute that should have been – had failed to open properly. Please try to imagine how I felt. I could not get it out of my mind that it should have been me who died. A thousand times I tried to imagine what it must have been like, plunging down to earth, terrified and knowing that you have only seconds to live. Believe me, I had terrible nightmares for months afterwards.

My nerve had gone, although I could not admit this even to myself at the time. Instead, stupidly, I blamed you. Why not? I asked myself. It was your order to jump that had been the cause of everything. What made it worse was that everyone else seemed to be regarding you as a hero for the way you had put the Lanc down and saved Geordie's life. That made my resentment even greater, although I tried hard not to let my true feelings show through. But when Barbara contacted me, I suppose that all of my suppressed spite came out. Here at last was an opportunity for me to speak freely with someone away from the squadron and smash the heroic myth that had been built up about you. At least, that was how I saw it back then.

The ridiculous thing was that I did not really consider it as telling lies, it was more a case of relating events to fit in with how I wanted them to be. By now, I practically believed my version of events anyway. Besides, how could I possibly tell a distraught and angry woman like Barbara that her husband would still be alive had I not picked up his parachute by mistake? A few small half-truths at the beginning rapidly grew into a totally distorted account. Although I do not deserve it, I beg your understanding and forgiveness.

Barbara will certainly over the years have related my story to her son. He in turn will have jumped to all the wrong conclusions about you. I hope and pray that this letter can in some way redress the balance.

Please Mike, do not seek to contact me. Within an hour or so I will be dead. Once again I beg you, please try to find it in your heart to forgive me. Things might have been so much better if I had used the correct chute.

Goodbye and God bless you,
Hughie.

***

Stafford finished reading and placed the letter back down on the table. Everything he needed to clear his name with Barbara and Alan was here. He could not have asked for anything more conclusive. But in spite of this, the only emotion he could feel at that very moment was a deep, all-consuming sense of sadness.

He dug into his pocket to see if he had any cigarettes remaining. There was just one. It would be the very last he ever smoked, he promised himself.

***

There was little time for Stafford to dwell on this latest development. As soon as he left the dining room, Phil appeared and wanted to be brought up to date. Shortly after that, Doug Short telephoned from his Cotswold cottage to enquire about any progress with Alan. He then gave his considered thoughts on the situation. Finally, within minutes of hanging up after this fairly lengthy talk, Geordie arrived back at the hotel. As ever, the big man was all for getting on with things immediately.

'Get yourself over to the hospital, Mike,' he said emphatically. 'We're all sad about Hughie, but moping around here won't help him. Alan's the one you've got to be thinking about now. He's the one who needs your help.'

Phil could not hide his surprise at Geordie's change of heart. Even so, he was quick to back up the big man's opinion with a similar one of his own.

'Okay, guys, you've convinced me,' Stafford told them. In spite of the sorrow he was feeling over Hughie, he could not deny that he was also eager to confront Alan with the evidence he'd demanded. This could be a major turning point.

Geordie looked pleased. 'I'll drive you over there myself,' he said.

***

It was a few minutes before noon when Stafford arrived at the hospital. While walking down the long corridor toward Alan's room, he spotted Barbara heading in his direction. Almost as a reflex action, his hand felt inside his pocket to make certain that Hughie's letter was still there.

But thoughts of the letter were quickly forgotten. As they drew closer to each other he could see that the woman was severely agitated over something. Twice she brushed away what he imagined to be tears from her eyes. Had she been arguing with Alan? he wondered. Did this mean that the kid was in a particularly bad mood today?

A moment later she saw him too. Her pace immediately quickened almost to a run. She stopped in front of him, breathing rapidly.

'I tried to call you at your hotel a short while ago,' she said.

'Okay, Barbara, take it easy. I'm here now. What's the matter?'

'It's Alan. He's disappeared! He's taken his clothes and run off some time during the night. No one seems to know exactly when.'

Her voice took a harder edge. 'I know he was angry when you didn't show up here yesterday evening. Why didn't you come back to see him like you promised?'

'Sure I promised to come back, but I didn't make any solid guarantee it would be that same evening. Something has happened that ...'

He paused, wondering how best to explain Hughie's suicide.

Barbara seemed to take his hesitation as an admission of guilt. 'There isn't time for your bloody excuses,' she said. 'The doctor told me just now that Alan is still very badly concussed. That's why he's been so confused and depressed ever since waking up after the car accident.'

'And why he's been so damn difficult to talk to,' Stafford added.

'Forget that! It's what's happening now that's important.'

Her voice rose. 'All kinds of wild thoughts will be going through his head. I've seen people suffering from concussion before. One minute they might be sensible, the next they can be in a rage. God knows how Alan might react if he thinks the police are after him. He's already told me there were two constables here again yesterday afternoon trying to force him into making a statement.'

Stafford could see she was literally shaking with emotion. A memory of something said to him that very morning then prompted him to place a reassuring hand on her shoulder.

'Try not to worry,' he said. 'Maybe we can find him before the police do. Geordie is waiting for me outside in the car. He'll drive us to where we need to go.'

She looked at him sharply. 'Do you know something I don't? Are you saying you might have an idea where Alan has gone?'

Stafford frowned. 'It's just a guess,' he told her. 'But it sure beats the heck out of staying here and doing nothing at all.'

TWENTY-SEVEN

Just like the first time he'd visited the Moor Tea Restaurant, Alan paused outside to look in through the window. There were far less customers than before. He was able to spot Sue waiting on a table almost immediately. Quickly, he drew back out of sight.

Keeping a low profile so far hadn't been easy. Although he'd been lucky enough to find a flat cap in one of the hospital cloakrooms to cover the eye-catching stitches on his head, the scattering of barely healed cuts over his face still left him feeling horribly conspicuous. It had taken several hours and three different buses to get to Scapdale. People were sure to remember seeing him if asked. Yet again he wondered why the hell he had taken the risk of returning here instead of just heading back to London. There were plenty of places he knew of in the East End where he could keep his head down for a while.

He sighed. He knew damn well why. The more he thought about it, the more he realised he couldn't leave the area without first knowing the truth about Sue. Was she in league with all the others who were planning to get him locked up, or had she been playing straight with him? And if she *was* genuine, he also needed to know if he'd completely blown his chances of ever seeing her again once he was in the clear.

Never before had a girl got to him anything like this. Why now of all times? he agonized. He was taking a huge risk.

Sucking in a deep breath, he stepped inside the restaurant.

***

Geordie drove in silence while Stafford travelled in the rear of the Rover with Barbara. After bringing her up to date on what he'd discovered, he handed over Hughie's letter, all the time watching her face for signs of a reaction. After only a few moments of reading she let out a series of deep sighs, at the same time slowly shaking her head. This told him that she must have already reached the part where Hughie admitted lying to her. She paused for just a second or two to glance up at him, but made no comment before returning her attention to the page.

By the time she was on the third sheet of notepaper she was chewing constantly on her bottom lip, and as she handed the letter back to him he could clearly see the enormous depth of self-reproach she was now suffering. He could feel nothing but pity for the woman.

Her voice was barely above a whisper. 'I should have known better. Jimmy always said he'd trust you with anything, and I know he could pick a wrong-un a mile off.' She gave a sad, faraway smile. 'Nobody ever put one over on my Jim.'

He smiled at her recollection. 'Once you read this to Alan he'll understand it wasn't your fault. You weren't to know that Hughie was stringing you a line.'

The mention of her son's name immediately injected the urgency back into Barbara. 'Are you sure we're going to the right place?' she demanded. 'Alan has never said anything to me about this girl Susan.'

'I can't be sure of anything,' Stafford admitted. 'But I did have a long talk with Doug this morning, and there's no one smarter than him when it comes to reading people. He's kept in close touch with Sue over the last few days, and from what she's told him, he reckons there's a good chance Alan's more taken with her than she realises. Quite a lot more, in fact.'

Barbara frowned. 'As far as I know, he's never let anyone get close to him. It's hard to believe that some waitress he only met the other day is going to have any influence over what he's doing now.'

'Well, we'll find out for sure soon enough.'

Stafford leaned toward the driver's seat. 'What do you reckon, Geordie? How much longer to Scapdale?'

'Half an hour at the most,' the big man told him.

***

Sue's reaction when she spotted him entering the cafe pleased Alan. There was surprise written all over her face, but nothing else. No hint of the fright and alarm that would have been almost impossible to hide had she really been one of those plotting against him.

She came over to his table immediately. Her voice was quiet and full of concern. 'You shouldn't be out of hospital yet. What are you doing here?'

'I wanted to see you. I didn't think you'd come back and visit me again after all those things I said, so I had to come over here instead.'

'I *was* going to see you again. I was coming over this evening.'

She hesitated before adding: 'If you must know...yes...you really did upset me the last time. But Mister Short said it probably wasn't your fault. He said you only acted the way you did because you were hurting a lot and that I should give you another chance.'

'Who the hell is Mister Short?'

'He's the man who ...'

Sue stopped to glance quickly around the café before speaking any further. 'Look, I can't talk very much right now, but I'm on the early shift today so I'll be finished in about twenty minutes. I'll explain more then. Why don't you just sit there and wait for me?'

'Yeah, I can do that,' Alan agreed.

Suddenly life was not feeling quite so shitty after all. At least he was now sure there was one person on his side worth believing in.

***

They walked together through the village, Sue pushing her bicycle alongside him while explaining who Doug Short was. Once she had described the man, Alan could remember seeing him around at the hotel. The heavy limp was a big giveaway.

They were soon approaching the bottom of Squire's Hill, causing another memory to take over. It was further up here that he had crashed Stafford's car, he recalled. That big bloke had been chasing him.

A convoy of lorries with brightly painted trailers attached drove past them and then slowed right down as they began climbing the steep incline.

Sue smiled. 'The fair's back in the village this weekend,' she remarked. 'They come here for the same couple of weeks every year. My dad rents out three of his fields to them.'

'Maybe we could go up there?' Alan suggested.

Already an idea was forming. He'd hung around different fairgrounds quite a lot in the past, and most of the travelling fair people he'd known had shown little regard for established authorities. It was like a private world they lived in, with its own customs and laws. If he could get a job with these people for a while, it would be the ideal place to keep his head down until the coppers lost interest in looking for him. It shouldn't take long before he was in the clear. It wasn't like he was wanted for murder or anything.

'There won't be very much to see just yet,' Sue told him. 'A few of them are set up already, but nobody starts operating properly until Saturday evening.'

'All the same, I wouldn't mind having a look,' Alan said.

The words were barely out of his mouth when he heard a sudden screech of tyres. A vehicle pulled up sharply on the other side of the road. His eyes darted across, fearing the sight of a police car. He tensed, ready to run if necessary.

For an instant he felt a wave of relief. There was no dark blue uniform sat behind the wheel. Then recognition kicked in. If anything, he would have almost preferred the driver to be a copper. It was Stafford's big angry mate. And behind him was Stafford himself. His mother too.

In a flash, realisation dawned. Alan's eyes flew back to Sue. 'You set me up. You called them while I was sat there like an idiot waiting for you to finish work.'

'No! I wouldn't do that to you. I don't know how they --'

He cut her off. He was in no mood to hear her excuses. 'You bitch! I trusted you. I bloody well believed what you said.'

'No! You've got it all wrong,' Sue insisted.

Stafford's voice called out. 'Alan! Please wait there. We only want to talk to you. It's not too late. I've got the proof you wanted to see.'

The bloke was already out of the car and moving toward him. There was no time to mess about. Snatching the bicycle from Sue's hands, Alan jumped into the saddle.

She let out a loud gasp of surprise. 'What are you doing? You don't need to run away.'

He ignored her. What the hell made her think he was going to listen to anything more she had to say? Pedalling furiously, he glanced back after covering about fifty yards. Stafford had already given up the chase on foot. He was now back inside the car and they were turning it around in the middle of the road so they could come after him.

He began pedalling even harder. Immediately ahead of him was the fairground convoy. The leading vehicle pulling two large trailers was crawling along at no more than a slow walking pace as it struggled to cope with the rapidly increasing slope. Alan knew that if he could just get past this line of lorries quickly enough, Stafford's car would be stuck behind them for a long time yet.

He caught up with the rear vehicle of the convoy just as the chasing car was closing in on him. In one sharp movement, he flipped the bicycle over onto the narrow pavement. By standing up on the pedals he was able to move quite a bit faster than the pace of the leading lorry. Little by little, he eased his way further along the line of vehicles, veering around a couple of indignant pedestrians in the process.

Halfway along he glanced behind once again, just to check than no one from the car was attempting to chase after him on foot. They were not. He grinned briefly. Stafford and his mate were both old compared to him. They knew as well as he did that he could easily outrun them.

After passing the lead vehicle, he steered back onto the road again. Soon he was at the top of the hill and in open country.

Moving far more quickly now and with the pressure of pursuit for the moment eased, his thoughts turned to Sue's betrayal. How could he have been so bloody stupid? It was making his head throb just to think about it. He should have known better. All his life he had got along okay by trusting no one. Why should he have expected it to be any different with her?

But there was no point in kidding himself. He wouldn't get far on a lousy bicycle, and the odds were stacking up higher and higher against him. Soon the coppers would be turning up as well. In fact, now he thought about it, he was surprised they weren't sniffing around the area already. Either Stafford or his mother was bound to have called them as soon as Sue told them he was in Scapdale.

The hopelessness of his situation rapidly grew, driving his anger to an even greater pitch. Ever since he could remember, everyone in authority had either lied to him or treated him with contempt, as if he was some kind an idiot. But that was bloody finished now. He would teach all those bastards to show him some respect.

Pulling up, he dropped the bike down close to a stone marker reading PICKERING 10 MILES. From here he set off in a straight line onto the moor, carefully counting out twenty paces.

***

More than ten frustrating minutes dragged by before the Rover finally reached the top of Squires Hill and Geordie was able to begin overtaking the long fairground convoy. Stafford, now in the front seat alongside his friend, felt a fresh surge of annoyance as the view ahead opened up. There was no sign of Alan, even though the road before them was fairly straight and level for a considerable distance. Had the kid turned off somewhere? he wondered. It was beginning to look as if he had given them the slip.

He turned to speak to Sue, next to Barbara in the rear of the car.

'You must know this area well. Where do you think he might – –?'

She called out, cutting him off in mid-question. 'Stop – stop the car!'

She pointed to a spot on the edge of the moor just behind them. 'There, that's my bike. I'd know it anywhere.'

Geordie reversed back to where the abandoned bicycle lay on its side. All four of them jumped out of the car. Stafford immediately began scanning the landscape, searching for any small clue that might help to show which way Alan had headed. The moorland appeared to be deserted. Only as his eyes shifted further to the right was there any relief from the vast expanse of heather and grass. Perhaps half a mile away, set well back from the road, he could see the thick undergrowth giving way to a large cluster of trees.

He tried to put himself in the place of a frightened and angry kid, on his own and with no proper knowledge of the local area. Knowing he couldn't possibly outrun them on a bicycle once their car had got past the lorries, Alan would have been desperately looking for a place to get out of sight.

Sue saw his gaze lingering on the trees. 'That's Stoner's Spinney,' she told him.

He turned to look at her. 'What's beyond the trees? Does anyone live over that way??'

'No, not really. But there are a few caravans and other stuff on my dad's land at the moment. He owns the fields on the far side of the spinney.'

She pointed back down the road to where the fairground convoy was coming into view once again. 'That's where all of those lorries are heading for. Some of the fair people have been here for a day or two already.'

Geordie chipped in. 'We may as well head over and take a look, Mike. It's the most obvious place, and there's no sign of him anywhere else.'

'Yeah, you're right,' Stafford agreed. 'But just the two of us, eh.'

He looked at the women. 'I'm not trying to cut anyone out, but it would be a big help if you two stayed back here by the car. That way you can --'

Barbara did not let him finish. 'How would staying here help?' she demanded. 'Alan is my son. I need to be with you and helping to find him.'

'And right now, doing what I ask is going to be the biggest help of all,' Stafford told her, his tone firming.

He swept an arm across the huge area of moorland on both sides of the road. 'We don't know for sure where Alan is right now. We're only guessing. He could be lying low almost anywhere amongst all this heather, keeping his head down and just waiting for us to go off in the wrong direction. Unless you want to take a chance on us losing him completely, someone needs to stay here and keep a lookout. It's the only way we can try to cover all the bases.'

'That makes sense to me,' Sue agreed.

The stubborn look on Barbara's face slowly dissolved. 'You'll let me know straight away if you see anything of him?' she asked.

'Sure we will. And I'm relying on you two to do the same for us. Just give three long blasts on the car horn and we'll head straight back.'

Barbara nodded, now as satisfied as she could be with the arrangement. 'I'll watch this side of the road, and you keep an eye on the other,' she said to Sue.

Stafford turned back to Geordie. Together, they set off across the moor leading directly to Stoner's Spinney.

***

Down on his knees behind a thick patch of foliage on the edge of the spinney, Alan watched as the two men began moving in his direction. He continued to suck in deep breaths. Coming so soon after his race uphill on the bicycle, the long sprint across open ground had taken everything out of him. He had only just managed to get under cover before Stafford's car appeared on the road. There had been no time to hide the bike. As he'd feared might happen, they had spotted it and pulled up.

He gave himself a few more moments to recover before raising the rifle to his shoulder and peering along the sight. Stafford and his mate were well out of range at the moment, but that would change before long.

Resting the rifle on the ground beside him, he removed the flat cap to gently touch at the row of stitches in his skull. Not that the wound itself was hurting him any more than before. But there was now a different kind of pain to deal with. The inside of his head felt like one of those pressure cookers when the steam was building up all the time but couldn't escape. The feeling had come on out of nowhere, almost straight after he'd clapped eyes on Stafford back in Scapdale.

Stafford!

Didn't the bloke ever give up messing with his head? Maybe the only way to get rid of the pressure was to get rid of the person causing it?

Yeah, that was it, Alan decided. Placing the cap back on his head, he glanced down at the rifle. At least this way he would get a bit of recognition and respect when he ended up in the nick. One half of his brain was shouting at him, telling him this was the very least he deserved. Go out in a blaze of glory just like in the American movies, it was saying. Mad Alan was what some people back in London called him. Okay, now was the time to prove them right.

But it wasn't that easy. Things never were for him. There was another side of his brain that wasn't shouting. It was trying to tell him calmly what a bloody idiot he was. That he should have given Stafford a bit more time to get back to him at the hospital before doing a runner. This voice was faint though, and anyway, it was now far too late to be thinking that way. In the end, the only thing he had to look forward to was a long stretch inside. And this time, according to those two gloating coppers who'd tried to question him at the hospital yesterday, it would not be in some approved school but the real thing.

'The cons inside a proper prison will make mincemeat out of a runt like you,' one of them had told him.

He'd repeated this to his mother when she came to see him that same evening. She'd told him not to worry, and that they were only saying things like that because they wanted to throw a scare into him and make him admit stuff. She reckoned they didn't have half as much to charge him with as they claimed. That he might even get away with probation or a fine. But what did she know? How could she talk like that? It wasn't like she was a bloody solicitor or anything.

A solicitor!

A tiny shaft of light suddenly stabbed its way into the darkness of his mood. Maybe she wasn't a solicitor, but now he thought about it more, he could remember her saying something about having gone to see some legal bloke in Wetherditch that same morning. The remark had barely registered at the time because he hadn't felt like talking to her when she first arrived for visiting. Now though, he couldn't help but wonder if perhaps she had been speaking with a bit of knowledge after all.

Frustration gripped him. Everything could have been different. Why hadn't Stafford come back to see him like he'd promised? He and his mother had both waited all evening for him to show up.

'It's not too late. I've got the proof you wanted to see.'

That's what Stafford had called out to him just now back in Scapdale. But if he hadn't got anything to show yesterday evening, what proof could he have come up with since then? The answer was nothing. Everything the bloke said was still bullshit.

But what if it wasn't?

What if Stafford *was* telling the truth?

What if his mother *was* right about the police charges not sticking?

And what if Sue really *did* care about him like she said she did?

If all these things were true, it could change his life completely.

He glanced quickly up and down the road. There was no sign of any coppers turning up yet. That didn't make much sense either. There had been plenty of time for at least one of their motorbike patrols to be here by now.

Maybe no one had called them after all?

His breathing was just about back to normal now, but the pressure inside his head was becoming greater than ever. Something had to give way soon or it would explode. Why was it so bloody hard to accept the possibility that everyone might have been playing straight with him all along? That it was nothing but his own messed-up way of thinking that made him keep pushing away the people who cared.

From nowhere, he could feel moistness developing in his eyes. He ground his teeth. What the hell was he doing? He couldn't possibly be crying. He hadn't done that since he was a baby. He was Mad Alan – a tough guy who took no shit from anyone.

So why…why…did he suddenly want to be with his mother?

He brushed away the tears and looked down at the rifle on the ground beside him. What the fuck had he been thinking of? He *was* bloody mad if he thought a gun was going to solve anything. If the coppers caught him in possession of a stolen firearm, everything would change for sure. No solicitor in the world would be able to keep him out of prison once they pinned a charge like that on him.

He shifted his gaze back to the moor straight ahead. Stafford and the big bloke were still at least three hundred yards away. Beyond them he could see the tiny figures of his mother and Sue. It was stupid, but even from this long distance he felt he could see concern for him on their faces.

As this final thought formed, something went pop inside his head. But it was a quiet, friendly kind of sound, not the explosion he'd been fearing so much. In an instant, the pressure that had been tormenting him was all gone. For almost the first time he could remember in his life, he could think totally clearly. It was a fabulous kind of release. Suddenly there were no longer any doubts holding him back from doing the sensible thing.

Do the sensible thing? Why not?

He was on the very point of getting to his feet and calling out to Stafford when he heard a small twig snap behind him. Before he had time to react, a powerful arm wrapped itself around his neck, squeezing painfully and dragging him backwards.

'Well, well. What we got here then?' he heard a faintly familiar voice say.

TWENTY-EIGHT

The forearm crushing against Alan's windpipe eased slightly, but still applied sufficient pressure to hold him firmly in place. With the back of his head forced right up against his attacker's chest, he was unable to see anything of the man's features.

There was no such problem in identifying the second arrival. The man who had spoken stepped fully into Alan's vision. About forty years old, with jet-black hair flowing over his shoulders and a vivid scar running all the way down his right cheek, he was an instantly recognizable figure. Alan's heart gave a sharp kick. This was the last person in the world he would have wanted to see right now.

The man picked up the rifle and held it out. Like several of the fairground people Alan had known in the past, he spoke rapidly, practically blurring his sentence into one long word.

'Now boy, where'd you get hold of this then?'

'I found it. Honest I did.'

Numb with shock, Alan was incapable of coming up with anything better at present. Even to him, the words sounded weak and unbelievable.

His interrogator obviously thought the same. 'Don't you be giving me none of that,' he sneered. 'I don't forget see, and I remembers you hanging around my place when we was set up on Wetherditch Common. That same night someone breaks in and one of my rifles goes missing.'

He shoved the weapon further forward so that it was only a few inches away from Alan's face. 'And blow me if this ain't the very one that was took. I know it's mine 'cos that's my mark on it, right here see.'

He pointed to a small symbol not unlike a dollar sign burnt into the end of the wooden stock. 'Everyone knows Seth Rawlings' mark.'

All Alan's hopes of talking his way out of the situation disappeared. He wouldn't be believed now, no matter what story he came up with.

'Okay, I p-pinched it,' he admitted. The stammer he hated so much was back again. 'But I don't want the bloody thing any more. Why don't you just t-take it back and let me go.'

Seth chuckled. It wasn't a reassuring sound. 'Oh, I'm taking it back all right. But you gotta pay for what you done, boy. What's right is right and all that.'

Alan didn't want to imagine what Seth might have in mind for him. He could remember all too clearly seeing rough justice being handed out to a thief at a fair on Mitcham Common in south London a year ago. The bloke had had the crap beaten out of him, and he'd only been trying to pinch some stupid prize worth next to nothing off the hoopla stall. What the hell was fairground justice for nicking a bloody gun, for Christ's sake?

He twisted sharply, hoping to wrench himself away from the arm still holding him down. Surprise briefly worked in his favour. For an instant he thought he was about to wriggle free. Then a second powerful arm came across, crushing both his hopes and ribcage.

'Two flatties heading this way,' his captor said to Seth after regaining control.

Alan knew he must mean Stafford and his mate. He had a vague idea that flatties was a term they used for all non-fairground people.

'I see 'em, Toby, Seth said. 'They're a good way off yet.'

He poked Alan's leg with the toe of his boot. 'Them anything to do with you?'

Alan shook his head.

'So why was you hiding here then? You got the sharpies after you or summat?'

'Sharpies?'

'Come on, boy. You know what I mean. Busies – peelers – rozzers.'

Understanding dawned. 'Yeah, the coppers are looking for me. So what?'

Seth laughed again. 'Thought so. Judging by the state of your face, you've been in a right old scrap.'

He motioned with his hand. The next thing Alan knew, the man called Toby had picked him up and slung him over his shoulder. It was done with no apparent effort at all. The bloke was massive, Alan realised. He was built like a bloody gorilla.

'Don't struggle and I won't tell him to break your arm,' Seth said.

With Toby leading the way they set off deeper into the spinney. Alan remained quiet as the huge man carried him along. He had no intention of struggling. For a start it would be a waste of time against someone of Toby's size, and anyway, Seth's threat had sounded horribly genuine. The irony of his situation was not lost either. Stafford and his mate – the very people he'd been running away from – now looked as if they may be his only hope of rescue.

Or were they?

Even if they did catch up with him, maybe they'd agree with these two bastards that he deserved a bloody good hiding?

A good hiding, or something worse?

Stafford good guy?

Stafford bad guy?

All the different possibilities and outcomes began bouncing around inside his head at crazy angles. Once again he couldn't think properly. But he had to try.

Up until now Seth had been walking behind Toby. Now he quickened his stride and moved ahead of them. Muddled though his brain was, Alan still managed to grasp the fact that this could well be his only chance. It might not help very much, but at least he'd have made some sort of effort.

After his earlier struggle with Toby, the red cap was already sitting very loosely on his head. It needed no more than a quick flick of his fingers to dislodge the thing completely. The action was well-timed. Only a few moments later they moved out of the trees and onto an open field. Alan caught a glimpse of some caravans and partly erected fair attractions scattered about. He could also see a few other people in the same field, but no one glanced at him more than once. The indifference on their faces said plainly that it would be a waste of time appealing to any of them for help.

They stopped at the first caravan they came to. Seth opened the door and quickly ushered Toby inside. With force enough to rattle his teeth, Alan was then dumped onto an upright wooden chair. The door closed behind them with an ominous thud.

Seth put the rifle down and placed himself squarely in front of Alan. 'Where'd your cap get to, boy?' he demanded. 'What you done with it?'

'It fell off.'

After a second or two of considering this, Seth shrugged. 'Makes no difference, I suppose.' He jabbed a finger at the now exposed row of stitches. 'Been in the wars proper good, haven't we?'

'I was in a car crash.'

'A car you stole?'

'Sort of.'

Seth grinned at Toby. 'Sort of he says. How'd you '*sort of*' steal a car?'

'All right, I bloody well nicked it.'

'Well don't be expecting no sympathy from me for getting yourself smashed up.'

From seemingly nowhere, Seth produced a large sheath knife. He allowed Alan's eyes to linger on the blade before speaking further.

'Right, boy,' he said. 'It makes no odds to me whether or not you wants to go around thieving. But it's time you learned yourself a proper good lesson.'

He moved closer. 'See, there's some people you should never rob from if you knows what's good for you. And Seth Rawlings is right at the top of that list.'

***

Stoner's Spinney was not particularly large, its cluster of trees standing up like an isolated island in an otherwise open sea of heather and grassland.

'You start looking at one end and I'll start at the other,' Stafford suggested as he and Geordie drew closer. They split up and began a systematic search of the woods by moving in from opposite points toward each other.

It was Geordie who made the discovery. He called Stafford over immediately. With its distinctive red and black check pattern, Alan's cap was easy for both of them to recall. Now sure that they were on the right track, they moved on a short way and surveyed the fields on the far side of the spinney.

Just as Sue had told them, fairground equipment and workers occupied three of these fields. The meadow immediately in front of them was quite sparsely populated, with just half a dozen caravans, a handful of people, and a small selection of attractions in various states of assembly. Amongst these were a coconut shy, a fortune-teller, and a .22 rifle range. A few men lounging around doing nothing in particular cast distinctly unfriendly glances in the newcomers' direction. There was certainly no evidence of Alan being anywhere around.

A narrow road separated this near field from two much larger ones further ahead. In these, far more activity was taking place and had people working with a genuine sense of purpose. Long established favourites such as dodgems and a gigantic carousel were already close to readiness. It was as if this was the real heart of the fair, and the travellers in the smaller field were nothing more than poor relations, shunted to one side and only tolerated under sufferance. For sure, Stafford considered, none of the people populating this bottom meadow looked as if they would be very disposed to answering questions from strangers.

Some of the vehicles from the convoy that had held them up earlier were now parking in the fields on the far side of the road. Standing alongside the largest of these lorries was a small group of men who appeared to be directing matters. One man in particular amongst them had a definite air of authority about him. As a source of possible information, he appeared to be their best bet.

Stafford pointed in his direction. 'Maybe I'll go and ask those guys over there if they've seen anything of Alan.'

'Aye, good idea.' Geordie glanced at the surly looking figures nearby. 'It'll be a waste of time asking this bunch of divvies anything.'

He made to move forward, but Stafford held out an arm. 'Barbara will be wondering what's happening. I think one of us should go back and bring her up to date.'

'When you say *one of us*, I get the feeling you mean me?'

'Well, it makes sense. You can bring Barbara up here in the car while I'm asking around. I may have dug up something new by then.'

Geordie nodded. 'Aye, you're right I suppose. I'll be as fast as I can. Just don't start anything until I get back.'

'All I'm planning to do is ask a few questions,' Stafford assured him. 'Nothing much is going to happen while I'm doing that.'

***

As anticipated, the group of men Stafford approached were friendly enough. Not that any of them were able to offer any practical help. All of his questions to the gaffer were met with a shake of the head.

'Ain't none of us seen no youngster like you describe over this way,' the man told him. He pointed to the far side of the lane. 'If he was coming out through them woods like you say, you'd be better off asking that lot over there about him.'

'Yeah, maybe I will,' Stafford said. 'I would have done that before, but they don't look to me like the kind of guys who take kindly to strangers asking questions.'

The gaffer nodded. 'Some of them floaters can be a mite unsociable.'

'Floaters?'

'That's what we call them that don't belong proper to any one fair. They floats around all over the place tagging on wherever they can.'

'So that's why you keep them all in a separate field?'

'Better that way. Leastways, I reckon so.' He shrugged. 'Each gaffer's got his own way of working.'

The man pointed to a caravan parked on the far side of the field well apart from the others. 'A word of advice. If you do start asking questions, I'd steer clear of that van over there. That belongs to Seth Rawlings and his cousin Toby.'

Stafford frowned. 'What's so special about them?'

'Well, it ain't Toby so much. But Seth can be real bad news. He drinks far more than is good for any man's liver, and he's got a terrible temper when things don't go his way. Even the other floaters stay well clear.' He sighed. 'The trouble he causes sometimes, I wonder why I bother letting him hang around with us at all.'

'I'll remember that. Thanks for the warning,' Stafford said.

After shaking hands with the man, he made his way back across the lane.

***

Alan's clothes were soaked with sweat, although the fear of what was to come was only partly to blame for this condition. A large, non-opening skylight positioned directly overhead was catching the sun's rays, making him feel as if he were inside a bloody greenhouse.

It must have been nearly half an hour since Seth had threatened him with the knife and told him what to expect. But his torment was far from over. Now that he knew his fate, they were playing mind games with him. The bastards were leaving him to sit here and sweat – literally – for as long as possible before the punishment was actually handed out.

'Make the punishment fit the crime is what I always says,' Seth had told him. 'You steals my rifle, so I'll cut off your trigger finger. That's fair, ain't it, boy? You think about it for a while.'

Alan could barely believe what he was hearing. He wanted to spit defiance at the man, but something warned him he would only be making things a whole lot worse for himself. There was little in Seth's expression to suggest that he would not carry out his threat, or take more than one finger if provoked.

Since then, he and the huge Toby had done nothing but drink several glasses of rum and play a few hands of cribbage. Very few words apart from those concerning the card game were exchanged between them. It was becoming obvious that Toby was not much of a talker. Occasionally one of the men glanced his way, but for most of the time he was totally ignored.

Alan watched Seth replenish both glasses from the now nearly half empty rum bottle. The pressure inside his head was as bad as it had ever been. Even so, he made a huge effort to try and weigh up his chances of making a successful dash for freedom. They appeared to be somewhere between very small and non-existent. His chair was now backed up against the far side of the caravan, and a five-foot long table had been positioned immediately in front of him. He was hemmed right in. First of all he would have to scramble around the table, then somehow get past the two men who were sitting on the other side. And even if he managed to do this, he would still need another second or two in order to get himself out of the caravan and start running.

Alan's eyes shifted over to the rifle, now propped up against the wall in a far corner. Making a grab for that was a waste of time. It would take him much longer to reach the weapon than it would the door.

He made his decision. No matter how bad the odds were on getting away, he had nothing to lose. Reaching beneath the table with both hands, he hesitated for a moment. This was it. Shit or bust.

Jumping to his feet, he forced the table sharply away from himself, tilting it over onto two legs. Seth let out a loud curse as the opposite edge was driven hard down into his lap. For a precious few moments both he and Toby were pinned into their chairs. Cards, glasses, crib board and rum bottle all tumbled to the lino-covered floor, adding to the confusion. Long before these had settled, Alan was already clear of the table and heading for the door. He grasped at the handle, tugging hard.

Nothing happened. The door wouldn't budge.

He tugged again. Still no movement.

Only then, with a rush, did Alan realise. This wasn't like a normal front door to a house. This one opened outwards. Why the hell hadn't he remembered that?

He pushed, and at last the door flew open.

***

Stafford had just crossed the lane when he heard raised voices coming from the far side of the field. His eyes flew over to the caravan parked closest to the spinney. The very one he had been warned about. The door was hanging open and there was no mistaking the figure of Alan as he fought to break free from the grip of a man with long black hair, in all probability the infamous Seth Rawlings.

It was over as quickly as it had started. After only a few seconds, Alan was dragged back inside and the caravan door slammed shut. No one else in the same field seemed to give a damn over what was happening.

Stafford's pace quickened to a run.

TWENTY-NINE

Stafford did not waste time wondering what kind of fresh trouble Alan had got himself into. The boy needed help. That was the only thing that mattered. Sharply aware of how the gaffer had described Seth Rawlings' violent nature, formalities such as knocking did not even enter his head. Yanking open the caravan door, he stepped straight inside and rapidly took in the situation.

Alan had ceased to struggle and was now being held easily under control by a powerfully built second man who Stafford figured must be Seth's cousin. Seth himself was bent over picking up some pieces of broken glass from the floor. There was an overpowering smell of rum.

For an instant, Seth appeared stunned by Stafford's entrance. Recovering quickly, he seized an empty bottle that was also on the floor by the neck, raising the weapon in a clear threat.

'What you want come bargin' in here?' he demanded.

It was obvious to Stafford that he stood little chance in a physical battle with these two. He would have to play it a bit smarter than that. He glanced over at Alan. The kid looked to be terrified and temporarily unable to say anything for himself.

'Take it easy, Alan,' Stafford told him. 'I'll work this out for you.'

'Work what out?' A tiny amount of the aggression left Seth's voice as he added: 'You the boy's father or summat?'

'A family friend.'

Stafford shifted his gaze from Seth to Toby. The big man's continuing silence and deep frown suggested he was still trying to work out how to react to this unexpected development.

'I'm not looking to make trouble for you,' Stafford told him. 'Just let the kid go and everything will be fine.'

'No, you keep hold,' Seth shouted. He glared hard at Stafford. 'Toby does what I tells him to.'

The big man's grip on Alan did not slacken. Almost like an obliging puppet, he nodded in agreement. 'That's right. Seth's my cousin. He's family.'

Stafford sighed. It was easy to see who had got the brawn and who had got the brains in this particular gene pool.

'Okay, so what has the kid done,' he asked Seth. 'Why are you holding him here?'

'He stole a rifle off me. That one standing right there in the corner. Now he's gotta be punished for that.'

'The bloke's bleeding mad. He wants to c-cut off one of my fingers,' Alan shouted out, at last finding his voice.

Stafford was stunned. 'Is this true?' he demanded.

'That's what I told him,' Seth admitted. 'Don't mean I meant it though. Just wanted to see the little shite cackin' himself for a while before giving him a few slaps and sending him on his way.'

He chuckled, as if relishing the prospect. At the same time, he tossed the empty rum bottle into a nearby cardboard box full of other rubbish. It was a clear signal to Stafford that he was not regarded as a serious threat any longer.

'No! He really was going to do it,' Alan insisted. 'He's got a knife in his back pocket.'

Seth swung round to face him. 'Listen, boy, you shut up. If I'd seriously been planning on having one of your fingers, I'd have done it by now. Don't be doubting that. You'd already be counting one short of ten.'

He turned his attention back to Stafford. 'Like I said, a few slaps. Nothin' more than that.'

Stafford still wasn't certain if the man was speaking the truth, but his discarding of the bottle was a move in the right direction. It was now time to step up the pressure.

'Look at the kid,' he said, pointing to Alan. 'See those stitches in his head? They're not there for decoration. He's been in a serious car accident and should still be in hospital. You hit him and anything could happen. You might even find yourself facing a murder charge.'

His final few words struck home. For the first time, Seth showed a hint of uncertainty. Encouraged by this, Stafford added: 'Is that what you want? Are a few slaps worth getting yourself hanged for?'

Seth's frown deepened further at the mention of the rope. 'So what do you reckon?' he said. 'You expect me to just let him walk out of here without any kind of making-up for what he's done?'

'You can't hold him here like a prisoner,' Stafford pressed. 'It's against the law. You know that.'

'Oh yeah – the law.'

A crafty look replaced the frown on Seth's face. 'He's wanted by the law, so he tells me. Is that true? Cos if it is, I'm sure they'd like to know all about him stealing that rifle over there from me. That would fetch him a proper tidy stretch inside.'

Stafford tried to weigh up the strength of this threat.

Seth saw his hesitation. 'Oh yeah, I reported it stolen. Did it all official-like days ago. Gave them sharpies the serial number and everything, just in case it ever got used on a bank job or summat else like that. Had to. It's the only way to protect meeself see.'

'Even so ...' Stafford began.

'And your boy's prints are all over it,' Seth continued. 'Won't be no argument about that. He's been in possession all right.'

It was not difficult for Stafford to see where this conversation was now leading. Pulling out his wallet, he removed two, ten-pound notes.

'Is this enough to make things easier?' he asked. 'It's all the cash I've got with me right now.'

Seth sucked in a deep breath. 'Twenty quid ain't very much to get him out of a possible five stretch,' he said.

'I've already told you, that's all I've got.' Stafford held out the wallet to show that it was now empty.

Seth thought for a moment. 'You a sporting man?' he asked abruptly.

'What are you talking about?'

'I'm thinking of you and me making a wager.'

'And if I win, you'll let Alan go free?'

'Free as a bird. You've got my word on that.'

'So explain,' Stafford told him.

'First off, let's be clear of what's in this for me. If I win I gets to keep your twenty quid, and the boy for a while longer. He can do some work for me to make up for what he did. That suit you?'

Stafford had no intention of leaving Alan behind, no matter what the circumstances. But this was not the right time to be making such a point.

'Sure,' he said. 'But you still haven't told me what the bet is.'

Seth pointed over to his cousin. 'See Toby there? He's the unofficial North Yorkshire arm wrestling champion.'

Stafford looked more closely at the big man. He wasn't surprised in the least at the claimed title. Toby's heavily tattooed forearms were even bigger than Geordie's.

'You don't imagine I can beat him, do you?' he said, astonished at the suggestion.

Seth laughed. 'No one's ever beaten Toby, so far as I knows. All you gotta do to win the wager is last out one minute against him.'

'Just one minute?'

'That's right. Are you on, or what?'

Stafford had no illusions. Although still reasonably strong in the arm himself, lasting even a single minute against such a powerful man was probably way beyond his ability. But at least he would be gaining a little more time. It shouldn't be long now before Geordie was back here and looking around for him.

'Okay,' he agreed. 'Let's do it.'

A wide smile cracked across Seth's face. He gestured Stafford to an upright chair set on the other side of the table. 'You sit there,' he instructed.

He turned to Toby. 'Bring the boy closer. He may as well have a proper look at what the man's doing for him.'

Seth then made a great show of locking the caravan door and pocketing the key. 'You behave yourself now or it'll be hard on you,' he told Alan once Toby had released his grip.

The big man sat down facing Stafford and placed his elbow on the table. Stafford did the same. As their hands gripped together he saw Toby exchange a look with his cousin. It was as if he was expecting something else to be introduced before they got started. The look was quickly explained. From a cupboard, Seth produced two nightlight candles.

'What's going on?' Stafford demanded.

His question was ignored. He could already guess the answer anyway. Seth placed a nightlight on the table either side of them, each one positioned so that whichever hand was forced down first, it would be hovering directly over a flame.

'Did I not tell you about our local rules?' Seth said, applying a match to both candles.

The grin on his face was wide as he added: 'You can quit any time you want. Just say the word. But if you do, I gets to keep the boy for some work remember.'

Even if Stafford had wanted to, he could not have backed out of things now. Toby's grip on his hand had become vice-like. 'How are we timing this?' he asked.

'I got a watch right here,' Seth told him. 'You'll just have to trust me to call it fair and honest.'

Once again he grinned, eager to get on with the contest. 'Both ready? One – two – three. Go!'

Stafford's teeth clenched hard together as every ounce of his being was channelled into resisting Toby's vastly superior strength. One minute. That was all he had to last out for. But even in these first few seconds his arm was taking an enormous strain. Already his hand had been forced an inch or two closer to the waiting flame.

Then he glanced up into Toby's face and saw with despair that his opponent wasn't even trying yet. This was never meant to be a wager in any proper sense of the word, he realised. Seth had set him up. He was merely providing entertainment for the sadistic bastard.

The seconds ticked by. Little by little the casually applied pressure intensified, driving him down ever closer to the candle. Already he could feel the painful tingle of heat on the back of his hand.

***

Being dragged back inside the caravan was the final straw for Alan. At that point, all hope had deserted him. His brain felt like a lump of rock, unable to create anything that might help. Even Stafford's sudden appearance had at first done little to bring about a revival. Only now, as the arm wrestling began, did his mind actually kick itself back into some sort of working order. The thoughts came with a rush.

The irony was almost painful in its intensity. His fate rested completely on a man who, until recently, he had hated so much that he'd wanted to see him dead.

Absolutely transfixed, he watched his former enemy straining every muscle in a vain effort to resist Toby. Stafford must have known he never stood a hope of lasting even half a minute against such a monster. So why the hell was he bothering to put himself through this? Alan could see little waves of hot air rising up from the candle flame already starting to attack the area of skin just below Stafford's knuckle.

It was still impossible to accept that the man was prepared to suffer any real amount of pain for his benefit. Any moment now he would shout out that he'd had enough. He'd then be free to walk away and claim that he'd done his best.

But the time continued to pass, and still no cry of surrender came. Stafford's hand was only a few inches away from the flame now. Sweat fell in great drops from his forehead; his face was screwed up in a massive effort to resist the agony he was so obviously going through.

'Fifteen seconds gone,' Seth called out.

The bastard was lying. He had to be. Alan had been counting in his head and knew that at least twice that amount of time must have passed by now.

'Wanna give in yet?' Seth asked. The smile on his face told clearly of how much he was enjoying every moment.

Stafford shook his head. Alan could see a large patch on the back of the man's hand turning an inflamed shade of red. He imagined he could even smell the scorching of flesh. The bloke must be in agony. And still he held on. For him!

More time passed.

'Twenty seconds,' Seth stated.

'That's bollocks!' The two words flew out of Alan's mouth.

Without even thinking, he leapt forward. His arm swept in a wide arc across the table, sweeping the candle as far away as possible from Stafford's hand. Still burning, it flew off the edge of the table and landed on the floor.

Seth made a grab for him, but he twisted away from the man's reach. And then there was a way through to the far corner – the corner where the rifle was still propped up against the wall. Dashing over, he grabbed the weapon and turned just in time to halt Seth's rush toward him. The same knife that Alan had seen earlier was once again in his hand.

'Think yourself smart do you, boy,' Seth snarled, still inching forward. 'This time I'll take more than a finger.'

A sudden cry of terror from behind made him look back over his shoulder. It came from Toby. The big man's chair flew back and toppled over as he jumped up in panic. A large area of the floor close to his feet was ablaze. Fuelled by more than half a bottle of spilled rum still on the floor, some of which had also splashed over the lower part of Toby's trousers, the fire had taken an instant grip. The big man's arms flailed wildly around but to little effect as he attempted to beat out the flames that were rapidly transferring themselves onto his clothing.

A few feet away from Stafford was an old blanket that was acting as a makeshift curtain separating the caravan's only bedroom. Ripping the blanket down from its flimsy fixings, he quickly wrapped it around Toby's legs to smother the flames. In spite of the man's huge size, Alan could see that he was now sobbing like a small child, mindless of everything else going on around him.

But the rest of the fire was already spreading. A mouldy looking stuffed armchair was beginning to smoulder, creating foul smelling black smoke.

'Unlock the damn door,' Stafford shouted to Seth.

'Not until I've taught this little shite a lesson. He ain't running away from me now, fire or no fire.'

Wild eyed, Seth once again inched closer to Alan, the knife in his hand weaving from side to side. The expression on his face said everything. He was now completely out of control: a man so crazed with anger and lust for revenge that not even the fire destroying his home was sufficient to divert him from this.

Alan aimed the rifle straight at Seth's chest, but he could feel his hands shaking badly. Seth saw it too. He was sure of that. The ability to defend himself was draining away. The bastard was almost hypnotizing him with those wild staring eyes and that swaying knife. This was a genuine mad man he was facing, not some kid like himself who went around pretending to be crazy in order to get some respect.

Stafford arrived in a flurry of movement, grabbing hold of Seth's long hair from behind and pulling hard. At the same time, his other hand reached forward for the knife hand. His fingers wrapped around the man's wrist.

With a bellow of rage, Seth swung around to face Stafford. For about half a minute they rocked back and forth, each straining for possession of the knife. Then Seth wrenched his hand free. The blade lunged forward in a direct line for Stafford's stomach. He jumped sharply back out of range, only to find his feet entangled around Toby's fallen chair. Carried on by his own momentum, he fell heavily onto his back. Teeth bared in a savage grin of triumph, Seth closed in for the kill.

'No, Seth. We've got to get out.'

Toby rushed forward to seize hold of his cousin's arm. He pointed desperately to the tiny kitchen area. 'That's a new bottle we had put in.'

The flames were now creeping dangerously toward a large gas container connected to the cooker there. Bolted into position the way it was, the hefty cylinder would be impossible to move without several minutes of work with a spanner.

The danger was immediate, and sufficient to wipe away the largest part of Seth's rage. All thoughts of revenge were suddenly forgotten. He moved quickly over to the door, feeling inside his trouser pocket for the vital key and cursing with impatience as he fumbled around.

'Hurry up,' Toby pleaded, just behind him. The tears continued to run down his face.

Choking smoke from the smouldering armchair was now starting to become thicker. New flames were also springing up elsewhere. Far too many to ever have a hope of extinguishing.

The danger of a gas explosion also helped to jerk Alan out of his trance. What the hell was he doing, standing around like some moron waiting for the world to end? He moved quickly over to Stafford, who was clambering back to his feet.

'Is that thing loaded?' the Canadian asked him, reaching for the rifle.

'Yeah, it's got seven rounds.'

'Give it to me then.'

The urgency in Stafford's voice warned Alan not to argue.

***

The key appeared in Seth's hand. Stafford knew he had to act fast.

'Don't open that door yet,' he shouted over. 'It's too late now. Let the air in through there and you'll start a fireball. We'll all burn before we can get out.'

Seth did not even look at him. 'Screw you,' he snarled.

There was no time for a second warning. Stafford fired the rifle just as Seth was about to place the key into the lock. The .22 round zipped viciously past the man's outstretched hand before burying itself into the wooden surround. So close did the bullet pass, Seth jerked violently from the shock, at the same time dropping the key. Swinging around, he glared at Stafford with a mixture of disbelieve and pure hatred.

'Step away from there. Both of you,' Stafford ordered. 'The next one will go straight in your leg if you touch that door again before I say so.'

The tone of Stafford's voice was enough to convince Seth that the threat was genuine. Still radiating hate, he shuffled back a few paces as instructed. Toby hesitated. For an instant it appeared as if he was going to make a wild grab for the key lying only inches away from his feet. A warning flick of the rifle changed his mind. He moved back to join Seth.

Stafford had never forgotten witnessing the devastating effect of a backdraft during a German bombing raid on York in 1942. One of the firemen on the scene had told him that the only way he knew of to help minimize the danger was to ventilate from above before entering the burning building. A tactic that was rarely possible.

But it was possible here.

Stafford fired two more shots, this time directly up into the large skylight. Around a dozen square feet of Perspex instantly shattered, although the majority of it remained in place. He turned to Alan.

'Grab that broom handle over there.'

Stafford did not need to complete his instructions. The boy quickly realised what was expected of him, even if he did not fully understand why. He began jabbing repeatedly at the skylight with the end of the pole. As more Perspex fell down, heat and smoke began rising up through the space like a large chimney. Within a matter of moments the air inside the caravan was starting to clear.

But the flames were still burning intensely. Stafford calculated that it would be no more than another thirty or forty seconds before they engulfed the gas bottle.

Seth tore his eyes away from the cylinder. 'Shoot if you want to, yer bastard. Anything's better than waiting for that thing to blow.' He moved quickly back to where the key was and picked it up. Toby did not make any attempt to follow him.

Was it safe to open the door yet? Stafford agonized.

Time had run out. He had to take a chance.

Seth shoved the key into the lock.

'Run like hell as soon as you get outside,' Stafford said to Alan.

To his astonishment, the boy actually grinned at him. 'That's the most obvious fucking piece of advice I've ever had,' he said.

The door swung open. Stafford held his breath in anticipation, but there was no immediate reaction to the sudden inflow of oxygen. He caught a glimpse of people gathering outside, standing well back and staring at the caravan. Then, like a greyhound out of a trap, Seth was through the doorway and off across the field. He was closely followed by Alan.

Toby remained exactly where he was. His panic of only moments ago now seemed to have transformed itself into a fatalistic acceptance of the situation. He was muttering incomprehensible words to himself, as if reciting a prayer or mantra.

'Come on! Move it,' Stafford shouted at him.

Dropping the rifle, he gave Toby a hard shove in the right direction. He didn't budge. It was like trying to push a tank along with one finger. Stafford slapped him across the cheek with every bit of force he could muster. The impact sent a wave of pain from his inflamed hand racing all the way up his arm.

'What the hell is wrong with you?' he demanded.

He glanced at the gas bottle again. Twenty seconds left. Twenty-five if they were very, very lucky.

The slap at least appeared to drag the big man back into a partial state of awareness. He allowed Stafford to begin guiding him in a slow shuffle toward the door. But their movements were nowhere near quick enough. Toby appeared to have lost all will of his own.

'Mike!'

From nowhere, Geordie's huge frame suddenly filled the open doorway. He took in the situation immediately.

'Get away,' Stafford yelled at him. 'This place is going to blow any second now.'

His friend ignored the warning. Positioning himself on the lowest step outside the door, he bent over to form a back. 'Drop him across here,' he instructed.

Like a massive rag doll, Toby flopped down, an arm dangling over each of Geordie's broad shoulders. Seizing hold of these two limbs to steady his load and still bent over at a steep angle under the burden of well over two hundred and fifty pounds, Geordie set off at a shuffling run. Stafford followed directly behind them, all the time doing his best to support some of Toby's weight at the rear.

He had no idea of how long they continued along like this. In reality it could only have been for a few seconds, but in many ways it felt like hours. The agony of expectation was with him every stumbling step of the way.

The caravan exploded.

Stafford felt a massive rush of hot air engulfing him. Hot, but far from fatal. His already exhausted legs collapsed completely. He fell face down into the grass, conscious that Geordie was also falling. Was this to be the only explosion, or was there a more severe, killer blast still to come?

Hugging the ground and gasping for breath, he could only lie there and wait for fate to decide.

***

There was no second blast.

Transfixed, Alan watched Stafford and Geordie carry Toby to safety with a mixture of anxiety and something that was entirely new to him: admiration. Never before, not even as a small kid, had he even come close to having any heroes. It had always been him alone against a world of people wanting to put him down. But all that changed in an instant as he gazed at the two men. They had both risked being burned alive in order to save someone who should have meant nothing to them.

Alan had fully expected Stafford to be right behind him when running from the fire. Discovering that he was still inside the blazing caravan struggling to get Toby to safety came as a massive shock. Why was he doing it? he kept asking himself. Even Seth hadn't bothered to hang around to help his own cousin. Bloody hell, only ten minutes ago Toby had been grinning like an idiot while putting Stafford through all kinds of agony. And yet he was still putting his life on the line in order to help the big bastard. It didn't seem to make any kind of sense at all.

He could maybe understand the reason for Geordie's actions a little better. All he had wanted to do was save Stafford. They were mates, and that was enough.

Alan shook his head in amazement at this thought. What kind of friendship was it that inspired such heroic behaviour?

Would he ever get to feel that way about another person?

Was he even capable of caring about anyone as much as that?

Alan looked at his mother standing beside him. She took hold of his hand, squeezing hard. He smiled at her.

'Look who's coming,' she told him.

He glanced across and saw Sue pedalling her bicycle down the lane toward them. She waved and called out to him. Like a ton weight lifting, suddenly all the pressure and confusion disappeared from his head.

Then he passed out.

THIRTY

Alan opened his eyes. For a few moments he was unable to focus, but gradually his eyes grew accustomed to the dim lighting. He realised that he was back in the same hospital room as before. The clock on the wall was showing just after five o'clock. The darkness told him that it must be five o'clock night-time. He had no idea of how long he had been out of it.

At first he imagined that he was alone. Then he saw his mother asleep in an armchair on the other side of the room. His first instinct was to call out to her, but quickly changed his mind. Let her sleep, he told himself. She was probably exhausted worrying about him.

Alan blinked, barely able to believe that such a considerate thought had entered his head quite naturally. But as he began to recall more details of his time trapped inside Seth's caravan, suddenly it did not seem so strange after all. There was no doubt that his thinking on a whole stack of things had been changed by what he had seen take place there that afternoon.

Almost as a matter of course, his thoughts began to centre on Stafford. This was one of the biggest changes of all. Everything was suddenly a clean slate between them. There was no longer even a small part of him that was capable of believing all the bullshit stories he had heard about the bloke. Not after what he had seen him do. Stafford had also claimed to now have proof of his innocence. Alan could hardly wait to discover what that was.

He was still thinking about this an hour later when his mother stirred. By now it was already becoming daylight. Once awake, she immediately got up out of the armchair and came over to his bedside. The huge smile on her face when she saw that he was awake said it all.

'Thanks, mum,' he told her.

'What for?'

'I don't know. Being here, I suppose.'

'I'm your mother. It's what mothers do. We never stop loving.'

Even for the new Alan – if that was what he had now become? – this conversation was becoming a bit too mushy. He quickly changed the subject.

'How long have I been back in here?' he asked.

'Only about twelve hours.'

'And am I going to be okay? Has the doctor told you anything?'

'He said you should be fine, just as long as you stay here and rest for a while longer.' She touched his hand. 'But you mustn't do anything silly like that again. You've been very lucky this time.'

Alan thought about this for a second or two before speaking further.

'Is he coming in to see me later? Not the doctor. You know …'

'You mean Mike Stafford?'

'Yeah.'

His mother sighed. 'I don't know. He might be here this evening, but he did say he had a lot of things to do today.' She shrugged. 'Maybe he's getting ready to go back home.'

Alan felt a huge surge of disappointment. Whether this was simply over the lack of an immediate visit, or the fact that the Canadian would soon be thousands of miles away once again, was hard to tell. It was most likely a bit of both, he felt.

His mother's expression brightened. 'Sue promised to be here this afternoon though. That should cheer you up.'

He smiled. Sue *was* important to him. Probably a whole lot more than he realised. He had a quick flashback of seeing her cycling down the lane and waving to him just before he'd passed out. For an instant he felt almost guilty for not asking about her sooner.

'And I've got something else here that I know you'll be very interested in,' his mother continued.

She went back across the room to pick up her handbag. From this she removed a letter and held it out for Alan to see.

'This is from Hughie Smith. We were talking about him. Remember?'

Alan nodded.

'Mike Stafford gave it to me so that I could read it to you.'

The look on his mother's face, and the tone of her voice, was significant. In a flash, Alan knew that this letter was going to be the key to everything. The answer to why she had told him all those wrong things about the man. At last, he would have the true story. He could suddenly feel a thousand nervous butterflies dancing around inside his stomach.

'You better do it then,' he said.

Settling herself down on a bedside chair, Barbara began.

***

It was approaching 7.30pm when Stafford entered the hospital main entrance. Halfway along the corridor leading to Alan's ward he passed a public cafeteria and was surprised to see Barbara sitting there alone at a table. Worried that something might be wrong, he hurried over to join her.

Her welcoming smile reassured him. 'I'm so glad you managed to get here this evening,' she said. 'Alan is dying to see you again.'

'How is he?' he asked.

'He's fine.' She motioned toward the half-eaten sandwich and cup of tea in front of her. 'I've been with him all day, but even mums get hungry sometimes.'

'Has he got any other visitors?'

'Sue was here for quite a long time, but she left about an hour ago. Alan's all on his own right now, and that's perfect. I'll stay here for a bit longer while you talk to him.'

He grinned. 'Then I guess you've already shown him the letter.'

'Yes.'

Stafford waited for Barbara to enlarge on this a little. He was surprised to see her eyes suddenly moisten. Then he realised it was happiness that was overwhelming her.

Dabbing away a tear, she spoke very quietly. 'When I first heard that you were coming back to England, I was devastated. I spent days cursing you for raking up all the bad memories again and making them fresh in

Alan's mind. I was terrified he was going to get himself into serious trouble by coming after you.'

'I can understand that. It must have been hard for you to make that first telephone call to me.'

'You don't know how hard.'

She took a sip of tea before continuing. 'But now – what can I say? Your coming back has been the best thing that could ever have happened for him. It's like a miracle how much he's already starting to change. Even more so since I read Hughie Smith's letter out to him this morning. Now he understands why I said all those awful things about you. He knows that I believed them to be true at the time.'

Her voice cracked slightly. 'You've given me my son back, Mike. I can never, ever thank you enough for that.'

A vision of Jimmy flashed through Stafford's head. 'To be honest Barbara, I didn't have a whole lot of control over events. Everything just kind of ...'

He hesitated. 'Kind of worked out, I guess,' he finished off. It felt lame.

She smiled at him. 'Go and see Alan. Talk to him. I'll give you two at least an hour alone together before I come back.'

***

Still under enforced bed rest, Alan heard the door to his room open. He looked across expecting to see his mother returning and instead saw Stafford. His feeling of pleasure was tempered only by a niggling uncertainty over how the Canadian might now regard him after everything that had happened.

Stafford grinned at him. 'How's it going, tough guy?'

Alan's doubts all but disappeared. 'I'm fine, Mister Stafford.'

It felt strange using such a title. Before this, the only people he had ever addressed as Mister were the so-called teachers at his approved school. And that had only been done under threat of a beating with the birch.

'Call me Mike,' Stafford told him.

'Okay – I will.'

Alan hesitated. 'About what happened in the caravan that time. I just wanted to say ...'

Awkwardness seized him. The words of gratitude he had rehearsed so carefully in his head suddenly felt clumsy and totally insufficient.

Stafford held up his newly bandaged right hand. 'You helped me out too remember, so I figure that makes us about quits.'

'But that bastard Seth was – –'

'You don't have to worry about him anymore. The rifle was destroyed in the fire, so there's no evidence left.'

'He might still try something.'

Stafford shook his head. 'No, he won't. His cousin Toby's promised to keep him in line from now on.'

Alan felt relieved, but cautious. 'Why would Toby do that?' he asked. 'Is it because you and Geordie saved him?'

'That's a part of it. But he was also in one hell of a rage with Seth for running off and leaving him. It turns out that both of Toby's parents were burnt alive in a caravan fire when he was still a small kid. Ever since then he's been terrified that he might die the same way. He gets regular nightmares about it. Seth knows all of this.'

Alan nodded. 'Like I said, he's a bastard.'

'Well, he's a bastard with a lot of bruises and several missing teeth right now.'

'You mean that Toby ..?'

'Yeah, he beat the crap out of him. Seth's hard man reputation is shot to hell. Toby might not be the brightest guy around, but he's the one running their show from now on.'

Alan could hardly contain his laughter. 'Oh bloody hell, I wish I could have seen that,' he said.

He was still laughing at the mental image of a battered and bruised Seth when he heard Stafford clear his throat, as if about to make a grave announcement.

'I don't want to bring you down, but I had a few words with the police about you earlier today,' he said.

For a second or two Alan's old guard came up. He had been wondering why he hadn't heard anything more from the coppers. His voice was wary.

'What did they say?'

'They were considering what charges they can bring against you.'

'And?'

A grin slowly formed on Stafford's face. 'To tell you the truth, they're in a bit of a fix. Just before I spoke to the police, I had a chat with that solicitor your mum hired. He told me how to handle things with them. He's a smart guy.'

Alan tried to copy Stafford's grin but failed. 'What do you mean?'

'It turns out that, without me wanting to make any official complaints against you, the only thing they're left with is the matter of the car you took. I couldn't do a whole lot about that. It was all in the hands of the hire company.'

'With my record that will be enough.' Alan's face clouded over. 'I'll get at least six months for nicking your car and smashing it up.'

'Yeah, you're probably right.'

'Thanks a lot,' Alan responded moodily. He then saw that Stafford's grin was becoming wider. 'Why are you looking so bloody pleased with yourself?' he demanded.

'Because I happen to know that driving without due care and attention is the only thing they're going to charge you with. And a small matter of no licence and insurance, of course. But like I said, your solicitor is a smart guy. He knows the angles to work. It'll be a fine and probation at the worst; he's confident of that.'

Alan could barely believe what he was hearing. 'What about me taking the car? The hire company wouldn't drop that charge. You just said so yourself.'

'No. What I said was that it's in their hands, and that *I* wasn't able to do anything about it. I didn't say that no one else could help.'

By now Alan was feeling more confused than ever. 'You're soddin' well enjoying this,' he accused.

'Maybe I am,' Stafford admitted.

He took a few more seconds to hang out the suspense. 'Geordie fixed it all up for you.' he said at last. 'I'm not the only one who's been busy today on your behalf.'

'Geordie! How could he do anything?' Alan felt his mouth literally dropping open with surprise.

Stafford's expression became more serious. 'You might not think so by talking to him, but Geordie's a real wealthy guy. And he's got a lot of influence. He owns one of the largest building companies for miles around, and they use a whole fleet of hired vehicles. Vehicles, it turns out, that come from the commercial wing of the same company who hired me my car. Geordie is one of their biggest customers.'

Alan began to get the picture almost immediately. 'So he threatened to take his business somewhere else if – –'

'It still cost him a packet,' Stafford cut in. 'But yeah, I reckon you could say he came to an arrangement with them. He's planning to put in a good word for you at the magistrate's court when your case comes up too. That's gonna help a lot.'

Alan could barely believe what he was hearing. 'Why the heck didn't Geordie come in here and tell me about this himself?'

'You'll understand why if you ever get to know him better.'

Alan thought for a moment. 'I think I'd like that. You know, that bit about getting to know him better. Will you tell him that for me?'

'Sure. He'll be pleased to hear it.'

Stafford's voice firmed. 'Understand, Alan, I've only told you all this because I want you to realise you've got a lot of people backing you up right now. Geordie's got as much faith in you as Sue and I have. He's helping you get a whole new start in life. Try not to chuck it back at him, huh.'

Their eyes met. 'I won't,' Alan promised solemnly.

He suddenly grinned. 'I might get a bit mad at times, but I'm not a bleeding idiot. Who the heck wants to upset a bloke that big?'

***

No longer classified as a patient requiring special attention, Alan was due to be moved into the main ward the following morning. On hearing about this, Geordie quickly stepped in and paid for him to remain in his private room.

'Mister Heatley said it was the only way he could be sure there were no restrictions on your visiting privileges,' the ward Sister explained to Alan.

Over the next few days the big Tynesider made full use of his purchase, visiting Alan at almost every opportunity. After a couple of his visits, Phil joined him. Their tales of life in the gun turrets were soon adding an exciting new dimension to Stafford's own stories. The two gunners were even able to relate small incidents involving his father that the Canadian knew nothing of.

It was by a mile the happiest ever period in Alan's life. But he also knew that it was not going to last for very much longer. At present it was like living inside a protective bubble, surrounded by people who cared and with everything provided for him. But in a few days' time he would be thrust back into the real world once again. His new friends all had homes they would be returning to far away from London. Without their encouragement and support, was he liable to slip back into bad old ways?

The prospect of not being able to live up to everyone's expectations was starting to weigh ever heavily on his mind.

***

'Thanks, Phil,' Stafford said, taking the car keys from his friend's hand.

In less than one hour he was due to meet Siggi. It was an encounter he was approaching with mixed feelings, especially after calling Alice early that same morning. He'd told her that he would not be coming home for a few more days yet, explaining that there was a funeral taking place shortly that he felt obliged to attend. She had of course understood. In some ways, she was too understanding. Her ready acceptance of everything he told her created a deep sense of guilt. It wasn't, he assured himself, that he had been unfaithful to her. Not in the true sense. Even so, this latest meeting with Siggi left him with an uncomfortable feeling that he was still somehow abusing Alice's trust.

He could not forget how he and Siggi had kissed, even though he continued to tell himself that what happened between them during their time trapped underground was motivated purely out of a need to control her fears. But he was also forced to wonder if he would have done the same thing had he not found her quite so attractive. This was a question he could find no truly honest answer to.

There was also the matter of how Siggi might respond to him now that she'd had a few days to reflect on their experience together. He had no idea what to expect from her. There was only one thing he was certain of. He liked and admired her as a person enormously.

He just prayed that she was not hoping for something more than that from him.

***

They dined together at a small restaurant in Wetherditch that neither of them had visited before. It turned out to be a good choice. Apart from the excellent food, each table was allowed a good amount of privacy thanks to carefully positioned room dividers bearing a variety of flowering blooms. The lighting was bright, which Stafford was grateful for. Had it been otherwise, the setting might well have been considered romantic. As it was, the atmosphere was comfortable and pleasant, but nothing more than that.

He shrugged off Siggi's enquiries about his bandaged hand by saying it was just a small skin infection, most probably picked up while they were stuck in the mine. She frowned, but did not enquire any further. Apart from this one brief interlude, their conversation throughout the meal continued easily enough.

But the small talk couldn't last for very much longer. Both of them had important things they needed to say to each other. The reasons for this might be a whole lot different to the circumstances when at the White Rose Inn, but the problems involved were uncomfortably similar for Stafford.

What were the right words to use?

And what might be her reaction to those he did eventually choose?

A lengthy silence developed as coffee was served. He was willing Siggi to initiate matters. It would be far better for him to know how she truly felt before touching on delicate matters himself. As if acknowledging the truth of this, she finally spoke.

'Mike?' She said his name as a question.

He gave her an encouraging smile, knowing that this was the beginning. 'Yeah.'

'You remember what happened between us when we were trapped in that terrible mine?'

'Of course I do.'

'Tell me honestly, what did you think of me then? Did you think that I was being ...?'

She paused, seeking the right English word to express her meaning properly.

'Being forward?' she eventually said.

He reached across the table to touch her hand. 'Never. Not for one second. I thought that we each acted in the way we needed to at the time. We both understand that everything was a whole lot different down there.'

'Yes, a whole lot different,' she sighed.

A distant look came over her. It was a look Stafford was unsure how to interpret. Had she taken his remark as a brush-off? It wasn't meant to be.

'You're a beautiful woman,' he told her. 'That hasn't changed.'

Even as he spoke, he realised how incredibly superficial and patronizing his words sounded. It came as a big relief when she did not pick him up on this. Instead, her distant look persisted. Her hand slipped away from his but did not move very far.

'You know, I can hardly remember the last time I kissed a man,' she murmured. 'I must have been nineteen years old at the time.' A reflective sigh slipped out. 'That was half my lifetime ago.'

He remained silent. There was nothing constructive he could add at this point.

A sudden change then came over her. With a visible effort, she became alert and bright-eyed. 'Perhaps the next nineteen years will prove to be better,' she said.

Stafford shifted in his seat, feeling awkward. 'I hope they are,' he told her. 'But whatever else you might think of me, I want you to know that ….'

Siggi took hold of his hand again, squeezing it hard to silence him. 'I know exactly what I am thinking. I have had more than a week to consider my feelings.'

He felt a stab of conscience. 'I'm sorry; I know I should have found time to see you before now. It's just that I've had a lot of things going on lately.'

His excuse sounded far from convincing, but it would have to do. He had made no mention to her of discovering Hughie's body, nor of his narrow escape from the blazing caravan. Any reference to these incidents would inevitably have required him to explain about Alan's existence, and then the part that his old friend's son had played in their time trapped underground. This was a side of things he had no wish to further complicate matters between them with.

She did not appear to be put out by the weakness of his excuse. 'It was good for me to have time on my own,' she told him.

She stirred her coffee before continuing. Her voice lowered. 'I will be very honest with you, Mike. Down there in that mine, I was terrified. Far more even than during the air raids on Berlin. If it had not been for you, I know I would have gone crazy.'

'Don't overestimate me,' he told her. 'Or underestimate yourself. You were brave for Tanya's sake.'

'Yes, maybe I tried to be for a while. But in the end it was you who got us both through it all. I still believe that they would not have found us in time were it not for the clever and very brave way you managed to get Tanya's handkerchief to the surface.'

Stafford was embarrassed, but it was plain to see that she was too.

She hesitated. 'Please try to understand that for many years I have chosen to avoid any personal relationships with men. I am how you might say, inexperienced in that direction. To be suddenly put into a situation where I am so much dependent on a man was a totally new thing for me.'

Her eyes cast downwards. 'It is something I will never forget. Nor will I ever forget the man involved.'

'I'll never forget you either, Siggi,' Stafford found himself saying.

Her eyes lifted once more, locking tightly with his. All the things that could have been between them had the situation been different were clearly there for him to see. With a sense of acute discomfort, he knew that she would also be seeing a similar message just as clearly in his own eyes. She was the first to shift her gaze.

'So!' Suddenly her voice had all its old Teutonic snap. 'I return home very soon now, and you also. Back to your family. You must be missing them very much.'

As a moment-breaker, it could not have been more effective. Their hands parted. Each of them eased back into their seats.

Stafford could only wonder at how much these final remarks had cost her. In the space of barely a minute she had opened herself totally up to him. Then, just as he caught a glimpse of what lay deepest inside, she had slammed the door shut. For both of their sakes. She was a truly remarkable woman in every sense.

A mental picture of Alice and Connie came to him, filling him with warmth. He smiled wistfully before replying to Siggi's question. 'Yeah, I'm missing them a lot. It's my daughter's birthday in three weeks' time.'

Siggi smiled with him. 'And speaking of young girls, Tanya wishes me to send you her love.'

This simple message touched him deeply. She was a great kid. A daughter anyone would be proud of.

Siggi continued. 'It seems that you are very much her new hero. Astrid bought her another pet this week. A tortoise. She has christened it Mister Stafford. That is just about the greatest honour she could bestow on anyone.'

He gave a soft chuckle. 'Well you better make sure you tell her how proud I am.'

He took a ten-pound note from his wallet and handed it across the table. 'Buy her something nice and say goodbye for me.'

'You could come to the house tomorrow before I leave and tell her yourself if you wish.'

Once more their eyes met. 'Do you really think that's wise?' he asked.

Siggi sighed. 'No, I suppose it is not. Perhaps it is best if we leave things the way they are. How do the Americans say – go out on a high?'

A silence followed while they finished their coffees. There was now an air of inevitable finality about the evening.

'Shall we go?' Stafford suggested gently.

Siggi nodded. 'Yes. I think that would be a good idea.'

***

He drew the car up outside Astrid's house. Neither of them spoke for a while as they sat together in the darkness, each silently accepting that this was to be the last time they would ever see each other.

'So, it is finally goodbye then,' Siggi eventually said.

'I guess so.' The words did not come easily to him. No easier than they had sounded for her.

'You have changed my whole life, you know,' she told him.

He tried to make light of her statement. 'That's a mighty big thing to accuse me of.'

'Please, I am not making a joke. I mean it.'

She touched him fleetingly on the cheek. 'How many more men are there like you in the world, I am wondering?'

'Millions of them.'

She shook her head. 'Only in the same way that they will also have two arms and two legs. But you – you have two hearts as well.'

He gave a soft laugh. 'I don't understand.'

'You have your own of course. And you also have mine.'

Before he could say anything suitable in response, she quickly opened the car door and stepped out onto the pavement. 'Please, allow it to remain with you until I am ready to give it to someone else. That is all I ask.'

The car door slammed shut. Seconds later she disappeared inside the house without once looking back. Stafford felt a great surge of affection for the woman.

'I hope that someone comes along for you real soon, Siggi,' he said softly to himself.

THIRTY-ONE

Hughie's funeral was held in Southport just two days after the inquest into his death recorded a verdict of suicide.

Grey skies and fine drizzle, the first rain for more than three weeks, added to the depression of the occasion. Apart from Stafford and his four remaining crew members, there was just Gloria and seven other people that none of the RAF veterans knew. It was a sad and scant gathering to acknowledge over fifty years of a man's life.

An agreement had been made amongst Stafford's group never to reveal the full reasons for Hughie's suicide. No useful purpose would be served by tarnishing the man's memory, nor by exposing Gloria to the humiliating details that had driven her husband to such desperate measures. Only Pete Cowley was excluded from this pact. He knew nothing of the truth anyway, and the others unanimously agreed that it was best left that way.

Pete appeared to have forged quite an attachment to Gloria. He remained close to the widow throughout the service, always ready with a quiet word of encouragement and generally being on hand should she require anything. Gloria, in turn, gave every impression of valuing his attention enormously.

As the small group of mourners slowly trickled away from the graveside, Gloria whispered something to Pete. She then approached Stafford's group alone, walking as she had done throughout the proceedings, proudly erect. Although no one doubted her genuine grief at Hughie's passing, she had chosen to display it in a controlled and undemonstrative fashion. Any cynic who might have imagined that she would take this opportunity to present them with a theatrical performance of the heartbroken widow was proved to be way off the mark.

'Could I have a word with you in private please, Michael?' she asked Stafford.

'Sure. What's on your mind?' he responded.

In truth, he had a very good idea of what she wanted to talk to him about, but there was little point in pre-empting the situation.

They drew aside from the others and walked slowly together toward the cemetery gates. For once, Gloria displayed uncertainty. Stafford even detected the trace of a tear on her face, something that had been noticeably absent up until now. He realised that he was witnessing a vulnerable side to the woman that few people were likely to see that day. There was no spotlight now, real or imagined.

'What made you come to visit Hughie last week?' she eventually asked.

Stafford offered a quick prayer of thanks that he had foreseen this very situation arising. 'It was a personal matter,' he began. 'I wanted to help put his mind at rest over a problem he had.'

Gloria sighed. Her tongue ran over dark red lips. 'So I take it you do know what he was referring to in that note he left for me. The bit about an old friend and comrade.'

'Sure, I know,' he admitted.

Then the lies started. 'We spoke a little about it at the reunion,' Stafford continued. 'Hughie didn't say much, but it was easy to see that he was still deeply troubled, even after all these years. That's why I felt the need to come to Southport and talk to him again. What I didn't know was just how bad things had got. If only he'd said more to me at the time, I might have been able to prevent this.'

The trace of a tear in Gloria's eye was now turning into something bigger. 'But this thing – this mistake or whatever – that he was so distressed over? What was it? You claimed to have no knowledge of this at the inquest, but I have a feeling that you do know something. So if you do, please tell me. What could possibly have been so terrible that he felt compelled to kill himself?'

She looked at him imploringly. 'Please, I've a right to know.'

She did have a right, Stafford acknowledged. But not to the whole truth. There was no reason at all why she should be subjected to that.

He took a deep breath. 'On the last op to Berlin our Lanc got badly shot up. So badly that once we were over home territory I ordered the crew to bale out rather than risk a landing with everyone on board. Purely by accident, Hughie took another guy's chute. The other guy's name was Jimmy.'

Gloria frowned. 'I don't understand. How could that possibly have anything to do with him wanting to…?'

She stopped, unable to complete the sentence.

'Jimmy died,' he told her gently. 'The chute he had been left with was Hughie's. It didn't open properly.'

Her gaze slipped to the ground. Her voice was now hushed. 'He didn't mention any of this to me at the time. Not a word.'

Stafford continued. 'You have to remember that we'd all been through a hell of a lot together. We were closer than most families. Hughie took his mistake as bad as any guy can. He never really managed to forgive himself. What made it a whole lot worse for him was that he realised he'd taken the wrong chute before he jumped. He very nearly came back to change it. The fact that he didn't made him feel even more responsible for what followed.'

Her eyes rose up once more, her expression incredulous. 'Are you trying to say that he would rather have taken the faulty parachute himself?'

'Who knows, Gloria? All I can tell you is that Hughie was a complex man. He had a unique code of honour that he built his life around. What happened might seem like a normal mistake to us, but to him he had done something that was unforgivably wrong.'

After a brief moment of thought, she nodded. 'Yes, I can see how that might be true; I know how deep he was at times. Even so, I still don't quite understand. Why now? Why after all these years did he suddenly think he needed to punish himself this way?'

Stafford sighed. 'It was the reunion I guess. Seeing all the old faces again must have brought everything back to him and made it a hundred times worse.'

'But the repercussions for an old comrade he wrote about? What were they?'

'They were all in his head, Gloria. You have to understand that Jimmy was one of the most popular guys in the squadron. Hughie got this crazy idea that some people there were still blaming me for Jim's death because of the order I gave, and that they wouldn't have felt quite the same way about things if he'd been the one to use the faulty chute. This was the one he'd been issued with, remember. We all tried to tell him it wasn't so, but he refused to go along with that. His mind was totally messed up.'

Gloria said nothing for a short while. Even through her heavy make-up, Stafford could see that she was visibly paling. For a few seconds her face quivered as if about to crumple completely. When she finally spoke, it was in an anguished hush.

'I can see now why he was so reluctant to go that weekend. And do you know what, Michael? I forced him into attending because I thought it would be fun. Why on earth didn't he explain to me how he truly felt?'

Stafford could have bitten his tongue off. In some ways he should have guessed that Gloria had been the driving force behind their attendance. Hughie had looked miserably out of place all weekend.

'You weren't to know,' he murmured. What else could he say?

She appeared not to hear him as she continued in the same low voice. 'I did love him you know. Whatever else you might think of me, I want you to know that. We had some good years together.'

'He said pretty much the same to me about you.'

Another lie, but Stafford was sure Hughie would have agreed with his statement. That made it okay.

A man's voice suddenly called out, shattering the mood.

'Gloria. Are you coming in the car with us?'

Close by, Pete Cowley looked daggers at the offender. He was not someone Stafford knew.

Gloria swung around. 'I'll be there in just one moment, darling,' she called back.

When she faced Stafford again, all trace of emotion had been erased. She was once again wearing the face that she wished to present to the world. That of a woman in complete control. Her next words came out with an almost artificial rush.

'I spoke to my agent in London last week, you know. He's very interested in your friend Peter's musical talents. Apparently, some of the songs he has written are very commercial.'

Stafford made a brief, non-committal sound. She was now talking merely for the sake of it. Both of them knew that their conversation was at an end.

She gave him one final lingering look. 'I simply must dash, Michael. But thank you so much for your help. At least I know the true facts now.'

For a moment it seemed as if she wanted to say something more. Then she changed her mind. An elegant hand briefly touched his and she was on her way.

'I'll see you back at the house,' she called behind her.

Stafford watched her go. Gloria would not grieve for very long; he was sure of that. She was far too strong a character. He had told her all she needed to know, and she had accepted what he said. It would soon all be water under the bridge.

With another deep sigh, he headed back to his own group.

***

Phil felt much better after a bath. Somehow it seemed to wash away much of the depression brought on by Hughie's funeral.

He had travelled back to Wetherditch with Mike and Geordie. Like Doug Short, they had not lingered for very long after the service. Small glasses of sherry and daintily cut sandwiches in the very house that Hughie had died held no great appeal for any of them. Within half an hour they all made their apologies and departed. After a quiet word of goodbye with each of them when outside, Doug Short then set off alone on the drive back to his Cotswold cottage.

Phil looked around the hotel room that had been his home for the last fourteen days. This was to be his last night spent here.

The decision to return home early had been made on the spur of the moment. With Mike already booked on a flight back to Canada tomorrow, and Geordie returning to full-time work on the same day, there suddenly didn't seem a great deal of reason to hang around in England any longer. And he did still have this business with Donna to sort out. He'd been lucky enough to get a flight out of London on the same day as the skipper, and they now planned to drive down south together in his hired car. Their flights left within two hours of each other, so it all fitted together quite neatly.

His mind turned to the coming evening. Geordie, Mike and himself were planning one final get together in the hotel bar. He dressed quickly. The other two were most likely already started and wondering where the heck he was. Briefly Donna crept once more into his thoughts, but he forced her out. Nothing was going to spoil this last evening for him.

With this thought in his head, he left the room and headed for the bar downstairs.

***

It was approaching closing time. 'Just one more drink,' Geordie suggested.

Stafford shook his head, grinning. 'It's okay for you. You won't be crossing any time zones on your way back to Newcastle tomorrow. Phil and I have got a bit further than that to travel.'

'Just one more,' the big man insisted, 'and then I'll tell you something that'll make you both happy.' He looked pleased with himself. 'It's something I've been saving up for the end of the evening.'

Phil emptied his glass and placed it on the bar. 'That sounds rather like blackmail to me, Mike.'

'And it looks like it's worked,' Stafford responded, also draining his glass. He regarded his big friend with a mock serious expression. 'This had better be good, pal.'

Obviously enjoying the suspense he'd created, Geordie took his time in ordering the round and then slowly counting his change.

'Get on with it,' the other two said, almost in unison.

'Well, lads, it's like this.' He paused for further effect. 'On my way down here I made a little detour and called into the hospital to see Alan. There was something I wanted to speak to him about.'

'He's determined to hang this out all night,' Phil said as Geordie paused yet again.

Stafford remained silent. His interest was now high.

'While I was at home, I started thinking,' Geordie continued. 'We need more help in the yard. I've got to take on someone anyway, so I wondered if Alan might like the job. It's nothing too special, not until he picks up the ropes. But it's a start. He can learn a good trade, and it'll also give me a chance to keep an eye on the lad. I can keep you up to date on how he's getting on.'

Once again Stafford marvelled at the change in his friend. It was clear that he was now developing a genuine affection for the boy.

'So what did Alan say?' he asked, already guessing the answer.

A wide grin formed on Geordie's face. 'He's coming up to see me as soon as he's out of hospital. That'll be in the next couple of days according to the doctor.'

He took a large gulp of beer. 'I spoke to Barbara as well. She knows it's a good opportunity for him, and she seems pretty happy for him to get away from all the bad old influences in London. I've told her she's welcome to come up and stay at our place whenever she fancies a visit.'

'I think there's someone else who might also appreciate that offer,' Stafford suggested.

Geordie's eyes twinkled. 'Aye, I've not forgotten young Sue. Her and Alan are getting along a treat right now, so we can find room for her too any time she wants to come. What's the point of having five bedrooms in the house if you don't use them all sometimes?'

Stafford punched the big man lightly on the chest in a gesture of regard. He shook his head. 'The bigger they come, the softer they are,' he said.

'I'll second that,' Phil joined in, raising his glass.

'Oh, and there is one more thing, Mike,' Geordie said. 'Alan asked me to give you this.' He dug into his jacket pocket and produced the old photograph of Stafford and Jimmy together.

'Read what's written on the back,' Geordie instructed while passing it over.

Stafford did as he was told. In the small space remaining beneath his own promise to Jimmy was a clumsy but legible script. Just six words were written.

Mission accomplished. With thanks from Alan.

'We wrote it together,' Geordie said in answer to the enquiring look. 'But it was all the lad's own idea to do it.'

Stafford did not know what to say. The sense of achievement was enormous.

Geordie picked up his glass. 'A toast,' he announced. 'To our old pal Jimmy.'

Phil quickly did the same. Both men then looked at Stafford. He too raised his glass. There was a huge sense of warmth inside.

'To our old pal Jimmy,' he repeated.

***

Their car was approaching London. 'Are you sure you don't mind?' Stafford asked.

'It's not a problem,' Phil told him. 'We've plenty of time in hand.'

They turned off from the airport road and headed for the city's southern suburbs.

'It's just along here,' Stafford said after a further half an hour of driving.

They pulled up. 'I'll stay in the car for a while,' Phil offered. 'I guess you'd like some time on your own to start with.'

Stafford thanked him and stepped out of the vehicle. Phil was right. He did need a short time alone with his thoughts.

Croydon Cemetery appeared to have changed little: a fact he found strangely curious considering how many new graves must have been dug here since he had last visited the place. It did not take long for him to locate Jimmy's headstone. He noted with approval that the grave was as well tended as Barbara had assured him.

He wasn't sure how long he just stood there staring at the stone, a thousand different memories passing rapidly through his mind. It was like watching a familiar movie played at high speed. The images flashed by, but no detail was missed.

The cemetery grounds were quiet with barely a soul around. 'I did my best, Jim,' he whispered. 'I figure Alan's going to be okay now. Geordie will help to make sure of that.'

To his own ears, the barely audible words gave an impression of floating upwards and then hovering in space somewhere just above him. It was an eerie sensation. Fleetingly, he wondered if he might receive an answer. Why not? Jimmy had spoken to him before, hadn't he? And what better place was there for them to communicate with each other than here?

No answer came. Just the singing of a nearby thrush intruded on the silence.

He began to wonder if the voice and presence he'd experienced when first arriving back in Wetherditch had been nothing more than his imagination playing tricks. Imagination or not, it had been so very real to him at the time. He continued to stand there gazing at the grave, heedless of the passing time. One final word was all that he was hoping for. One final sign that Jimmy was now truly resting in peace.

The words came from out of nowhere.

'You did good, Brandon Boy. Nobody could have done better.'

This time there was no mistaking that the voice was real. Too darn real! Stafford swung around to see Phil standing directly behind him only a few yards away.

He stared at the Kiwi. 'Why did you call me that? No one used that name except Jim.'

His friend suddenly looked embarrassed. 'I don't know, Mike. I don't even know why I said anything at all. I've been standing here watching you for at least five minutes. It just kind of came out. It was almost like someone else was speaking.'

'Someone else speaking.' Stafford repeated the words slowly. A huge sense of release surged through him. All at once he felt good.

Phil frowned. 'Are you okay?'

'Sure. Couldn't be better, pal.'

Stafford took one final lingering look at the headstone. It was done. All that he could have hoped for, and far more besides.

As he turned away he found his thoughts immediately switching to Alice and Connie. The urge to be back with them was now very strong indeed.

'Let's go, Phil,' he said. 'We've a couple of planes to catch. It's time we went home to our wives.'

Full of his own anticipation, he failed to catch the less than enthusiastic note in Phil's reply.

'Yeah. Back home to the wife,' his friend replied.

THIRTY-TWO

The large airliner was just over one hour away from its scheduled arrival at Auckland airport. Phil gazed down through the window at the Tasman Sea many thousands of feet below. He was nearly home.

After more than twenty-four hours of travelling, he was also very tired. There had been a couple of periods during the long journey when he'd managed to snatch a few minutes of sleep, but that was about the limit. Hour after hour spent debating his and Donna's future together had prevented any substantial period of rest. Still, he consoled himself, at least his mind was now finally made up.

If this trip had taught him anything it was that personal contentment and peace of mind, no matter how simply attained, were priceless. He thought of the years of torment that Hughie had put himself through, and the tragic end that his unhappiness had finally driven him to. There was Alan as well. All of his childhood had been spent in anger and mental turmoil. There were so many wasted years. But at least the kid could hopefully now put all that behind him.

On the other side of the coin there was Doug Short. The quiet single life he had deliberately chosen for himself didn't exactly fit in with convention, but that was how the man wanted it to be. He was happy in his own way. It was impossible to imagine anyone ever forcing Doug to live his life in the hustle and bustle of the city. He would never be able to adapt.

Phil frowned. No more than he would ever be able to.

So it was settled. Donna, of course, would go mad, and there were sure to be more bitter rows. But the truth was, all he'd ever really promised was to give the move to Auckland some serious thought. Well now he'd done that, and she would either have to accept him for what he was or call it a day on their marriage. If she did choose the latter, he wished her well.

The firm decision not to leave Tauranga helped to lighten Phil's mood a touch. All he was dreading now was the backlash. The pair of them breaking up pretty soon seemed inevitable, but before that there were sure to be more weeks of arguments and unpleasantness. Donna would hit him with everything from emotional blackmail to threats and abuse. This depressing prospect soon dragged his spirits back down. What a welcome home he had to look forward to. At last, fed up with this mental see-saw, Phil closed his eyes. There might just be time for a quick bit of shuteye before landing.

Even as his eyelids dropped, he knew that he was hoping for the impossible.

***

The taxi dropped him off directly outside his house. Everything looked exactly the same as he had left it. He paused by his boat, still sat on its trailer in the driveway, to run a hand lovingly over the hull. This was the one lady in his life he knew how to handle. The other one was going to prove a lot more difficult to deal with. He moved on toward the house, mentally preparing himself.

It came as a small surprise to find the front door locked. Dropping his suitcase on the step, he let himself in and called out Donna's name. There was no reply.

He shrugged. She had probably gone shopping. That, or she was out visiting one of her friends. Moving into the living room, he regarded the settee that he had spent his last night on before leaving. The memory of this did little to ease his dread of the immediate future.

His eyes then shifted to the table. Propped up against an empty flower vase was an envelope with his name written across the front. He recognised Donna's handwriting immediately. But why would she have left him a note when she wasn't expecting him home for another week yet?

He paused as a hint of what the envelope may contain slowly formed. Surely she wouldn't have done – would she?

By the time he removed the single page from inside he was at least partly prepared. Even so, as he read her words they still came as a shock. He sank down onto the settee to read the message for a second time, just to make sure that he had not misunderstood anything. There was no mistake.

It was all worded very nicely with phrases like *'in complete fairness to us both'* and *'I can fully appreciate your own reluctance to leave Tauranga'*, but it still amounted to the same thing. She had left him. There was no forwarding address.

At first he felt angry. There wasn't any way in the world that Donna could have written a letter like this by herself. Such fancy phrases simply weren't in her vocabulary. He wondered who had helped her to compose the message, and if the helper was now providing her with more than just grammar lessons.

A quick check in the bedroom confirmed that all of her things were gone. He returned to the settee, speculating further on this unexpected departure. But as the minutes passed, so his anger faded. It might be a bit lonely at present, but at least his homecoming would not now consist of the rows and tantrums he'd been dreading. This comforting thought was still lingering when he heard a scuffling noise behind him. Before he knew it, a cold wet nose was being shoved up his trouser leg.

'Dag, you old mongrel!' he exclaimed. 'Where have you been?'

'I've been looking after him for you,' a voice from the doorway said.

His mate Gavin stepped inside. 'I saw the door open and your case on the step,' he continued. 'We weren't expecting you back yet.'

Phil got to his feet and shook hands. 'I decided to come home early.'

He held up the envelope. 'Did you know about this? Donna's buggered off and left me. Packed her bags and gone.'

Gavin looked shocked. 'Jeez no. All she said to me was that she was going to Auckland for a few days and would I look after Dag until she came back.' He scratched his head. 'That must have been nearly a week ago.'

'She's gone all right, and she sure as heck ain't coming back.'

'I don't know what to say, mate.' Gavin shuffled his feet. 'What are you going to do now?'

Phil gave him a wry grin. 'I was just thinking about that when you came in. After I've caught up on a bit of shuteye, I reckon I'll get the boat back in the water and do a spot of fishing.'

'But Donna? What are you going to do about her?' Gavin persisted.

Phil's grin grew wider. 'She'll be right mate.'

***

Siggi frowned while returning to her comfortably furnished office. She was annoyed with herself. It was always the same when something like this happened.

She sat down behind her desk, the frown still in place. A few minutes earlier her boss had introduced her to an important new client of their advertising agency. They were now in a meeting together.

The new client had impressed her. He was of similar age to herself, and already he was the marketing head of a major international motor company with a huge advertising budget to spend. This was excellent news for the agency of course, but there had been something about the man that triggered a memory buried deep inside. Even though his name did not ring any bells, Siggi still felt certain that she had seen him somewhere before. What's more, from the way he had glanced at her on a couple of occasions, she had a suspicion that he was also thinking exactly the same thing.

If they had indeed met in the past, it would have been only briefly and a very long time ago. Siggi was certain of this. The face she was struggling to remember was many years younger.

She sighed with frustration. This would not do. During her time in England a backlog of work had built up: the kind of highly confidential work that her boss would not entrust to anyone but her. She must continue attending to this and stop such silly daydreaming. The memory would come back eventually if it wanted to.

It wasn't as if it was going to change her life in any way.

***

Two hours later she was still hard at work. By now it was approaching the time when she would normally finish for the day, but there was still a small amount of correspondence left to catch up on. Siggi wondered if she should stay late and attempt to clear it all up before leaving.

The knock on her office door broke into this train of thought. A moment later the door opened and she saw the new client standing there. He smiled at her; it was a friendly, genuine smile. Once again she began struggling to remember where she had seen him before.

'I'm leaving now,' the man said. 'I just thought I would look in and say goodbye.'

'That's nice of you,' she replied, wondering if she should just come out with it and say what was on her mind. But his status made her think twice.

To her surprise, in spite of his expensive suit and importance to the agency, he suddenly appeared to be a little unsure of himself.

'We did meet once before many years ago,' he said.

His words were such a relief to hear. 'I know,' Siggi told him. 'I've been trying to remember when.'

Instantly, she began to feel more at ease with him. At last she was going to have an answer to her mystery.

'It was March, nineteen forty-four,' he said. 'We were on the Dresden to Berlin train together.'

The memory returned with a rush. Both of Siggi's hands flew up to her mouth.

'Yes, March the twenty-fourth. That was the date! The night the bombers came back to Berlin.' She stared at him. 'You were that soldier who helped me off the train when everyone else was panicking.'

He smiled once more, regaining some of his confidence. 'You do remember me now. I was hoping that you would. I have certainly never forgotten you. I have seen your beautiful face a great many times in my mind since then.'

Siggi could feel herself blushing. Why should that be? It wasn't as if she was unused to receiving compliments from men. They usually meant nothing at all.

'I don't know what to say,' she told him. 'I'm flattered.'

He gave no sign of noticing her embarrassment. 'I was too shy to tell you how much I liked you at the time,' he continued. 'Also, it did not seem right. There were the bombs, and you were so concerned for your family.'

He hesitated. 'I hope that your mother and sister were still safe when you finally got back home to Steglitz. I did hear later that the area was hit quite badly.'

Her mother's death was still too painful a memory for Siggi to share with a relative stranger. With Mike Stafford the circumstances had been very different. This was just a casual conversation.

'They both got through the air raid in their different ways,' was all she said.

He seemed to sense that the vagueness of her reply concealed heartache, but did not press further.

He glanced at her left hand. 'Have you never married? There must have been many men who wanted to ask you.'

She shook her head. 'My career here has left me with little time for relationships.'

'Then we have one thing in common straight away. For me also, the demands of business have always seemed to get in the way of making a personal life.'

Siggi found this perfectly believable. The war had only been over for seventeen years. And even after that there had been the rebuilding process. For him to have risen from an infantry corporal to the marketing head of a major international company in such a short space of time must have demanded absolute dedication. Not to mention a great deal of ability.

He gave a small, self-conscious laugh. 'Maybe now is the perfect time for me to start changing some of that.'

Once again he hesitated. Then the words came out quickly. 'Would you do me the honour of having dinner with me this evening, Siggi? Of course, I understand if you have another engagement. But on the chance that you do not?'

He allowed this final sentence to hang.

Siggi was thrown. Maybe she should have seen this coming? It was not the first time a client of the agency had asked her to join him for dinner. She had even accepted on a few occasions in order to help further her career, but only if there were others such as her boss also present.

This time it was different. He was asking her out on a genuine date. The Siggi of recent years would have immediately refused, politely but firmly.

But now – now she reminded herself – her experiences in England had made her determined to open up to life a lot more. This man was kind and considerate; she already knew that from their time together on the train. Maybe this evening would lead to nothing, but she would never find out unless she gave it a chance. She could see that he was anxiously waiting for her response.

She smiled. 'No, I was not planning to do anything special this evening. What time would you like us to meet?'

Mike Stafford would be happy for her, she felt.

***

It was the Sunday morning of Stafford's first weekend back home. Alice had noticed the change in him immediately. She could see it in his every movement and gesture. There was absolutely no doubt in her mind that something very special must have happened in England to bring this about. But eager as she was to know more, she had so far held back from asking too many questions. It would be far better if she allowed him a little time to adjust first. Mike would talk to her when he was good and ready.

The house was now quiet. Connie had gone to visit her friend Sandy. With a host of presents from England to show off, she was in her element. An LP record titled The Young Ones by someone called Cliff Richard had particularly captured her imagination and she was anxious for her friend to hear it. With everything temporarily so peaceful and relaxed, Alice considered that this might be a good time to see how Mike was feeling.

She found him sitting on the rear porch.

'So, honey, it's back to work for you tomorrow,' she said, selecting a chair beside him.

He smiled at her. 'Yeah, that's right. But I reckon insurance is going to seem pretty darn tame for a while after all the stuff that went on in England.'

She took hold of his hand gently, noting again the still visible traces of what looked like a burn on the back. Several times she had wondered what might have caused this.

'Why don't you tell me about your time over there?' she said. 'I get the feeling you're about ready to talk now.'

He gave a wry grin. 'A heck of a lot happened, that's for sure.'

'And Jimmy?'

'He's fine.'

Alice frowned. 'That's a funny way of putting it.'

'I suppose it is,' he agreed after a few seconds thought. 'But it's true, all the same.'

Separating his hand from hers, he placed an arm around her shoulders.

'Okay, honey. Let's give you the full story.'

***

He began slowly and methodically. But as the story developed, so did his openness. He told Alice everything, including the finer details concerning Siggi and himself during their time spent trapped in the mine. The only part of the story he tried to play down was the level of danger he'd faced while underground, and also later when inside Seth's blazing caravan. But even this censored version of the risks involved was sufficient to shock and horrify her.

By the time he was finished he felt totally purged.

He awaited Alice's reaction. Apart from her expressions of concern for his safety, she had remained silent throughout the telling. Even now her face gave little indication of what she was feeling inside. She simply gazed at him with moist eyes for what seemed like an eternity.

At last, her hand reached out to gently stroke the side of his face. He could see nothing but love in her eyes. 'Welcome home, Mike,' she whispered.

At that precise moment, the telephone rang.

'Heck!' Stafford exclaimed, rising from his chair. He walked quickly through into the hallway and picked up the receiver.

'Hello.'

'Hello, Mike. It's Doug Short here.'

'Hi, Doug. This is a surprise. What can I do for you?'

'I just thought that I'd give you a call to make sure you arrived home safely. You know, after everything that happened.'

Stafford grinned to himself. 'No need for you to worry, Doug. Everything is fine.'

'I'm so pleased. I really am.'

Short hesitated slightly before continuing.

'Look, while I'm talking to you anyway, I may as well just mention this. I'm already looking to organize something similar for next year. How do you feel about coming? I know it's probably rather early to be asking, but if I can just get a rough idea of numbers ...'

His voice trailed off.

The suggestion was so unexpected that Stafford did not have a clue how to respond. Sure he wanted to return to England some time. But next year? That may be rushing things a little bit too much.

Or would it be? he suddenly considered. By then, the temptation to see for himself how things were working out for Alan and Geordie would be strong. And this time there was no reason why the reunion should not be just a small part of a proper family holiday, with all three of them going over together.

His eyes moved to the window, through which he could see Alice waiting for his return. Their eyes met.

'I guess I'll have to call you back on this one, Doug,' he said. 'But you can sure put me down as a possible to attend.'

He replaced the receiver. Right now he had a loving wife who needed his company. That was the only thing on his mind as he made his way back to the porch.

A FINAL WORD: Thank you for reading this novel. I really do hope it provided you with a few hours of enjoyable escapism. If you did find it an entertaining read, please will you consider leaving a review on Amazon, or indeed any other relevant website or blog? Reviews are the lifeblood for all authors, and you will have my sincere thanks if you take the trouble to write a few words on your thoughts about this book.

You may be interested to know that BURIED PASTS is a companion novel to I SPY BLETCHLEY PARK, a similar literary tribute that I wrote to my mother who served as a WAAF at the famous code breaking centre for two years during WWII.

Here's the blurb.

BLETCHLEY PARK IN PERIL

Deeply embittered by the government's seizure of her financially ruined father's Buckinghamshire estate, Lady Margaret Pugh swears revenge on all those in Westminster. With World War II looming, Hermann Goering then makes her an irresistible offer if she will agree to spy for him.

Before long, the many curious comings and goings at nearby Bletchley Park capture Margaret's attention. And as she starts putting all of the pieces together, so Britain's most vital war secret becomes increasingly in peril of a devastating bombing raid.

In response to this suspected threat, a young working-class WAAF is thrust untrained into the world of counter-espionage. Thanks to a prodigious musical talent, Betty Hall is uniquely placed to infiltrate Margaret's private life. But matters suddenly escalate, and the fate of Bletchley Park soon hangs entirely on Betty becoming ever more deeply and dangerously involved.

With countless lives at stake, two most determined women find themselves fighting a very private war.

Thanks once again for your support.
George Stratford   www.georgestratford.com

Printed in Great Britain
by Amazon